TO KISS A SPY

Also by Jane Feather
in Large Print:

Virtue
The Accidental Bride

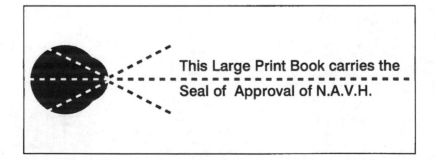

This Large Print Book carries the
Seal of Approval of N.A.V.H.

TO KISS A SPY

Jane Feather

Thorndike Press • Waterville, Maine

Published in 2002 by arrangement with Bantam Books, an imprint of the Bantam Dell Publishing Group, a division of Random House, Inc.

Thorndike Press Large Print Core Series.

The tree indicium is a trademark of Thorndike Press.

The text of this Large Print edition is unabridged.
Other aspects of the book may vary from the original edition.

Set in 16 pt. Plantin by Rick Gundberg.

Printed in the United States on permanent paper.

Library of Congress Cataloging-in-Publication Data

Feather, Jane.
    To kiss a spy / Jane Feather.
       p. cm.
    ISBN 0-7838-9739-1 (lg. print : hardcover : alk. paper)
    ISBN 0-7838-9746-4 (lg. print : softcover : alk. paper)
    1. Great Britain — History — Edward VI, 1547–1553 — Fiction.
    2. Large type books. I. Title.
    PS3556.E22 T6 2002
    813′.54—dc21   2001058533

TO KISS A SPY

Prologue

●

High Wycombe, England, July 1550

The attenuated cry of an infant pierced the black miasma of exhaustion. The woman on the bed was slumped motionless against the pillows, her eyes closed, her skin the color of old parchment. At the baby's cry her eyelids fluttered but didn't open and she sank once more into merciful oblivion.

Not one of the three other women in the stifling chamber glanced towards the bed. The baby's mother didn't interest them. They worked quickly and in silence and when they had done what had to be done they left the chamber soundlessly, closing the door behind them.

More than three hours passed before Pen emerged from her stupor. She was soaked with sweat. The room was like a furnace, the windows tight closed, the fire blazing in the deep hearth. She heard whispers and with a soft moan tried to raise herself on the pillows but her body ached as if she'd been racked, and she had barely sufficient strength to open her eyes.

"Ah, you are awake." It was the voice of her mother-in-law. Effortfully Pen opened her eyes.

The Dowager Countess of Bryanston looked down at her daughter-in-law. Her hard brown eyes were dispassionate as stones, her mouth a thin line above a heavy jutting chin. She made no attempt to disguise her contemptuous dislike of the frail young woman on the bed. The young woman who was the widow of Lady Bryanston's elder son. The widow who had just labored for some twenty anguished hours to bring forth her husband's posthumous son, who from the moment of his birth would inherit his father's titles and estates.

"The baby," Pen said, her voice coming as if from a great distance through her cracked lips. "Where is my baby?"

Lady Bryanston said nothing for a moment, and there was a rustle of skirts as another woman joined her at the bedside.

Frightened now, Pen gazed up at the two faces bent over her. Her heart felt squeezed. "My baby? Where's my baby?" Panic rose in her voice.

"He was stillborn," Lady Bryanston said without expression. "He was born early, four weeks too soon. He did not live."

"But . . . but I heard him cry," Pen said. "I *heard* him."

Her mother-in-law shook her head. "You were unconscious when we pulled him from you with the forceps. You heard nothing unless 'twas in your dreams." She turned from the bed with a dismissive gesture and left the chamber.

Pen closed her eyes on the tears that filled them, on the despairing weakness that swamped her anew. Since Philip's death she had lived for the child growing in her womb. Philip's child, the child of their love.

"Let me make you more comfortable, madam." A brisk voice accompanied firm hands, and Pen kept her eyes shut as the woman cleansed her, changed her smock, pulled from beneath her the wadded sheets that had protected the feather mattress.

Pen wanted her mother. It was a childlike want, an all-consuming need. Her mother was on her way, making the long journey into High Wycombe from Mallory Hall in Derbyshire to be at her daughter's confinement, but the baby had come early and the Countess of Kendal had not yet arrived. Instead, Pen had endured the cold ministrations of her mother-in-law, and the women, all strangers, whom Lady Bryanston had appointed to assist at the birth.

And it had all been for nothing. Those dreadful hours had been for nothing.

But she *had* heard the baby cry. The baby had entered the world alive.

Pen opened her eyes and fixed her attendant with a clear and commanding look. "I wish to see my son's body," she stated, pushing aside the cup of warmed wine the woman held to her lips.

"Madam, he was buried immediately," the woman said. "In this heat, it's not wise to keep a body unburied." She hurried to the window and drew back the heavy velvet curtains. The pitiless midday sun poured into the already sweltering chamber.

Pen had endured the last weeks of her pregnancy amid one of the hottest summers in memory. Bodies did not remain unburied. Pen slid down in the bed and closed her eyes again. She opened them immediately at the sound of the door latch lifting followed by a heavy tread approaching the bed.

Miles Bryanston, her husband's younger brother, stood beside the bed. His eyes, malicious, brown, cold, so like his mother's, regarded her with a degree of complacency. "Sister, I'm sorry you have had such ill luck," he declared.

" 'Tis an ill wind that blows nobody any good," Pen returned with a cynical smile that despite her weakness came easily. Miles was now the Earl of Bryanston. Red-faced, heavily built, thick-witted, strong as an ox, the absolute antithesis of his elder brother. Philip had been thin and quick, but physically frail. A dreamer, a poet, a musician. Everything his brother was not.

And Pen had loved him.

She turned her head aside, away from her brother-in-law's smug countenance.

She *had* heard her baby cry. She *had*.

One

●

London, December 1552

"What I propose is a matter of some refinement, my dear sir. A scheme of some complexity." Antoine de Noailles paused to lift a silver chalice to his lips. He drank with an assessing frown, then nodded his satisfaction and gestured to his companion to drink from his own chalice. He waited to see if the wine found favor with his guest before he continued speaking. "Yes, a complex scheme, a two-pronged scheme. Very neat." Noailles smiled happily. "One perfectly suited to your own particularly delicate methods, Owen."

Owen d'Arcy contented himself with a raised eyebrow. Antoine de Noailles, the French ambassador to the English court of the young king Edward VI, delighted in taking his time when revealing to his master spy an intrigue that he considered especially ingenious.

Owen d'Arcy was a tall man, lithe and slender, and when necessary as deadly as the rapier in the chased silver scabbard at his waist. His black eyes were never still, they missed nothing, and the fertile brain behind them ceaselessly absorbed, sorted, and acted upon the information they transmitted. He knew now without being told that the ambassador was about to drop a choice plum in his lap. He sipped his wine and waited.

"I believe that the king is dying," Noailles said calmly. "His Privy Council think to keep the truth of the young man's health a state secret, but . . ." He shrugged and smiled at the absurdity. "The issue, of course, is what happens on the boy's death."

"The crown goes to Mary," Owen said, his voice surprisingly dark and rich with a musical lilt to it.

"It certainly *should*," the ambassador agreed. "King Henry so decreed it. After Edward, if the boy has no issue, Mary is next in line, Elizabeth is second." He paused, and again Owen waited with no sign of impatience.

"I fear, however, that our friend Northumberland, the Grand Master of the Realm, has some other plans," the ambassador said in a musing tone.

The two men were standing before the fire in a small paneled chamber in the ambassador's residence at Whitehall. Outside, snow was falling softly, dulling the ceaseless sound of traffic along Whitehall, the clop of hooves, the clang of iron wheels on the cobbles, the shouts of barrow boys.

The chamber was lit only by the fire, and a many-branched candelabrum on the long table that stood against the wall opposite the clerestory window. In the shadowy gloom the ambassador's scarlet gown glowed in vivid contrast to his companion's black velvet, and when he moved his plump hands the firelight caught the jeweled rings on his fingers in flashes of green and red and turquoise.

Owen left the fire and refilled his chalice from the flagon on the table. "Do we know what Northumberland is planning?"

Noailles extended his chalice to be filled. "That, my dear Owen, brings us to the crux of the matter."

"Ah." Owen tipped the flagon and watched the red stream of wine arc into the silver vessel. "This is where I come in?"

"Precisely." Noailles turned back to the fire. "There's a certain woman who attends Princess Mary who is particularly well placed to provide us with the most intimate information about what goes on in the princess's household. She is a trusted confidante and a party to Mary's thoughts and intentions."

Noailles glanced over his shoulder at Owen, who still stood beside the table in the flickering candlelight, his black eyes sharp and alert, belying the impassivity of his countenance.

"You could perhaps become . . . shall we say, acquainted . . . with the lady," Noailles suggested. "It's a task most suited to your talents, I believe." He chuckled, his round face shining.

Owen did not respond to the ambassador's amusement. "And the other prong to this attack?" He took a sip of wine, regarding the ambassador thoughtfully over the lip of the chalice.

Noailles beamed. "Ah, yes. Here lies the beauty of it. The lady is closely connected to a man, her stepbrother in fact, who is a trusted friend of the Duke of Suffolk and his family. I hardly need tell you that Suffolk is an intimate of Northumberland's. Their interests lie closely bound, and whatever Northumberland is planning, Suffolk will be a part of it. 'Tis not unreasonable to assume that Robin of Beaucaire is privy to some of their secrets."

"And we assume that the lady in question exchanges confidences with her stepbrother," Owen stated, setting down his chalice. He walked to the window, his short black velvet gown swinging from his shoulders.

"They are very intimate and they spend a great deal of time together when they're both in London."

"As happens to be the case now, I presume." Owen looked down at the street below. The snow was falling heavily.

"Yes, both Princess Mary and Suffolk are in their London residences for the Christmas festivities. I understand that Edward ordered his sister's presence. She'll find it hard to celebrate a Christmas mass under the king's eye."

Owen drummed a finger on the glass. The religious differences between the fanatically Protestant King Edward and his equally fanatical Catholic half sister Mary were of little interest to him except where they impinged upon his work. He was much more concerned with the lady who was to be his quarry.

"Exactly how intimate are the lady and her stepbrother?" He turned back to his companion.

Noailles offered a very Gallic shrug. "I've heard no whispers of scandal, but they are *very* close. And Lord Robin at the ripe age of twenty-eight has never married."

"And the lady. What's her situation?"

"The Lady Pen has been a widow close to three years now. Her marriage to Philip, the Earl of Bryanston, was promoted by the king and Princess Mary, and to all intents and purposes seemed happy. But Philip died and she gave birth some months later to a stillborn child. Her brother-in-law inherited the earldom and is ruled, it's generally believed, by his mother. He's something of a dolt." The ambassador's lip curled. "Like most inhabitants of this nasty island."

Owen smiled slightly. The Frenchman was not happy in his present diplomatic position and made no secret of it to his intimates.

Noailles drank wine and then continued. "The Bryanstons have little or nothing to do with Philip's widow. She lays no claim to any part of her late husband's estate. She doesn't even take the title of dowager countess, leaving that to the sole use of her mother-in-law. 'Tis clear there's no love lost there."

Owen nodded. He ran a hand over his clean-shaven chin. "Is the lady ripe for plucking?"

"When have you ever failed to *persuade* the fruit to fall from the tree?" Noailles smiled.

Owen did not return the smile. "In the interests of business," he said somewhat curtly.

"Oh, of course, only in the interests of business," the ambassador agreed hastily. Owen d'Arcy's private life was a closed book, or had been since that unfortunate business with his wife. As far as Noailles knew, the man lived the life of a monk except when seduction suited his purposes. And then he was a true artist.

"Is she pleasing, this Lady Pen?" A frown crossed Owen's black eyes. "A strange name. Is that truly how she's called?"

"Penelope . . . but I've never heard her called anything but Pen, even by the princess. 'Tis a family name and she's very close to her family. I think you'll find her pleasing. She's not strikingly beautiful but has a certain sweetness of countenance. She's of middle height, neither fat nor thin."

"She sounds singularly unexciting," Owen observed aridly. "Do you have any views on her temperament?"

Noailles pulled at his neat dark beard. "She is somewhat reserved," he said finally.

Owen gave a sharp crack of laughter. "I had hoped at the very least that you would tell me this nondescript creature would exhibit some passion once in a while."

The ambassador opened his hands in a gesture of resignation. " 'Tis said she took the deaths of her husband and child very hard."

Owen shook his head and picked up his gloves from the table. He drew them on and strode to the door where his thick hooded cloak hung. He slung it around his shoulders, observing, "It seems you've set me quite a task, Noailles. I hope I'll be equal to it." The door banged shut on his departure.

Oh, you'll be equal to it, my friend. The ambassador took up his chalice again. He went to the window, peering down through the driving snow at the street below.

After a minute the black-clad figure of Owen d'Arcy emerged from the house, a page at his heels. He paused for a second, casting a quick glance up and down the street in a manner quite familiar to the watcher above. The master of intrigue never took a step without first assessing his surroundings. Then he walked off quickly in the direction of the Savoy Palace and was immediately lost in the swirling white.

Antoine de Noailles smiled to himself at the absurd idea that Owen d'Arcy would not succeed in bedding Pen Bryanston. Her confidences behind the bedcurtains would keep the French ambassador informed not only of Princess Mary's schemes with her cousin, the Holy Roman Emperor Charles V, but also of whatever intrigue was plotted in the two great ducal houses of Northumberland and Suffolk.

★ ★ ★

The great hall of the Bryanstons' London residence on the banks of the Thames at Westminster was thronged. Pen stood in the gallery looking down on the hall, where jewels glittered and sparkled against rich velvets, damasks, and satins under the great wheels of candles suspended from the ceiling. From above, the mass of people resembled a gigantic, brilliantly colored wave that ebbed and swelled. Voices were indistinguishable, the sound was a featureless rumble that occasionally became a roar which drowned the sweetness emanating from the minstrels' gallery.

It was hot in the gallery. The heat from the massive fireplaces, the many candles flaring in sconces high on the walls, and the press of heavily clad bodies rose to envelop Pen, and she dabbed at her forehead with an embroidered handkerchief.

It was hot but it was also secluded and afforded her the best view of her mother-in-law. The Dowager Countess of Bryanston was at the far side of the hall among the ladies surrounding Princess Mary. She was unlikely to leave that circle and her royal guest for some time, but even if she did she would have no reason to come up to the gallery. And even if she did have a reason, it would take her at least fifteen minutes to push her way through the throng and make for the stairs to the place where Pen stood.

She had at least fifteen minutes, Pen decided.

18

Her eyes searched the throng for the Earl of Bryanston and his lady. They shouldn't pose a threat but Pen knew she would feel safer if she located them. She leaned forward slightly to get a better look and was suddenly blinded as a pair of hands came over her shoulders to cover her eyes.

Even as she started she knew to whom they belonged, and a delighted cry broke from her as she wrenched the hands away and spun around. "Robin! You scared me!"

"No, I didn't. Of course you knew it was me." Her stepbrother grinned at her, his brilliant blue eyes alight with pleasure at seeing her. He was a stocky man, square built, with a shock of springy nut-brown curls on which his velvet cap perched somewhat insecurely. His dress was rich and yet somehow awry. Pen automatically reached to brush a piece of fluff from his doublet, and while she was about it resituated the jeweled brooch he wore in the lace at his throat.

"Where have you been? I haven't seen you in weeks," she asked, kissing him soundly.

"Oh, out and about," he responded. "Out of town, anyway."

Pen regarded him shrewdly. Robin would never disclose whatever it was that took him away for these long absences but she had a fair idea. Her own years in the devious world of the court had taught her that very little was as it seemed. "On the duke's business?" she asked in a neutral tone.

He shrugged and changed the subject. "What are you doing all alone up here?" He peered over the gallery rail.

Pen's eyes followed his. Her mother-in-law was still at the princess's side, and now she saw Miles Bryanston and his wife at a card table at the far side of the hall, their large faces glistening in the heat. They would be occupied all evening.

"I felt the need for some quiet," she said. "It's so noisy down there and so *hot*."

"It's hot up here," Robin pointed out, looking at her closely.

Pen shrugged. "I'll go down again in a minute. I have need of a privy and, as I recall, there's a commode behind the arras in the passage behind the gallery. You go down and I'll find you. I want to hear all your news."

She smiled, hoping to convince him, trying not to think about precious time wasting, trying not to look down to check on her mother-in-law's whereabouts. Robin, in company with the rest of her family, worried about her obsession, and if he thought she was following its impulses again he would certainly try to prevent her.

Robin hesitated. They had known each other for sixteen years. When they had first met they had been smitten with each other, caught in the pangs of first love. Then their parents had married and in the hurly-burly of family life, that first love had become a deep, abiding, loving friendship. Robin thought he knew his stepsister better than anyone, better even than her mother or her younger sister Pippa.

And he knew she was not being honest with him.

"What's the matter?" Pen demanded. "Why would a need for the privy cause you to look at me like that?" She laughed at him.

Robin shook his head. "I'll see you in a few minutes." He turned to walk away, and Pen set off in the opposite direction. As soon as she had disappeared at the end of the gallery Robin followed her, soft-footed despite his stocky build. He turned into the narrow corridor behind the gallery and saw her ahead of him, hurrying as she might well do if she were in genuine need of the commode. Halfway along she twitched aside an arras and disappeared.

He frowned, pulling at his unruly beard. Perhaps he'd been wrong and she had been telling the truth. He turned and retraced his steps down to the great hall.

From behind the arras, Pen watched him depart. She'd been certain he'd follow to check up on her. She knew Robin at least as well as he knew her. When the coast was clear, she slipped out into the corridor and hurried towards the chamber that served the Bryanston family as both office and library. The only member of the family who had delighted in stocking the library had been Philip. Pen's derisive grimace was automatic and unconscious. The present Earl of Bryanston was barely literate and she'd never seen him open a book. Even his mother, for all her sharpness, couldn't add two and two or do more than scrawl her name, and now that Philip was gone she relied on a chamberlain to manage the family's affairs.

She entered the chamber, glancing over her shoulder as she did so. There was no one around to see her. The servants were all busy with the revels below.

She closed the door softly and stood with her back to it, looking around the room where she and Philip had spent so much companionable time. She was not the scholar he had been, but she had grown up in the care of a mother who was as learned as any man, and Pen knew well the pleasures of a still and silent companionship disturbed only by the rustle of turning pages or the scratch of quill on parchment. She could almost hear those quiet sounds now, almost see Philip at the big oak table, his fair head bent over the tablets he always carried with him in case the muse struck unexpectedly.

Suddenly she was hit by a wave of grief. It was a familiar occurrence although it happened less often now, three years after Philip's death. But it was as sharp, as piercing, as ever. Dry-eyed she waited for it to pass, for the tightness in her chest to ease, the great ball of unshed tears to dissipate.

If only she had his child, the child they had conceived in so much love . . .

Her expression cleared, her mouth set, her hazel eyes focused. There were no more shadows in the chamber, no more memories. Only purpose. The hard-edged driving force of her existence. A child had been born. Somewhere in this room among ledgers and Bibles there would be some record of that birth. Even a stillbirth had to have its place in family records.

She had been so ill after the dreadful labor, her body racked with fever and pain, her spirit with inconsolable grief. Her mother and stepfather had arrived and removed her instantly from the Bryanston home in High Wycombe. It had taken close to twelve months under their loving care for Pen to overcome her illness and to put her grief aside, although she knew it would always be a presence in the deepest recesses of her soul. This evening marked the first occasion she had been under a Bryanston roof since the birth. It provided her with the first real opportunity to look for some record of her son's birth. The Bryanstons behaved as if it had never happened, and her mother and stepfather encouraged her not to think of it, to put it behind her. But Pen could not accept that the child who had grown inside her, who had kicked and hiccuped and been a physical part of her, a child she had labored so sorely to deliver, could be so utterly dismissed from the world.

And neither did she believe that the child had been born dead. She had heard him cry.

This was her obsession. This was what drove her as she returned to the princess's household and the life she had known before her marriage.

To all intents and purposes Pen was her old self, but below the surface raged the conviction that somewhere her child lived.

Her eye fell on the great family Bible on the lectern in the window embrasure. Births, deaths, marriages were all recorded there. She stepped quickly across the chamber, hurrying to the lectern. The Bible was open at the Book of Psalms and she feverishly turned the wafer-thin pages to the front of the volume. The pages stuck to her fingers, which had grown damp in her haste and eagerness. She wiped them on the gray damask of her skirt before continuing. The front of the Bible carried no record of the stillbirth of her son on July 7, 1550. The date itself was not inscribed. She looked down the long list of marriages, births, deaths. Her marriage to Philip was there. Philip's death was there. Miles's ascension to the earldom was there. In bold letters, bigger it seemed than any other entry. But, of course, Miles was the favorite son. The son his mother was convinced should have been her firstborn and always treated as such.

Pen's eyes swept the chamber. How much time did she have left? Where else could she look? She went to the cabinet where she knew the estate papers were kept. How often she had watched Philip working on them. The key was in the lock. She opened the cabinet and began sorting through the ledgers.

The door opened behind her. The door she had forgotten, in her eager haste, to lock.

Her heart raced, her scalp contracted. Slowly she turned. At best it would be Robin, at worst her mother-in-law.

But it was neither. For a moment speechless, she stared at the stranger, her first thought that he was a servant. But it was a fleeting thought instantly dismissed. No servant was ever this elegant, or ever bore himself with such cool arrogance. Was he an intimate of the Bryanston family? If so, not one she knew.

Black eyes beneath a broad brow and prominent but shapely eyebrows assessed her in the pregnant silence, and Pen returned the scrutiny with a slight lift of her chin. He had a long straight nose, a pointed chin, and a calm mouth. He held himself very still and yet she could feel a surge of energy around him. She couldn't guess at his age. He was certainly older than Robin.

She found her voice at last. "The revels are in the great hall, sir. You seem to have lost your way."

He bowed. "Owen d'Arcy at your service, madam." His voice was musical, rich and soft, and Pen puzzled over the curious lilt. It wasn't quite a foreign accent and yet like his dark complexion it was not purely English either.

"I have no need of any service, sir," Pen observed tartly. She felt on her mettle, somehow. A prickle of irritation mingled with something else as he continued to regard her with a glimmer of amused speculation. It was as if he knew something that she did not.

25

Everything about the man unsettled Pen. His clothes were curiously exotic, like his voice and his complexion. He wore doublet and hose of black satin worked with threads of Venetian gold, his shirt was of black silk, the collar fastened with black enameled clasps. A short cloak of black velvet lined with crimson silk hung from his slender shoulders. He carried a rapier and a dagger in black velvet sheaths at his waist. It was immediately obvious that he knew how to use such weapons. Pen had the absolute conviction that he was dangerous.

"You seemed to be looking for something," he said pleasantly, as if she had not spoken. "Perhaps I can help."

"I cannot imagine why you should think so." Reluctantly Pen closed the cabinet and turned the key. She could not continue her search in his company, or indeed any company, and she was filled with resentment at the stranger's intrusion. There was no knowing when she would have such an opportunity again.

"Are you closely connected to the Bryanston family, sir? Familiar with their affairs, perhaps?" She swung back to him, her expression as challenging as her tone.

There was more to her than met the eye, Owen thought. At first sight she was as Noailles had said, fairly nondescript with her brown hair, regular features, and undistinguished figure. But her eyes. Now they were something else altogether. Very large, very clear, and a wonderful mixture of green and brown shot through with gold. They reminded him of sunlight on a forest pool. Noailles had been wrong about the temperament too, he decided. There was a distinct flash of spirit there. For the first time, Owen felt a stirring of interest in this task.

"I must confess total ignorance of all things Bryanston," he said with a smile. "But I find myself very interested in you, madam. I couldn't help but follow you when you left the hall." He bowed and gave her his most winning, inviting smile.

Pen looked at him incredulously, her annoyance vanquished by this absurdity. "Are you attempting to flirt with me, sir?" She gave a peal of laughter. "You have the wrong sister, I'm afraid. My sister Pippa is an incorrigible flirt and will repay your efforts much more than I. I'd be happy to introduce you." Still laughing, she swept past him to the door, her skirts brushing against him.

Owen was rarely disconcerted, and chagrin was a most unusual visitor. However, he was aware of both as he followed Pen from the chamber. Something had to be done about it.

"Lady Pen," he called softly but with a degree of urgency.

She stopped in the passage, glanced interrogatively over her shoulder at him, wondering how he knew her name. They had definitely not been introduced. He stepped up to her. He caught her turned chin in the palm of his hand and swiftly before she had any idea of his intention pressed his lips lightly against hers.

"Forgive me," he said. "But I have been wanting to do that all evening."

"How extraordinary!" Pen declared. "Why on earth should you?"

He had expected shock, maidenly horror, indignation, fluster at the very least. Instead he received only this blank astonishment, this implication that he must have lost his senses. Surprise usually had a good effect in Owen d'Arcy's experience. But not in this case, it seemed.

He looked at her closely, his eyes suddenly narrowed. "I have no idea," he said slowly. "Forgive me."

"Why, there's nothing to forgive," Pen returned with another laugh. "If you'll excuse me."

She hurried away, leaving Owen d'Arcy for once in his career nonplussed. Clearly he was going to need some more refined technique to gain the lady's confidence. And he was damned sure she was not going to laugh at him again.

Two

●

"I have just had the strangest encounter," Pen said as she descended from the gallery and found Robin awaiting her return at the foot of the stairs. She was still laughing, although with some puzzlement. She'd reacted at the time of that kiss with honest astonishment; in its aftermath she was aware of a deep pulse of excitement that confused her.

"I thought you were a long time," he said, regarding her with a tiny frown.

"Who are you to question how long I take in the privy?" Pen returned with feigned exasperation.

Robin shrugged, accepting defeat. Whatever Pen was up to she was not about to share it. "What was this encounter?"

Pen glanced around, then indicated a deep window embrasure. "Let's go over there." She moved ahead of him, her step quicker than usual.

Curious, Robin followed. Pen seemed to exude an unusual energy this evening. He often thought that the twin tragedies of her life had left her somehow diminished, had bled the color out of her, so that she sometimes seemed to him only a shadowy reflection of the vital person he had known so well. Tonight, though, she was different. In the gallery he had sensed her impatience, sensed that pleased though she was to see him, he had interrupted something important. And now she seemed excited, her eyes larger and brighter, more alive than they had been for almost two years. She had taken on some emotional color again.

In the window embrasure they were secluded, set apart from the noisy activity in the main body of the hall. Pen looked out into the night, where the darkness was pierced by the flaring light of pitch torches planted at intervals around the garden leading to the water steps. Torchbearers paced the snow-covered pathways and manned the landing stage where the guests' barges awaited, their cressets flickering like a plague of fireflies as the boats bobbed in the river.

Robin propped himself against the wall, hands thrust deep into the pockets of his blue-and-silver-striped gown, careless of the way the rough movement caused the delicate satin to pouch. "Strange encounter?" he prompted.

"Oh, yes." Pen turned back to him, shaking her head self-deprecatingly as if she'd completely forgotten what she'd intended to tell him. "It's nothing really, I just thought it was a little odd. In the passageway upstairs I ran into a man. He said . . . he said he found me interesting so he'd followed me. And then . . ."

She paused, half embarrassed, and yet her

eyes were if anything even brighter. "He kissed me, Robin. On the mouth, as if we were the best of old friends. Or . . . or . . ." She couldn't bring herself to say there was something loverlike about that kiss.

"I can't imagine why he would wish to flirt with me," she continued. She gave another little laugh that failed to disguise her inner turmoil. "If he hadn't known my name, I'd have assumed he'd mistaken me for Pippa. She's the family flirt after all."

Robin acknowledged this truth with a vague smile but fond though he was of his younger stepsister, Pippa could never distract him for long from Pen's concerns. And he was now very interested in Pen's response to a stranger's kiss. Despite her dismissal of the incident as unimportant, something had caused her present liveliness and the renewed sparkle in her eye. He certainly didn't think she had found the encounter disagreeable, and she wasn't asking him for brotherly outrage at a stranger's unwonted familiarity. He asked, "Who was the man?"

"I'd never seen him before, but he knew who I was. Maybe you passed him on the stairs? When you were going down and he was coming up?"

Robin frowned in thought. He had brushed past someone but they hadn't made eye contact. He'd been too involved with his own thoughts. "I may have done, but I wasn't really looking."

"Well, he said his name was Owen d'Arcy."

Robin turned abruptly to look out at the revelers, and Pen didn't see the flash in his eyes, the sudden tightening of his mouth.

What could Owen d'Arcy want with Pen?

"Do you know him?" Pen inquired, looking across the hall herself, her eyes searching for the slim dark man who had accosted her, who had so unsettled her.

"No," Robin replied, reflecting that it wasn't a complete lie. He didn't know Owen d'Arcy but he knew of him, knew what he did. Robin was in the same business himself but he freely acknowledged he was nowhere near d'Arcy's equal. The other man was a true master of his trade. Robin was still a tyro, far beneath Owen d'Arcy's notice.

"I don't think he's English," Pen mused. "Although it's hard to know why. He doesn't have a foreign accent exactly, but there's something strange about him. Something not ordinary."

"D'you see him here now?"

Pen shook her head. "No, but it's so crowded it would be easy enough to miss him." But even as she said this she knew it wasn't true. If he was in the hall she would see him. He was such a distinctive figure, so dark and calm amid the peacock brilliance of this chattering throng.

"Your mother-in-law appears to be coming this way," Robin observed, not sorry to change the subject. He didn't want to give Pen any indication of his own interest in d'Arcy; and she was so intuitive, particularly where her stepbrother was concerned, it wouldn't take much for her to start probing.

Pen stiffened beside him. "I have nothing to say to her."

"You must at least exchange the courtesies."

"I have already done so at the beginning of the evening." Before Robin could remonstrate further, Pen had slipped away, gliding into the throng and out of sight. He braced himself to greet Lady Bryanston. He knew how badly she had treated Pen, and like the rest of Pen's family considered barbaric her precipitate removal of the stillborn baby before its mother had had a chance to grieve over its loss. But he was a guest in her house and the proprieties had to be observed.

He bowed as the lady billowed up to him. She was heavyset like her son Miles, and like him had an inordinate fondness for the most elaborate dress. This evening she was arrayed in puce damask trimmed with silver fox fur and encrusted with diamonds. Robin guessed that beneath her jeweled headdress she wore a wig. It was difficult to imagine that that particular shade of bright red could be natural, and the high color on her cheeks certainly owed its origins to paint, he thought scornfully.

"Lord Robin." She acknowledged his bow with a faint nod. "I thought I saw Pen with you."

Robin looked around with the appearance of surprise. "I don't see her, madam."

Lady Bryanston's thin lips almost disappeared. "I have something to say to her. When you see her, tell her so."

"May I also tell her what it is you wish to say to her?" Robin inquired, trying to keep his voice bland, his angry contempt from his countenance.

"She has something of Philip's that I believe rightfully belongs to the earl." Lady Bryanston was not a clever woman, but she had a certain malicious cunning, and an overweening avarice that masqueraded as intelligence. Her brown eyes glittered with spite as they fixed upon Robin, then she gave another nod and left him, making her way across the hall to where her son and his wife were still at the card table.

"Bitch!" Robin muttered. She was probably after some memento of Philip that was particularly precious to Pen. It would be her way. He looked around for Pen but there was no sign of her.

What did Owen d'Arcy want with her? It was possible that his interest in Pen was quite innocent, that he was simply attracted to her. Robin could well understand that. But he also felt that Pen wasn't dramatic enough to attract Owen d'Arcy. He felt rather disloyal thinking this, but in cold clarity it was true. So d'Arcy must have some purpose in his pursuit.

Robin was only beginning to learn the intricate art of espionage, but knowing what he did, it wasn't hard for him to guess at that purpose. Pen was an intimate of Princess Mary's. D'Arcy worked for the French ambassador. If they wanted an opening into the mind of Mary and the designs of her cousin, the Holy Roman Emperor, with whom the princess was in close but clandestine touch, Pen could provide the key. In the present volatile climate, with a sickly king who had no offspring, such insights would be invaluable to the French.

Pen was no fool, and like Robin she'd lived among court intrigues for most of her adult life. She would not be easily taken in. Robin was fairly certain that she had guessed at his own involvement in the world of espionage although she respected his reticence, but d'Arcy was a master of his art and surely Pen would be no match for him.

Robin decided he needed to discuss Owen d'Arcy's interest in Pen with his own people. There might be nothing sinister in it, but it was not a judgment he could make alone. Robin took one last look around for Pen but there was still no sign of her.

The Duke of Northumberland was in the group around the princess, and as Robin approached, a pale thin girl also in the group smiled shyly at him. Her dress was very plain compared with the richness of those around her, and she looked uncomfortable, shifting from one foot to the other, glancing longingly towards the door.

Robin felt sorry for her. In his years in the Duke of Suffolk's household he'd had ample opportunity to witness the general bullying and browbeating that the duke's daughter Lady Jane Grey suffered at her mother's hands. He put an arm around her as he came up and squeezed her shoulders with the easy intimacy of a family friend. She smiled up at him, grateful as always for any show of kindness.

Northumberland turned his fierce gaze to Robin. His customary air of haughty disdain softened slightly. "You wanted to speak to me, Robin?"

"When your grace can spare me a moment," Robin said cheerfully. He had learned from his father, Hugh of Beaucaire, now the Earl of Kendal, the art of never being intimidated by the wealth and position of those around him. He was never awed and he never flattered. It brought him the genuine liking and respect of both the young king Edward and the lofty members of the Privy Council.

Northumberland nodded and moved away from the circle, indicating that Robin should accompany him.

Pen hastened along the passage to the library, the cone-shaped farthingale that supported her damask skirts swinging from side to side with the speed of her progress. She had taken no precautions this time to ensure a discreet departure from the hall while her mother-in-law was engaged with Robin. She was filled with a sense of recklessness that she knew had something to do

36

with her encounter with Owen d'Arcy. If the Bryanstons discovered her going through family papers, so be it.

She entered the library, and this time locked the door at her back before opening the cabinet. The ledgers it contained were mostly account books, and she was about to discard them when her hand fell on the ledger for the year 1550. She turned the pages, looking for July, and then for the entries under the day of her son's birth. The midwives would have received payment. They had all been strangers to her, brought in by Lady Bryanston when Pen had suddenly gone into labor four weeks before her due date.

Maybe she could get a name from the ledger, some way of contacting some woman other than her mother-in-law who had been present in the chamber on that dreadful day.

She found the page and stared down at the list of entries. There were names, sums allocated to the names, but no indication of what service the names had performed to warrant payment. Pen's fingertips prickled as if with pins and needles. Without thinking, she tore out the page, folded it, and slipped it into the small embroidered purse suspended from the fine gold-linked chain she wore at her waist. Then she replaced the ledger, locked the cabinet, and left the library.

She was alert, her heart pounding against her ribs. Now that she had something to hide, she feared discovery. No one would consult a ledger from two years previously unless they had reason to do so, and she mustn't arouse the least suspicion.

She entered the gallery above the hall and noticed immediately that the level of noise was much diminished. She looked down and saw that the hall was rapidly emptying, guests summoning their servants to call for barges, horses, or carriages.

Princess Mary's departure would be the signal for the party to break up and Pen saw that the princess and her ladies had indeed left, which meant that the royal barge would be gone from the water steps. Mary disliked late nights since she was up at her prayers well before dawn. She would not have worried about leaving Pen behind, simply assuming that she would remain under her mother-in-law's roof overnight.

Pen had no intention of seeking Bryanston hospitality even if it meant she would have to jostle for a place in one of the public barges. The crowd at the water steps would be huge and she could expect to wait for at least an hour before the public conveyances could get close enough to take on passengers.

Unless Robin was still around. He would escort her home even if he was on horseback and she had to ride pillion behind him. She examined the thinning throng but couldn't see him, and then she became aware of Miles Bryanston's upturned countenance from the floor just below. He was looking at her but she couldn't be certain he either saw her or recognized her. He was well in his cups, his great moon face crimson, the little brown eyes bloodshot and unfocused. She ducked back into the shadows and hastened down the stairs to the hall, hoping he was sufficiently befuddled to have been unaware of her.

Owen had seen the princess's departure and noted Pen's absence from the party. He stood in the small hallway that separated the great hall from the front door, a space designed to keep the frigid outside air at bay. The door stood open now as people crammed the small hall and pressed through the doorway, yelling for servants, huddling in furred cloaks. It was no longer snowing but the ground was covered with ice that cracked like glass beneath booted feet.

A group of chattering men and women emerged from the great hall behind him, eddying around him as they grumbled at the cold and the difficulty of the journey home. Pen was among them, pulling the furred hood of her cloak over her head. She saw Owen, in fact if she thought about it she would have said that she felt his presence the instant before she saw him. He smiled at her, and without volition she smiled back. He took a step towards her but a couple pushed between them, and Pen made no attempt to resist the tide of humanity that carried her out of the hallway and into the bitter night.

Owen's page scrambled back through the crowd, his cheeks red from the cold. " 'Twill be a two-hour wait for a barge, sir. And 'tis freezing hard."

Owen merely nodded, his expression customarily impassive except for a gleam in his dark eyes. "Then the sooner we leave the better, Cedric." He put a hand on the lad's shoulder.

" 'Tis powerful cold," Cedric muttered, looking longingly at the brightly lit hall behind his master. "We could wait here a bit, sir, just until the crowd's gone."

"I've no desire to linger, boy. A walk will warm you. Come." He propelled the page ahead of him out of the house.

Pen, when she reached the water steps amid the crowd, stamped her feet, hugged her arms across her chest, and looked around disconsolately. The line of barges and wherries waiting to pull into the steps seemed infinite, their bobbing cressets visible in the far distance across the black water, and the number of people ahead of her in the line was more than she could count. It was going to be an inhumanly long wait for passage.

She thrust her gloved hand beneath her cloak and clasped the little embroidered purse. She could almost feel the crisp fold of parchment within. Once she got back to Baynard's Castle and the privacy of her own chamber she could examine it properly. A surge of excitement ran through her, warming her despite the bone-chilling air. She forgot her fatigue, and her frustration at the crowd and the long wait became an impatient need to do something decisive. If she stayed where she was she wouldn't see her bed before daybreak.

She stepped back from the throng. The Horseferry water steps were no more than a ten-minute walk and the crowds would be much less there.

Of course the walk would take her through the maze of dark lanes surrounding the Bryanston mansion. In daylight she wouldn't have thought twice about it, but on such a bitter black night . . .

Suddenly making up her mind, Pen looked around for a torchman to light her way. A sullen fellow, a Bryanston servant, came shivering to answer her call. He set off ahead of her, holding his torch high to illuminate the dark alleys they had to thread to reach the Horseferry steps.

Huddled in her fur-lined cloak, Pen picked her way carefully over the icy ground trying to keep up with his light, but he was impatient and his booted feet had a firmer grip of the ground than her thinner-soled sandals. She cursed him under her breath, and would have cursed herself for missing the princess's departure and a brazier-warmed journey home on comfortable cushioned seats out of the wind, except that the same excitement, the residue of her earlier reck-lessness, and a surging anticipation infused her.

The sudden "Holla!" from behind her startled her. She spun around and found herself instantly surrounded by ragged dark-clad figures, men, some women, even children. She yelled for the torchman, who looked behind him and then ran into the darkness, holding his torch aloft.

"Cowardly scum!" Pen exclaimed between her teeth, for the moment too angry at his desertion to feel fear. But that lasted barely an instant, to be followed immediately by the desperate certainty that she should have stayed at the Bryanstons' steps and waited it out among the crowd. Instead she had yielded to a stupid impulse, with possibly deadly consequences.

She tried to push her way through the group around her but they closed in tighter, gazing at her with hungry eyes, slack mouths that showed toothless gums. For a minute no one moved, then one of the men reached out and touched her arm. It was the signal for the rest. The women came closer, pushing, pulling, prodding. And now Pen was breathless with terror. She tried talking to them but they didn't seem to hear her. Dirty fingers plucked at her cloak and the gem she wore at her breast was revealed, flashing a white light in the darkness. They came at her then, clawing, hissing, like evil wraiths robbing a grave.

Pen heard her own scream even as she fought them with a frenzy she would never have believed she possessed. And then suddenly they were falling back with cries of pain, of alarm. Cries that now sounded human.

A man in black was in their midst, wielding a rapier to deadly effect. He was silent, the silver blade slicing through the air with lethal efficiency. At his side a smaller figure plied a dagger with the same dexterity.

Pen found herself freed from the circle. She had no weapon by which to add her mite to her rescuers' efforts, so she gathered herself together, running a mental inventory over her body and then her possessions. Her cloak was torn, the index finger of her right glove ripped away. But she was still on her feet and for the moment aware of no injury.

The alley was emptied as quickly as it had filled. Owen d'Arcy reached for her and, instinctively it seemed to Pen, drew her against him. For a minute she rested in the circle of his arm, hearing his heart beat beneath his cloak as slowly and steadily as if he'd never raised a rapier. She rested against him, realizing as she regained some measure of strength and composure that she hadn't believed it possible to know such terror.

"My thanks, sir," she murmured finally, pulling out of his hold when it seemed to her that the longer she stayed so close against him the less will she would have to move away. "I had a torchman but the coward ran as soon as I was attacked."

" 'Tis a bad road for a woman with only a torchman for protection," Owen said, sheathing his rapier. "I saw you leave the water steps but couldn't credit that you would strike out on your own in such fashion. Cedric, light a taper."

Cedric drew a tinder box from the leather

pouch he carried at his waist. Flint scraped on steel, the tinder sparked, and a light glowed, a small golden circle that enclosed the three of them. Owen reached out and caught Pen's chin as he had done earlier that evening. He held her face and examined her in the light of the torch.

Pen shivered suddenly, her legs quivering so that she leaned against the wall of the hovel at her back. It had nothing to do with the strange power in the black eyes bent upon her, nothing at all to do with the compelling calm that surrounded him. It was simply the aftermath of her ordeal. It was perfectly natural to suffer a shock once the need for strength was gone.

"You're hurt," he said in that lilting voice. "The kennel scum cut you with something." He touched her neck, moved aside the collar of her cloak, and traced a line from her ear to her shoulder. His finger came away wet and sticky with blood. Pen felt the pain of the cut for the first time, just as she also became aware of many other spots of soreness on her body. She had fought hard for those few terror-stricken minutes and her body was telling her so.

"It's ragged. They must have used a sharpened stone or some such. Anyway it needs attention," Owen said. "And soon. There's no knowing what filth was on it." He moved her cloak back over her shoulder. "There's a place nearby."

"What kind of place?" Pen hung back slightly as he took her elbow and began to move her along the alley, Cedric holding the taper to light their way. She didn't know this man and he unsettled her. She knew he had saved her life and she was immensely grateful for that but there was something disturbing about him. Sufficiently disturbing for her to feel that she shouldn't accompany him to some strange venue, that anything could happen in his company. Why had he pursued her from the great hall earlier? Why had he kissed her? What did it mean that she interested him? And just what was it about him that interested *her?*

Pen decided she was in no fit condition to explore the latter question. "I'll take a wherry at the steps," she said firmly. "I'll be home in an hour. My own servants can take care of the wound."

Owen didn't want to frighten her but neither was he willing to let this heaven-sent opportunity go by the board. He said with soft reassurance, "There's no need to be afeard, Lady Pen. Not in my company at least. But the longer the wound remains uncleansed the greater the chance of mortification. There's a tavern hard by the Horseferry steps where I'm known. They will have hot water, and bandages, and I trust a decent sack posset. After which I will convey you myself to the princess's residence."

The wound throbbed in her neck, and when she touched it tentatively the skin was hot and her finger came away bloody. She thought of the kind of weapon they might have used, a stone from the gutter coated in filth, a sharpened piece of iron found in a dung heap. And she knew her companion was right. It was imperative to cleanse it immediately. And a tavern would have servants, an innkeeper and his lady. All quite ordinary and safe.

"Very well," Pen said.

They walked quickly to the steps and Pen was aware that she had begun to rely on the support of his hand beneath her elbow. Her own body was letting her down. She forced herself to stand upright, to stiffen her watery knees, to take firm steps. It seemed vitally important that she show no weakness. Why she felt this she didn't know. But she was convinced that he wanted something from her and she must be on guard against it lest it creep up upon her.

Nothing that had happened since Pen first met Owen d'Arcy had changed her opinion that he was a very dangerous man.

Three

●

"She was in the gallery, you say?" Lady Bryanston glanced up at the gallery that ran along one side of the great hall.

"Aye, I saw her up there just after the princess and her entourage left." Miles Bryanston's words were a little slurred, his eyes on the contents of the goblet he held.

"What could she want up there?" demanded Lady Joan, his countess. Her face glistened with the heat. Her eyes followed her mother-in-law's upwards to the gallery.

"Poking and prying as usual," Lady Bryanston declared, her lips a thin line above her heavy chin. "She won't let it go. She's as stubborn as an ox."

"Even though her own family don't believe her," Miles commented. He belched and drained the contents of his goblet, then yawned noisily.

Servants moved around them, clearing up the debris of the revels. The candles were now guttering, the logs in the great fireplaces burned to embers, and cold edged aside the last breath of warmth left by the recently departed crowd.

" 'Tis to be hoped they don't," muttered his mother. The Kendals were a formidable pair

47

with powerful connections. If they once decided to interest themselves in their daughter's obsession, there was no knowing how far they could take it.

"Why should they?" Joan asked, stifling a yawn. "It's been two years. What could they find? There'll be nothing left of a dead child now!"

"No, but they could be a nuisance," her mother-in-law said evasively.

If Miles had done his work well, there would indeed be nothing to find.

She gave her son a quick glance that held just a degree of doubt. Much as she adored him, she had to admit that he was not as quick-witted as he might have been. Unlike his elder brother, whose wit had been pure quicksilver, bright and swiftly moving. But where Philip would not be ruled by his mother, Miles obeyed her every dictate with the faithful devotion of an old dog. Where Philip would have refused to touch anything remotely underhand, Miles would have followed her instructions to the letter and relished every moment. No, surely he would have done his work well. He would have left no traces.

She glanced at Joan, whose attention had as usual wandered. Lady Bryanston spoke softly to her son. " 'Tis probably time to check the arrangements. If there's anything left, make another move. Do it soon. You understand me?"

Miles grunted a response and called for more wine.

48

"You have no need of more wine," his mother said impatiently. "I want to know what you discussed with the Duke of Northumberland. You were in his company for close on twenty minutes."

"Hunting," Miles said, extending his goblet to the servant who'd run up with a flagon. "We talked of hunting."

"Is that all? You didn't discuss the king's health as I told you to?"

Miles hiccuped. In truth he had completely forgotten his mother's instructions; they had somehow become lost in the wine wreathing through his brain. But he couldn't admit to that. "It didn't arise." He looked soulfully at his mother. "I couldn't just open the subject myself, could I?"

Lady Bryanston sighed. "Yes, Miles, you could have done. Everyone is interested in the king's health, it would not have been remarked upon. If you don't talk with the duke or try to gain his confidence, how can you suggest the possibility of a new treatment? Sometimes I think —"

She stopped, for her son was not listening, or if he was he was not capable of absorbing anything she said. "We will discuss this when your head is clear," she declared with a snap. "I am going to my rest. I bid you both good night." She swept to the stairs.

" 'Tis possible I angered her," Miles muttered into his goblet. He raised bloodshot eyes and looked at his wife, whose attention seemed to have returned. "D'you think 'tis possible, Joan?"

"Maybe," she said mournfully. " 'Tis not wise, Miles. You should have remembered to talk of the king's health."

"I know but my head was full of the cards and I could think of nothing else." He tipped the contents of his newly charged goblet down his throat. "Let's to bed, sweetheart."

He gave her something very like a leer but Joan knew from experience that the leer promised nothing. The spirit might be willing but the flesh would be definitely droopy. Sometimes she thought her barrenness might have something to do with her husband's infrequent ability to perform adequately in the marriage bed, but of course she knew that couldn't be so. The inability to conceive was always a woman's problem. Her womb was barren, unfriendly to her husband's seed, and she knew her mother-in-law blamed her. The dowager countess's anxiety to have the succession tied up was almost as much of an obsession as Pen's with her dead child.

With a tiny sigh, Joan followed her husband's stumbling progress up to their bedchamber.

The tavern was set back from the Horseferry steps in its own garden. It was lime washed, half timbered, with a low-pitched thatched roof from which smoke curled in the bright freezing air. Its windows, however, were dark behind their shutters.

"They're all abed," Pen said as Owen, still holding her elbow, unlatched the gate to the path. "I'll take a wherry at the steps."

"Nonsense," Owen said placidly. "Mistress Rider will be pleased to assist us."

"She'll not be pleased to be woken," Pen protested, hanging back.

"She will be pleased to be woken," Owen responded with cheerful serenity. "Cedric, run around to the back and see if anyone's up in the kitchen."

Cedric trotted off, and Owen adjusted the hood of Pen's cloak so that it covered her more tightly. The clouds had dissipated and the night was crisp and clear, the moon washing all around them with a pale light now that they were out of the huddle of dark lanes.

Pen's face was white in the moonlight, her hazel eyes both wide and very dark. The natural ease with which he'd adjusted her hood had startled her. Owen smiled at her and she felt a measure of reassurance. Some warmth flowed back into her chilled and aching body.

The front door opened. A woman stood there holding a lantern high. "Come you in, sir. Cedric says you've a wounded lady."

"Aye, Mistress Rider." Owen propelled Pen in front of him. "We had an encounter with a tribe of beggars. They cut Lady Bryanston and the wound needs cleansing immediately."

Pen stepped into a narrow passageway and returned the interested gaze of a round-bodied woman wrapped in a shawl over her kirtle and chemise. "Forgive us if we roused you from your bed, mistress," Pen said.

"Oh, 'tis no trouble, madam. I'm used to the chevalier turning up at all hours. Come this way." She bustled ahead of them, holding the lantern high so that it threw its light along the passageway.

They came into a large square kitchen where a kettle sat on a trivet over a brightly burning range. Three yellow lurchers lying by the door to the yard raised their heavy heads, then lumbered to their feet, tails wagging, to greet Owen like an old friend. He stroked them, let them lick his hands, and after a minute they returned to their places, dropping their heads back to their folded paws with breathy sighs.

Cedric was revolving slowly before the fire, making sure every side of him was exposed to the heat. He had a satisfied air. On such a night a warm kitchen was infinitely preferable to hanging around the water steps waiting for transport.

"If ye'll just warm yourselves 'ere, I'll 'ave the chevalier's bedchamber prepared in a trice," Mistress Rider said. " 'Tis all ready, just needs a light to the fire. We wasn't expectin' you back this evening, sir."

"No," Pen said hastily, throwing out a hand to stop the woman as she made for the stairs. "There's no need to prepare a bedchamber. This will take but a minute."

"I believe it will take a little longer," Owen

said easily. "You'll be more comfortable before a fire above stairs, and Mistress Rider will prepare a sack posset while I cleanse the wound."

"Aye, that's right," the woman said cheerily. "You, young Cedric, bring a bucket of 'ot coals from the fire, we'll have the chevalier's chamber warm as toast in no time."

Cedric shoveled hot coals into a bucket and followed Mistress Rider from the kitchen.

"Come to the fire," Owen said, going over to the range. "There's no need to be afeard."

"Isn't there?" Pen returned somewhat dryly. Nevertheless she followed him to the fire, bending to warm her hands. The ripped gloves had offered little protection from the cold on their walk to the tavern and her fingertips were reddened and numb.

"I would expect that anyone reckless enough to strike off on her own through the dark alleys of London would be a stranger to fear," he commented with a raised eyebrow. "I assure you, if it's me you fear, I'm a deal less dangerous than a tribe of beggars."

That I doubt. But Pen kept that thought to herself. She was not afraid of him at all, but she was deeply disturbed by him. Or was she disturbed by the simple fact that he *did* disturb her? She sucked her fingertips in an effort to get the blood moving again.

"I do not fear you. And if the torchman had not run away I would have been better served," she responded a mite defensively. "But you mustn't think I don't know you saved my life. Or, indeed, that I'm not grateful."

"Well, as I said once before, you interest me, Lady Pen. I seem to find myself following you whenever I see you." There was no smile as he said this and his gaze was cool and steady resting on her face. Pen could detect no humor in the statement, it was entirely in earnest. For the moment she could find no suitable response.

Owen appeared content with the silence, and it seemed to Pen that she was slowly and inexorably enclosed by the calm stillness that flowed from him. The quiet of the kitchen was disturbed only by the heavy breathing of the dogs by the door and the crackle of the logs. She began to feel her aches and pains anew and the gash in her neck was throbbing, the skin around it was tight and sore. That made her afraid, if nothing else did. If the wound were poisoned, she had much more to fear than Owen d'Arcy's calmly determined pursuit, incomprehensible though it was.

Cedric returned to the kitchen. "Mistress Rider says I'm to take up hot water, sir. She's fetching some special salves and bandages from the stillroom."

Owen merely nodded and said to Pen, "Let us go up then."

It seemed, Pen thought, that she had little choice. Her hand went to the purse suspended from the chain at her waist. She felt the fold of parchment beneath the embroidered silk. This strange encounter in a waterside tavern seemed all part and parcel of the force that had driven her all evening. Maybe Owen d'Arcy was in her destiny.

She must have a fever, Pen thought disgustedly, to entertain such a ridiculous notion. Destiny, indeed! Her life was her own. Her choices were her own. She was like her mother, strong and in control of the forces that affected her life. She *chose* to be here with Owen d'Arcy, and she *chose* to allow him to minister to her hurts. And that was that.

With a lift of her chin she preceded him out of the kitchen and up the stairs from the narrow passageway.

Owen followed, wondering what she had been thinking to cause that sudden stiffening of her shoulders, the challenging lift of her chin. Something to do with him? It seemed likely. And that was all to the good. Anything that piqued her interest whether favorably or not served his purpose.

Mistress Rider greeted them at the head of the stairs and lit their way to a small chamber under the eaves, where a fire burned comfortingly in the hearth and sconced tallow candles threw golden circles of light onto the shining waxed floor.

"There's witch hazel for the bleeding, marigold cream for cleansing, and comfrey to help the healing," Mistress Rider said, indicating a basket on the table. "Will I tend to the lady, Chevalier?"

"No, I'll do it myself. I've a powerful need for a cup of aqua mirabilis and the lady would benefit from a sack posset. If you would see to those needs, mistress, I'll be well content."

"As you wish, sir." The woman bobbed a curtsy and bustled out.

The chamber was warm, cozy, and utterly inviting. Pen sank down on a stool by the fire and unclasped her cloak, letting the heavy hood fall back. The thick furred garment slipped to the floor. She cupped her hand over the throbbing gash in her neck as she leaned closer to the flaming logs.

Owen watched her for a moment, enjoying the graceful curve of her back. She wore the long hood of her headdress pinned up as prevailing fashion dictated and it accentuated the porcelain column of her neck. It struck him that she was not really nondescript at all. It struck him for the second time that night that his seduction of Pen Bryanston might afford more pleasure than he'd anticipated.

Pen felt his eyes upon her and slowly turned her head to look up at him, her hand still cupping her throat. Her arrested gaze held his and for a long moment neither of them moved, strangely connected by their reflections in the dark orbs of the other.

Pen could hear in her ears the suddenly accelerated beat of her heart. The muscles in her belly contracted. Her mouth was dry as she read the flash of pure desire that crossed his black eyes, belying the absolute stillness of his countenance. Philip had looked at her with desire and passion many times but under Philip's gaze she had never felt as she did now. Owen d'Arcy's desire would burn, would devour. She had the fanciful notion that if she was ever touched by that desire she would cease to exist as the person she knew. And deep within her she understood that this was what made Owen d'Arcy a dangerous man.

Cedric came in with hot water and the moment passed, the connection was broken. But something lingered in the air, and the page glanced curiously at the couple beside the fire. Then Owen without urgency moved backwards, away from Pen.

"Set the water on the table, Cedric, then go down to the kitchen and help Mistress Rider with the sack posset." His voice was calm and neutral.

Pen opened her mouth to say that Cedric should stay. She didn't want to be alone with Owen, alone while he ministered to her hurts, put his hands upon her body as he would have to do. But then she didn't know how to express this to the page without it sounding either silly or insulting. Instead she watched Owen's hands as he unclipped the velvet sheaths that held his rapier and dagger and laid the weapons on the table beside the hot water.

Those hands were so long and slender, so fine boned. A musician's hands, she thought. Rather like Philip's. But Philip had been more hesitant in his movements, less sure. He would not have handled arms the way Owen d'Arcy did. As if the rapier and dagger were extensions of himself.

"Do you live here?" she heard herself ask in an attempt at ordinary conversation.

"Mostly, when I'm in London . . . although tonight I had other plans."

"I disturbed them then?"

"They're all the better for being disturbed," he responded, his eyes smiling. "Would you remove your headdress? It will be easier for me to work." He spoke casually as he shrugged off his black velvet cloak. The crimson lining glowed in the candlelight as he tossed it carelessly onto the bed. He turned to the basin of hot water on the table. The firelight sparked off the gold thread in his black doublet, gleamed in the black enamel clasps of his black silk shirt.

Such a contained figure, she thought. Contained and yet surging with vitality and purpose. Such a man could be irresistible if he chose to make himself so.

Almost as if she were dreaming Pen stood up and removed the jeweled circlet that adorned her hood. She laid it carefully on the wide mantel above the hearth, then unpinned the hood and the crisp white coif beneath. She laid the long gold pins beside the circlet, and the hood and coif on the chest at the foot of the bed. She felt curiously naked. Her hair was parted and looped over her ears, and a whisper of a draft from the shuttered window touched her bare neck and throat.

In the same silence she resumed her seat on the stool before the fire and folded her hands in the lap of her gray damask gown.

Owen came over to her holding a steaming cloth that he'd dipped in the hot water. "Could you tilt your head to one side?"

Pen did so, closing her eyes because it seemed easier not to look at him as he bent over her, so close she could feel the warmth of his breath on her cheek.

He worked swiftly, surely, offering no apologies for hurting her as he cleansed the dried blood from the open wound. The stinging was inevitable and Pen was glad that he didn't refer to it, merely got on with the task as quickly as he could.

"What instrument do you play?" she asked, breaking the silence that had become uncomfortable for her, although not, she suspected, for him.

He paused in his ministrations and asked with a note of surprise, "What makes you think I play at all?"

"You do, though, don't you?" she challenged, opening her eyes and turning her head to look at him so that his hand dropped from her neck.

"Yes," he agreed. "I play the harp. Could you bend your head again? I'm almost finished."

Pen obeyed. "The harp. That's an unusual instrument. I thought maybe the lute or the lyre."

"It's the Welsh in me," he said with a soft laugh, and Pen realized what it was about his voice: those lilting cadences were Welsh. "I sing a passable tenor, too," he said, and now it sounded as if he were teasing her.

"But your name is French and Mistress Rider gave you the title of chevalier. A French knight's title."

He put a hand on her head, a warm palm steadying her, and the sudden intimacy of the touch sent a jolt through her belly and brought the fine hairs of her nape on end. "Hold still, please." He bent closer, applying the hot cloth like a compress.

"How bad is it?" Pen asked, struggling to regain her composure.

"Not as bad as I first thought. But it's ragged and I'm afraid it might scar." He straightened and dipped the cloth in the basin again. The water turned pink.

He continued to talk in his calm fashion as he returned his attention to her wound. "Anyway, to answer your question, my father was French, my mother is Welsh. I spent most of my growing years in France, mostly at court, but when I speak English my mother's accent takes over."

"I like it," Pen said, wincing at the sting of witch hazel as he splashed it into the wound.

"Why, thank you, madam." He laughed a little and she found she liked his laugh too. It was light and soft and seemed to indicate that he found more than the issue at hand amusing. In fact she was beginning to think that he was the most relaxing person she'd ever been around. Which was a curious paradox when she was also utterly convinced that he was the most dangerous person she'd ever been around.

He smoothed soothing cool salve into the cut, and the contrast after the heat of the water made her shudder. "So what were you looking for in the Bryanstons' library?" he inquired casually.

Pen's head jerked upright. "What makes you think I was looking for anything?"

"I have eyes and can in general put words to what they're seeing. . . . There now, I'll put a bandage over it and a physician can decide when you get home whether it needs to be stitched." He suited action to words, binding a soft pad over the cut with a strip of bandage that circled her throat.

"You were married to the Earl of Bryanston, I understand?" he continued in the same casual tone.

That would not be hard to discover, Pen thought. It was perfectly common knowledge. *Why was he interested in her?*

"Yes," she agreed.

"Perhaps you were looking for something that had belonged to your husband," he suggested, turning to the door as Cedric entered with a tray. "Good lad, put it down there and then find yourself a bed in the kitchen. We'll not be going anywhere until it grows light."

"But I must go home!"

"I'll escort you as soon as it's light." He brought a pewter tankard over to her. "This will soothe whatever aches and pains you still have."

"Thank you," Pen said faintly, taking the fragrantly steaming tankard from him.

"I see no virtue in going back into that frigid night when we can sit and drink companionably before a warm fire," Owen pointed out, hitching another stool to the fire with his booted foot. He sat down with his own cup of strong distilled waters and took a deep draught.

"Your husband died nearly three years ago, I believe. Did he fall ill?" His melodious voice was so gently interested, his tone so intimately confiding, that Pen found herself answering him without hesitation.

"Yes, it was very sudden. One day he was fit as a fiddle . . . he was never very strong, quite the antithesis of his brother." Scorn laced her tone. "Miles has a weak brain and a strong body. Philip was the opposite."

She paused, then continued into the inviting silence, "But he was well that autumn. Stronger than I'd ever seen him, and he was so delighted about the baby. . . ." Her voice faltered. She drank from the tankard.

Owen waited peacefully, his steady gaze revealing nothing of his thoughts. He believed he had found the key to this seduction. This was not a woman to be swept off her feet with flattery and passion. But if he once gained her friendship and confidence, then she would be open to temptation. She was a woman in whom emotions ran deep, he decided, and she was holding something close to herself, a sadness and an anger that he must understand before he could approach her.

"There was a child?" he prompted softly when it seemed she would not continue.

Pen raised her eyes from the fire and he almost flinched at the blaze of fury in the look she gave him. It was so fierce as to be almost mad, he thought.

"I had a son," she stated, turning her gaze back to the fire. "Six months after Philip's death. Philip was well and happy one day and then suddenly he was sick. He died in three days, no one could do anything for him." Her voice was now cold but the fury was still there. The white bandage around her throat accentuated her pallor and the flaring mélange of color in her eyes.

She looked up at him again and spoke clearly, articulating every word. "And then I was told that my son died, that he was dead before he was born. But I heard him cry."

She stared at him fixedly and he read the challenge she was throwing. "No one will believe me. But I *know* my son was born alive. They wouldn't show me the body. It was as if they wanted me to believe that he had never existed, that I had not carried him for eight months."

No little brown mouse this! Owen leaned forward, resting his elbows on his knees, his cup held loosely between his hands. *This was a woman capable of deep and abiding passions.*

"So what were you looking for in the Bryanstons' library?" he asked, looking intently into her eyes.

"I don't know. Something . . . anything . . . that would tell me what happened the night my child was born." She lifted her embroidered purse and unfastened the little gold clasp. "I tore this page from the accounts ledger for that day. There are names and payments; I thought maybe I'd be able to track down someone who was there. One of the midwives, perhaps."

She looked at the paper that she held between her hands. Now that she'd started on this tale it seemed she couldn't stop, although why it would interest the calm, attentive man sitting opposite her she couldn't imagine. "Towards the end I was barely conscious. It was a long and difficult labor, brought on early by something . . . I don't know. These things happen. . . ."

She shrugged as if trying to dispel the intense concentration in the chamber. "He was born before my mother could arrive from Derbyshire. Only my mother-in-law was in attendance, and some women she hired."

She looked across at him. "Of course everyone says grief and exhaustion played tricks on my mind; that I couldn't have heard my son's cry because he was born dead. But I *did!*"

Owen nodded. He spoke with softly melodic sympathy. "To be disbelieved on such a matter

64

must have made your loss unendurable."

"Yes," she agreed, her hand passing restlessly over the paper on her lap, smoothing out the creases where it had been folded. "Even my mother . . . my sister . . . Robin even, think that I was unhinged by grief. But it was not so."

"Robin?" he queried. He knew perfectly well, of course, but it wouldn't be wise to reveal the depths of his knowledge about her family.

"My stepbrother. Robin of Beaucaire. When his father was created Earl of Kendal, Robin took Lord Hugh's previous title. His father and my mother have been married for fifteen years. Or is it sixteen? I can't remember exactly."

Owen nodded again. "I see." Then he frowned. "Do you believe your child is still alive?"

"I don't know." She shook her head wearily. "My goal is very simple at this point. I would like to talk to someone who was there."

"Your mother-in-law is no help?"

Pen gave a short bitter laugh. "My mother-in-law was all too happy with the outcome. Miles is now the earl and under her thumb. She could not control Philip and she detests me."

"An unpleasant picture." A moment's silence followed the arid comment, then Owen extended a hand to the paper in Pen's lap. "May I look at that?"

She handed it to him in surprise. It almost seemed as if he believed her. The novel thought nonplussed her and she watched in startled silence as his eyes ran down the list.

"Are any of these names familiar to you?" he asked.

"One or two of the men. Tradesmen who supplied the household. But I don't recognize any of the women's names. And the women who attended me at the birth were all strangers . . . with the exception of Lady Bryanston, of course. My mother was to have been with me at the birth but I went into labor before she and my stepfather could arrive."

"I see," he said again. He glanced down the list once more. "There are three women mentioned here. It would be interesting to see if their names appeared on any other date in the ledger. If they were often employed by Lady Bryanston in some household capacity, one would expect to see regular payments made to them."

He didn't disbelieve her! Astonishment, excitement, gratitude tumbled in her head. She understood that not disbelieving didn't mean that he actually believed her, but it was going a great deal further than anyone else had done.

"Perhaps I can get back into the library and take another look," she said, her eyes glowing in her pale face. "There must be some way."

"Alternatively, one could go to High Wycombe and find these women," he mused. "They would presumably be local. In my experience, village gossip can be most enlightening."

"What kind of experience?" Pen sat up very straight on her stool, fixing him with an intense gaze.

"Oh, the Welsh can never keep secrets," he responded with a smile. "The village where I spent summers in my childhood was a hotbed of gossip and scandal. Reputations were ruined as easily and as frequently as a batch of scones."

"I know what you mean," Pen agreed slowly. "But I don't see how I could go to High Wycombe without the Bryanstons' discovering it. And they'd know immediately if I started asking questions." Fatigue suddenly swamped her. Her shoulders drooped and she rubbed her eyes with the tips of her fingers.

Owen rose and went to the window. "It wants but an hour until dawn. Why don't you rest on the bed until daylight?"

Pen glanced at the deep feather bed with its tapestry curtains and tester. It looked very inviting. She hesitated, glancing back at him.

"Go on," he said. "I assure you I'll not disturb you."

"But I'll be taking your bed. What will *you* do?"

"Sit by the fire and drink," he returned, folding the paper. He handed it back to her and with his head he gestured to the bed. "Go on," he repeated. "I have little need of sleep. If I do, Mistress Rider will find me a cot. It's been a rough night for you and you're dead on your feet."

Still she hesitated, then she asked, "You don't think I've made up some mad tale, do you?"

He shook his head. "Why would you do that?"

"Grief, they tell me."

"I think you're too strong, too levelheaded,

Pen Bryanston, to lose your wits in an orgy of grief," he replied. "I also think you have enough common sense to take the bed that's offered you without worrying that you'll be raped or murdered in your sleep." He smiled and lightly touched her cheek. "Believe me, I like my partners to be both willing and awake."

To her annoyance, Pen felt her cheeks warm at this. "I was not worried about that at all," she denied.

"Good. Then go to it." He turned and threw more logs on the fire.

Pen sat on the bed and surveyed her sandaled feet. They seemed to be a long way away from her, all the way down on the floor. Just the thought of bending to take them off filled her with a kind of desperation. With a sigh she fell back on the bed.

Owen straightened from the fire. He came over to the bed and slipped the sandals from her feet. She murmured something but didn't stir. He threw over her the fur coverlet that was folded at the end of the bed, then resumed his seat at the fire.

What an extraordinary story she had told. Could there possibly be any truth to it? He stretched his feet to the andirons, linking his hands behind his head. Owen d'Arcy had a great understanding of the depths of human depravity. He would not discount Pen's story out of hand. And he could begin to see a way to turn it to good use.

Four

●

Pen came awake with a jerk. Disoriented, she stared up at the unfamiliar pattern on the tester. She turned her head on the pillow, wondering for a moment why her neck hurt. She put up a hand and felt the bandage. Then she remembered.

She pulled herself up against the pillows, aware of a general soreness throughout her body. She had fought hard during that wild struggle with the beggars.

The chamber was empty although the fire burned brightly with fresh logs. The shutters were closed against the cold but sunlight shone through the cracks. It was well past dawn, Pen realized. A hue and cry would start up if she didn't soon appear at Baynard's Castle in Thames Street, where Princess Mary was presently residing as a guest of the Earl of Pembroke.

She pushed aside the fur coverlet and stood up groggily. Her sandals were laid neatly side by side at the end of the bed. She sat on the stool before the fire to put them on. Her eyes felt gritty, her gown was hopelessly creased, her hose were twisted. There was no mirror in the chamber but she had little difficulty imagining how she looked.

Her eye fell on her discarded coif and hood. She glanced up at the mantel, where the jeweled circlet and pins still lay. She touched the loops of her hair. They had come loose and tendrils were escaping the pins. She had no comb, she had no mirror.

Impatiently Pen released her hair and shook it down her back. Better that than half up and half down. She ran her fingers through the thick mass to get rid of the tangles.

All of these things she did with little attention. Her mind was a welter of emotion. She was confused, excited, apprehensive. Owen d'Arcy had believed her, or at least had not disbelieved her. She was so accustomed to having her obsession gently but firmly dismissed that she didn't know quite how to respond to someone who accepted it as possible.

But it wasn't just that that confused her. The man himself confused her. Sometimes she felt as easy and comfortable in his company as in Robin's, and at others he disturbed her so powerfully it almost scared her. He had some motive in pursuing her, of that she was certain, but what could it be?

Pen had few illusions about herself. She had not her sister's mischievously flirtatious manner that drew men like flies to the honeypot. She was pleasant enough to look at but nothing startling. Philip had loved and desired her but he had not

70

been the kind of man to draw swooning women to his feet. They had loved and desired each other. There had been passion and companionship but never this confused turmoil of contradictory emotions.

Why was a man of Owen d'Arcy's ilk interested in her? He was an exotic. A man of sophisticated elegance, one who moved through the courtier's world with supreme confidence and competence. A man who counted tavern keepers among his friends and whose skill with a rapier was that of a trained assassin. It was a conundrum.

And the thought of solving it brought goose bumps tingling over every inch of her skin.

Pen turned abruptly as the door opened. Owen came in carrying a laden tray. "Good morning," he greeted cheerfully, setting the tray on the table.

"Good morning," Pen responded in the same tone. He looked immaculate, as if his black silk shirt had been freshly laundered, his doublet and hose new pressed.

"I've brought breakfast. You're probably hungry."

Pen thought about it. "I suppose I am. But mostly I ache and I feel filthy. I must look terrible." Suddenly self-conscious, she pushed her hair away from her face. Her untidiness seemed even more noticeable when compared with her companion's morning freshness. It was unreasonable and inconsiderate of him, she decided resentfully.

"You are not in your best looks, I would agree," he replied. "But that's hardly to be wondered at. Should I carve you some ham?"

He might have had the decency to lie, Pen thought. But there wasn't much she could do about it. "If you please." She stood up and went to the table. She poured a cup of small beer from the pitcher on the tray and drank thirstily. "Did you sleep at all?"

"A little." He gave her a quick smile as if to reassure her that he didn't begrudge her the bed. He handed her a bread trencher thickly piled with ham.

"You look as if you slept the sleep of the just for a full night and awoke to freshly laundered clothes," Pen observed, not troubling to conceal her tart note.

"Appearances can be deceiving," he said mildly.

"I imagine Mistress Rider has an accustomed hand with your wardrobe. Since you lodge here."

"She looks after me very well," Owen agreed. "I've sent Cedric to summon a wherry to the steps. I imagine people will be worried about you."

Pen regretted her momentary sourness. It had been ungracious and smacked of ingratitude. She smiled and said, "The princess will assume I stayed at Bryanston House."

He raised an eyebrow. "An uninformed assumption no doubt."

"Completely," Pen agreed. She took her bread

and ham to the window and unlatched the shutters, flinging them wide. Frigid air flooded the
chamber, setting the logs flaring in the hearth.
The day was bright and sharp as ice crystals. The
bare branches of skeleton trees stood out, etched
against the pale clear blue of the sky. She could
see the river, a silver-gray stream crowded even
at this hour with boats.

Owen glanced sideways at her as he sliced
more ham. He liked the way her hair tumbled
down her back, liked its thickness and the little
kinks and curls that a brush would smooth out.
It was brown, at first sight a very ordinary
brown, but it was enlivened with streaks of gold,
little rippling lights in the cold pale sunlight.

Pen shivered and pulled the shutters closed
again. "It's a pretty day but it's too cold to have
them open." She went to the fire to warm her
hands.

Owen noticed that the bandage around her
neck was bloodstained. "It might be wise to look
at the wound and change the bandage. It's been
bleeding while you slept."

Pen put her hand up to her neck. "It feels stiff
and sore, but 'tis not throbbing anymore."

He came over to her and caught up a swatch of
her hair in one hand, lifting it clear of her neck.
He twined it around his hand, savoring its soft
silkiness.

Pen stood very still. There was an intimacy to
this touch that was much greater than his earlier
ministrations, greater even than the kiss he'd

given her. The fingers of his free hand worked the bandage loose and unwound it. Gently he lifted the pad that had covered the gash.

"Why do I interest you?" Pen asked abruptly.

Owen debated his answer for only a second. Flattering lies would do him no good with this woman. "I don't know," he said with a rueful laugh. "I don't mean to offend you, but I honestly don't know."

Now why, Pen thought, did she find this response so reassuring? Except, of course, that it was so credible. "I'm not offended," she said.

"No, I don't imagine you are," he responded. "And that, I think, is one reason why I'm so drawn to you. You're different, Pen Bryanston. In the midst of this serpentine world of deceit and lies and affectations you're straight, I believe, and honest."

Pen turned her head against the pressure of his hand and looked up at him. "How could you know that? You couldn't have known anything real about me before you followed me to the library yesterday."

"Ah, well, there I was following a hunch." Still holding her hair, he leaned sideways to the table where the basket of salves and bandages remained from earlier. "If you could hold your hair clear for me, I'll dress the wound again."

Their fingers brushed as she took the swatch of hair from him and her spine jumped with a sharp current of energy. "And where does this interest take you, Chevalier?" She bent her neck sideways under the gentle pressure of his ministering hand.

"That rather depends upon you, madam." There was a laugh in his voice. "As I said, I like my partners willing."

"And awake, as I recall," Pen returned in the same bantering tone. It was mad to be having this conversation, and yet with that energy racing through her it seemed perfectly natural.

"Certainly awake," he agreed, winding a fresh bandage around her throat. "There, at least you won't return to your friends and relatives looking like a bloodstained veteran of battle."

Pen let her hair fall again. She touched the bandage with her fingertips. "Is it healing?"

"The wound is closing nicely. I doubt there'll be a scar. Let us go now. Cedric will have a wherry waiting." He picked up her heavy furred cloak and draped it around her.

Pen pulled up the hood and tucked her loose hair out of the way. The high collar was torn where her neck had been gashed. The jeweled circlet and gold pins of her discarded headdress were still on the mantel. She selected a pin and craned her neck to fasten the rent material together.

"I'll do that." He took the pin from her, brushing her hands aside as naturally and easily as Robin would have done.

Pen found she was becoming accustomed to this confident and friendly manner. It seemed absurd to think of him as a stranger now, even though common sense told her that he remained so. She knew a little about him, but probably less than she knew about any other of the myriad slight acquaintances she had among the king's courtiers. But she had never before spent such a curiously intimate night with a bare acquaintance. At the thought she was aware once more of that strange sensation of energy prickling her spine.

Owen gathered up the rest of her pins and gave them to her. Pen opened the little purse at her waist, dropping the pins inside. The folded sheet of paper from the accounts ledger rustled against her fingers.

Would Owen d'Arcy help her? He seemed to believe her. But would he help her?

"What is it?" he asked as she stood in reverie, immobile, a tiny frown drawing her brows together, her lower lip caught between her teeth.

"I was wondering if you would help me try to discover what happened to my child," she answered slowly.

"How could I help?"

She met and held his gaze. "You talked of going into High Wycombe, asking some questions. . . ."

"I suggested it as a possible avenue," he agreed.

"One that you might help me take?" Pen asked directly.

He was silent for a minute and she could hear her heart thump in the stillness. "I will think about the problem," he said finally.

Pen would have preferred a more definite response but she would take what was offered. She felt that in this man lay her only hope. How or why that should be was a mystery, but it was true, and her spirits lifted.

She said simply, "My thanks, sir."

She withdrew a silver coin from her purse but hesitated a second before laying it on the table. The circumstances had been so peculiar that it might be considered offensive to offer to pay the landlady for her services. But Mistress Rider was still a woman in business and Pen knew her obligations. "I would like to leave Mistress Rider some token of my thanks."

"Of course," Owen said easily. "She will not refuse, I assure you."

Pen nodded, laid the coin on the table, and dropped the circlet into the deep pocket of her cloak. She picked up her ruined gloves and drew them on, wiggling her fingers comically through the torn leather. "These will do me little good."

"Wear mine." He handed her a pair of black gloves. The leather was the softest doeskin. "My hands rarely feel the cold."

Pen was not going to argue with this. Her hands and feet chilled far too rapidly for polite remonstrance. His fingers were longer than hers, she noticed absently as she drew on the gloves, longer and very slender; the gloves enclosed her fingers very tightly.

Cedric waited at the wherry, stamping his feet,

blowing on his hands. The boatmen grumbled at their oars as the boat knocked against the water steps. It was too frigid a morning to be sitting still.

"Where to, m'lord?"

"Baynard's Castle." Owen stepped into the wherry and offered Pen his hand. She jumped lightly in beside him. The sun glittering on the water was almost dazzling and the frosty air hurt when she drew it deep into her lungs.

She was going to find explaining the events of the night rather difficult, Pen realized as the little boat shot across the river, darting in and out of the traffic. Her reckless decision to plunge off into the night to make her own way home was not going to be popular with her nearest and dearest. And she didn't know how to explain it. She knew she couldn't confess to the truth, that the theft of the ledger page from the Bryanston library had driven all thought of danger from her mind.

And then she would have to explain what had happened during the remainder of the night. The truth was awkward, but a lie was impossible. She had a wound on her neck to make nonsense of any peaceful fabrication. Besides, she was a hopeless liar.

The wherry turned into the mouth of the Fleet River and drew up at the water steps of the imposing Baynard's Castle, once a royal palace, now the home of the Earl of Pembroke. Princess Mary, in her childhood, when she was King

Henry's pearl, as he'd liked to call her, when her mother, Catherine of Aragon, was still his beloved wife, had spent many happy times in the palace with her mother. In memory of those times she had asked her half brother King Edward for permission to reside there during her visits to London. The request had been granted, and Pembroke himself turned a diplomatically blind eye to the clandestine Catholic masses said in his royal guest's private apartments.

"There's no need to accompany me any farther, Chevalier," Pen said, hearing the sudden formality of her tone. "You have been very kind."

Owen looked at her in amusement. "Afraid I'm going to be hard to explain, madam?"

Pen flushed slightly. "As it happens, yes."

He laughed and jumped ashore, offering her his hand. "I will not rest easy until I see you safe inside." Pen Bryanston was to be his password to the tight circle around the princess. It stood to reason the princess would gratefully receive her friend's rescuer.

Pen hesitated, unwilling to seem ungracious, and yet certain that she could explain what had happened to her much more easily without his presence. Facts could be simply described when not muddied by emotional confusion.

"If you'll return this afternoon, sir, I'd be happy to —"

"Pen . . . Pen!"

She broke off at the sound of the high voice.

She spun around to look up the redbrick path that led from the water to the gate in the wall around the castle. A young woman, a flash of crimson and emerald, was running down towards them, her bright skirts caught up to free her stride, words tumbling from her mouth.

"Pen . . . Pen . . . where on earth have you been? We've been frantic with worry."

Pen sighed. All hope of concealing any part of the truth was gone. Pippa would ferret out every detail. And yet despite this she hurried to meet her younger sister as she arrived at the foot of the stairs. Pen hadn't seen Pippa for close on a month and as always she had missed her.

"Pippa, I wasn't expecting you for another three days." She hugged her tightly. "Are Mama and Lord Hugh here too?"

"Yes, at Holborn." Pippa's gaze had immediately found Owen d'Arcy. Her eyes widened and she whispered into her sister's ear, "Who's that?"

Pen turned, her arm still around her sister's waist. Owen d'Arcy stood smiling expectantly. She was about to make the introduction when a loud hail from the path distracted her.

"Oh, it's Robin," Pippa said, momentarily forgetting Pen's companion. "He has been *beside* himself. Robin . . . Robin . . . it's all right, Pen's here now. She's quite safe!" she cried. "Someone brought her back."

"Chevalier d'Arcy at your service, madam." Owen took his cue and stepped forward. He bowed, his bland countenance hiding his swift appraising scrutiny of Pen's sister.

Robin arrived beside them, out of breath, his cap in his hands, his thatch of nut-brown curls windblown. His brilliant blue eyes held a mixture of anxiety and relief.

"What happened? Where have you been?"

"Princess Mary said you had stayed overnight at Bryanston House," Pippa chipped in. "But we knew perfectly well you would never have done that." Even as she spoke her gaze remained on the chevalier.

"The water steps were so crowded and it was so cold that I foolishly decided to strike out on my own," Pen explained. "I ran afoul of a crowd of beggars. Fortunately, Chevalier d'Arcy happened on the scene and came to my rescue." Her hand went fleetingly to her bandaged neck.

Robin's gaze swiveled to the man still standing by the wherry. Suspicion darted across his countenance. *So this was Owen d'Arcy. Was his rescue of Pen pure coincidence?*

He looked back at Pen and noticed her torn cloak and the glimpse of bandage beneath. For the moment he dismissed Owen d'Arcy. "You're hurt!" He stepped quickly up to Pen.

Pen shook back the hood of her cloak to show the bandage. "It's not as bad as it might have been. The chevalier took me to an inn he knows at the Horseferry steps. The tavern keeper was very kind, although it was so late at night. She had salves and bandages so I could cleanse the wound. It needed to be done immediately," she added, wishing she didn't sound so apologetic. It made it seem as if there had been something wrong about Owen's intervention. Something she needed to hide.

Was there?

"You had an adventure," Pippa declared in a tone of wonderment. "How strange, Pen. It's usually me who has adventures."

"I assure you, Pippa, you're welcome to them," Pen said. "That one will last me a lifetime." She laid a hand on Robin's arm and said, "I don't believe you're acquainted with the chevalier d'Arcy, Robin. Chevalier, this is my stepbrother, Robin of Beaucaire."

Robin bowed stiffly to Owen, his mouth tight. "I'm honored, sir."

Owen returned the bow with an ironic little smile. Pen's stepbrother was not in the least honored by the meeting. "The honor is all mine," he murmured.

Pen frowned at Robin. She could feel him as prickly as a hedgehog, his usual courtesy and good humor quite absent. Why would he dislike Owen d'Arcy? Maybe it was because the smooth, immaculate Owen was such a contrast with his own somewhat haphazard appearance. The chevalier had not a hair out of place. Robin on the other hand was tousled, his hose and doublet were ill-matched, his shirt collar was un-buttoned, and his short gown was slipping from his shoulders as if he'd dressed in haste. This indifference to his appearance was perfectly usual for Robin and ordinarily she would barely notice, but this morning his dress seemed particularly careless.

She said swiftly, "I'm not exaggerating, Robin, when I say that the chevalier saved my life."

Robin looked directly at Owen d'Arcy, mistrust and suspicion still clear in his gaze. "Lady Pen's family stand in your debt, sir," he said in clipped tones.

"Not at all," Owen responded cheerfully. "It was fortunate I happened to see her leave the water steps."

"As Pen hasn't seen fit to introduce me, sir, I must introduce myself," Pippa announced. She regarded Owen with her head on one side. "I'm Pen's sister Philippa, Chevalier." Her hazel eyes, the twins of her sister's, sparkled mischievously as she subjected him to a full and frank assessment.

Owen bowed over her hand, carrying her fingers to his lips. "*Enchanté,* my lady."

"Oh, how pretty!" Pippa cried. "I think we are to become great friends. After all, you saved Pen's life and that means we can dispense with all sorts of formalities."

Robin and Pen exchanged speaking glances. Pippa was at it again. She was an incorrigible flirt but for some reason no one ever took her liveliness amiss.

"Well, that is certainly something I look forward to, Lady Philippa," Owen returned gravely.

"Pippa," Pippa corrected. "No one ever calls me Philippa. Not even the king, and old King Harry never did either." She smiled at him, setting dimples dancing at the corners of her mouth.

"I can see how that might be," Owen said with the same gravity, well aware that she was flirting with him. "Pippa suits you much better."

Her smile became a grin and Owen could easily understand how men were attracted to her. She was far from pretty in any conventional way, quite the contrary. Her nose was long and pointed, her chin sharp, her countenance liberally sprinkled with freckles. She was thin and quick, and in her crimson and emerald silk she reminded him of a brightly plumaged little bird, not an exotic though, more like a sparrow in borrowed feathers. The French had a word for women like Lady Philippa. *Jolie-laide*. Her plainness was somehow attractive. But for his own money, he found her sister infinitely more appealing.

He turned away from the sparrow and back to Pen, who he decided reminded him of a thrush — brown, speckled, bright-eyed, and very sure of who she was and where she was going. A no-nonsense bird. He spoke with deliberate formality although his eyes had a very different tone. Their message was one of intimate complicity. "I can see I have no need to see you safe inside, madam. I leave you with Lord Robin and your sister. But I trust you'll permit me to inquire after your health tomorrow."

"I shall be happy to receive you, Chevalier," Pen returned with the same formality. "I should like to present you to Princess Mary."

"I would be deeply honored." He leaned forward and kissed her full on the lips as he'd done once before and said softly, "In the meantime, I'll consider that other matter." Then he turned away and said calmly, blandly, "Lord Robin . . . Lady Pippa . . . I bid you farewell."

"Don't wait too long before you come to call upon Pen," Pippa said. She had barely noticed the kiss.

"Believe me, Lady Pippa, I will not." He stepped into the wherry where Cedric was waiting impatiently, although the page had found the exchanges on the water steps most interesting. The oarsmen took up their oars and pulled out into the current.

Owen stood in the bow with his hands clasped at his back, gazing across the river. A thrush, or a dove? No, definitely not a dove. Too sickly sweet. No, she was a thrush. Seemingly nondescript but a sweet-tongued yet tough dweller of the hedgerow. He smiled to himself. Then he recollected her stepbrother and a grimace twisted his mouth. Lord Robin could prove to be a nuisance.

Owen had made it his business to learn all he could about Pen's brother. He knew that the man was more than a peripheral member of Suffolk's household, that he did more than just walk the halls of the ducal houses of Northumberland and Suffolk. Robin of Beaucaire took an active part in their diplomatic intrigues. He was nowhere near as accomplished a spy as the chevalier, but he was no fool.

It was clear from the last few minutes that de Noailles had not exaggerated when he'd said that Pen and her stepbrother had a special closeness. And Lord Robin would know of Owen d'Arcy's own affiliations.

Owen could see that he would have to forestall any tale-telling.

"How dare he kiss you!" Robin exploded as the wherry pulled away.

Pippa saved Pen the trouble of answering. "Everyone kisses everyone, Robin. You know that. Particularly if they're really close friends, and if someone saves your life how could he be anything else?"

The reasonable side of Robin knew that he couldn't argue with this. Such salutations were indeed quite unremarkable between friends. But Owen d'Arcy could not possibly be a friend of Pen's. He could only mean her harm. But Robin couldn't tell her this.

The Duke of Northumberland had been adamant that they leave the relationship to develop. Something useful might come of having Robin's sister involved with a French spy. He had made this declaration in his coldly decisive manner and Robin had held his tongue. A man did not argue with John Dudley, Duke of Northumberland, unless he was prepared to forfeit everything. And it seemed to Robin that he'd be more useful to Pen with his head still attached to his body.

His frustration took its own path, however. "How could you have done something so foolhardy, Pen? To set off on your own like that?" he demanded as they climbed up the steps to the castle. He glanced over his shoulder and saw that the wherry bearing d'Arcy away had reached midstream.

"Robin, if you insist upon scolding me you must wait until I've soaked myself in a hot bath and a physician has looked at the cut on my neck," Pen declared, weariness making her acerbic. She stepped up the path with a strength she didn't have. "Pippa, I hope you haven't said anything to Mama and Lord Hugh."

"Oh, but . . ." Pippa looked stricken. "I beg your pardon, Pen, but when I arrived here this morning and you weren't here I sent a message to Holborn to see if you'd gone there. So, I'm afraid . . ." She bit her lip ruefully.

Pen sighed. "I am quite old enough to make my own decisions and my own mistakes. But of course no one will accept that."

"You're not old enough to make them when they nearly kill you," Robin snapped.

"Oh, don't be so sanctimonious, Robin!" Pen

marched through the gate in the wall into the quiet garden beyond. "You'd be more helpfully employed by riding to Holborn and telling Mama and your father that I'm back safe and sound. I'm going to have a bath and summon a physician. Pippa, will you tell Princess Mary that I'm back and will attend upon her as soon as may be?"

"I'll tell her, but I think you need to sleep before you do any attending," Pippa said frankly, examining her sister with concern. "You really do look dreadful."

"Well, thank you!" Pen said. "That's all I needed to know. That really improves matters." She pulled her hood up over her head again, stalking away from them towards the palace.

"Oh, dear," Pippa said. "Something's happened. I don't mean just the beggars, but something else. I wonder what."

"If anyone can find out, you can," Robin said, not sounding exactly as if he was conferring a compliment.

Pippa, however, took it as her due. "Yes," she agreed. "But if you're going to be disagreeable I won't tell you what I discover."

She went off in her sister's wake, leaving her stepbrother to his anxiety and frustration as he rode to Holborn with the news of Pen's safe return.

Five

●

"You're covered in scratches and bruises, Pen!" Pippa exclaimed as she entered Pen's bed-chamber after delivering her message to Princess Mary.

Two maids were filling the copper tub before the fire. Pen was naked, examining her body inch by inch with a small Italian hand mirror of silvered glass. Pippa was not exaggerating. Her arms and breast were crisscrossed with scratches, some of which had oozed a little blood. There was a big bruise on her belly and she seemed to remember being kicked. Bruises on her thighs and shins certainly backed up the memory.

"It was horrible!" she said, shuddering as she relived those few ghastly minutes. "It didn't last long before the chevalier arrived but . . ." She crossed her arms over her breast with another shudder.

"He must have arrived just in time," Pippa observed, arranging herself on the deep window seat, paying particular attention to the fall of her crimson silk gown that opened over an emerald-green taffeta underskirt. Pippa shared with Princess Mary a passion for rich materials and bright colors, unlike Pen, who followed her mother's

89

taste for a more subdued elegance.

"So, a dramatic rescue!" Pippa declared, clearly settling in for a good chat. "Tell me everything. What an adventure. I'm quite envious. Did the chevalier beat them off all by himself?"

"His page was there, using a dagger. But Owen used a dagger and a rapier. Like an assassin, Pippa. An avenging angel. He was everywhere and they just melted away before his sword."

"Owen?" Pippa questioned quickly. "You didn't use his first name before."

Pippa never missed a trick, Pen thought, cursing herself for allowing the familiarity to slip out. "I was introducing him before," she retorted. "But we met in somewhat unusual circumstances." She set the mirror aside and went over to the fire.

"When someone saves your life and then spends the night in the same inn chamber it seems silly to be formal." She dipped a toe in the water in the bathtub. "Add a little more hot, will you, Ellen? And dried lavender and rose petals, please."

"Yes, m'lady." The elder of the two maids fetched another steaming copper jug from the fire and poured its contents into the tub while the younger sprinkled lavender and rose petals into the stream so that the fragrance filled the chamber.

"Oh?" Pippa's eyes narrowed, but she said no more for the moment.

Pen stepped into the water, saying to the maids, "You may leave me now. I'll ring when I need you again."

Only when they had curtsied and left did Pippa continue her questions. "So what did you do in the chamber all night?"

"Talked mostly." Pen slid into the hot water and rested her head on the edge of the tub, closing her eyes as the warmth laved her and her tight muscles began to relax.

"Talked? What about?" Pippa sat forward, her hands resting on her knees.

"This and that," Pen murmured. "Then I slept for a couple of hours. When I awoke, the chevalier escorted me home."

Pippa frowned, convinced she was not hearing the whole story. "So who is the chevalier? Had you met him before?"

"I met him for the first time earlier that evening, at the reception." Pen wondered whether to tell Pippa about that strange meeting and the very unexpected kiss. Pippa would relish the story, but then she would extract from Pen exactly what she'd been doing in the library when Owen had surprised her. However hard she tried to keep it secret, her sister, given half a chance, would ferret out all the details and then her mother would know and everyone would be sad and vexed again. It wasn't worth it. And most particularly not now when all her hopes were centered on Owen d'Arcy.

She continued carelessly, "As I understand it

he spends most of his time at the French court. I assume he's newly arrived in London."

"Does he have a wife?"

"How should I know?" Pen demanded, sitting up so abruptly that the water splashed over the edge of the tub onto the waxed floorboards.

"Well, I thought you might have asked," Pippa responded. "I would have done."

"Yes, I'm sure you would have done. I didn't consider it relevant to any discussion we were having."

"Oh." Pippa was for the moment nonplussed. "Aren't you interested in finding out?"

"No."

"He's very . . . um . . . very striking," Pippa said. "Not handsome, that's too ordinary a word. But he's . . ." She searched for the word she wanted.

"Exotic," Pen supplied, and Pippa laughed and clapped her hands.

"Exactly so. Exotic. So why wouldn't you be interested in knowing whether he was married?"

"I'm not a flirt."

"And I am."

"Deny it if you can." Pen laughed, turning to look at her sister over her shoulder. "You're an outrageous flirt. Are you ever going to get married?"

"I don't see the point," Pippa said. "I'm enjoying life too much just as it is. I don't want to be proper and tied down. And I most certainly don't want a mother-in-law. Not after your experience."

"Well, you may understand that for the very same reason I've no interest in acquiring another, so the married status of Owen d'Arcy matters not a whit to me," Pen declared roundly.

"But you do find him attractive?" Pippa pressed.

Pen closed her eyes again. There was no point denying it. And no point denying to herself that his attraction had very little to do with the possibility that he might help her in her quest. "I suppose I do."

"I wonder how Robin's going to take that."

" 'Tis no business of Robin's!"

"He'll think it is," said Pippa with perfect truth.

At that moment the sisters' tête-à-tête was interrupted. The door flew open and Lady Kendal entered in a rustle of silk and velvet. She was followed by a very elderly woman with a pronounced dowager's hump.

"Pen, my dearest girl! What happened to you? We have been out of our minds with worry."

"Mama!" Pen stood up in a shower of water. "Oh, believe me, 'twas nothing. Pippa reacted too quickly. There was no cause for concern." She put a hand to her neck as if to conceal the bandage.

"Ay . . . ay . . . ay, chuck!" the old woman muttered, hurrying to the bathtub. "Look at you, girl! All scratched and bruised."

"Tilly, 'tis nothing serious. A cut on my neck, a few bruises and scratches." Pen smiled reassuringly at the woman who had been her mother's nurse and then her own, and was now so old that their young half sister Anna thought she had been living forever.

"Standing there dripping in this cold, you'll catch your death," Tilly scolded, gathering up a thick towel and wrapping it around Pen. "Let me look beneath that bandage."

Pen stepped out of the tub, drawing the towel tightly around her. She sat on a stool by the fire and submitted patiently as Tilly, tutting to herself, unwound the bandage.

"I think I need a little more explanation, Pen," her mother said, regarding her eldest daughter with a frown in her dark purple eyes. At forty-three, Guinevere was still a lovely woman. Her hair, once palest gold, was now silver, and the faint tracery of lines upon her face served only to accentuate the intelligence and humor of her character. She was as elegant as ever, sapphires blazing against the black velvet of her gown.

"Pen fell among thieves," Pippa said. "And she was rescued by a Chevalier d'Arcy who —"

"Pippa, I can tell my own story!" Pen interrupted.

"I suppose it was *your* adventure," Pippa agreed. "But I wish it had been mine."

"Pippa, I would discuss this alone with Pen," her mother said firmly. "Would you please go to Lord Hugh? He's paying his respects to Princess

Mary and he has Anna with him. She's most anxious to see Pen. Would you go and find her and bring her back here?"

Pippa knew quite well that she was being sent on an unnecessary errand to get her out of the way. Anna was perfectly capable of finding her own way to Pen's chambers. But Pippa was slow to take offense and even the most pointed snubs rarely hit home. She went off with a cheerful wave at the towel-wrapped Pen.

Guinevere sat down on Pippa's vacated window seat and drew off her gloves. "Now, love, tell me please what's happened."

Princess Mary's presence chamber was crowded as Pippa entered. She saw her stepfather, the Earl of Kendal, and her half sister, Anna, in the circle around the princess, who sat by the fire in a carved chair, an open book in her lap. Even when giving audience, Mary was rarely without a volume at hand and would frequently disconcert visitors by suddenly withdrawing her attention and turning her eyes to her page.

This morning, however, her attention seemed wholly focused on those around her. Despite the relative poverty forced upon her by the king and his council, she was dressed with great richness in a French gown of gold brocade heavily embroidered and studded with emeralds. A gift from her cousin, the Holy Roman Emperor. Her small hands were smothered in rings, and a great diamond blazed at her breast.

95

Mary was a handsome woman who wore her thirty-six years lightly. She was small and slight and her auburn hair and fresh complexion gave the lie to the ill health that plagued her, exacerbated by her constant anxiety about her personal safety amid the snares and conspiracies that surrounded her.

Pippa edged through the crowd and curtsied as she reached the princess. Her stepfather laid an affectionate hand on her shoulder as she stood beside him.

"How is Pen?" Mary asked with an air of concern. "I don't understand why she didn't remain at her mother-in-law's house last night. If I'd known she intended to come back here I would have sent someone to escort her."

"It's most unlike Pen to do anything so foolish," the earl said with a frown. "I'm sure she must have had good and sufficient reason, madam."

"She has a cut on her neck and many bruises and scratches," Pippa informed all and sundry. "It was a very narrow escape and so fortunate that the chevalier happened to have followed her when she left the water steps."

"Who is this chevalier?" asked the princess.

"The Chevalier d'Arcy," Pippa replied promptly.

Mary raised a delicately arched eyebrow. "I am not familiar with the name but he has my thanks. Has the physician been sent to Pen?"

"Tilly is with her now so I doubt she'll need a

physician, madam," Pippa responded. "And Mama is there too."

"I see. But I insist the physician visit her as well. She must remain abed today." Mary turned to one of her ladies. "Matilda, would you send the physician to Pen's chamber?"

"At once, madam." The woman curtsied and withdrew.

"And now, if you'll excuse me, Lord Kendal, I must go to my prayers." The princess rose from her chair. She smiled at the fourteen-year-old Anna, who stood close to her father. "Such a pretty child. Bring her to see me again, Lord Kendal."

Hugh bowed his acquiescence and his daughter curtsied, her cheeks pink with a mixture of embarrassment and excitement.

Mary left the chamber, her hand resting on the arm of the Spanish ambassador, a saturnine gentleman whose dark complexion contrasted with his neat gray beard and mustache.

Anna turned to Pippa. "Did you hear her? The princess said I was pretty!"

"Well, so you are," Pippa said matter-of-factly. "If you were at court, you'd have more suitors than you could count. Wouldn't she, Lord Hugh?"

"Quite possibly," Hugh said with a dry smile. "But I'm not about to let her loose on the world just yet. What do you know of this business with Pen, Pippa?"

"Only that she set off on her own after the

Bryanstons' revels last evening, and was set upon by beggars and was rescued by this chevalier, Owen d'Arcy. Did Robin tell you that we met him when he brought Pen home? Do you know him, Lord Hugh?"

"Not to speak to. But I believe he's a close acquaintance of the French ambassador, Antoine de Noailles."

"He didn't sound French."

Hugh shrugged. "That means little." He stroked his chin, wondering if there was any significance in Owen d'Arcy's friendship with the ambassador. It was possible that he was involved in the French king's undercover diplomacy. Every foreign power had an undercover presence at the Court of St. James's. If so, Hugh wasn't sure that he wanted his stepdaughter to further her acquaintance with the chevalier. He may have done her a service, but spying was an unsavory business.

It was bad enough that Robin dabbled his toes in that murk. Hugh disliked his son's involvement in the intrigues of the Duke of Northumberland. The Duke was a dangerous man and the young king was no more than his puppet. When so much power was centered on one man, the stability of the kingdom was inevitably threatened.

Hugh did not interfere in his son's choice of loyalty but he watched him and the situation a deal more closely than Robin was aware.

Princess Mary was the heir to the throne. So

far there had been no overt challenges to the succession, but Hugh had a feeling that the dukes of Northumberland and Suffolk had something up their sleeves. They were certainly manipulating the sick young king and managing to feather their nests in the process. If the dukes plotted treason, then Robin would be tarred with their brush. And his father would not then stand aside.

By the same token he needed to probe into the character and situation of this Chevalier d'Arcy who had managed to attract Pen's attention so dramatically. The role of paterfamilias was an onerous one, Hugh reflected, but with an inner smile. He would not have it any other way. He adored all four of his children and drew no distinction between the two he had sired and the two he had not.

"I must seek out the chevalier and thank him once I've had a chance to talk to Pen," he said. "Run ahead, Anna, and ask if she's able to receive me yet."

"So, how goes the pursuit, Owen?" Antoine de Noailles straightened his doublet and peered in the small mirror on the table to adjust the jewel in the lace at his throat. A pool of golden candlelight illuminated the mirror and the table, but the rest of the chamber was as dim as the gray day beyond the window. Owen stood in the shadows, outlined against the arras, one hand idly playing with the hilt of his rapier, his gloves held loosely in his other.

"A promising beginning," he said with a shrug. "Circumstances played into my hands."

Noailles turned from the mirror. "How so?"

Owen laughed softly. "Leave me to my business, Antoine, and I'll leave you to yours."

The ambassador shook his head. "You'll at least tell me if you think you'll succeed."

Owen did not immediately respond. He turned his gaze to the window, where a bare branch scraped irritatingly against the pane. The ambassador was asking whether the chevalier believed he would succeed in getting the lady into his bed.

With vague surprise, Owen realized that he was less than confident about that. He realized that he had no interest whatsoever in seducing Pen Bryanston in order to steal her secrets. He realized that he *wanted* to make love with Pen Bryanston, but for quite other reasons than her usefulness to the French government. He had, however, a task to fulfill. But there were other routes to the same goal.

"I believe you may safely leave matters in my hands," he said when the silence seemed to have stretched into infinity and the ambassador was staring at him in some puzzlement.

"So how d'you find the lady?" de Noailles asked curiously as Owen drew on his gloves. "As uninteresting as you expected?"

Owen regarded him with a slightly mocking curve to his well-shaped mouth. "You were the one who described her as uninteresting, my friend. Reserved and nondescript as I recall. How should I have found her any different?" He raised a hand in salute and left the chamber as soundlessly as his shadow.

Owen left the ambassador's residence, Cedric falling in behind him. It was a cold gray morning, a far cry from the bright crisp sunshine of the previous day. The snow had turned to dirty slush and an icy drizzle was just beginning.

Owen turned up the collar of his cloak. "This is an accursed climate," he muttered. There were times when he could agree with Antoine de Noailles's oft-repeated description of England as "this nasty island."

The rain in Wales, on the other hand, as he remembered it, was a soft fall that turned the hilly countryside a lush green. Gentle on the eyes, gentle on the soul. It had been three years since he'd been back to his mother's homeland. Three years since he'd taken Andrew and Lucy to his mother.

His step quickened and Cedric was forced to trot to catch up with him. "Where are we going, sir?"

Owen glanced over his shoulder at the page, and his black eyes were so cold and bleak that Cedric regretted the question. He didn't see that look very often, but when he did he knew that it was best to keep a still tongue in his head. He pulled his cap down over his eyes and fell back.

"To Baynard's Castle, Cedric. We pay a visit

to the Princess Mary."

Cedric was surprised to get an answer and even more by the seemingly equable tones in which it was delivered. But he didn't venture a reply and concentrated on keeping up with the longer legs of his master.

Owen walked fast to the water steps, as if he would outdistance the bitter drizzle. "Whistle, Cedric."

The page obliged with two fingers to his mouth. His whistle brought two wherries to the steps, competing for custom, their oarsmen huddled in frieze cloaks. The oarsman in the leading wherry cursed his rival, pushing his boat away with an oar. The air rang with richly blasphemous oaths.

Owen, his face dark, his eyes black as agate, stepped to the edge of the quay. His rapier appeared in his hand, a flash of silver in the wet gray light. "You!" he pronounced, his voice a harsh monotone, pointing with his weapon to the first wherry.

The oarsmen fell silent with their mouths opened on the next execration. Then the second boat moved backwards, yielding the field, and the other pulled in to the steps, throwing a rope that Cedric caught with an expert hand.

Owen stepped into the wherry. "Baynard's Castle."

The oarsman took one look at his customer's face and mumbled something to himself. As soon as the youth had followed his master into the boat the oarsman pulled away strongly, as if he were trying to outdistance the devil himself.

Owen forced himself to relax, driving the blackness away. Only thus could he concentrate on the task ahead. The drizzle had turned to sleet and he raised his face to receive the stinging icy drops on his skin. They scoured his face as he scoured his mind, banishing everything that would interfere with the task that lay ahead.

Pen's face came to him. Its intensity, the passion as she talked of her lost child. It was the intensity of her passion that drew him, that and her strength and humor. She had little patience for fools, he was convinced.

Even if he was prepared to seduce her in cold manipulation she would not fall for the smooth lines, the practiced moves that had always stood him in such reliable stead. He remembered how she'd laughed at him in genuine amusement when he'd first approached her with the kiss that was intended to throw her into confusion. She had made him feel foolish then. And she would certainly do so again in the same circumstances. For some reason, although the joke was on him, Owen couldn't help a wry smile.

But there was another way. He would use her straightforward, no-nonsense, rational mind. He would offer her a bargain she would not be able to resist. She might hate him for it, but at least everything would be in the open.

There was something pleasingly neat about a device that would also kill another bird. It would ensure that if Robin of Beaucaire decided to tell Pen what he knew of Chevalier d'Arcy, he could tell her nothing that she did not already know. And what Owen d'Arcy didn't tell her, Lord Robin himself could never discover.

His pleasure in the neatness of this plan faded. The faces of his own children as he'd last seen them three years ago rose in his mind's eye with a cold clarity. Andrew had been three, Lucy two. They had their mother's eyes. Green as moss. What would they remember of him now? Not much. He had told his mother never to mention his name to them. They were as lost to him as Pen's child was to her.

But his loss was his own doing. He believed he had had no choice, and it was too late now for second thoughts, or the wisdom of hindsight.

The black cloud of a familiar depression loomed large and he thrust it from him with an almost physical effort. He had done what he had had to do and he would live with it. Now he had a task ahead that would require all his ingenuity.

The wherry pulled up at the water steps of Baynard's Castle. Owen gave the oarsman a penny and stepped out, Cedric on his heels. Owen glanced at the page and seemed to acknowledge him for the first time in an hour. He adjusted the lad's hat in a paternal fashion and said, "Come, Cedric, you need to get in the warm. You look half frozen."

"I am, sir," Cedric agreed, beaming now that the world had come to rights again.

Owen flung an arm around the youth's shoulders and strode up the path with him. "There'll be fire and succor within," he said cheerfully. "What a miserable master I must be."

"Not at all, Chevalier," Cedric denied with absolute sincerity. "I wouldn't wish to learn from anyone else."

"I'm honored, lad." Owen laughed and the last residue of bleakness vanished from his eyes.

The porter at the wicket gate received the chevalier's credentials and sent a lad running with them to the controller of the princess's household.

"If ye'd care to wait within by the brazier, m'lord." The porter gestured invitingly to the small gatehouse.

Owen nodded his thanks and stepped into the relative warmth of the gatehouse. Cedric scuttled in gratefully behind him.

As he waited, Owen took his dagger from its sheath and idly pared a loose thumbnail. The porter watched him covertly. The tall, slender, dark man, whose lustrous black velvet cloak seemed blacker than black against the lamplight, made his skin prickle. The man seemed so calm, every movement was considered, gentle almost, but nothing would escape those eyes, they seemed to follow a person around without seeming to move at all.

No one who came to visit Princess Mary was without power, but the porter, who had a fanciful turn of mind, thought the devil's power could well be sitting on this visitor's shoulder. Surreptitiously, he crossed himself and went to stand in the door, looking across the courtyard for the controller's messenger.

The messenger came at a run. He bowed, his message breathless in its hasty delivery. "Chevalier d'Arcy, Princess Mary is most anxious to receive you. If I may escort you . . . ."

"You may," said Owen, sheathing his dagger. "Come, Cedric."

Owen saw everything as he was escorted across the courtyard and through the corridors of Baynard's Castle. He noticed the insignificant as much as the significant. He saw who spoke to whom; who glanced at him with interest or acknowledged him with recognition; who should have recognized him and didn't . . . or pretended not to. He noticed and committed to memory where doors and corridors connected. He didn't hear what was spoken among the people as he passed but he speculated, and sometimes concluded. Owen d'Arcy knew the lords who inhabited the corridors of London's palaces a great deal more intimately than anyone in those same corridors could claim to know him.

And then he entered the princess's private parlor and he saw Pen Bryanston. She raised her eyes from the purse she was netting, saw him, and smiled.

A feeling almost like fear crept over him. For the first time in his adult life he was uncertain. He had never met a situation that he could not

106

dominate, a person he could not use. But he knew in his soul that Pen Bryanston presented a challenge he was by no means confident he could meet.

Six

●

Pen set aside the purse and rose to her feet. "Chevalier, pray allow me to present you to Her Highness." She came to him with swift step, one hand outstretched in welcome.

She had a lovely smile, Owen thought, as he bowed over her hand, feeling the warm dry palm and the slight flutter of her fingers against his own. A generous smile, without flirtation or artifice. He noticed for the first time that her teeth were slightly crooked, giving a certain wryness to her smile. His fingers tightened over hers as he held her hand a minute longer than courtesy required.

She wore her hair loose again, confined at the brow with a jeweled band and drawn over her shoulders in an effort to conceal the white bandage that still encircled her neck. He moved one hand up to her neck, beneath the fall of her hair.

"How is it?" he murmured, and Pen heard his soft melodic voice as a caress that stroked her with the same sensuality as the warm brush of his fingers against her skin.

But she had no time to respond.

"Chevalier d'Arcy, you are most welcome."

At Princess Mary's clear tones, which carried just the slightest hint of hauteur, Owen released Pen's hand. His eyes held hers for an instant, his mouth curved in an unmistakably conspiratorial smile, then he moved gracefully across to the princess's chair, leaving Pen to wonder if anyone else in the parlor had been aware of that moment of contact. It had been so intense, although so short, that it was impossible to imagine everyone in the chamber had not felt it.

A quick glance at the assembled company, however, showed her only the expected degree of interest in the new arrival. No one was looking in her direction. She followed Owen to the princess's chair.

Owen swept his jeweled cap from his head and bowed very low. "Princess Mary, you do me much honor."

"We all owe you thanks, sir, for your timely rescue of Lady Bryanston."

"I count myself fortunate that my assistance brought me to Your Highness's notice."

"Pretty words, sir." The princess gave him a look of approval. "I spend little time in London, otherwise I am sure we would have met before."

"I have paid few visits to England in the last years," Owen said. "I prefer a quiet life." He smiled slightly as he took the stool the princess indicated beside her. "My estates and vineyards in Burgundy provide me with all the excitement I could wish for."

"Indeed, sir?" Mary raised a disbelieving eyebrow. "You do not have the air, Chevalier, of a man who lives retired from court."

"Appearances can be deceiving, madam," Pen said demurely, quoting Owen's own comment in the inn. Owen flicked a glance up at her, an appreciative glimmer in his black eyes.

Mary nodded and looked quickly between them. "Pen tells me you fought off her attackers single-handed. No mean feat for a man who likes a quiet life."

"One can enjoy a retiring life but still be capable of dealing with the . . . with the less peaceful side of a more public existence," Owen observed.

"The chevalier is a harpist, madam," Pen said. "A reflection of the quiet Welsh side of his nature, I daresay." She felt very lighthearted suddenly. Playful almost. A most unusual sensation. She hadn't felt such a thing since Philip's death.

"An unusual instrument for a man, Chevalier," Mary said with surprise. "Would you play for us now? One of my ladies plays the harp and has a fine, well-tuned instrument."

Owen glanced at Pen, and she gave him a look of pure mischief that took him aback. He knew her to be sharp and intelligent. He knew her to be passionate to the point of obsession. But he would not have guessed her capable of girlish mischief. Her sister Pippa, yes. But Pen had more gravity. She had suffered too much, he would have thought, to evince an impish appreciation of catching him on the hop.

"I would prefer to come prepared, madam," he demurred, flexing his fingers automatically. "I haven't played in some weeks and my fingers have lacked the exercise."

"With a harp, perhaps, Chevalier, but not with a rapier," Pen observed. "For which I, for one, am very grateful."

"Perhaps you will play for us one afternoon, Chevalier," Mary said. "With sufficient notice, of course."

Owen bowed. "It will be my pleasure, madam."

A stir at the far end of the parlor drew their attention. The Earl and Countess of Kendal entered the chamber and Pen smiled at the sight of them. Affection as always mixed with pride. They were such a handsome couple, so much more striking than anyone else in the room. "You are not acquainted with my parents, I believe, Chevalier."

"I await the honor," he returned, noting her pleasure at the prospect of her parents' company. He wondered how closely involved they were in their daughter's life. They didn't support her passionate obsession about her lost child, but it was such a strange tale that their disbelief could be rooted in concern for Pen.

"Pen, my dear, should you be up and about today?" Lady Kendal said, coming over to them.

"I am perfectly recovered from my foolishness, Mama," Pen replied, choosing her words carefully in the knowledge that she had not yet been fully forgiven for her recklessness. "May I present the Chevalier d'Arcy? I owe him thanks for my deliverance."

Guinevere heard the ironic note and chose to ignore it. She turned to her husband, who said calmly, "Yes, indeed, we all owe the chevalier our thanks."

Hugh smiled at his stepdaughter. "I give you good day, Pen. You are certainly in best looks this morning. One would not think you had undergone such an ordeal."

Pen's cheeks pinkened as she offered her step-father a curtsy. He nodded benignly but turned to Owen d'Arcy.

"I was hoping for the opportunity to thank you in person, sir. As was Pen's mother."

Owen met the steady appraising eyes of the Earl and Countess of Kendal. His question had been answered. It was as clear as day that the Kendals were very concerned about their daughter and kept a close watch on her doings. How much influence they had remained to be seen.

He bowed, his expression pleasantly bland, his returning scrutiny calm. "Lady Kendal . . . my lord."

"We cannot thank you enough, Chevalier," Guinevere said. "Pen has taken no lasting hurt, thank God."

"The chevalier's timing was faultless," Pen said with more than a touch of acidity. She was growing tired of the criticism of her implicit in the thanks heaped upon Owen. "I will stand for- ever in his debt."

Hugh caught Guinevere's eye. It was time to drop the subject. Pen had had all the lessons she needed. "I think that expresses everyone's feelings," he said. "Tell me, Chevalier, are you long in London?"

"I arrived a few days ago, my lord. I have some business to attend to and I thought to enjoy the Christmas season in London. It's been many years since I spent that time in England. Not since I was a boy." His smile was open and confiding.

"Then may we be among the first to welcome you, sir," Guinevere said warmly. "I hope you'll honor us with a visit at our house in Holborn during the Christmas festivities."

"I should be most honored, Lady Kendal." Owen glanced at Pen, and there was a glow of amusement in his eyes. He could feel her impatience with these pleasantries. "May I have your permission to walk a little this morning with your daughter?"

"A question best addressed to Pen, I believe," Hugh observed.

"Yes, indeed, Chevalier," Guinevere said. "You have no need to ask my permission. Pen is well past the age of consent."

Owen looked at Pen, one eyebrow raised in question.

Pen was in fact eager to talk privately with Owen. He had said he would consider her problem and surely by now he had done so. Perhaps that explained the tingling, expectant fascination she was feeling in his company.

Philip's face flashed across her mind's eye and with it came a hot wash of guilt. She felt her cheeks warm and turned aside, feeling for her handkerchief, feigning a sneeze.

"I trust you haven't taken a chill in addition to your cuts and bruises," Owen said. "It was a frigid night."

"No, not in the least," Pen denied. "Just a tickle."

His eyes still glowed with amusement. "So, Lady Pen, would you show me the long gallery? I understand there are some interesting Holbeins."

"My great-uncle, King Henry, was Holbein's patron," a rather childish voice stated.

Jane Grey had crept up to them, a thin figure clad in a dull lavender gown. She turned instantly to Guinevere, her expression now eager. "Lady Kendal, I was hoping to discuss with you that text from Tacitus that was mentioned the other afternoon. I was wondering if perhaps you had a moment now when . . ." She glanced towards the door and seemed to flinch.

Guinevere understood immediately that the girl was afraid her terrifying mother would enter the room and put an end to any discussion of scholarship. She put an arm around Jane's skinny shoulders and said, "But of course, my dear. I remember the discussion well." She bore her off to a secluded corner of the parlor.

Hugh paused for a minute, his eyes resting on the chevalier but his expression unreadable. Then he smiled, reiterated his wife's invitation, and followed.

Pen laughed slightly. "Poor Jane, she would have done well to have had *our* mother. Mama has never said Pippa and I disappoint her, but I know she finds our lack of interest in scholarship puzzling to say the least. And Anna isn't much more promising."

Owen laid a hand gently on her arm, turning her towards the door that led to the long gallery. "Your mother is very learned?"

"Oh, yes! She defeated old King Harry himself . . . the machinations of Lord Cromwell, the Lord Privy Seal, and the king's entire Privy Council when they put her on trial in the Star Chamber." Pen shook her head in admiration. "No one is as clever as Mama."

If only her mother and Lord Hugh had believed her about the baby . . .

But only one person had ever seemed to believe her. Deliberately she turned her face up to Owen's and smiled at him as they left the parlor. She had made a copy of the page taken from the ledger and the names and sums were now burned into her memory. Before the afternoon was over, the chevalier would promise to go to High Wycombe and investigate those names for her.

There was something guileful about that smile, Owen reflected. Quite unlike Pen's usual open friendliness. Experienced as he was at intrigue, Owen recognized that Pen wanted something from him. Well, she would find a receptive audience.

The long gallery was bustling with servants, ushers, heralds. The ill-fitting glass rattled in the windows and gusts of wind blew through cracks in the panes, sending the heavy arras billowing against the cold stone walls behind. Pen walked briskly. It was not a place for secrets.

"Are we not to look at any of these paintings?" Owen inquired on a plaintive note. "I am most interested in Holbein's work."

"Later," Pen said. "I wish to talk to you."

"Can we not talk and look at the same time?"

He was teasing her, but she was too impatient to play games.

"Let us go this way." She set off towards a side corridor.

Owen followed, his long stride keeping easy pace with her quick steps. He found this aspect of Pen Bryanston fascinating. She had the same air about her as she'd had when he'd followed her into the Bryanstons' library. Both secretive and urgent. He was about to be recruited by a very passionate and strong-willed woman.

Pen led the way through a series of passages until she reached a closed door at the end of a windowless corridor. "I wish to talk privately with you," she said, opening the door to her own chamber.

"I had rather gathered that," he replied, following her in.

"Since we have already spent the greater part of a night together, I see no reason why we should not be private in here," Pen declared a mite defensively.

"No, indeed," Owen murmured. "What possible reason could there be?" He closed the door quietly at his back.

"You had best leave the door ajar," Pen said.

"Ah." He opened the door again. "Wide open? Or just a crack?"

"You're laughing at me," Pen accused.

"Perhaps," Owen agreed, opening the door a fraction. "But, forgive me, Pen, if I point out that we are both at an age and stage in life when such proprieties are no longer necessary. Your mother said as much."

"I suppose that's true." Pen sighed heavily. "A widow of six and twenty summers is practically in her dotage. Reputations belong to the young, do they not, Chevalier?"

"Now *you're* laughing at me," he declared, watching laughter light her eyes. She only chuckled.

Owen looked around the chamber, looking for signs that would give him more clues to the person Pen Bryanston was. It was warmly furnished, richly colored tapestries adorning the stone walls, embroidered rugs on the waxed floor. A fire burned in the grate; there was the smell of pinecones; wax candles sent streamers of golden light upwards from the wall sconces, flickering off the thick black beams of the ceiling.

It was a richly comfortable guest apartment in the Earl of Pembroke's residence, and it contained little that was personal to its present occupant except for a large and somewhat ancient ginger tomcat who lay upon the bed. He blinked green eyes and stirred infinitesimally in what was clearly a gesture of greeting.

"This is Nutmeg," Pen said as if the introduction were de rigueur. She bent over the old feline, burying her face in his belly. He purred and rolled over, stretching his feet, claws extended in a leisurely ecstasy of welcome.

"Nutmeg's sixteen," Pen said, gathering the cat into her arms. Ginger fur and long legs spilled over her arms. "Pippa has his sister, Moonshine. We brought them from Derbyshire when we first came to London."

She nuzzled the cat's face before putting him gently back on the bed, saying with a chuckle, "He cannot bear to be left behind so I have to bring him with me whenever the princess travels. I can't imagine how many litters he's sired over the years."

"A splendid animal." Owen gently pulled the old tom's ears in a fashion that indicated he knew a great deal about the likes and dislikes of the feline species.

Pen regarded him with approval. "You like cats."

"I feel a certain kinship with them. They don't compromise and they're not easy to know."

"That's certainly true," Pen said, suddenly uncertain of her ground.

There was a short silence. Owen looked at Pen and thought she seemed nervous. The laughter had died from her expression and she was twisting her hands together in the folds of her gown of olive taffeta. It was a color that suited her multihued hazel eyes. And those eyes were fixed intently upon him.

"You said you would think about my problem," she said. "I need your help."

He nodded slowly as he continued to scratch between the cat's ears. "To look into your son's death?"

"To look into his life!" she insisted fiercely. She moved a hand to brush her hair aside and golden lights danced against the darker brown. "I cannot do it alone and no one else will help me."

"If I help you," Owen said, "I cannot promise what I will find."

"I know that!" She turned aside, looking into the fire. "He may be dead, but I need to know that. I need *proof*." She leaned forward slightly, her hands crossed over her belly, as if trying to contain some pain deep within.

Owen moved to the door and very gently closed it the last inch. He stepped across the room, his booted feet soundless, and came up behind her. He circled her body with his arms, burying his lips against the top of her head.

For a moment Pen didn't stir, then she turned into the circle of his arms, her cheek resting against the midnight-blue silk of his doublet. She felt his heart beating steadily. He moved a hand up and over her back, his fingers tracing the sharp edges of her shoulder blades, the knob at the top of her spine. She felt his heart skip into a faster beat. His breath was hot on the top of her head. He cupped her chin and lifted her face. Her own heart began to race.

Her lips moved against each other. In anticipation . . . invitation? Pen neither knew nor cared. There was only this moment, the scent of wine and cloves on his breath, and then the hard yet pliant feel of his mouth on hers. She leaned into him, her arms reaching up to hold him tight against her. His spread hands spanned her back but he was utterly motionless, only his mouth and tongue moved, exploring her own. And the stillness enveloped her as the kiss seemed to invade her every pore, reaching down even to her toes.

This was a kiss by a master, Pen thought when she could think at all. There was no urgency, no demand, just this sweet possessive joining. It was like a gift and for the moment she was content simply to take.

When at last he moved his mouth from hers and raised his head, he held her and himself very still, so that she began to feel the lines of his body as almost indistinguishable from her own. They seemed to have been standing together, touching in this way, for an eternity, for long enough to have blended into one form. And it felt so natural, so right. She closed her eyes and thought her body swayed slightly, involuntarily, in the calm blackness. But he still held her as if with butterfly wings.

Owen kissed her ear and whispered, "So, Pen Bryanston?"

It took her a moment to come to herself. She opened her eyes and the room, softly lit though it was, seemed as bright as the noon sun at midsummer. She blinked, and as his hands dropped from her she stepped away, feeling the heat of the fire on her back, hearing the tap of her shoes on the floor as loud as a thunderclap in the silence.

"I'm not accustomed to kissing strangers in such fashion," she murmured, her voice shaking slightly.

"So what should we do about this strange business?" He quirked an eyebrow.

"I think we should open the door wide," Pen said, trying to laugh but managing only to sound doubtful.

"Just in case it happens again?"

Pen shook her head. She was confused. There was no reason why she shouldn't indulge in a little harmless flirtation with the chevalier. There would be no scandal in that. And a little voice reminded her that this was certainly one way to ensure his cooperation in her quest. But her response to the man, and to that kiss, frightened her a little. She had the sense that she could lose control of things if she didn't keep a clear head.

"Are you married?" she asked abruptly, remembering Pippa's question.

The light left his face. It was only for a second but Pen was chilled by the shadows that gathered in the hollows beneath his eyes, that passed across the sculptured planes of his face. Then his expression was once more bland, his smile neutral. "No," he said definitely. "No, I am not married. Does that make a difference?"

"Yes, of course it does," Pen said. "If I'm going to be kissing you like that again, I want to be sure I'm not poaching."

Owen chuckled. "Straightforward as always. Do you think you will be kissing me like that again?"

Pen put her head on one side, as if considering the question. "Maybe, and maybe not. More to the point, Chevalier, I would discuss my business with you. I don't see how I can go alone to ask questions in High Wycombe village. Someone is bound to recognize me and word will get back to Lady Bryanston. I thought perhaps you could make discreet inquiries for me. I have made a copy of the list of names I took from the ledger."

She took a key from the purse that hung at her waist and went with swift step to a small coffer in the corner of the chamber. Gracefully she knelt, her skirts spreading in a corolla around her, the silk shimmering in the candlelight. She unlocked the chest.

Owen watched her in considering silence.

She rose with a folded sheet in her hand. "Here are the names. Will you go for me?" Anxiety made the question abrupt and her gaze was fixed upon his face with painful intensity.

He took the sheet from her and tapped it thoughtfully in the palm of his hand. "You're moving just a little fast for me, Pen." He laid the sheet, still unfolded, on a side table.

The light died in her eyes. "So you won't help me?"

"I will, in exchange," he replied.

"In exchange for what?" She stared at him, dismay and confusion chasing each other across her countenance.

"I have a proposition to make." He moved towards her and she jumped back. "No," he said with a smile. "Not that kind of proposition. Although," he added, his smile deepening, "if you would consider it in addition to the one I have in mind, I would be more than happy."

Pen realized that her startled jump had put her back against the wall. She stood still as he came up to her. "Don't play games. . . . What is this proposition?" she demanded.

"Well, now, my business in London concerns the princess," he said, cupping her face in his hands. "I would like your help in that business in exchange for mine in yours."

Pen pulled free of his hold. "Speak plainly!"

"Very well." He placed his hands on the wall on either side of her head. He was so close she could feel the heat of his body and she couldn't tear her gaze away from the deep black eyes that seemed to read her every thought.

"I need a pair of ears in the princess's household," he said bluntly. "If you will agree to tell me everything that is said by the princess and her advisors, inform me of any change in plans and —"

"Enough!" Pen cried in horror. "You would have me spy on the princess?"

"Spying is a harsh term," he said.

"It is the correct term!"

"Listen to me for just a minute," he said. His expression was calm, unmoved by her outrage, but when she tried to push him away so that she could move from the wall, he remained where he was, keeping her in place.

"I don't mean to trap you," he said quietly, "but if I stand aside you'll run away, and I need you to hear me out."

Pen set her lips and said nothing, but her glare spoke volumes.

"My government has the princess's best interests at heart. We mean her no harm, but with the king on his deathbed her position is very vulnerable. No one knows what Northumberland is plotting but we're almost positive it is *not* in Mary's best interests. We need to know what he's doing and we need to know what Mary is thinking and planning."

He paused, then ventured, "Your stepbrother is in a position to know some of what goes on in Northumberland's head and perhaps he confides in you?" He raised an inquiring eyebrow.

Pen continued to stare at him with contempt and disgust. "You would have me prick my brother for his secrets?"

"I would have you believe that if you love the princess you will help her by cooperating with me," he returned sharply.

After a minute, when it was clear that Pen was going to say nothing further, he said, choosing his words, "I would think you would be more dismayed if I talked of doing Northumberland's dirty work." He watched her closely.

Pen's sharp inhalation and the rush of color into her face told him that she knew about her brother's affiliation. Brother and sister clearly had no secrets from each other.

"The world of espionage is a small one," he pointed out. "We make it our business to know those who inhabit it with us."

Pen still said nothing but she understood that it was obvious spies would know one another. Robin would know of Owen's involvement in that underworld, which presumably explained his hostility to the chevalier.

"So, is it not better to be working in Mary's interests rather than Northumberland's?" he pressed.

Pen could not let pass an attack on Robin, whatever her own thoughts about Northumberland. "I am sure that Robin is inspired by loyalty to both Northumberland and Suffolk. They have stood his friends and protectors since he was a lad," she retorted, still flushed. "You, on the other hand, will play whatever field suits your purposes."

"I am loyal to France," he corrected softly. "I see no difference between us, except that your brother serves a man who is motivated only by personal ambition and I serve king and country."

"Do not criticize Robin!"

"Forgive me. I merely sought for a defense."

"Well, you will not find one on that road," she fired.

"Very well." Owen shrugged.

"Why should I believe you? Why are the French more likely to help Mary than . . . than the Spanish, say? Her own cousin, the emperor, has sent ships to escort her to Flanders if she chooses to leave. What has France done?"

"If she leaves England, she loses all chance for the throne. You know that and so does she. Which, I'm sure, is why she hasn't taken flight already. We will help her in her struggle with Northumberland and his council."

"In your own interests!" she declared, almost spitting the words at him.

"Of course," he replied calmly. "I'm not pretending there's any altruism in this. I'm offering you a straight exchange. Information for my help in discovering the truth about your son. I am

126

very good at discovering truths, I might add."

"So I should imagine," she said scornfully. "It's a spy's stock-in-trade."

"It is a very necessary trade, Pen," he said. "There isn't a court or a government that doesn't practice it. You must know that."

Pen turned her head aside. She knew he spoke the truth. Her love for her stepbrother was in no way affected by his own involvement in that world. However scurrilously Northumberland played his deep games, Pen was convinced that Robin would not do anything dishonorable. Robin would not use someone's pain and grief for his own ends.

Owen waited for a response, and when it didn't come he said simply, "So, do we have a bargain, Pen?"

She wished she could get away from him. His closeness was confusing her. The only emotion that ought to matter was the knowledge of his betrayal. This was what he'd been after all along. That first kiss, the steady pursuit, his apparent interest in *her*. All for his own ends.

She knew she should turn him down, tell him to take his dirty bargain and never come near her again. She knew she should do that. But he could help her. If anyone could find out the truth, Owen d'Arcy was that person. And maybe he was right that the French wanted to help Mary. Pen was in no doubt that the princess was threatened. Mary had been in danger throughout her adult life.

But he'd betrayed her, led her to believe something that wasn't true. Then she told herself coldly that it didn't matter. She had been using him, or at least *intended* to use him. So what was the difference between them?

But even as she thought this, she knew that there had been something more — something that now she could no longer explore. Confusion swamped her anew and she pushed hard on his chest, desperate to put some space between them.

Owen dropped his hands from the wall and stepped back. Pen moved around him, her breath coming in deep urgent gasps as if she'd been deprived of air. She stood in the middle of the room and faced him.

It had been so long since she'd had any hope.

He was her only chance to bring her wretched uncertainty and confusion to a close. She had lived with the misery for so long, she looked at the world through its veil, the edges of daily life were blurred by it, everything faded and insubstantial against the hard reality of her obsession. It was her first waking thought and her last.

"Very well, an exchange," she said flatly.

He nodded, then said quietly, "I could wish you didn't now view me with such loathing, Pen."

"What do you expect?" she shot back. "You force this odious bargain upon me . . . what do you expect me to think of you?"

"I would like you to see me for the man I am,"

128

he replied. "A man with a mission, a pragmatist, a man who plays in the world's arena. Just like your brother. Is that so very bad?"

"Do not *ever* put yourself in the same category as Robin. You are a spy and a trickster," she declared with a bitter smile. "And you deceived me. You pretended to . . . to . . . Oh, I cannot talk to you!" She pushed at the air as if she could thrust him from her.

"I pretended nothing, Pen," he said, taking her hand. "I have not deceived you in any way. I have been utterly truthful with you." He raised her hand to his lips. "We will be partners, you and I."

It was a whispered promise, ambiguous and yet Pen heard it in the way she knew he intended. Her fingers curled in his grasp as if in angry denial she would rake his palms with her nails, as if in the hot surge of passion she would rake his palms with her nails. . . .

"Pen . . . Pen . . . are you in there?" It was Robin's voice outside the door.

Pen jerked her hand out of Owen's clasp. Her face was suddenly hot as if she had been caught in some dishonorable act. Of all the moments for Robin to arrive, playing that impatient tune on her door with his knuckles.

She spun to the door and opened it wide. "What is it, Robin? Does the princess want me?"

Robin stared over her shoulder to where the chevalier stood by the fireplace, an expression of bland indifference on his face, his dark eyes cool and quiet as they met Robin's. Robin's mouth tightened and angry spots of color appeared on his cheeks. "Forgive me, Pen, I hadn't realized you were *entertaining* a guest in your chamber."

"I would not outstay my welcome, madam," Owen said softly. He came across the chamber, his step as soundless as always. He offered Robin a bow and a courteous smile. "How pleasant to run into you again, Lord Robin. I trust it will not be the last time."

Pen set her lips, and Robin could do nothing but return the bow in stiff silence.

The chevalier left, still smiling, and Pen closed the door gently. She was conscious now only of the part she had to play. The world must believe that she and the chevalier were on the best of terms. Robin must never guess what she knew of Owen d'Arcy. "What is it, Robin? Why do you look so disapproving?"

"You should not be closeted with a stranger in your bedchamber," he stated, his mouth stubborn.

"Oh, don't be ridiculous. I am not answerable to you for my conduct, Robin! I'm a widow, not some innocent virgin. And I will talk with whom I please, where I please."

"You know nothing about Owen d'Arcy," Robin said. "What makes you think you can trust him?"

"Trust him to do what?" Pen met his gaze with one as stubborn.

130

"You know what I mean!" His ruddy cheeks grew brighter.

Pen could no longer pretend to be angered. She and Robin were too close, and she knew his concerns were only for her. If only she could tell him the truth, explain her devil's bargain. But for the first time in all the years they'd known each other, she had to keep something from him.

She asked with seemingly mild curiosity, "Why do you dislike him so much?" He wouldn't tell her, of course, but it was only natural that she should ask.

Robin turned aside from her clear gaze. He bent to the fire, poking at the logs until scarlet flames shot up the chimney and a billow of smoke filled the ill-ventilated chamber.

Pen coughed, waving at the smoke. "Leave the fire, Robin. It was fine as it was."

" 'Tis cold in here," he said in half-apology.

Pen went to the side table and poured a goblet of wine from the flagon that stood there. "Maybe this will warm you." She handed him the goblet. "Now, tell me why you dislike Owen d'Arcy. You said the other night that you'd never met him."

Robin drank deeply. For two pins he would tell her what he knew of d'Arcy. But he couldn't do it as yet. Loyalty still forbade him to disobey Northumberland's orders, at least until his growing distrust of the duke was justified. There were too many plots twisting in the wind around the young king's unstable throne, and a wise

131

man would thread a careful path through them. Robin could not afford to act prematurely.

"There's just something about the man," he muttered, concealing his frustration at the half-truth. "He makes me uneasy. I worry about you, Pen."

"Oh, I know you do." She put her arm around his shoulders and kissed his cheek. "And I worry about you. But there's nothing to worry about, Robin. I'm quite capable of taking care of myself."

"You think you are," he mumbled, returning the kiss. "But what do you know of the man?"

Pen hesitated. "Not much," she said, then added deliberately, "But I like being in his company."

"You're not falling in love with him?" Robin stared at her in horror.

"*No!* Of course not," she said with a laugh that she knew sounded convincing. Earlier that evening it might not have done. "But I can amuse myself a little, can't I? Pippa does, and no one objects."

"Pippa's different. Everyone knows she's not serious. But people know that you are, that you do take things seriously."

"Perhaps I do." She kissed his cheek again, hating herself, hating Owen d'Arcy, hating Philip's mother with a power even greater than hitherto. Her heart had turned to stone.

"I love you dearly, Robin, but you cannot take charge of my life. I'm sorry if you don't like

Owen, but I do. And unless you can give me good reason why I shouldn't trust him, I see no reason why I shouldn't trust my own instincts and inclinations. Do you?"

Robin had no answer. He would give his life for Pen, but he knew, too, that she would do what she believed in. He knew her strengths. He admired them and wished he shared more of them than he did. Pen didn't sway in the wind like so many people in their world. She clung steadfast to her views unless or until she had good reason to change them.

But how could he protect her without confiding in her? The question tormented him because for the moment it had no answer.

Seven

●

The parlor reeked of tallow candles, woodsmoke, and over-blown perfume poured on hot flesh. The drapes were drawn tightly across the windows in a vain attempt to block the drafts that needled their way through every cranny between the creaking shutters.

Miles Bryanston shuffled his feet and wrinkled his nose at the stale smell that rose from the rushes that he thus disturbed. How long had it been since they'd been changed? he wondered with an unusual fastidiousness. The sole of his boot seemed to have stuck to something unsavory on the wooden boards beneath the rushes. He shook it free with a disgusted oath and turned at the sound of the door opening.

"So, my lord, welcome. We wasn't expectin' to see you for another two weeks. 'Tis not your usual time to visit." The voice was a curious blend of obsequious whine and sharp suspicion. A strong fog of aqua vitae accompanied the words.

"Circumstances have changed, Mistress Boulder." Miles tried to sound brisk and commanding even though the madam of this South Bank brothel emasculated him with every piercing glance from her rheumy eyes. Miles couldn't imagine how she could encourage men to take advantage of her whores. His balls shriveled at the very sound of her foot on the stair. But fortunately that was not where his business lay. He just wished his mother would take on Mistress Boulder instead of leaving it to him. She was much more the woman's match.

"Oh?" the madam said, her eyes narrowing, her mouth pursed into what struck Miles as a good resemblance to a chicken's arse. "And 'ow might that be, *my lord?*"

"We . . . my mother . . ." Miles gathered his forces. "The dowager Countess Bryanston and I have decided to make other arrangements, Mistress Boulder. You will, of course, be paid up until the end of the month."

"We 'ad a contract, my lord. Six months." She bent over a low table to fill two tin cups from the leather flagon of aqua vitae. " 'Ere. This'll put 'eart in ye, dear sir." She leered at him but he was not deceived. He shook his head at the cup and laid a hand on his sword hilt. It made him feel more in control even if it didn't convince the fearsome Mistress Boulder.

Mistress Boulder drained both cups with one swallow each. She wiped her mouth with the back of her hand. "Now, you can't be expectin' me to give up six months of income, not you nor 'er ladyship," she continued. "I'm a businesswoman, my lord, and I've got me own responsibilities. I've got me girls to look after. By all means I'll consider our contract ended, jest as long as you pays me my due. Six months was what we agreed. You pay that now an' you can leave 'ere wi' what you come for and no questions asked."

Miles tried to summon his mother's image to his aid. But he wasn't sure whether even the redoubtable dowager countess could make short work of Mistress Boulder. "I have coin to pay you until the end of the month," he said, reaching into his pocket, hoping that the sight of actual money might sway the woman. "I daresay I could add a couple of guineas extra, for goodwill." He shook the leather purse so that the coins chinked invitingly.

The woman regarded him with evident disappointment. "Now, now, m'lord, that won't do at all. A deal's a deal, an' I've done me part. You don't 'ave no complaints, I trust." There was no mistaking the menace in her voice or the challenge in her bloodshot little eyes.

"No . . . no," Miles denied hastily. "No complaints, but circumstances have changed. We have to make other arrangements."

"I see." She folded her arms across a skinny bosom. "So, if there's no fault to be found, my dear sir, then you'll understand that I'm entitled to me full due. Six months' payment, as promised." She held out a grasping hand, the fingers curled slightly. The nails were broken and black with dirt. Miles repressed a shudder.

There were more salubrious stew-houses in

this brothel-strewn stretch of riverbank opposite St. Paul's, but Lady Bryanston had instructed her son to find one that would not be frequented by any man who moved in their own social circles. Mistress Boulder's establishment certainly fitted that bill, but by the same token it was unfamiliar territory for Miles himself, and he found his usual bullying bluster inadequate in the face of a brothel keeper who was accustomed to dealing with the toughest customers. Sailors who spoke every known tongue piled riotously off the trading ships that sailed up the Thames estuary to the London docks.

"Of course," she mused, her hand still outstretched, "there's folk what might pay a pretty penny for what I know." She leered at him again, but the menace was yet more pronounced. "Not that I'd be spreadin' the word, mind you, but word gets around all on its own, y'know."

Miles was between the proverbial rock and a hard place. If he yielded to the woman's demands, his mother would be furious. She detested spending a groat more than she had to, and kept the family purse strings firmly in her hands despite Miles's occasional bleats that as the earl he should have access to more than the paltry allowance his parent gave him. But he could not refuse to satisfy Mistress Boulder's greed in the face of this blackmail.

"I'll pay you for four months," he tried, but without much conviction.

Mistress Boulder shook her head. "Can't

stand 'ere all day, my lord. I've work to do. My girls are wakin' up and the customers'll be bangin' on the door any minute now. You want what you come for, just pay me what's right an' proper and you can be on your way wi'out another word spoken."

Miles gave in with a little sigh, and his shoulders hunched in defeat so that he looked rather like a deflated frog. He drew another leather purse from his pocket and counted out a pile of gold and silver under the madam's sharp scrutiny. She counted with him, under her breath, and as soon as the last coin joined the pile she swept them up in a movement so swift and clean it was as if a magician had waved a wand. She unlocked an iron-bound casket on the table and deposited the coins.

She turned to him, all business now. "Right, I'll get what you come for."

Miles waited impatiently. He would have to hurry if he was to complete his business on the South Bank before the bells sounded for curfew and London Bridge was closed for the night. His mother would want a report on the afternoon's business before she sent him off with his wife to Greenwich Palace for the Twelfth Night revels. There he was supposed to accost the Duke of Northumberland. . . .

A heavy sigh escaped him. He'd be hard-pressed to enjoy the traditional unlicensed roistering of Twelfth Night when he'd have to keep a clear head to do his mother's bidding. There were times when he longed for the carefree days before Philip's death, when he could carouse with his friends, hunt, frequent decent brothels for their true purpose without question or hindrance. But his mother had had other plans.

He sighed again as the door opened and Mistress Boulder returned, a bundle of rags in her arms.

Miles went out into the frigid late afternoon with his burden. Black-edged clouds raced across the gray sky and the air smelled of snow. He hastened to an establishment in a back alley away from the riverbank. A tall narrow house with overhanging gables and dingy plaster. A rickety wooden staircase on the outside gave access to the upper floors. It was a house not dissimilar to the one he had just left.

The ill-hung door opened a crack at his knock and he entered the narrow passage, again wrinkling his nose at the unsavory odors. The bishop's inspectors wouldn't bother with this stew-house, and it was inevitable that the women would be diseased. No one he knew would darken the doors of such a place. At least that would please his mother.

The transaction with a slatternly woman, whose rheumy eyes shifted beneath drooping lids, took a bare fifteen minutes. Miles, no longer burdened, retraced his steps down the narrow alley to the riverbank, drawing the cold air deep into his lungs, trying to rid himself of the noxious air of the brothel. He passed an open door from which wafted a rich scent of cloves, nutmeg, and wine. Women's laughter sounded from within, light and full of promise. There was the sweet sound of a plucked lute. He could smell roasting meat.

Miles hesitated, sniffing like a bloodhound on the scent of quarry. Duty called him across London Bridge, but then he'd have to face his mother and admit to his cowardly submission to Mistress Boulder's demands. Joan would look mournful and disappointed as Lady Bryanston uttered her sharply contemptuous opinions of a son who was incapable of fulfilling a simple task. Sometimes Miles wondered why his mother had always favored him over Philip. Philip had been so much cleverer than he.

But somewhere in Miles's generally befuddled brain lurked the knowledge that whereas he would always meekly do his mother's bidding, Philip had had a mind of his own. Lady Bryanston did not look with favor upon those who had minds of their own. If Pen had not shown her own strength of will, her mother-in-law might well have chosen a different course of action.

Miles grimaced, thinking of the recriminations ahead, followed by an abstemious and inevitably uncomfortable evening trying to find the opportunity for an apparently casual interview with Northumberland. The duke barely knew who he was.

Another heavy sigh escaped him, and on the

exhalation he followed his nose without another coherent thought through the open door into the hot, sweet-smelling world of warm-fleshed women and spiced wine. A well-regulated world where the bishop's inspectors examined the women every month, and comfortable apartments opened off a cloistered garden where torches kept the encroaching dusk at bay. He rubbed his hands together in anticipation as an elegantly dressed woman billowed across the spacious hall to greet him.

He didn't notice the man standing just beyond the circle of light thrown by the flaming torch that lit the entrance to the brothel.

Owen tapped his mouth with his gloved fingertips, a slight frown between his brows. He had been leaving the Bishop of Winchester's palace after a particularly fruitful discussion with one of his grace's manservants who kept his ears open for France. Then he'd recognized Miles Bryanston scurrying out of one of the squalid alleys that opened onto the broader thoroughfare of the South Bank. Even if it weren't for Pen, the instincts of his profession would have prompted him to follow a man who could not possibly have business in the unhealthy stews where a woman could be had for a groat, with robbery and disease thrown in as part of the deal.

But it seemed that whatever the earl had been doing in the dark, dank lanes behind the lights of the established world of sex for sale, the world that catered to men of his rank and fortune, he hadn't been grubbing for a woman. A satisfied man did not leave one pair of thighs and instantly dive between another.

Unless, of course, Bryanston had some interesting perversions, Owen reflected. It wouldn't surprise him. Owen had been doing some probing of the Bryanston family, wanting to be sure that Pen's story wasn't the crazed fabrication of a grief-stricken widow that everyone else believed it to be.

The picture that emerged hadn't been particularly pretty, and it had convinced Owen that there might be something to Pen's story. Miles was widely considered a dolt and a barbarian, ruled by his own appetites and his mother's ambition. When people spoke of the Dowager Lady Bryanston and her ambition it was in generally mocking tones. She was considered greedy and not very clever.

Owen, however, was not inclined to dismiss her so easily. It was always possible that she would trip herself up as she reached for the moon, but in his experience greed, cunning, and a complete lack of scruple made for a dangerous opponent.

Miles's brother Philip, on the other hand, had been well liked and respected, his premature death mourned by those who'd known him.

Possibly Miles had been satisfying his more brutish appetites in the back streets before seeking conventional relief in more sanitary surroundings. Then again, maybe there was more to it.

Owen turned under the lights and entered the brothel. An elegant woman appeared immediately. She welcomed him with a gracious smile and a small page proffered a tray with wine.

"Come this way, my lord." The brothel keeper glided ahead of him into a handsome paneled chamber, warmed by fires at either end and dimly lit by oil lamps. Women stood around the walls, chatting in groups. They cast covert glances at the newcomer, sizing him up, he thought with some amusement, like a prize stud at the market fair. No matter that the shoe should be on the other foot.

Miles Bryanston was standing before the fire at the far end of the chamber. He held a pewter tankard of mead and wore an air of smug satisfaction as he looked the women over. Before Owen could approach, he drained his tankard in one swallow and tossed it to the floor, then he beckoned to one of the women, wrapped an arm around her waist as she came up to him, and bore her from the room, brushing rudely past Owen without any acknowledgment.

"Pleasant man," Owen murmured with curled lip.

"A regular customer, my lord," the brothel keeper said with a discreet smile. "Will you make your choice?"

"I'm not interested in a woman tonight, except as a companion while I take my wine. If one of your women is blessed with wit and the art of conversation, I'll be well pleased in her company," Owen said.

The brothel keeper considered. She had a honed instinct when it came to customers and this one would pay well, even if his inclinations were not quite the usual. She said, "If you've a mind for some music, my lord, Sally has a delicate hand on the lute."

"That will suit me well," Owen said. "Bring me a flagon of burgundy and I'll take my ease by the fire. When our friend comes down again, I would have him join me in a glass, if you would mention it to him when his business is done."

"Certainly, my lord." The woman went over to the girls clustered along the wall, and after a soft-spoken exchange one of them separated herself from the group and came over to where Owen now sat on the long settle.

She curtsied, examining him with frank curiosity, clearly wondering why a man would come to a whorehouse just to listen to music. "I give you good even, my lord. I'll fetch your wine and my lute, if it pleases you."

Owen nodded pleasantly. "It does indeed please me. Sally, is it?"

"Yes, sir." The girl blushed as if she were an innocent and had not been a whore for the last six months. Privately she thought she had never had such an attractive customer.

Owen passed the next half hour sipping his wine and listening to the girl's playing, which, if not technically perfect, showed a delicacy of feeling. His face gave no sign of his tension as he

144

waited for Bryanston's return.

He had barely a half hour to wait before the earl appeared in the doorway, the brothel keeper at his side. He blinked at the room, his prominent gut pushing against his doublet, his face mottled with drink and exertion.

Owen rose to his feet and motioned to the girl that she should leave. He extended his hand as Miles weaved a somewhat uncertain way towards him.

"Don't know I've had the pleasure, sir," the earl said thickly. "Can't think what you want with me."

"Why, we are well met, indeed, my lord. Chevalier d'Arcy at your service." Owen gestured to the opposite settle. "Will you join me in a cup of our hostess's very palatable burgundy? I have been so hoping to make your further acquaintance."

"Oh," Miles said stupidly, wondering what this elegant figure could want with him. "Can't think what I can do for you, sir. Never seen you before."

Owen turned a dazzling smile on him and said with his soft lilting voice, "Forgive me, I should have made myself known when I attended your reception for Princess Mary."

"Oh . . . oh, yes, of course." Miles wondered if he had committed some social solecism by not recognizing this man who had been a guest in his house. He hastened to make amends. "I didn't recognize you, Chevalier." He gave a lascivious and distinctly lopsided leer. "Had something else on my mind, don't you know."

"No reason why you should recognize me," Owen murmured soothingly. "We have not had the advantage of a formal introduction." He smiled. "I tend not to stand out in a crowd."

Miles, once he looked closely at his new companion, wasn't at all sure of the truth of this. It seemed to him that once met, the chevalier would be hard to forget.

Owen sat down. He stretched his long legs sideways and propped his boots on the andirons. Miles took the place opposite him.

"Will you take wine, my dear sir?" Owen reached for the flagon that reposed on a small table beside the settle.

"Yes . . . yes . . . thank you, sir, most good of you." Miles leaned forward eagerly for the cup that Owen had filled. He took the scent of the wine, his head bobbing in his enthusiasm. "Oh, yes, very good . . . very good indeed."

Owen sipped his wine. "Forgive my bluntness, Lord Bryanston, but I have always felt it wise to come to the point quickly."

Miles hauled his nose from his cup and regarded his companion blearily. "Yes?"

"Your sister-in-law, Lady Pen Bryanston." Owen wriggled his toes in his boots, smiling pleasantly.

Miles's expression became a curious mixture of befuddlement and sudden attention. "What of her?" he demanded.

"I find her interesting."

Miles stared at him. "Why?"

"Is it so unlikely?" Owen inquired, one eyebrow lifted. "Your brother, for instance . . ."

"Philip . . . she trapped Philip. She wanted the title," Miles declared, but his eyes slid sideways before he reached for the flagon and refilled his cup.

Owen shrugged. "That's a history that doesn't concern me, my friend. I find myself interested in the widow."

Miles peered at him, all greedy suspicion. "She has nothing from the estate. Not even her dowry. That was held in trust for her son. No one can touch it now, since the child died. Not even Lady Kendal can bend that law to her will. 'Twas her own daughter's choice. And with the child dead, the money's lost to her."

Miles drained his cup and smacked his lips. His host without prompting refilled the vessel.

"Can't think why you'd find her interesting. In fact," Miles continued confidentially between long sips, "can hardly bear to be in the same room with her, myself. Thinks she's too good for the rest of us." He upended his cup and peered into it in search of a drop that might have evaded him. "Powerful good, this. Keeps out the cold."

"Indeed." Owen proffered the flagon again. "So your family didn't approve of your brother's choice for wife?"

Miles's glazed eyes blinked once or twice and he leaned closer. "She wasn't my mother's

147

choice," he said significantly. "Too fond of her own way to suit my mother. But it was a love match and the king and Princess Mary both promoted it, so what could my mother do? Had to smile on it. But by the mass how she hated it!"

"That must have made sharing a house rather difficult," Owen remarked neutrally.

"Oh, you should have seen the fur fly!" Miles picked up the flagon again and shook it. He drained the last of its contents into his cup seemingly unconcerned that his companion had not once refilled his own.

Owen gestured to the ever-watchful Sally, who swept the empty flagon from the table, with a resigned expression allowing Miles to paw her haunches as she passed.

Owen leaned back against the settle, cradling his still-full cup between his hands. "Lady Pen strikes me as of mild temperament," he observed.

"Oh, you don't know her, Chevalier. Sly as an asp, she is. She got under my mother's skin. With just one look. She and Philip. They ignored her, see. Can't stand being ignored, my mother." Miles held out his cup to Sally, who now stood at his elbow with a full flagon.

His words were slurred, his eyes ever more unfocused. He shook his head. "Ignore my mother at your peril. They found that out."

"How so?" Owen sipped from his cup; his dark gaze seemed casual as it rested on his companion's suffused countenance.

148

A crafty look crossed Miles's little brown eyes. He tapped the side of his nose. "Word to the wise," he declared. "Word to the wise." He gave a sinister little smile. "Cross my mother at your peril. They certainly found that out." His expression managed to combine smugness with malice.

"So you'd advise me not to pursue the widow?" Owen asked.

"Wouldn't touch her with a barge pole," Miles declared with an unexpected surge of energy. "Not quite right in the head, either, you know." He dropped his head again and mumbled, "Mother wouldn't like it either."

Owen's expression remained impassive. He wanted to put his hands around Miles Bryanston's thick neck and squeeze. He could almost feel the pulse of the carotid artery under his fingers. *Just what was this doltish lump of scum hinting at?* He could get the truth out of him in minutes under the right circumstances. But that pleasure, and it would be a pleasure, would have to wait.

He observed blandly, "I'm grateful for the advice. I assume Lady Pen returned to her own family after your brother's death?"

"Oh, no." Miles shook his head emphatically. A mouse skittered across the floor at his feet and he kicked out at it automatically. "Mother wouldn't have that." He looked down at the stunned mouse and raised a heavy boot to stamp on it.

149

Owen, without knowing why, swept the mouse under the settle and out of harm's way with a swift sideways movement of his foot. He had no time for mice himself, but found he couldn't sit there and watch Bryanston stamp it to death.

Miles appeared to accept the disappearance of his intended victim without surprise. He continued as if he hadn't been interrupted. "Pen was pregnant, see. Caused quite a ruckus. Mother said the child was a Bryanston and had to be born under the Bryanston roof but the Kendals insisted that Lady Guinevere be present at the delivery. Mother didn't want them there. She knows how tricky they are."

Miles nodded significantly. "She knew they would probably try to whisk Pen away and it made her mad as fire. Child was heir to the earldom after all." He drank again, coughed, spluttered, wiped his mouth with the back of his hand. "But it was all taken care of in the end."

Owen's eyelids flickered almost imperceptibly. "How so?"

"Pen went into labor a month early, before the Kendals could arrive. Mother had the managing of it."

Managing of what? Premature labor or just the delivery?

Owen's expression remained bland. "And the child died?"

Miles looked up abruptly, his gaze seemed to

150

focus. "Aye. What of it?" he demanded with sudden aggression.

"Nothing. It's hardly an unusual occurrence," Owen said.

"Aye, it died," Miles stated. "Stillborn. Known fact. Everyone knows it." He peered at Owen, his eyes narrowing. He said slyly, "Pen ever talk about it to you?"

Owen shook his head. His fingers twitched as if with a life of their own. But he said, "Only in passing."

Miles continued to regard him with the same sly look. He wagged a finger. "Well, if she does, don't you listen to a word she says. Got some bee in her bonnet. Don't want to encourage it. Even her family don't like her to talk about it. Told you she wasn't quite right in the head."

"I'm most grateful for your advice, Lord Bryanston. I might have made a very serious mistake."

"That you might have done," Miles mumbled. "Wouldn't touch her with a barge pole. You remember that, Chevalier. Word to the wise." Miles slumped back against the settle and closed his eyes. Within seconds, deep snores rumbled from between his slack lips.

Owen removed the cup from his loose grasp before it fell to the floor. He regarded the slumbering drunk for a minute with an expression of savage contempt, then he stood up and brushed down his hose with a fastidious flick. His eyes met those of the mouse, which, now returned to

151

its senses, had stuck its nose out from under the settle. Its whiskers twitched.

"I should go back to your hole before your luck runs out," Owen said. "Either the cat will get you or the maid's broom." The mouse seemed to consider this, then it shot out and scuttled for a hole in the wainscot.

Owen drew his cloak around him as he walked back briskly to the palace of Westminster, where his horse was stabled. Pen was expecting him at the banquet that would begin the Twelfth Night festivities and he would make better time by road than by water.

He had not seen Pen since the king had summoned the princess and her household to Greenwich Palace for the New Year and Twelfth Night celebrations. He told himself that by now she would have some information for him. But that was not the chief reason that he put spur to his horse.

Eight

●

Princess Mary examined her reflection in the long glass in her bedchamber at Greenwich Palace. "Do you think the ruby breast jewel or the emerald, Pen?"

"The ruby, madam," Pen said without hesitation.

Mary held the ruby pendant against her gown of ice-blue satin. The red jewel sparkled against the pale satin and accentuated the gold undersleeves and underskirt of the gown.

"How right you are," Mary said. "You have excellent taste, Pen. So like your mother's."

Pen smiled and helped the princess fasten the pendant. "Pippa's taste is rather different," she observed.

"Yes, but she knows what suits her," Mary responded. She adjusted the jeweled band of her headdress with a critical frown. Her gaze caught Pen's in the glass and her frown deepened.

"You seem distracted these days, Pen. Do you not find Christmas revels at Greenwich to your taste?" There was more than a touch of irony in her voice. The princess herself had resented her brother's command that she remove from Baynard's Castle to Greenwich Palace.

153

Pen could not admit the real reason for her distraction: that at every moment she was on tenterhooks waiting for the princess to tell her something that she would be compelled to pass on to the French agent if she was to fulfill her side of the devil's bargain.

She chose a partial truth. "I would have liked to be closer to my family, madam," she said. Unlike Greenwich Palace, Baynard's Castle was but a short distance from the Kendals' London home in Holborn.

"My brother takes no such considerations into account," Mary said with a sigh. "Although I'm sure my lord Northumberland had a hand in the decision to summon me here."

"I'm sure," Pen agreed.

Mary turned from the mirror, worry etched on her countenance. "In truth, Pen, I am in constant fear while we remain here. I haven't been permitted to visit the king, my brother, for two weeks. I have no way of telling if his condition has deteriorated. There's no knowing what's being plotted."

Absently it seemed she ran her rosary through her fingers. "But I know full well, Pen, that the Privy Council have no wish to see me succeed my brother. I am terrified Northumberland and the council will make some attempt to secure my person and confine me in the Tower on some pretext. If I am dead, I can hardly be queen," she added with a sardonic lift of an eyebrow.

" 'Tis said that the king's to attend the banquet tonight, madam, although not the revels afterwards."

Mary shook her head. "I doubt we shall see him. They would keep him from me. I feel like a mouse waiting for the cat to spring."

She sighed again, playing with the rings on her fingers, then she looked up and said decisively, "I have decided to take to my bed. To buy myself some time. I have been told that the king will not permit me to return home to Woodham Walter and I've been given no date when I might leave here."

Her voice hardened as she added, "The duke merely smiles and cracks his fingers and murmurs platitudes whenever I seek information."

Pen was silent. She wanted to scream at the princess not to confide in her. She was no longer her friend, her trustworthy confidante. But she kept silent.

Mary continued inexorably with her confidence. "Only you and my physician will know that I am in truth perfectly well. I would not have any of my other ladies aware of the fiction. The duke will not molest me while I remain secluded under a physician's care, and my brother might be sufficiently concerned to grant me an interview. If I can once manage to talk with him without the duke's intervention, I'm certain I can secure his permission to leave."

Pen nodded. Mary had suffered ill health since puberty, and one particular ailment that could lay her low with fever for many months at a time, particularly in the winter. On occasion they had despaired of her life. Such a deception now would certainly buy her time and might indeed induce the king to grant her an interview.

"If the London people know of your illness, madam, it will be even harder for the duke to make a move against you while you're here."

Mary smiled her approval. "That is good thinking, Pen. The people do love me. They will rally to me at my brother's death. We must make sure the news of my illness is broadcast."

"If you're taken ill very suddenly, in public . . ." Pen suggested.

"This evening . . . during the banquet . . . under many eyes," the princess said, thoughtfully now. "The news will soon spread. You will watch for my signal. . . . What shall it be now? Oh, I will drop my fan to the table, like so." She illustrated with the delicately painted Italian fan she carried.

"When you see the signal you'll come to me immediately, express concern . . . you will know what to say, you have such quick wits."

The quick wits of a betrayer. Pen inclined her head in acknowledgment.

"Then I will insist that the revels continue in my absence and leave the banquet. You'll escort me to my chamber, and then report to the duke and the council that I have my old infirmity and must remain under the physician's care in the seclusion of my own bedchamber. That will do, I believe?"

"I believe it will, madam."

Mary looked at her closely. "Are *you* quite well, Pen? You're very pale."

"Oh, I'm just a little tired," Pen said. "Like you, madam, I don't rest easy at night in this place."

Mary nodded, satisfied. She went to the prie-dieu at the end of her bed. "My mind is more at ease now that I have made a plan, and I know I can trust in your help. You may leave me; I must attend to my devotions." She knelt and took up her prayer book.

Pen left, closing the door quietly. The antechamber beyond the princess's bedchamber was a long narrow room, chilly despite the fire and the light of many candles. The other ladies who attended the princess were busy with their own dressing for the evening and a pleasant buzz of conversation rose in the drafty air as they helped one another to tighten laces, curl fringes, adjust headdresses.

"Has the princess need of anything, Pen?" Lady Matilda Harlow leaned into the mirror, plucking distressfully at a pimple on her nose.

"She's at her prayers," Pen answered. "She'll ring when she's finished."

"Pen, what can I do about this spot?" Matilda wailed softly. "It's as big as a house!"

"Hot water and witch hazel," Pen advised, trying to brighten her tone. Her position as the princess's closest confidante drew little resentment from the twelve ladies who attended Mary;

indeed they looked to her for advice much as her own sister did, even though she was younger than some of them.

She sat down and took up her embroidery frame, hoping that the occupation would still the turmoil in her brain. Owen would be at the banquet this evening, and afterwards the doors would be thrown open to even the lowliest hangers-on at the king's court for the Twelfth Night revels. The king himself would not attend the wild party. He considered the night when the Lord of Misrule held sway to be a pagan rite, not suitable for good Christian folk.

Somehow, while she was treating Owen with the flirtatious ease that formed part of their deception, she would have to tell him of her conversation with Mary. He would want to know of the princess's fears and the true nature of her illness.

Her scalp crawled and her fingers slipped. The needle jabbed her fingertip and blood smeared the delicate linen she was embroidering.

She sucked her finger, cursing under her breath. Blood was the very devil to get out. She was working on a cap for the infant daughter of one of Pippa's friends, a young woman so happy in motherhood, so adoring of her first child.

Pen set down the embroidery frame. Her scalp no longer crawled and her heart was once more cold and determined. She would do what had to be done. She would believe that the French meant Mary no harm. They wanted information in order to plan a quick response to whatever situation developed after the king's death. As long as she didn't betray the princess to Northumberland's spies, then the bargain was harmless.

But supposing it would suit the French to disclose Mary's plans to Northumberland?

Her head began to ache. Everyone was devious, no one trustworthy. Except her own family. She yearned to discuss her bargain with them, but she couldn't. In this she was as alone as she had been during the long grim hours of her labor and its dreadful aftermath.

She had made a devil's bargain with Owen d'Arcy and she would keep it.

Leaning sideways, Pen rang a handbell for a maid, and when the woman appeared she gave her the soiled cap. "Try what you can to get the blood off this. I pricked my finger."

"Yes, indeed, my lady." The maid took the stained linen but she looked a trifle surprised. Small children pricked their fingers as they sewed, not the sophisticated ladies of the court.

Mary's door opened and the princess entered the antechamber. She looked serene, as she always did after her prayers. "Well, my ladies, are we all assembled?"

The women gathered around her in their pearl-strewn brocades, their embroidered velvets, their furred overgowns. She had a word for each one, an appreciative comment on their dress, a personal inquiry here, a general remark there. These women were her bulwark against the machinations of her enemies and she knew how to ensure their loyalty.

"I'll summon the heralds, madam." Pen went to the door that opened onto the corridor. Two heralds, trumpets in hand, pennants unfurled, awaited their orders to sound the arrival of Princess Mary in the great banqueting hall below.

The trumpets sounded as the heralds preceded the party. The Tudor Rose flew on the pennants. Mary and her ladies followed. At the foot of the staircase the heralds waited on either side as the princess and her party descended, walked between them to a renewed tucket, and were received by the Dukes of Northumberland and Suffolk.

Pen saw Mary's rigid response to the oiled smiles of the Privy Council as she was escorted to her place at the high table beside her brother's high-backed chair with the Lion of England embossed in gold on the scarlet canopy above.

Pen took her own place just below the high table. She was neither royalty nor married to a man of political influence and so had no claim to a place of honor on the dais. But she was seated close enough to Mary to see and respond when she gave the signal.

She glanced around the hall at her fellow guests. It was a relief that Robin was not present at the table, although he would come later, escorting Pippa to the revels that would follow the feast. It distressed Pen dreadfully to find that she no longer looked forward to seeing him. The knowledge of her deception made her awkward and distant with him, and she knew he continued to look with disfavor upon her apparent flirtation with Owen d'Arcy, although he no longer discussed it with her.

"Lady Bryanston . . . may I take my seat?"

At the soft courteous tones, Pen turned without surprise to greet the chevalier. She had known that he would engineer a place at her side. She gave him a smile as bright and brittle as the ice-covered puddles in the courtyard beyond the long windows.

"Pray be seated, Chevalier. It has been too long since we last met."

"Far too long," he replied, swinging a leg over the long bench with an adroit management of his sword that reminded Pen of the night he had saved her life.

It was not a reminder she relished.

"You have been well, I trust." He arranged himself on the bench beside her with the same deft twitch of cloak and black velvet sleeve, turned back to reveal a pearly gray lining. "You look well, if I may say so."

The melodic lilt to his voice, the warmth of the smile in his eyes was almost too much to withstand. But she would not let him see that. With a faint responding smile, she turned her attention to the high table, where heralds stood at either side of the king's chair, waiting to signal his arrival.

Owen swallowed a sigh of discouragement and refused to be disheartened. Ever since they had struck their bargain, he had steadfastly ignored Pen's coldness, the falseness of her smile as she played the game. And she played it impeccably, he had to admit. But in all other respects she would not give an inch. He knew she was as affected as he by the powerful tug of their mutual attraction, by the strange current of sensual energy that connected them, and he knew she was resisting him purely through willpower.

She had a damnably strong will!

Conversation faltered as the wait continued. Great wheels of wax candles flared above the long tables, servants stood ready with flagons of wine and mead. Butlers had knives at the ready before the carving tables. The smell of roasting meat was rich in the stuffy air. And still there was no tucket of trumpets to herald the king's entrance.

Pen glanced up at Mary, who sat pale but composed, her brother's empty chair on one side of her, the Duchess of Suffolk on the other. The duchess bent to say something to the princess, an expression of sympathetic attention on her sallow, angular countenance. Mary nodded at her cousin's remark with an air of indifference.

The duchess offered a thin smile to the company at large and sharply pinched her dreaming daughter who sat beside her. Jane came out of her reverie with a little gasp, rubbing her forearm, a blush of pain and mortification coloring her pale face.

"I wonder what could be keeping His Highness," Owen murmured.

"Perhaps he's mislaid his britches," Pen returned with a sardonic snap, although she maintained her public smile.

"Oh, so sharp you could cut," Owen said, with a note of appreciation. He stretched his long legs beneath the damask-covered table and appeared to take his ease. "I own I would like my glass filled, but in that absence, let me tell you what I have been doing this evening."

Pen turned her head and couldn't help the spark of eagerness that lit her eyes. "You have discovered something?"

"Well, more a confirmation than anything definite." He watched the light die.

"Confirmation of what?"

"Some mischief surrounded your son's birth."

"I told you that. You didn't believe me?" she accused.

"I am careful about what I believe," he replied. "I didn't *not* believe you, but before I embark on a mission, I like to satisfy myself that the cause is good."

"As indeed do I, Chevalier," she said.

"Ah." He regarded her thoughtfully. "So you have some information for me."

"Maybe." She met his gaze unsmiling. "Maybe, Chevalier. But I only give in the same measure as I receive."

"I would not have expected otherwise. Should I begin?"

She was prevented from a response by the high note of a trumpet that heralded a messenger in the king's livery approaching from the staircase.

He stopped behind the Duke of Northumberland's chair and whispered something in his ear. The duke listened impassively, then waved the messenger aside. The man bowed and stepped back, standing at attention behind the duke's chair.

Northumberland rose to his feet, his dark brooding gaze sweeping the hall. "My lords, I regret to have to inform you that His Highness says that pressing business will keep him from us this evening. The king bids us feast and be merry." He sat back in his chair and gestured impatiently to the page at his elbow to fill his goblet.

So Mary had been right, Pen thought. The duke had shown neither surprise nor concern at the messenger's news. He had not expected Edward's attendance tonight. Had he kept the king away so that he would not have an opportunity to talk with his sister? Or was the king's health so far deteriorated that he could not appear in public, so the council had to find a fiction to explain his absence?

"Interesting," Owen commented, glancing at Pen. "Did you have the sense that the king's pressing business was not unknown to Northumberland beforehand?"

Pen merely raised an eyebrow at this accurate reading of her thoughts. She moved her arm aside to allow a page to fill her own and the chevalier's goblets. She waited until she had been served a portion of roast peacock before she said, "You were about to begin, Chevalier."

Owen drank from his goblet. "I happened upon your brother-in-law this evening."

"And?" she prompted with admirable calm.

"The baby was born prematurely, as I understand it."

"Yes, a month early." Pen realized that she didn't want to go near the subject of the baby's birth. Not even with someone who was pledged to help her. "Why is that important?"

"It would be important if premature labor was induced." His voice was quiet, distant almost, as if he understood that he was treading on the most delicate ground.

Pen stared at him. "How could that have been?"

"If your mother-in-law wished to ensure that you gave birth before your own family arrived, there are ways she could have done so." He signaled to the page standing behind his chair to serve him from a dish of larks' tongues, giving Pen time to absorb this and compose herself.

"Did Miles say something to imply that his mother had done something like that?" she asked finally.

He nodded. "He was in his cups, but it seemed clear to me that that was what he was implying.

Is the countess capable of such a thing?"

Pen stared down at the cooling meat on her plate. She had no appetite, indeed could not imagine ever being hungry again. "Yes," she said. "She's capable of anything."

"I was wondering if she wanted the child born before your parents arrived in order to see what sex it would be. A girl would be unimportant. A boy would disinherit Miles." Owen kept his eyes on his plate, his voice neutral.

"Dear God! How could she . . . ?" She lifted her head and looked at him, her eyes ablaze with passion. "My child . . . my son, was born alive. I *know* it." Her clenched fist rested white-knuckled on the table.

"Then we shall find out the truth." Owen laid a hand over hers, his fingers, warm and firm, working her fist open until her hand lay flat. "Try not to show your feelings, Pen."

"I don't have your mastery of deceit," she retorted. "I came late to spying." And yet she made no immediate attempt to pull her hand free of his. The physical connection sent a jolt through her belly, and the longer their hands remained joined the more it seemed impossible to separate them. Then abruptly she jerked her hand free and dropped it to her lap. "We have a business agreement," she said curtly. "I see no reason to hold hands."

He shrugged. "As you wish. However, we must at least preserve the appearance of friendliness, if not something a little more."

Pen took up her goblet. Thoughtfully she ran a finger around its rim before giving Owen a dazzling smile. "Your company gives me so much pleasure, Chevalier."

"I'm not sure anyone would find that convincing," he responded aridly. "The frown has a distinctly more genuine air." He leaned back and surveyed the tables, saying in a conversational tone, "So, you have something of interest for me?"

Her gaze darted to the high table where Northumberland and Suffolk sat. "I cannot tell you here."

"Let me explain a little trick of the spy's trade," he said in the same easy tone. "A public gathering is the safest place to communicate the deepest secrets. As long as we appear to be having a perfectly ordinary conversation, no one will pay us any particular attention. Use your normal voice but keep the tone even, almost a monotone, just as I'm doing now."

"It's enough to put me to sleep," Pen observed.

He gave a short laugh. "Exactly. So, try it."

Pen played with her goblet. What Owen had just told her he suspected filled her with such cold fury that she knew she would do anything; there was nothing she would stop at to get at the truth and be avenged upon Philip's mother.

Keeping her voice to the correct tone, which she found helped her to distance herself from what she was saying, she told him of Mary's fears and her planned seclusion.

Owen merely nodded, crumbling a piece of bread between finger and thumb. "She's right to suspect a threat from Northumberland."

"She always expects such a threat," Pen said shortly. "But her brother's continued illness makes it more likely. And now that he hasn't made an appearance this evening . . ." She shrugged.

Again Owen nodded, and Pen asked, "What will you do with this information?"

"Pass it on to the ambassador."

"You will not betray it to Northumberland?" She couldn't help the question or her anxiously belligerent tone.

He turned his head and smiled at her. "No, sweetheart. Do you still not understand that we are as interested in thwarting Northumberland's plots as is the princess?"

The soft-spoken endearment shocked her. It was like an affirmation of some kind, as if something had happened that gave him the right to address her in the language of a lover. His eyes glowed as they rested on her taut, pale face. "There is no need for us to be so at odds," he said.

Pen shook her head, tearing her eyes away from his. "There is every reason."

He changed the subject. "Your family were not bidden to the king's feast?"

"They were, but my sister Anna has been unwell and they made their excuses."

"For Lady Pippa too?"

"Pippa will come later to the revels with Robin. She'll share my bedchamber tonight." This conversation was so normal, so matter-of-fact, that Pen felt her color returning, her heart slowing to a reasonable pace.

"Your sister is not seriously ill, I trust?"

"Oh, no, she has a slight cold." Pen laughed suddenly. "According to Pippa's letter, Anna could well have been left at home in Tilly's charge, but Lord Hugh wouldn't hear of it. He treats her as carefully as if she were made of glass."

"Clearly a devoted father," Owen said, and his voice had a sudden chill.

Pen, in the resurgence of her own pain, didn't notice. "None more," she returned dully. The conversation had come full circle.

She glanced up at the high table and caught Mary's eye. The princess suddenly dropped her fan and touched her forehead with her napkin. She had no need to feign illness, Pen thought. The princess was pale as death.

Pen gave a distressed little exclamation and rose hastily to her feet. Owen, forewarned, moved to assist her. Her neighbors in some surprise rose with her. Pages moved the bench so that she could step away from the table.

She hastened to Mary's side. "Give the princess some air. Madam, take a sip of wine." She bent over the woman, who was now leaning against the high back of her chair, her eyes half closed.

"What is it?" demanded Northumberland even as Lady Suffolk took up the dropped fan and waved it vigorously in the princess's white face.

"The princess is unwell, my lord duke," Pen said. "She was complaining of the headache earlier but didn't wish to disappoint the king by taking to her bed."

Mary murmured, "Forgive me, my lords . . . my ladies. I must retire."

Her other ladies crowded to the dais but Pen waved them away. "I will attend the princess alone."

The duke, however, insisted upon giving Mary his arm and helping her from the banqueting hall, escorting her as far as her chamber door. He looked at her as she wavered in the open doorway, annoyance clear in his gaze. "I trust you will be more yourself in the morning, madam."

"I fear the princess has one of her fevers, my lord," Pen said smoothly. "If you would be so good as to send someone for her physician, I will help her to bed now."

Northumberland's eyes snaked to Pen's open countenance. He bowed and left.

"Well done, Pen," Mary whispered as Pen closed the door. She stood, her hand on her heart, still so pale that Pen was genuinely concerned.

"Madam, are you truly ill?"

"No, I don't believe so, but if 'tis possible to

die of fright, I could almost imagine myself at death's door," Mary responded, her voice growing stronger, a slight smile now touching her eyes. "But I believe we have outmaneuvered my lord Northumberland, at least for the moment. He knew my brother would not attend this evening."

"Yes," Pen agreed. "Let me help you to bed before the physician arrives."

Mary's physician was loyal and knew his part. It was one he had played before. Nothing was said to him as to the true nature of his patient's illness and he asked no awkward questions, merely agreed that the princess was suffering from a severe fever and chills that if not cared for would inevitably go to the lungs. He suggested purging and cupping and Mary agreed to both, knowing that she would be left so weak after the treatment, her headache so severe, that if the duke had any suspicions, they would be soon laid to rest. Even her attendants would be convinced of the seriousness of her illness.

When the man had done his draconian work and left, Mary spoke feebly from the bed.

"Pen, I wish you to attend the revels and inform the duke that I will be unable to receive visitors for at least several days. Make certain that the seriousness of my condition is known to as many people as possible. Attend me in the morning."

Pen curtsied and left the darkened chamber. From downstairs she heard the sounds of an army of servants clearing the banqueting hall of its tables and benches in preparation for the Twelfth Night madness. The strains of musicians tuning their instruments came from the gallery that surrounded the hall. The dinner guests, those not resident in the palace, would be refreshing themselves and adjusting their dress in the two long galleries set aside for them.

Would Owen be among them? Or had he left, his spy's work done? Was he even now on his way to the ambassador with her information?

Pen went to her own bedchamber to wait for Pippa, before carrying her message to Northumberland and the rest of the court.

Nine

●

"Pippa, are you here already?" Pen said in surprise as she entered her bedchamber and found her sister preening in front of the mirror.

"We arrived half an hour ago." Pippa turned in a swirl of green-and-yellow-flowered turquoise taffeta. "They said you were with the princess. Such talk there is! She fell ill at dinner?"

"Yes, one of her fevers, she's laid very low," Pen replied. She had to keep from her sister, from whom she rarely kept anything, a secret she had revealed to a French agent. The reflection chilled her and abruptly she turned her attention to Nutmeg, who yawned, stretched, and rolled over, offering his belly for a rub.

"This is a very ordinary mask," Pippa said with a hint of disapproval, indicating the article in question that lay on the dresser. "Couldn't you have found something a little more imaginative?"

She tied on her own choice, a delicate feline disguise of green velvet with embroidered black silk whiskers and slitted eyeholes. It was such a perfect match for its wearer's swift and mercurial temperament that Pen laughed.

"It really suits you, Pippa. But I prefer something less conspicuous." Pen tied on the simple ivory silk mask that concealed little of her countenance. The Lord of Misrule had decreed that all the guests at the revels should be masked. His word was the only law to prevail on this traditionally wild night of feasting and mockery.

"You should see Robin's mask." Pippa bent to the mirror and pinched her cheeks to make them rosier. "It's a lion's head with a full mane. I would have chosen something different for him if he'd asked my advice."

"Robin has no interest in his appearance," Pen said. "He probably picked the mask up somewhere and just decided it would do."

"More than likely," Pippa agreed.

"How's Anna?"

"Fine, and cross as two sticks because Lord Hugh wouldn't let her come tonight. They're riding over in the morning, though. Mama says she hasn't seen you for far too long."

Pen sighed. "I know. I feel that too." She glanced at the brass clock on the mantel. "We should probably go down."

Pippa opened the door and stuck her head into the corridor. "The musicians are playing." She glanced at Pen over her shoulder. "Is the Chevalier d'Arcy going to be here tonight?"

"Perhaps," Pen returned with a convincing shrug. "He was at the banquet, but I don't know if he intended to stay for the revels."

"Why would anyone come to the feast and not

join in the fun afterwards?" Pippa asked robustly.

"I didn't have the chance to ask if he was staying because the princess became ill and I had to leave the table very suddenly."

"Ah." Pippa nodded. "If he thought you weren't coming back, he probably *would* decide to leave."

"Now, what's that supposed to mean?"

"You know perfectly well," Pippa said airily. "You flirt with him enough. Let's go down and find out if he's there." She linked her arm through her sister's and bore her off.

Pen left it at that. She and Owen had tried to give the impression that they enjoyed each other's company, so she could hardly resent it if they'd succeeded. It rankled nevertheless. It was so far from the truth.

The atmosphere in the great hall had an edge to it, the laughter louder than usual, the dancing more uninhibited. The masks gave a sense of anonymity, although identities were never really in doubt, but with the masks came a feeling of license, as if everything was permitted and for this one night consequences did not exist.

The Duke of Northumberland was standing at the bottom of the stairs, and as the sisters came down he put a foot on the last step, effectively barring their way. "Lady Bryanston." He cast a brief glance at Pippa, acknowledging her with a bare nod that made it clear how unimportant he considered her.

"How is the princess?"

"Very feverish, my lord duke. The physician cupped her and we can only hope that she will have improved in the morning."

Pen shook her head gravely. "I would not be honest if I said I believed that likely. The air here is damp, my lord, and the princess is very susceptible to cold. It goes quickly to her lungs. Not unlike His Highness, her brother," she added, watching the duke's reaction through lowered lashes.

"The king's condition is improving," the duke said icily. "I would have thought you, Lady Bryanston, would be better employed at the princess's bedside than taking part in this unbridled revelry." He gestured scornfully to the noisy scene behind him.

"I obey the princess's orders, my lord," Pen said with a sweet smile, and waited for him to move his foot. For some reason she was not afraid of Northumberland although she knew he was a dangerous man to anger.

The duke hesitated, then stepped aside. Pen smiled, curtsied, and swept past him, Pippa at her side.

"I detest that man," Pippa said. "But I would not anger him, Pen."

"If Robin is not afraid of him, I see no reason why we should be," Pen replied.

Pippa's attention was claimed by one of her host of admirers, and she was swept into the dance before she could respond, lost to sight in the mayhem.

Pen moved around the walls where groups were gathered, chattering, laughing, deep in gossip. She paused frequently as she made the circle, choosing her audiences for their gossip-mongering or for their ability to disseminate information beyond the palace walls. To each she gave the impression that the princess was gravely ill. And all the while, her eyes searched the throng for Owen.

She didn't want to be looking for him. She told herself that it didn't matter whether he was there. She had done what she had to do, and it was now time for him to fulfill his side of the bargain. They didn't need to play the game of flirtation anymore.

It was a game that Owen made the most of. He'd touch her or kiss her mouth with the casual intimacy that seemed to come so naturally to him, and she couldn't push him away without drawing unwelcome attention.

To make matters worse, she knew that a part of her she could not control longed for that contact . . . the scent of his skin, the feel of his hands on her, the firm hard press of his body against hers.

She would conjure Philip in her mind's eye in an effort to dispel the longing. But she seemed to have lost the sound of his voice, and even the lines of his face were growing blurred at the edges as if he was receding into a far distance. And that made her angry confusion even worse.

She would not find peace until Owen d'Arcy

was out of her life, and he could not leave her life until he had helped her. And she would never find peace if she did not find the truth about her child. Once again she told herself she had made the only decision possible. The physical restlessness, the *longing,* that Owen d'Arcy engendered was a minute price to pay if she could finally put to rest her obsession.

"Ah, there you are. Why such a deep and terrible frown?"

His voice was so startling that Pen literally jumped, knocking over a stool.

"God's bones! I don't ordinarily have such an effect," Owen said, righting the stool. "What's troubling you?"

"Nothing . . . nothing at all. I have been talking to people," she said distractedly.

"That is what one normally does on such occasions," Owen said. "That and dance. Let us do the latter." He took her hand and led her into the dance, sliding them both effortlessly into the stately movements of a pavane.

"So, what have you been talking to people about?"

"The princess . . . her illness . . . it seemed sensible to spread the news abroad as far as possible."

"Very wise. I can help there. I know a publisher of one of the popular broadsheets. A word in his ear will have the news cried throughout the streets of London by tomorrow evening."

The offer was not one to be refused just because it was not made for altruistic reasons. It would serve his own interests, although Pen was still not sure what those interests were. Any more than she was confident that they would not suddenly change, and assisting Princess Mary would no longer be their object. She contented herself with one of her bright and brittle smiles and turned gracefully in the movement of the dance.

"Why are you looking so miserable, Robin?" Pippa bounced up beside her stepbrother, who was standing morosely in a window embrasure, his hands thrust deep into the pockets of his short gown of peacock-blue velvet.

"Even under your mask I can see how cross you are."

"I'm not miserable or cross," Robin lied. "I just wish Pen would find someone other than d'Arcy to flirt with."

"He's very exotic," Pippa said. "I expect he adds a little excitement to her life. It's been very dull for her since Philip died . . . and then the baby. . . ." Her voice faded and she bit her lip.

Robin turned to look at her, his eyes brilliantly blue in the eyeholes of his mask. The full-maned lion's head looked incongruous atop his stocky and somewhat rumpled figure. "Is that all she's looking for? Excitement? Pen's not that shallow, Pippa."

"I know." Pippa looked out at the dancing couples. Pen's rose-pink gown floated around her in bright contrast to Owen d'Arcy's silver-edged black velvet. Their hands were joined, held high in the dance.

"Actually," Pippa said slowly, "I don't know what Pen's up to. See how she seems to be laughing? But she's not really amused."

"How can you know that?" Robin followed her gaze. He could see the soft glow beneath the creamy pallor of Pen's complexion, and her hazel eyes, their rich depths of color accentuated by the ivory mask enclosing them, picked up and held the lamplight. "She looks radiant."

Pippa shook her head. "She's all tied in knots. That's why she looks flushed and her eyes are so bright. You know what she's like when she gets upset."

Robin looked at the couple with new eyes. "You think she's not happy?"

"I don't know for sure," Pippa said slowly. "But I do know that something's engaging her attention. There's a sort of passion about her . . . and that's the first time since . . . well, since. You know how it seemed that she wasn't really here anymore? You know what I mean?"

"Aye," Robin agreed morosely. "I know."

"Well, it's not like that now. For whatever reason. Something's touched her. Either she's angry, or she's in love, or she's confused. But at least she's reacting with some emotion."

"I *know*," Robin repeated with vehemence. "For God's sake, Pippa, I'm not blind."

Pippa hesitated. She was not offended by

180

Robin's brusqueness. "You don't like him?"

"No."

Pippa looked at him curiously. "Do you know something about him?"

Robin deflected the question. "I don't like the effect he's had on Pen. We can't be in the same room together anymore without arguing. Everything I say she picks holes in."

Pippa said with customary bluntness, "You're both wearing that shoe, Robin. You seem to look for quarrels."

Angry denial was on the tip of Robin's tongue, but he knew Pippa spoke the truth. He looked across to where Northumberland stood with Suffolk at the edge of the dancers.

Northumberland's cold gaze swept the hall, settled for a moment on Jane Grey, who was dancing in lackluster fashion with his own son, Guildford Dudley. Robin suspected that a match was being made there. A match that would unite the ducal houses of Northumberland and Suffolk. It would be an impeccable match except that Jane was already contracted to Lord Hertford. There would have to be compelling reasons to break such a contract.

So what was the duke plotting? Robin no longer believed that Northumberland had the king's best interests at heart. Robin had access to the anterooms and offices of the two great ducal houses, his presence so familiar it was barely noticed, and he'd heard and seen much that troubled him in the last weeks since the king had

181

disappeared from public view. And if the duke was faithless, Robin considered himself released from his own vow of loyalty.

He no longer felt obliged to obey the duke's instructions to keep Pen in the dark about d'Arcy's French affiliations, but he couldn't decide what to tell her, or how, or when. For all he knew, it might not even shock her. She had lived with the devious tricks and connivings of the court for years now. Probably nothing would surprise her. But if she was being used against her knowledge . . .

He looked closely at the dancing couple again. *Was she happy?* He could feel from this distance the simmering attraction between Pen and Owen d'Arcy. It wasn't so much *simmering,* he amended grimly as he watched them in the dance, as about to boil over. Pippa was right about the passion. Pen exuded it like an aura. But she was also right that Pen did not seem happy.

Pippa glanced again at Robin and saw his fixed stare on the dancers. She left him to his reverie and went to choose a partner for herself from among the group of masked young men standing beneath the holly boughs and fat clumps of pale mistletoe that decorated the walls of the hall. They all brightened noticeably at her feline approach and the air around them suddenly crackled with competition.

Pen felt Robin's scrutiny as she went through the motions of the dance, and it made her uncomfortable. If she could just tell him the truth, if she could just reassure him that she knew all about the chevalier . . .

She brushed against Owen as they passed in the dance and her skin contracted. Involuntarily she turned her face up to his. His black gaze seemed to devour her. He had chosen a mask of an eagle's head, with a harsh predatory beak. His eyes were black points of light in the sockets. He was as dangerous, as fierce, as brilliant and fascinating as the bird whose mask he wore. And there were moments, like this one, when Pen felt like the shrew in the grass watching the predator circle slowly overhead, talons, wicked and grasping, ready to pounce.

Ridiculous, she told herself. But she could not break the chain that held her gaze fast to his. And she could not ignore the ironic little voice that said that if only circumstances had been different, the shrew in this case would probably be throwing herself into those talons.

He lifted her hand and for an instant held it against his heart. He dipped his head and his lips brushed her neck behind her ear. The skin there burned and her thighs quivered as the movement of the dance turned her away from him.

Owen savored the scent of her, the taste of her on his lips where they'd touched her skin. A soft dewy taste with a hint of salt. He could feel the blood flowing in his veins, hot and fast. Pen Bryanston was rapidly becoming an obsession.

183

His gaze was suddenly distant. He saw another ballroom, a beautiful, flirtatious woman with no knowledge of the consequences of the deadly game she played. . . .

"What is it?"

He came back with a start. Pen was once again facing him in the dance. He noticed the dew of perspiration on her brow. She was frowning at him.

Pen was not Estelle. Pen understood consequences. She was no naïf. She knew what he was about, just as she knew what she was about.

He smiled down at her but his eyes were still distant. "Nothing, why?" He took her hand, holding it high as she revolved around him in a graceful measure.

"Your face," she said, dropping a sweeping curtsy.

"You can't see my face." He raised her and exchanged places with her in the line.

"I can see your eyes and your mouth," she returned. "And whatever you were thinking, it was not pleasant. If the wind changes, you'll look disagreeable for the rest of your life."

"Ah, and then I suppose what little patience you have with me will be quite dissipated," he said with a mournful sigh.

Pen ignored this and concentrated on her steps. The expression she'd surprised on his face had disturbed her. He had looked somehow devastated, hurt even.

The dance ended and she dabbed at her forehead with a scrap of lace that passed as a hand-kerchief.

She caught Robin's stare from the other side of the hall. He hadn't moved from the embrasure the entire evening, and as far as she could tell he hadn't taken his eyes off her either.

She turned her eyes from Robin's and said brusquely, "I believe it's time you paid your debt, Chevalier. I have paid mine."

Owen beckoned a footman who carried a tray of goblets. "It's an ongoing debt, but I agree we should discuss my part very soon." He handed her a goblet of cool rhenish.

Pen took it. She touched the cold glass to her neck and her temples and felt her body cool. "I believe that we should discuss it now." Her tone was even.

Owen sipped from his own goblet. "Must it be now?"

"We've discussed matters of interest to you in such public circumstances."

"True enough." He reached out and touched his fingertip to a droplet of moisture on her neck. "Believe me, Pen, I will not renege. I will give you what you need."

She heard the double edge to the soft promise. The spot on her neck burned. She stared at him from behind her mask.

He returned her look, his gaze quite steady, but she read the message and she knew that she was sending the same.

Acceptance.

A great roar came from the dais at the far end of the hall, where the Lord of Misrule, in a devil's mask, sat upon his throne wielding a trident. Instantly a pack of small boys, all in devils' costumes, darted around the room, dodging between the masked guests who now stood transfixed, waiting for what the Lord of Misrule was about to decree. The little devil figures wielding snuffers on long poles extinguished all the candles and within minutes the great room was dark, except for the light from the massive fireplaces at either end.

There was a stunned silence, then whispers and laughter. The Lord of Misrule bellowed his order for everyone to turn around three times, take six steps backwards, then reach out and seize hold of the first person of the opposite sex that they could reach. Laughter rang out as the entire masked company tried to obey, bumping into one another, stepping on toes.

Pen felt Owen take her hand. She couldn't see clearly in the shadowy gloom as people stumbled around her, but the clasp of his hand was tight and warm and suddenly urgent. He led, she followed, snaking through the now riotous crowd. Everyone had hold of someone; hands grasped her as she passed, lewd hands that stroked, patted, grabbed at her buttocks. Laughter, shrill cries, the occasional little shriek punctuated the uproar. Blindly Pen followed where the hand led her. The excitement surged around her, through her, became a part of her. Everything was unreal, uncharted. For some reason she kept her eyes shut, locking herself into the surreal crimson world behind her eyelids.

Then she felt cooler air on her face and there was a strange quiet as if they had stepped into another world. She opened her eyes. Owen let fall the arras he had moved aside, an arras that covered a door into a small, windowless, round chamber lit by a single candle in a sconce high on the wall.

Pen looked around, blinking as her eyes adjusted. "Where is this?"

"Somewhere I thought we could discuss my side of our bargain away from active ears," he said, closing the door and turning the key.

The noise from without continued unabated. "No one will miss us." He untied his eagle's mask and tossed it to the floor.

"No," Pen agreed, her fingers busy with her own mask. She was trembling as if with cold, but her hands were warm, her skin flushed with heat. When he came towards her she went into his arms. Here, in the quiet and the dimness, passion flared. Obsession became a flicker . . . for the moment.

"You're trembling," he murmured, moving his lips to her ear even as he worked on the pins of her hood.

"So are you," she returned, sliding her hands inside his doublet, feeling his ribs, the hard swell of muscle beneath his fine silk shirt.

"I know." He laughed softly. Her hood

slipped from her head. His breath was warm on her neck as he kissed the tender skin behind her ear.

"I want you, Pen." The words were suddenly fierce and his hold tightened, his mouth urgent now as he brought his lips to hers.

Pen felt herself drowning, melting into his body. His mouth was hot and hard upon her own, and she inhaled deeply his own special fragrance, where warm male flesh mingled with lavender and crisply ironed linen. She felt his body on hers, the hard jut of his penis pressing through her damask skirts. She wriggled her fingers inside the tiny pearl buttons of his shirt, desperate to touch his skin. She sucked on his lower lip, her tongue probed deep within his mouth. Her eyes were tightly closed and she was conscious of nothing but her need, the ever-tightening spiral of passion. The screams, crashes, and shrieks of laughter outside the round chamber seemed to exist on another planet.

Owen's fingers were deft on the laces of her stomacher, and her gown opened and slid from her almost without her being aware of it. With the same swift expertise he untied the tapes of her Spanish farthingale and the awkward structure was cast aside so that she stood in nothing but her lace-edged chemise and gartered silken hose, her slippered feet lost in the frothy puddle of rose-pink damask at her ankles.

She fumbled with the laces that fastened his

hose to the waistband of his doublet even as she rubbed her other palm against the bulge of his penis, aware only of her frenzied need to hold him.

He helped her, opening his hose, and she gave a little sigh of satisfaction as finally she got what she wanted. She enclosed him in her hand, reveling in the feel of the hot shaft of flesh, the corded veins pulsing against her palm. She felt blindly for the tip, easing back the little hood of skin with two fingers. She brought her finger to her mouth, tasting the drop of moisture that she'd gathered in her exploration.

His lips were pressed to the soft swell of her breasts rising from the lacy chemise. He opened the bodice and cupped her breasts in his palms, bending to kiss each in turn, sucking on her nipples that rose hard against his mouth. She shuddered against him, her thighs parting as she struggled to lift her chemise to her waist, baring her lower body.

Owen lifted her free and she curled her legs around his hips. She bit his lower lip and tasted blood.

He carried her to a table in the center of the chamber and Pen fell back, her legs still twined around his hips. He slid his hands beneath her backside, holding her up as he entered her, plunging to her core in one smooth deep movement. She moaned with satisfaction as she closed around him, holding him tightly within her.

Owen held himself very still. "Sweetheart, I

daren't move," he whispered. "You have rendered me as incontinent as a virgin on his initiation." He smiled ruefully down at her, the candlelight falling across his face.

Pen opened her eyes for the first time in hours, it seemed. "I, on the other hand, am no virgin, and I need you *now!*" The demand astounded her even as she made it. She had never made such a demand before and as she thrust her hips upwards, tightening her inner muscles around him, she laughed aloud with joy and the absolute sense of her own mastery.

Owen cried out as the orgasmic rush took him. He had just enough control left to pull out of her before he was completely lost. His fingers were buried deep in the soft swell of her bottom, gripping with bruising strength as he held her, his head thrown back, his eyes closed in ecstasy.

Slowly Pen returned to awareness, to the feel of the table hard beneath her back, the hands beneath her, the juices of love drying on her belly. She blinked in the candlelight, which seemed very bright, and reached up to touch his face.

Owen opened his eyes and gently slid his hands from beneath her. She lay on the table, for the moment unable to imagine making her languid limbs work enough to enable her to get to her feet.

Owen fastened his hose, then took her hands and pulled her into a sitting position. "That was very unceremonious, Pen. Next time, I'll do better." He bent to clasp her face between his hands and kissed her.

Next time? Pen sat on the table. Her body still gloried in its satisfaction, her spirit still sang with pleasure.

But slowly she felt the icy tide of reality.

Dear God, what had she done?

She had given in, yielded control, lost herself, lost sight of her goal. She could think only that in lust and in passion she had betrayed her child. In her animal arousal. She had forgotten her child, forgotten Philip, forgotten her oath to honor his memory by finding the truth.

She gazed up at Owen but his features were blurred; he seemed like some figment of a strange and dreadful trance. There was no glory now, only a confused self-disgust. No residue of pleasure. Her body was cold, and she was vulnerable in her seminakedness.

She slid off the table and with almost desperate haste grabbed up her discarded clothing.

"Wait . . . wait a minute." He took the clothes from her.

Slowly he came back into focus and Pen saw that while he was still smiling, his eyes still soft with the afterglow of desire, there was a wary puzzlement in his steady regard.

"What's happened, Pen?"

"Nothing, I don't know . . . nothing," she mumbled, tucking her breasts back into her bodice with shaking fingers. *How could she possibly explain to Owen what she couldn't explain to herself?*

He frowned. "Are you regretting what happened between us?"

"It shouldn't have happened." Pen snatched her farthingale from his hands and fumbled with the ties at her waist. She felt that by yielding to that wild, all-consuming passion, she had somehow lost the moral right to insist that he fulfill his side of their bargain. Some part of her mind knew it was unreasonable to think like this. She was blaming Owen as much as herself, and that was not in any way reasonable. But she couldn't seem to help herself.

"Shouldn't . . . ?" he began, then with an impatient gesture Owen moved her hands aside and fastened the ribbons himself. He could feel her desperation even if he didn't as yet understand it. Without another word he helped her into her gown.

Pen smoothed her skirts over her farthingale, and bent to pick up her hood. She couldn't see the pins anywhere, they must have rolled into the dark shadows of the chamber beyond the candlelight. She stood holding the silk hood, wondering in distant perplexity how she was to put it on without pins. As if it mattered.

"You have to do what you promised," she stated, staring over his shoulder towards the door leading to the great hall. "That's why we came in here."

But she knew that it wasn't and she wasn't surprised when Owen said incredulously, "What *nonsense* is that, Pen?"

"It's not nonsense. We came in here to talk about when you would fulfill your side of our bargain." Still she couldn't bring herself to meet his gaze.

"We came in here to do exactly what we did," Owen stated, articulating each word with careful deliberation. "To make the passionate love that we did." He turned his palms up in a gesture of puzzlement, and anger now mingled with the confusion in his dark gaze. "It was agreed between us before we set foot in this chamber."

He was right. So right. That moment in the great hall when their eyes had spoken together. When they had acknowledged the power of lust and accepted its inevitable conclusion. She remembered it in every devastating detail. But now she pushed the knowledge from her. It merely twisted the knife of her remorse and self-contempt.

"I want you to tell me when you will do what you promised," she insisted, ignoring his statement.

"God's blood, Pen! There's a time and a place for your obsession, but this is neither. Not after what we have just shared." He regretted the harshness even as he spoke, but it was too late.

She paled. He was betraying her. Dismissing her overpowering need just like everyone else had done. "The only thing that matters to me is finding out what happened to my child. We had a bargain. I would like to know when you will live up to your end of it."

He pinched the bridge of his nose until the skin whitened as if only thus could he contain his anger at himself and his frustration with her.

"When do you want me to go?"

The simple question was all Pen needed. She felt relief, but none of the jubilation or satisfaction she would have expected.

She frowned, considering the question. It was in the early hours of the morning now, he would need some sleep. "Later today. It's thirty miles to High Wycombe but hard riding will take you most of the way in an afternoon. You can go on to the village the next morning and make inquiries. I will send you the page I copied from the ledger. Will you be lodging with Mistress Rider?"

"Most probably."

Pen turned to the door. Then she paused. "No, I'll bring it to you right now."

He shrugged. "By all means. I'll await you here."

Pen heard the frustration in his voice just as she heard the resignation, but she ignored both.

She slipped through the door and out from behind the arras. She threaded her way through the shadowy couples in the great hall and hurried up the stairs to her chamber. She thought only of her goal. She wouldn't think about what had happened between them, and soon it would be as if it had never happened.

She unlocked the chest and took out the list of names and figures. It held the key, she knew it did. And Owen d'Arcy was going to find it for her.

Then she paused. How could she be certain he would exert his best efforts in her cause? Why should he? It was not his child. It was not his quest. And he too had called it an obsession.

How could she trust him now?

Pen sat down slowly on the bed. She looked at the parchment in her hands. How could she trust anyone to act for her? She had lived for so long alone with her desperation, with her secret conviction that informed every minute of her days, and every dream of her nights. She could not sit by while someone else, even someone as skilled at spying and extracting information as Owen d'Arcy, unraveled *her* mystery.

She would have to go with him. It was a very simple answer to the problem, one she should have thought of long ago. Its execution, however, was not so simple. How was she to get away? How was she to escape the confines of the palace and the close-knit world of Mary's household? How was she to keep such a journey from her family? They would never countenance it. No one would.

Pen tucked the folded sheet into her bodice and rose to her feet. Now was not the moment to discuss her new intention with Owen. He was angry and frustrated enough as it was. She needed to work out how to execute the plan first. He would be much easier to manage if presented with a *fait accompli.*

She returned to the hall and stood for a moment against the wall, looking for an opportunity to approach the arras amid the frenetic whirl of shadows around the darkened chamber.

"Pen?"

Her heart sank and she turned reluctantly to the shadow beside her.

Robin held his flowing lion's mane in his hand; his curly hair was sorely in need of a comb. He stood awkwardly, as if the last place he wanted to be was here beside her.

"Where did you go, Pen?"

"Just now? Upstairs. I needed something from my chamber." She tried to smile, to hide her impatience. If she waited too long, Owen might leave.

"No, before. You disappeared from the hall."

She laughed and it sounded unconvincing to her own ears. " 'Tis Twelfth Night, Robin. Everyone is playing games. Don't question mine." She kissed his cheek and melted into the crowd.

Robin slammed his mask against the paneled wall behind him in frustration, then turned on his heel, leaving the Lord of Misrule's kingdom to its revelry.

Pen slipped behind the arras and back into the small chamber. Owen was perched on the edge of the table, idly swinging one leg, his expression a mixture of irritation and boredom at the delay. He was anxious now to be gone from here, to get this business over with.

"Here." Pen took the parchment from her bodice and held it out to him.

It was warm and faintly perfumed from her skin. Owen felt his frustration fade. "Sweetheart —"

"No!" she interrupted, holding out her hand as if to ward him off. "It can't happen again, Owen. We are partners, we have a bargain, that's all that we have. Do what you promised to do." And she was gone.

He pocketed the parchment.

A glimmer of gold caught his eye in the empty hearth and he bent to pick up the pins from Pen's hood. He held them in his palm, staring down at them.

Ten

●

Pen slept fitfully. In her dreams she heard the attenuated cry of an infant, saw the hard brown eyes of her mother-in-law, heard her voice with a strange complacent edge to it.

The child is dead.

She awoke when Pippa crept into the bed beside her close to dawn.

"Are you asleep, Pen?"

Pen didn't answer. She couldn't face an intimate conversation with her sister just now. She lay breathing deeply and steadily until Pippa's own rhythmic breathing indicated that she had fallen asleep.

Pen rose soundlessly, trying not to disturb the covers too much, and slipped on her furred night robe. The room was frigid, the fire a mere ashy glow, but a maid would be in before cockcrow to riddle the ashes and rekindle the logs before the ladies were ready to get up and dress.

She left Pippa asleep behind the tightly drawn bedcurtains and let herself out of the chamber. The princess's suite of rooms opened off the corridor at the far end. A sleepy page with two lidded buckets of night soil came towards her, his head down, his slippered feet scuffing the waxed floorboards. He stepped aside, pressing himself against the wall in the narrow passage as she passed.

The princess was abed when Pen entered her apartments. She lay propped up against a mountain of pillows, a prayerbook in her hands. When she saw Pen she dismissed the maid who was tidying the chamber and laid down her book.

Pen approached the bed. "I give you good day, madam." She regarded Mary with concern. She looked genuinely ill. "How are you feeling?"

"Weak," Mary said. "The physician did his work all too well. Did you talk to Northumberland last even?"

"Aye, madam. He was not best pleased, but the word has gone out that you're gravely ill."

"Good . . . good." Mary closed her eyes for a minute. "I will stay in seclusion for a week and send each day to my brother for permission to visit him while I still have some strength. If I can but talk to him directly, I am certain he will give me leave to return to Essex."

Pen had spent much of the night working on the best way to present the request she was about to make. She knew how the princess's mind worked. If Pen was at all apologetic or tentative, Mary would attach little importance to her petition and reject it, so she spoke now with calm assurance.

"Madam, since you are to stay secluded for a week, you will have little need of my services. I would ask leave to visit my parents for a few nights."

Mary frowned. She was not unreasonable but she relied upon Pen, upon her counsel and her friendship. None of her other ladies comforted her in the same way. And none of her other ladies was aware of the present deception.

"My little sister Anna has been ill," Pen said into the silence. Pippa had said that Anna was now fit as a flea, but Mary didn't know that. She knew only that the girl had been sufficiently unwell not to attend the Twelfth Night festivities.

Still Mary hesitated, and Pen waited quietly. If she didn't capitulate to Mary's disapproving silence, the princess would eventually agree.

Mary sighed heavily. "I can ill spare you, Pen, but I know that you've been separated from your family since we came to Greenwich."

"I would dearly love to spend some time with them before we return to Essex, madam."

"Oh, very well." The princess turned her head aside on the pillows in an almost petulant gesture. "I daresay my other ladies will attend me well enough. But no more than four days."

"My thanks, madam." Pen curtsied. "Will you break your fast now?"

"I cannot be seen to eat heartily when I am upon my sickbed," Mary snapped.

"A little porridge perhaps?" Pen suggested. She was used to the princess's moods. Mary did not like to be inconvenienced.

"Very well."

Pen rang the handbell for the maid who awaited outside, and gave the order, then she returned to the princess's bedside and brushed Mary's hair in soothing strokes, chatting cheerfully until the woman's temper had mended.

"I shall miss you, Pen," Mary said as her breakfast arrived and Pen laid down the brush. "You're the only person I can really talk to."

"I'll be gone but four days, madam," Pen said firmly, recognizing a two-pronged appeal to her conceit and her sympathy. She rose to her feet and drew her night robe around her. "With your permission, I'll go and dress now."

"You needn't return before you leave," Mary stated, digging a spoon into the porcelain bowl of porridge. "I'm sure you're anxious to be on your way." She frowned at the spoonful of porridge. "Are you sure they put honey in this?"

"I'm certain they have, madam. They know your tastes." Pen curtsied and left, heaving a sigh of relief when the door was safely closed behind her.

She hurried back to her bedchamber. It was now full daylight, and a thin ray of chilly sun fell across the floor from the large easterly facing window beyond the bed. Pippa was sitting beside the newly kindled fire eating bread and bacon with gusto.

"There you are. Were you with the princess?"

"Yes, she's no better," Pen said, taking a crispy piece of bacon from the platter and popping it in her mouth. "She'll keep to her bed for several days. What time are Mama and Lord Hugh due to arrive this morning?"

"Around nine o'clock, I would say." Pippa proffered the ale jug.

Pen drank, and broke a crust off the loaf of bread that was still warm from the oven, its rich fragrance mingling with the scent of burning logs and pinecones in the hearth.

She regarded her sister covertly. Despite a certain air of dishevelment, Pippa looked as fresh and rested as if she'd slept the night away instead of falling into bed at dawn.

Pippa selected another piece of bacon, holding it between finger and thumb. "What happened to you last even?" she asked, a mischievous glint in her narrowed eyes. "I lost sight of you."

"You would have done. They snuffed the candles," Pen pointed out.

"Oh, but I *did* see you go off with the chevalier behind that arras."

"How could you have done?" Pen demanded. "When it was dark?"

"I was a cat, remember? Cats can see in the dark." Pippa chuckled and ate the bacon. "I lost sight of you *after* you disappeared behind the arras."

Pen merely shrugged and allowed a little conspiratorial smile to touch her mouth. It helped her scheme that Pippa had seen them leave the great hall. It would make her motive seem more believable.

"So, did you have an amusing adventure? Did you have a night of unbridled passion, Pen?" Pippa's eyes gleamed.

"Mind your own business," Pen retorted, but still with the smile.

"You are my business," Pippa responded. "When I see you with the chevalier I can't work out whether you take pleasure in his company or not."

"Of course I do!" Pen exclaimed. "I'd hardly spend so much time in his company if I didn't enjoy it."

"If that's so, I'm glad! It's time you came out of the doldrums at last. We were all so worried about you." Pippa paused, then said hesitantly, "You were so unhappy and we were so worried when you wouldn't think about anything but the baby. . . ." Her voice trailed off as she saw Pen's face close, her mouth set.

Resolutely she continued on a slightly different tack, her tone once more as bright as before. "So, is he married?"

"He says not." Pen sat down at the dresser and picked up her hairbrush.

Pippa frowned. "Don't you believe him then?"

"Of course I do. Why would I not?"

"I don't know. You just sounded a little uncertain."

Pen said nothing as she pulled the brush through her sleep-tossed hair. She was remembering the strange shadows that had gathered in Owen's eyes when she'd asked him if he was married. All the light had left his countenance.

She turned on the dresser stool. "I'm not uncertain at all, not about anything, Pippa. And I need your help."

Pippa's eyes widened. She leaned forward eagerly. "How?"

"I need you to lie for me," Pen said simply. "I want to go away for a few days. I have the princess's leave to spend four days with my family, but that's not where I'm going. I need you to tell Mama that I'm closeted with the princess during her illness and cannot see anyone. Mary will not let me out of her sight until she feels better. That's happened before. It will not be such a great untruth."

"It *will*," Pippa said fervently. "It's a terrible, big lie."

Pen sighed. "I know. But will you do it?"

"Yes, of course I will. But where are you going?" Now there was neither mischief nor laughter in the younger woman's penetrating gaze.

Pen turned back to the dresser mirror. The king's palace at Greenwich was amply supplied with the precious objects, all of Italianate design. A rare luxury even for Pen, who had grown up in its lap.

She began to braid her hair, concentrating on the movement of her fingers making order out of the thick brown mass. "If I tell you that it concerns the chevalier, will you leave it at that?"

Pippa whistled soundlessly. She came to stand behind her sister. "You are going to have a tryst with Owen d'Arcy? A four-day tryst!"

Pen met her astounded gaze in the mirror. "Yes."

"Well, you are a dark horse," Pippa said after a minute. "I just hope to God no one finds out."

"There's no reason why they should so long as Mama and Lord Hugh don't have any conversation with the princess. At least until I get back. If they find out then, I'll deal with it." She sounded calm and definite.

Pippa stared at her. This was so unlike Pen. Not the calm composure, that was very much her sister, but for Pen even to think of such a deception, let alone put it into practice! That was just totally out of character. Pippa didn't think she would dare to do it herself, and she was much more adventurous than her sister.

"This is just *passion*?" she asked after a minute's incredulous silence.

"And why not?" Pen was beginning to enjoy her sister's reaction. It was so unusual for anyone to be able to throw Pippa off balance. "You're no stranger to passion yourself, are you?"

Pippa frowned. "I flirt, I play games, but *passion!* No." She shook her head firmly. "I can honestly say that's something I have never felt."

Pen raised an eyebrow. "No sex?"

Pippa grinned suddenly. "Not of the passionate kind, Pen. Only the playful. Believe it or not, I'm very careful."

Pen nodded. It didn't surprise her. Pippa was

no fool, despite her apparent volatility.

There was a tap at the door and they both turned, annoyed at the interruption. Their little sister stuck her head around the door. "Oh, good, you're both awake." She came in without waiting for an invitation.

"We weren't expecting you so soon," Pen said, rising from her stool to kiss Anna, concealing her dismay. She had hoped to be well away by the time the Kendal party arrived so that Pippa's fiction would be all the more believable.

"Oh, we left almost at daybreak," Anna said, hugging Pen and turning to do the same to Pippa. Pippa gave Pen a comprehending nod over the girl's dark head. They would need to modify their plan.

"I had such a *dull* Twelfth Night!" Anna complained, darting around the bedchamber, alighting on her sisters' scattered possessions, examining them and moving on like a honeybee in a flower bed. "I was perfectly well by the afternoon. We could have come easily enough."

She pouted slightly. "My father really doesn't want me to appear at court at all. He uses any excuse to keep me at home."

"He doesn't want you to grow up too fast," Pen said, exchanging a look with Pippa. Their stepfather adored his daughter and could barely tolerate her spending a night under any roof but his own. His wife, his son, and his stepdaughters derived considerable amusement from this single-minded care and devotion. Its recipient, however, who as a child had basked in it, was now beginning to find it somewhat irksome.

"It's not just," Anna complained. "Jane Grey is only fifteen, and she's been going to revels and dances and feasts for years."

"Jane Grey is the king's cousin," Pippa stated. "She's expected to be on display. You don't have to be."

"That's very true, Anna," Pen agreed. "You can be thankful that you're not Jane. Her life's a living hell with that dreadful mother of hers, who's always pinching at her and criticizing her in front of everybody. You know she's going to be forced to marry whoever suits the duchess and the king's council. At least no one will coerce you in that way."

"No, but I'll have to marry someone, and how can I meet someone if my father will never let me out of his sight?" Anna declared, pirouetting in front of a long mirror. "Do you like my gown? Isn't it pretty?"

"Very," her sisters agreed.

Anna darted to the armoire. "May I help you dress? What will you wear, Pen?"

Pippa joined her at the armoire. "I think Pen should wear this." She took out a gown of flaming orange velvet.

When she saw Pen's frown she forestalled the coming objection. "I know you don't like bright colors as a rule but I'm sure that today you would wish to look your best." She raised a meaningful eyebrow.

Pen shot her a warning glance, recognizing that her sister was now in a teasing mood. "Anna, could you pass me my shift?"

Anna passed her a white linen shift delicately embroidered at the neck and wrists.

Pippa said, "Anna, love, would you go and take our respects to Mama and Lord Hugh and say that we will join them in half an hour?"

"Oh, they know that," Anna said cheerfully.

"They may do, but we would not be lacking in courtesy," Pen said. "We cannot just ignore their arrival and wander in when we're ready. You know that's discourteous."

"Oh, very well," Anna said and left.

"Now, dress quickly," Pippa said. "As soon as you're gone I'll go to them and say that after Anna left you were summoned urgently to the princess. I'll pretend that then you sent a message saying that you're unable to leave her bedside . . . the physician is gravely concerned. They won't question it."

"No," Pen agreed. "And then they'll return to Holborn. If they can't see the princess and they can't see me, there'll be no reason for them to stay."

"And if the Duchess of Suffolk should appear, they'll flee all the quicker," Pippa said with a chuckle. "Mama can't abide to be in the same room with the woman. Are you riding to this tryst?"

"Yes," Pen said. She had already decided that

in broad daylight she could safely ride alone from Greenwich Palace into the city. It would take her little more than an hour. Once there, she was fairly certain she could find her way back to Mistress Rider's tavern.

Owen would surely make a leisurely start. He'd not exactly been champing at the bit to go on this errand. But if he'd already left, then she would follow him out of the city on the High Wycombe road. She would catch up to him somewhere.

"You'll need these if you're riding." Pippa handed her stiffened petticoats to substitute for her less pliable farthingale, which was impossible to wear on horseback.

"What else do you need to take?"

"Just money," Pen said. "There's a purse in the chest." She stepped into the underskirt and pushed her arms into the orange gown her sister held for her. There was no time to consider what possessions she needed to take with her on such an errand. She would have to contrive as she went along.

"I think you should take your dagger," Pippa said seriously. "You're riding alone. You can't be too careful. Particularly after the last time."

"A dagger wouldn't have helped me with that crowd of thieves," Pen said in perfect truth. But Pippa was right. The little silver dagger that she could carry in her sleeve would give her some sense of protection.

Her heart was beating too fast. She pulled in

her stomach as her sister tightened the laces of her stomacher.

"Suddenly I feel sick," she said.

"You're not made for adventure," Pippa observed, adding, "But then I feel sick too, so probably I'm not made for it either. At least, not this kind. Not this *real* kind . . . Come, you must hurry, in case Anna comes back. Where are your boots?"

She rummaged in the armoire while Pen fastened her braided hair into a netted snood that would secure it beneath the hood of her cloak when she was riding.

Pen took her boots from Pippa and pulled them on, smoothing her skirts down over them. Her appearance was irrelevant to the business in hand and yet she couldn't prevent herself from glancing in the long mirror.

The orange velvet gown opened over an underskirt of black damask embroidered with tiny green flowers. The sleeves were full to the elbows and tight to her forearms and wrists. A small lace ruff rose at the back. The deeply scooped neckline cried out for a breast jewel, but she told herself again that her appearance was irrelevant and such adornment was absurd in the circumstances.

But even without jewelry it was a very elegant outfit. The color did seem to impart a glow to her skin and to deepen the mélange of colors in her eyes. Although perhaps that was just because she felt in the grip of a raging fever.

"Here's your dagger." Pippa handed her the small knife. It was secured to a thin leather strap that Pen fastened around her wrist. "And here's the purse."

Pen threaded the leather pouch onto the gold chain she wore at her waist. It was reassuringly heavy. Money was a form of protection too.

"Cloak and gloves." Pippa held them out for her. She was being calm and orderly, not showing any of her anxiety.

Pen wrapped herself in the thick black velvet, fur-lined cloak, drawing the wide hood over her head. She pulled on her gloves. She swallowed a rather large lump in her throat. "Are you sure you don't mind, Pippa?"

"Oh, for pity's sake, Pen. Go!" Pippa cried, pushing her towards the door. "We'll both get cold feet if you hesitate."

Pen knew that she would not get cold feet. However nervous she felt, even guilty at compromising her sister in this way, she was resolute. Whatever she had to do she would do. Whatever she learned on this journey, it would bring her peace of some kind.

An ending if it had to be, but maybe a beginning. Just maybe a beginning.

Pippa opened the door and peered out. "Quickly," she said. "There's no one around. Don't use the main staircase."

"I wasn't going to," Pen said. "I'll return in four days." She squeezed Pippa's hand and hurried away, her black cloak tight around her.

Pippa waited until Pen had disappeared down the narrow staircase that led to the back regions of the palace, then she returned to the chamber to throw on her own clothes. She twisted her hair into a knot and concealed its still somewhat untidy appearance beneath a silk hood.

Her busy fingers stilled in the process of inserting the pins. She frowned into the mirror, no longer seeing her own reflection.

What was Pen up to?

All that talk of passionate trysts. Pippa didn't believe for one minute that that was the whole truth.

Pippa could think of only one thing that would drive her practical, levelheaded sister to practice any kind of deception, particularly one so dangerously impulsive.

The baby.

And if that was it, was Pippa helping her or making things worse? If Pen was returning to the dreadful state she had been in after she lost the child, her sister was doing her no favors by aiding and abetting her.

Pippa's heart quailed. Lying to her mother was hard enough under any circumstances, but if she was doing Pen harm it would be unforgivable.

But she had promised. And she would not let Pen down, whatever the consequences.

Eleven

●

On this bright sunny morning the roadway from Greenwich to London was crowded. Carters' wagons jostled with foot traffic; women balancing flat baskets on their heads, or suspended from heavy yolks across their shoulders; men pushing hand trolleys filled with sea coal unloaded from the barges at the docks.

One or two people glanced at the cloaked and hooded woman on her dappled gelding, but for the most part Pen drew little attention. Her horse was obviously of good blood and her cloak was thick and rich, but her face was barely visible beneath the hood. She kept her eyes on the road, looking neither to right nor to left.

She rode as fast as she dared without drawing attention to herself. William, despite being gelded, had a rather skittish temperament, but he was the largest of the three horses she owned and had the most stamina. He had seemed the obvious choice for a journey that would require hard riding, and she had perfect confidence in her ability to hold him.

It was a confidence that wavered slightly when he reared and sidled when they came upon a small boy leading a ragged bear on a chain. A pack of dogs ran at the bear, barking and yelping. William snorted and threw up his head, pulling hard against the bit.

The small boy threw stones at the dogs and a laughing crowd gathered, jeering good-naturedly at the boy's desperate attempts to drive off the pack. At last several men took pity on the lad and helped him drive off the snarling animals. While bearbaiting was an amusing and lucrative entertainment, everyone knew it should take place in a bear pit and not by the side of the road with a nonpaying audience.

Pen soothed her horse and gave him his head until they'd left the melee behind. Action always calmed him. The road followed the curves of the river flowing to her left. She could see through the winter-bare trees along the bank to the fields and hamlets spread out on the far bank. Soon she could hear the sound of London's many church bells that seemed to ring incessantly, and she could make out the jumble of roofs on the outskirts of the city.

Mistress Rider's tavern was close to Westminster, where the Bryanstons had their London mansion. A Horseferry crossed the river at a relatively narrow point, just beyond Lambeth Palace on the south bank, ferrying its passengers to Westminster on the opposite side. The only other way of crossing was much farther up at London Bridge, and, while the bridge was a safer and more comfortable crossing, Pen didn't want to waste time going so far out of her way.

She turned her horse towards the river at the palace to wait on the bank with an assorted group of merchants and laborers for the sturdy flat ferry to return from the other side.

The ferry docked. The passengers loaded amid profanities and shouted instructions from the ferrymen. William shied and bumped another horse as she tried to ride him onto the floating, swaying platform. Both animals reared their heads, nostrils flared.

"Lead 'im on!" a man yelled at her as he took her penny fare. " 'E'll 'ave us all in the water!"

Pen dismounted, flushed with embarrassment at William's bad manners and her conspicuous incompetence. The only other time she had done this, there had been a groom to take charge of her horse. She led the animal onto the ferry, holding the reins tight just above the bit, talking softly to him as he shifted and snorted, looking distrustfully around at his fellow horse passengers, who now all seemed perfectly at home.

"First time fer 'im is it then?" a stout foot passenger in a homespun jerkin inquired cordially. "Looks a bit 'igh strung to me. Good breedin' though." He stroked the gelding's withers with a knowledgeable air. "Nice bit o' leather that, too."

Pen's saddle was of beautifully tooled leather; her silver stirrups glittered in the sunlight. She felt a tremor of nerves. Her horse, as if sensing it, stamped. The ferry creaked and swung, and one of the oarsmen bellowed an obscenity.

The man probably meant her no harm but she felt his curious eyes on her even as she averted her gaze, pulling the hood closer over her head.

"So, where you goin' then, mistress?"

Pen ignored the question.

"Not used t' being out on yer own, I shouldn't wonder," he observed, laying a hand on the saddle. "No groom wi' you?"

Pen kept her silence, staring rigidly down at the muddy water slipping beneath them. The leather purse beneath her cloak seemed suddenly very heavy and conspicuous even though it was well concealed. Had he seen it when she'd paid her fare?

The man stopped talking, but he kept his hand on the saddle and whistled tunelessly through a wide gap between the blackened stumps of his front teeth. The ferry drew closer to the opposite bank.

The other horses, who seemed to know the routine, began to move forwards. William shivered uncertainly at the sound of shifting hooves around him. Pen felt very vulnerable as she stood in the midst of all this powerful, palpitating horseflesh with the man beside her still whistling, his eyes still on her. She had an overpowering sense of menace. An absolute premonition of danger.

The ferry touched the wooden dock and the men on the bank grabbed the ropes to make it fast. Pen took a tighter hold of the gelding's reins. Desperate though she was to get off, she would have to wait to lead him until the others had disembarked, otherwise she risked being trampled underfoot. Their fellow passengers clattered off the ferry and onto the dock, the man in the homespun jerkin stayed back, his hand still resting on Pen's expensive saddle.

"Come, William." She tugged on the reins, fear now hard in her throat. She was sure the man was going to try to stop her and she couldn't remount without a block. The gelding surged forward, so anxious to reach dry land that Pen almost lost her balance, nearly slipping beneath his hooves.

"Steady on there," the man said, putting a rough hand over hers on the bridle. He bent his head towards her and she tried to turn her head away from the reek of raw onions and stale beer on his breath. "Let me 'elp you 'ere, mistress, since y'are all alone like."

She jabbed her elbow into his belly; then, in the moment it took him to recover, she slid the dagger from its strap and drove it into his hand as he reached again for the bridle.

The man fell back with a vile curse, clutching his hand. Blood poured from the wound. He yelled at her as she ran with William, leading him onto the dock. Her skirts caught at her ankles, her cloak swirled around her, impeding her movement. Faces stared at her, men began to move towards her.

She still held the knife dripping blood in one hand as she dragged William to an upturned log.

She clasped the hilt in her teeth and scrambled with more speed than elegance onto his back, crooking her knee over the rest on the sidesaddle. She kicked the gelding hard in the flanks.

Surprised, William took off with a jump start along the narrow lane that led up from the river. Behind her Pen heard curses and pounding feet but William rapidly outdistanced the pursuit.

Her destination lay close to the Horseferry water steps just a short way from the ferry dock, but now she couldn't go there immediately as she'd intended. She would have to wait for the disturbance to die down.

Only when she had reached the maze of lanes and alleys away from the river did she take the knife from her teeth, but she didn't return it to its sheath. She felt safer with it ready to hand.

She was on familiar ground now, the area around the Bryanston mansion. Even in bright daylight, when the streets were busy with ordinary traffic, she couldn't repress a shudder at the memory of the assault on that night before Christmas. It was a dangerous world for an unescorted woman, she reflected acidly. Not that that would come as any surprise to a sensible person. But then sensible people didn't put themselves into positions where they'd have to go around stabbing folk with daggers.

She passed the roadside gates to the Bryanston mansion and instinctively drew her hood even closer about her head. She glanced up at the turrets and saw that the Bryanston pennants were flying in the swift breeze. It was confirmation of what she had known, that the family were still in residence in London. But it was reassuring to have such confirmation. She would not have been able to ask her questions freely if they had removed to their country estate. Here they were some thirty miles away from High Wycombe, and she could probe for gossip among the Bryanston tenants without fear of intervention.

After a few streets, she turned back towards the river, coming at the Horseferry steps from the opposite direction. She drew rein at the corner of the lane and peered out from the gable overhang to look downriver. The river traffic flowed by, children scrambled in the mud looking for eels or cockles and whelks. The ferry itself was now in midstream, returning to Lambeth with a new cargo. All was quiet at the ferry dock.

Pen emerged from the lane. The tavern was exactly as she remembered it, set back from the steps in its own garden. Smoke curled from the thatched roof and the windows were shuttered against the cold morning.

She dismounted at the garden gate and led William up to the front door. The brass knocker was shiny against the heavy oak door. Pen knocked and waited. She found she was remarkably calm now that she'd reached her destination. She was in control once again, perfectly sure of what she had to do and how she would do it.

A small girl opened the door and gazed up at her, one finger in her mouth.

"Is Mistress Rider in?"

For answer, the child called, "Mam!" over her shoulder, then returned her wide-eyed gaze to the visitor.

Mistress Rider came to the door. "Get back to your pots, Ellie," she instructed, turning the child away from the door. She examined Pen. " 'Tis the young lady who came with the chevalier," she said. "You was hurt."

"Yes, that's right," Pen said. "Is the chevalier here, mistress?"

"He's still abed," the landlady said. "Came back after dawn, went straight to 'is bed. Young Cedric too."

So he hadn't rushed off at the crack of dawn to keep his promise. Well, she hadn't expected it. Why else was she here?

Pen stepped around Mistress Rider and into the hall. "I'll go up then," she said calmly. "Would you ask Cedric to take care of my horse, please? Oh, and the chevalier will be needing to break his fast, and he'll need hot water for washing. He's going on a journey for a few days."

Mistress Rider's mouth fell open. Her gaze was riveted to the dagger Pen still carried in her hand. "He didn't say nothing to me, madam."

"No, I daresay he was very tired when he got in this morning. But you'll find that that's exactly what he's going to be doing. So if you could send up breakfast . . . whatever he likes. I'm sure

220

you know." With a sweet smile, Pen swept up the stairs.

She remembered exactly where the chevalier's chamber was to be found. She knocked briskly on the door before raising the latch. The door swung open; she stepped inside.

"Cedric . . . God's bones, lad, I didn't call for you!" an irascible voice declared from behind the bedcurtains.

Pen opened the curtains. "Good morrow, Owen."

Owen sat up, instantly awake, instantly in full possession of his senses. *"Pen!* What in the devil's name is this?" He caught sight of the dagger. His eyes narrowed, his dark gaze sharpening abruptly. "What are you doing with that knife?"

"Oh, this." Pen looked down at the knife. She'd been holding it for so long it had almost become an extension of her hand. "There was a man on the Horseferry. I think he had evil designs and I wasn't prepared to give him the benefit of the doubt." She laid the dagger on the table beside the bed.

Owen pushed aside the coverlet as he swung his feet to the floor. He was naked. Powerfully and beautifully so. Last night in the round chamber behind the arras she had not seen him naked. Pen turned her eyes away. A loose gown hung on a hook by the door and she took it down, holding it out to him wordlessly.

Owen waited a fraction longer than necessary

before taking it from her. He could think only that the night had caused her to regret her abrupt withdrawal after their lovemaking. She had come to him now in this startling fashion to make matters right between them again. His blood stirred as he looked at her, remembering now with vivid clarity the joyousness of her responses to him, the wondrous glow in the forest pools of her eyes as she moved beneath him.

He smiled slowly as he shrugged into his gown. "This is an unexpected surprise, sweetheart, but an utterly delightful one."

"It's not what you think." Pen stepped swiftly away from him as he reached for her. She went to the fire, vigorously poking at it before throwing on fresh kindling.

Owen was aware of a wash of disappointment, renewed anger and frustration hot on its heels. It appeared that the distance was as frigid a wasteland this morning as it had been last night. So what the hell was she doing here?

His eye fell again on the little silver dagger. He saw with a mixture of horror and bemusement that rusty bloodstains adorned the blade. "You *used* this?" he demanded, picking it up from the table. The blood was congealed but still sticky.

"There's little point carrying a knife if one's not prepared to use it," Pen returned. "I'm sure you'd agree."

Cool as a cucumber! Well, two could play at that game.

"Certainly," he replied dryly, adding in a tone

222

of tutor to erring pupil, "But you should always clean your weapons after use. The blade will tarnish if you don't. You should know that if you intend to make a habit of stabbing people."

He took a cloth from the washstand and washed the blood from the blade before running a finger along its edge. He raised an eyebrow. "It's keen enough, at least." He handed it back to her. "Here. Where do you carry it?"

"In my sleeve." Pen slipped the weapon back into its strap. "And I don't intend to make a habit of using it. To be honest, I don't usually carry it, but my mother taught us that we should be able to defend ourselves. Pippa made sure I brought it, and I'm glad she did."

For a moment there she'd sounded like her usual self. She seemed to be switching both mood and manner on him at every turn, and he still didn't know what the devil lay behind this visit.

He asked with a slightly ironic edge to his voice, "Pray enlighten me, Pen. Just why did you put yourself at the mercy of unsavory characters on the Horseferry in order to wake me from my slumbers?"

Pen did not answer directly. "I know it must have been late when you reached your bed, but I had thought you would at least be ready to leave by *now*," she said.

"Ah." Comprehension glimmered and he didn't like what he understood. "You have come to see me on my way to High Wycombe?"

"Not exactly," Pen said judiciously. "I've come to accompany you on your way."

Owen absorbed this in silence. Pen intrigued him, aroused him, amused him, confused him. But before last night she had never angered him. Now he looked at her calm, determined countenance and understood that she was permitting him no leeway in this matter. She would compel him to do *what* she wanted, *when* she wanted.

He had struck a bargain. But he hadn't expected to be driven like an ox at the plow. "Just let me get this straight," he said slowly. "Am I right in assuming that you don't trust me to fulfill this commitment I've made to you?"

Pen was not deceived by his calm tone. She realized that she had insulted him and made haste to explain herself. "It's not that, Owen, indeed it isn't. But I find that I need to be there," she said reasonably. "This is *my* quest. You see it only as part of a contract. I need your help, but I've realized that I need to play my part."

"And just how are you going to leave the princess for such a time?" But even as he asked the scornful question he realized that Pen, of course, had already managed the details.

"I've taken care of it," she replied, shrugging.

A knock on the door interrupted them. He spun around, opening it with less than his usual controlled grace.

Cedric stood there with a jug of hot water sitting in a basin. "I took my lady's horse to the stable," he said. "Mistress Rider sent me up with hot water. She said we're going on a journey, sir." His eyes slid around Owen to where Pen stood before the fire.

"Leave the water, Cedric, and bring the horses around," Owen instructed.

"My lady's too, sir?"

"Yes, Lady Bryanston's too," Owen stated. "Lady Bryanston is returning to Greenwich Palace. John Rider will escort her. Tell him to saddle up as well."

"Aye, sir." Cedric deposited the jug and basin and left, casting an interested glance at Pen. The chevalier's clipped orders told the page that his master was dangerously close to anger and Cedric could only assume that the lady was its cause.

"No," Pen said as the door closed on the page. "I am coming with you, Owen."

"Don't be absurd." He poured hot water into the basin. "There's no need. I can do your errand for you perfectly well. You will return to Greenwich. Mistress Rider's son will provide you with more than adequate protection in case of further menace on the Horseferry."

"No," she said again with the same finality. "No one can do this for me. I need your escort . . . and your . . ." She hesitated, choosing her words carefully. "Your professional expertise," she said. "I have helped you, now you will help me."

Owen dipped a towel in hot water and held it to his face. He was too angry at her uncompromising tone to respond immediately, concentrating instead on the methodical routine of his ablutions. He draped the towel around his neck and began to sharpen a flat blade on a leather strop.

To her dismay Pen realized that she was disturbed by the intimacy of his actions, an intimacy that deepened as he began to shave. Philip had worn a beard, a neat triangular beard that suited his thin face. She held on to the image of Philip's face; she conjured memories of the times she had watched him shave, and slowly her composure returned. She was doing this for him. For *their* child.

She removed her cloak and took a stool by the fire. It was the one she had sat on while Owen had dressed her wound.

The recognition came and went. She waited quietly. He was angry but that didn't matter. Indeed it helped to increase the distance between them that she so desperately needed if she was to stay single-minded, focused only on her quest. The answers were so close now. Nothing else mattered.

Owen cast aside the loose gown and reached for his hose. Pen stared into the fire, forcing herself to think of anything but Owen d'Arcy and his nakedness.

Owen glanced over at her and his anger faded. He could read her reactions as clearly as if she had written them out. Every muscle of her rigid back told him how hard she was fighting to keep herself from responding to him. She had clearly not thought through this situation. It had not occurred to her that there would be anything disturbing about mounting guard in a man's bedchamber while he performed such personal tasks.

His lips twitched in a slight albeit reluctant smile. Single-minded she might be, but she hadn't anticipated every possible problem.

He buttoned his shirt, considering. What harm would it do for her to accompany him, at least on the first leg of the journey? Obviously she couldn't be around while he was asking questions around the Bryanston estate. She would be recognized, and then they'd never get any honest answers. But up until then, they could travel together.

After several days of keeping close, indeed intimate, company he could surely wear down this resistance. Seduce Pen Bryanston anew.

And this time Owen d'Arcy would be conducting a business that had nothing to do with French diplomacy.

"Well, I suppose if you must you must," he said carelessly, sitting down to pull on his boots.

Pen turned abruptly, surprised at such sudden capitulation. "What changed your mind?" She stared at him suspiciously.

Owen shook his head. "There's no pleasing you, it seems. You insist. I agree. And now you question my motives."

"You're not insulted then?" Pen asked. "Not anymore, I mean."

He shrugged. "As you said, it's your quest. You have the right to see it through."

"Thank you," Pen said, the wind quite taken out of her sails.

Owen merely nodded and silence fell. He completed his dressing and when Mistress Rider brought him a substantial breakfast he ate in the same silence. At one point he gestured in invitation to the table, but Pen merely shook her head. She was impatient to be gone. She only had four days. One and a half days to get there, the same back. There was no time to waste on coddled eggs and sirloin.

She sat on the stool and stared into the fire, wondering just why he had capitulated without further argument. He had been so definite, and so definitely angry. What had happened to change that? A faint suspicion niggled but she couldn't think how to broach the subject before he did. She didn't want to invite a mortifying snub. And yet if she said nothing, she might be implying consent. Which she most certainly was not!

Owen finished his breakfast and gathered his possessions, packing into a leather bag a night robe, a change of linen, a razor, a pair of boots.

Pen turned from the fire, watching his preparations curiously. She found that if she concentrated on his actions she was less affected by his presence.

He took a folding leather standish from the dresser and packed it in the bag. Pen wondered why he thought he was going to be writing letters on such a journey but she didn't ask.

Cedric came back and announced that the horses were saddled and ready. "I gave my lady's horse some oats," he said. "He seems very high strung."

"He gets nervous in strange places," Pen said. She smiled at the page. "Thank you for taking care of him."

Cedric blushed. "My pleasure, my lady."

"I'll need to take one bird, Cedric," Owen stated, clasping his short cloak at his throat. "You can carry the cage. Strap my bag to my horse. We'll be down in a minute."

"Aye, sir." Cedric picked up the bag and hurried away.

Pen's curiosity got the better of her and she broke her resolute silence. "Bird?"

"A homing pigeon," he explained. "Believe it or not, I have work to do that is not directly related to your interests."

"Oh," she said. She now understood the need for the traveling writing case. "You mean reports to write, dispatches, things like that?"

"Precisely."

He had hoped to discomfit her just a little, to bring her to some recognition of how importunate she had been, but he failed.

Pen merely said, "Well, then it's good that you have everything you need. Your standish and such like. We won't be able to reach High Wycombe until tomorrow so you'll be able to work this evening. . . ."

She hesitated, praying that her color would not betray her. "You will be glad to spend the evening on your dispatches wherever we stop . . . stop for the night. I shall be no company for you, I fear."

There, she thought, that should have made all clear.

Owen drew on his gloves. His black eyes sparked with lively amusement. "Indeed?" he murmured, before turning on his heel and striding from the chamber.

Exasperated, Pen swung her own cloak around her shoulders and followed him downstairs. That exchange had not gone as she'd intended. She would be forced to tell him straight out that if he had any ideas he had best forget them.

Mistress Rider bustled from the kitchen regions when she heard them on the stairs. "So y'are going away for a few days, sir?"

"Yes. I'll be back in a few days."

"Aye, Cedric said as much. Our John's ready an' waiting to escort miss."

Pen smiled at Mistress Rider and said, "Actually, I won't be needing your son, mistress. I go with the chevalier."

The innkeeper looked confused. "But the chevalier said —"

"My error, Mistress Rider," Owen said cheerfully. "It appears I didn't quite understand the situation."

A young man stood holding William in the lane just beyond the front garden. A broad-backed placid mare cropped the dry winter grass of the verge. Cedric was strapping Owen's bag behind the saddle of a handsome black horse. A cage containing a ringed pigeon was on the ground beside the page's smaller horse.

Pen came down the path. "I thank you, Master Rider, but I shall not be needing your services after all. I explained to your mother. But you may help me to mount, if you would be so good."

"There's no need, John. I'll assist the lady," Owen said as cheerfully as before. "Come, Lady Bryanston." He put his hands at her waist and lifted her bodily into the saddle.

Pen caught her breath at this unorthodox assistance, but it was accomplished with such speed and absence of fuss that she decided to ignore it. She busied herself arranging her right leg over the knob on the sidesaddle and settling her skirts decorously around her. William tossed his head and whinnied.

Owen frowned. "I don't like the temper of this beast. Was he the best you could find?"

"He's the fastest," Pen replied. "It seemed to me that speed was the most useful quality on this journey."

"More haste, less speed," Owen observed, still frowning. "An adage often proved right."

"William will do very well," Pen said, taking a firm grip of the reins. "We shall not delay you, Chevalier. That I promise."

"Well, bear in mind that I'll hold you to that," he said aridly. "The horse is your responsibility."

He mounted his own horse and turned him in the narrow lane. Cedric fell in at his side, and Pen set William to follow.

Twelve

●

"It's such a shame we weren't able to see Pen this morning," Guinevere said as she dismounted outside the half-timbered stone house that was their residence in Holborn. It was modest when compared with the great stone mansions that had been constructed along the banks of the Thames in recent years. But Guinevere and Hugh despised the newly rich who made such show of their wealth, a wealth for the most part stolen from those who lost it with their loss of power and influence in the turbulent politics of the Tudor court.

No one, however, confused the Kendals' unostentatious London lifestyle with lack of resources. Guinevere had long shared her vast wealth with her husband, and she continued to devote her legal knowledge and her accounting and administrative skills to the management of their estates and to building that wealth.

"The princess must be gravely ill," Pippa said, dismounting beside her mother, "to keep Pen with her all the time." She brushed down her skirts, lowering her head to hide her eyes as she wished that she was a more accomplished liar. She'd never had much need for deception and was quite unpracticed.

"You're back early." Robin came down the steps to greet them. "I thought you were to spend time with Pen."

"Oh, Pen had to stay with the princess," Anna informed her brother importantly. "The princess said she couldn't possibly bear it if Pen were not at her side."

"She didn't say anything so dramatic, Anna!" Pippa declared. "Pen's message simply said that she couldn't leave. There was little point to our staying at the palace when Mama couldn't see Pen or the princess."

"And the Duchess of Suffolk was there," Anna piped up. "So — we came away quickly, before Mama was obliged to speak to her."

"Anna, you mustn't say such things," Guinevere scolded gently as she mounted the steps to the front door.

"But it's only to Robin," the girl protested.

"That may be, but it's still indiscreet," her father declared, propelling her ahead of him into the house.

Robin remained on the step, regarding Pippa with a frown. "The princess's summons must have been very sudden. Pen was enjoying herself so much at the revels, you'd never have thought she was worried about Mary's health."

"Perhaps she wasn't then," Pippa said, moving past him as she entered the house. "Mary didn't send for her until dawn."

She knew that the more she was forced to discuss the subject the more likely it was that she would trip herself up, and most particularly to Robin. "I have some letters to write." She hastened up the stairs to the privacy of her own chamber.

She was not left alone long enough to do more than greet the dainty silver cat curled up on the window seat. Pippa's Moonshine was as old as her litter mate Nutmeg but much sprier in her dotage, despite countless litters. She was a slender, dainty feline who merely closed her eyes and raised her chin for the expected caress.

Robin entered on a perfunctory knock.

"I might have been standing here in my shift!" Pippa protested, sitting beside her cat on the window seat.

"I was on your heels, you've barely had time to take off your gloves," her stepbrother replied carelessly. He had never stood on ceremony with his stepsisters any more than they had with him. He leaned against the door, running both hands through his hair so that it stood up in a halo. "Where's Pen?"

Pippa couldn't help a startled little jump. The cat expressed annoyance. Hastily Pippa resumed her attentions.

"I told you already. Pen's closeted with the princess."

"Something's not right about that," Robin stated. "Come on, Pippa. You can't fool me. What's going on?"

Pippa gently pulled the cat's ears. It would be

a huge relief to share the burden, and Robin would no more betray Pen than she would. But Robin was so hostile to Owen d'Arcy and he and Pen had been at odds over the chevalier for weeks. But if this flight *did* have anything to do with Pen's dead child perhaps Robin would have some idea how Owen d'Arcy was involved.

"You won't like it," she said after a minute.

"D'Arcy?" he said instantly.

Pippa nodded. "She said it was a tryst, four days of passion."

"Passion!" Robin exclaimed in disgust. "Pen would never say anything so . . . so unlikely!"

Pippa shrugged. "Well, she did." Then she said almost to herself, almost as if she didn't want Robin to hear, "But I don't think she meant it. I think it was an excuse."

Robin's brilliant blue gaze raked her face with an electric intensity. "For what?"

Pippa hesitated. She needed so much to confide in Robin. She needed his opinion. She said in the same low voice, "I'm afraid it might have something to do with the baby."

Robin paled beneath his weather-bronzed complexion. "Not again?"

"I don't think she's ever put it away," Pippa said. "She doesn't talk about it anymore because we all get so upset, but it's still there."

She chewed her bottom lip in the ensuing silence, which told her that Robin also believed that Pen had not let go of her obsession. Then tentatively Pippa broached the one aspect of the subject no one had ever discussed before: "Robin, do you think it's possible . . . I mean I just wonder . . ."

"Wonder what?" Robin prompted in sharp concern. It was so unlike Pippa to beat about the bush.

Pippa took a deep breath. "I just wonder whether there could be anything in it . . . in Pen's obsession, I mean."

Robin stared at her. "What are you talking about, Pippa?"

Pippa met his fixed gaze. "I think you know, Robin. Just *why* would Pen hold on to this all this time if there's absolutely nothing in it? It's not as if she's out of her mind or anything. She's the most rational, sensible person I know. Even more than you, I think," she added.

Robin heaved the sigh of a man who carried the burdens of the world upon his shoulders. "I won't say it hasn't occurred to me," he muttered. "But it doesn't make sense, Pippa. Why would anyone tell her the child was born dead when it wasn't?"

"Perhaps she's gone to discover the answer to that," Pippa returned. "But how can Owen d'Arcy help her do that?"

"More to the point, *why* would he?" Robin demanded.

"Passion?" Pippa suggested, almost immediately wishing that she could keep a firmer handle on her mischievous sense of humor. Robin did not look at all amused. But in fact, she reflected,

it had not been an altogether frivolous sugges-
tion. Something powerfully out of the ordinary
was going on between Pen and the chevalier.

Robin began to pace the chamber, from the
window to the door. He had made up his mind
to tell Pen what he knew of d'Arcy, but now
she'd gone away with the man before he could
even open his mouth. And he couldn't tell Pippa
the truth about the Frenchman before he'd discussed it with Pen. It was all so damnably com-
plicated.

"All we can do is wait for Pen to come back,"
Robin said. "What else can we do? I wouldn't
know where to start looking for her."

Pippa heard his desperation. She went over to
him, laying a hand on his shoulder. "She'll be all
right, Robin. Pen's stronger than any of us give
her credit for."

Robin wasn't counting on it. In fact, he was
going to look further into Owen d'Arcy. There
was one man who could tell him every discredit-
able secret there was to be known about the
French agent. If Pen chose to continue her
passion — God's bones but the word stuck in his
craw — then she would do so with her eyes
open.

He spoke with soft-voiced savagery. "I swear
to you, Pippa, that if d'Arcy injures her in any
way I'll run him through." He laid his hand on
his sword hilt as if in emphasis, then turned
without a word of farewell and left Pippa.

As if that would solve anything, Pippa thought.

Just like a man, in this situation that cried out for delicacy.

"I don't think he'd get very far with Owen either," she observed to the cat. The chevalier had never been anything less than charming in her presence, but Pippa, like Pen, had sensed the danger, the contained power, beneath the sophisticated, elegant facade.

Owen chose to leave London through Aldersgate. The crowds along Fleet Street were thick and Pen had to keep a tight rein on William, who was inclined to shy and prance at any strange smell or unexpected movement in the throng, of which there were many. She should have brought the docile mare, Lightfoot, Pen realized, as they were surrounded by the jostling crowd waiting to cross London Bridge with its gruesome frieze of severed heads on spikes staring out over the river.

The lanes leading out of London were crowded with local traffic, but as they left the city behind them they rode among laden pack trains and groups of well-dressed merchants heading for Oxford's gleaming spires. Farm carts loaded with turnips and cabbages rumbled towards them on their way to the London markets.

It was close to noon when they had passed through Aldersgate and Owen rode as fast as the traffic would allow. He intended to stop before dark at Gerrards Cross, twenty-two miles from

London. It was a reasonably comfortable distance for the horses and would leave only twelve miles to cover the following morning. A day at High Wycombe should give him what he needed, if indeed there *was* anything to discover.

He glanced over his shoulder to where Pen was riding on the verge, where her skittish horse had less to distract and disturb him. The animal was the very devil, he decided. Pen was so fully occupied in holding him that there was no opportunity for conversation. And without conversation one could not expect to renew intimate companionship. He would have to do something about it when they stopped for dinner.

"Are we going to stop for a bite of dinner soon, sir?" Cedric spoke Owen's thoughts with uncanny accuracy.

Owen laughed. "Are you hungry, lad?"

"Well, it's close to two o'clock and I was thinking the horses could do with watering and a feed."

"Ah, yes, the horses. Of course," Owen agreed solemnly. "How right you are to remind me. We'll stop at Northolt, it's the next village."

He turned in his saddle and again looked at Pen. He wondered when she had last eaten; she'd refused to share his breakfast.

He called over to her, softly so as not to spook her horse, "Pen, we're going to stop at Northolt for dinner. Are you hungry?"

"Famished," she said succinctly. It seemed an eternity since she'd shared her sister's bread and bacon at dawn. She tightened her hold on William's reins.

They were approaching the village of Northolt and the sound of church bells came across the fields. A gibbet stood at a crossroads, a nearly fleshless carcass hanging in chains, swinging forlornly in the wind. Crows on the crossbar set up a violent chattering as the travelers approached.

William shied, then plunged off the verge and into the roadway. Pen hauled back on the reins and the horse reared in terror as the crows soared into the air in a wild gaggle of noise, protecting what remained of their feast.

Pen hung on grimly until William got all four hooves back on the ground. "That is the most unschooled horse!" Owen declared, leaning over and grabbing the reins. "He's quite unsuitable for a woman's mount."

"He's well enough behaved on his own land," Pen replied defensively. "There's no need for you to hold his reins, Chevalier." She flicked indignantly at his hand with the tip of her whip.

Owen twitched the whip from her fingers. "There are some things I don't take kindly to," he observed with a distinct chill to his voice. "You'll find another mount when we stop, or you go no farther on this journey." He handed her back her whip and moved away.

Pen grimaced at the curt instruction but made no comment, deeply regretting that derisory flick of her whip. It had been automatic, but very unwise.

The Rising Sun stood on the green in the village of Northolt. It was a commodious inn, well placed to cater to travelers on the busy London to Oxford road. Owen dismounted at the main entrance, handing his horse to an ostler who came running from the stables.

"I'll join you in the inn," Pen said, her tone rather subdued. Without waiting for a response, she directed William around the inn in the direction of the stables at the back.

The negotiation and instructions for William's care took a little time and a little more coin, and when Pen entered the inn's busy taproom she found Owen and Cedric at the common table addressing a fricassee of mutton with buttered greens and roasted chestnuts.

She stood in the doorway, tossing back her hood before unclasping her cloak. The rustic fare on the table made her mouth water. Owen beckoned her over and slid over on the bench to give her room.

Pen hesitated but could detect no hint of his earlier vexation in his calm countenance. She had been forgiven for that ill-considered gesture, it seemed.

She hung her cloak on a peg by the door, and hitched up her orange skirts to climb over the bench.

"That's a most elegant gown," Owen observed as the skirts settled around her. "More

242

suitable for a palace than a tavern." He stuck the point of his dagger into a thick bread trencher on the board in front of him and passed it to her.

"I don't have any gowns suitable for a tavern," Pen responded. But she realized she should have resisted Pippa's choice. In the dark-raftered taproom among the rough homespuns and somber country hues of their fellow diners, the orange dress was as conspicuous as a sunburst in a stormy sky.

"No reason why you should have," Owen replied with a neutral smile. He continued in an equally neutral tone. "Have you found a substitute horse?"

There were no utensils at the table. Before answering, Pen folded her bread expertly into the shape of a shovel. She dipped it into the common dish of fricassee and carried a generous scoop of meat and gravy to her mouth.

"Yes," she replied through a full mouth before scooping greens onto her trencher. "A dull-looking animal, one used to traffic." She nodded decisively. "He won't give me any trouble. Would you pass the ale jug?"

Owen obliged. "Then perhaps we can ride rather more companionably this afternoon," he observed.

Pen couldn't see how that could be avoided. But she would use the time to discuss how they would proceed in High Wycombe. She wondered if he had a plan. She certainly had her own ideas. They would pool their suggestions, that should make for a productive and relatively safe journey.

She drank from the jug, then took her own dagger from her sleeve and speared a piece of particularly succulent mutton from the pot. She separated the gristle from the meat with the knife point and ate the mutton. Daggers were useful for more than defense, she reflected. No wonder her mother had urged her daughters to keep one about them. Of course, Pen did not ordinarily dine in the absence of utensils at the common table of a roadside tavern.

The food was good, though. She hadn't realized how hungry she was. She leaned sideways to allow a stout servant girl to reach over her and set an enormous fig pudding on the table. The girl wiped her sweating forehead on her sleeve and plunged a spoon into the center of the pudding. Steam escaped with a hiss.

The pudding was passed down the long table, its communal spoon going with it. Pen watched her fellow diners and when the pudding reached her decided that she was no longer hungry.

Owen too declined, but Cedric plunged in the spoon when it was handed to him and ate with enthusiasm.

"Unfastidious youth," murmured Owen. "It knows only appetite." Pen smiled, for the moment forgetting the need to keep her distance. It was all too easy to forget it when he was sitting beside her in this way, so companionable and easy.

He touched her neck just behind her ear, a light press of his fingertip just behind the line of the delicate half-ruff that rose at the back of her gown. Pen was very still. His finger rested on her skin. She felt his pulse beating against her skin. She held her breath. Then she turned her head away, and his hand dropped.

"We should be on our way," Owen said as if that moment had never happened. "Come, Cedric, you've eaten enough to sink a barge of coal. Have the horses brought around. Lady Bryanston has arranged for a substitute for the excitable gelding."

Cedric scrambled from the bench, grabbing up his hat, which had fallen to the floor. He ran off, picking unnameable scraps from the flat brim.

"I'll join you outside," Pen said. "I won't be many minutes."

"There's a privy next to the henhouse," Owen offered helpfully. "I'll take your cloak."

"My thanks, Chevalier." She dropped a mock curtsy and went off to the dark and noisome shed in the back regions.

She emerged quickly, it was not a space to linger, and hurried up the path that led around the side of the tavern.

Owen was examining the broad-backed cob that Pen had hired. He laid down the hoof that he had been checking with the point of his dagger. "I think he'll carry you. He seems adequately shod."

"I'm not without some knowledge of horse-flesh," Pen informed him with a touch of asperity.

He merely inclined his head in acknowledgment, and refrained from commenting on the gelding's unsuitability for crowded roadways.

"Shall I put you up, or would you prefer to use the block?"

Pen touched her neck almost reflexively. She remembered the way he'd lifted her into William's saddle that morning. "I prefer the block."

"As you wish." He gestured to the groom to lead the horse to the mounting block, and swung onto his own horse.

Pen mounted. The animal wore her saddle so it was not as unfamiliar as it might have been, but it still took her a while to get used to the cob's gait. She went at her own pace and Owen, after a murmured word with Cedric, slowed his own mount to a walk.

"Take your time," he said. "Cedric has gone ahead to arrange accommodations for us at the Bull."

Pen listened for a smug or patronizing note but heard neither. He was as charming and as attentive as if he had begged her to make this journey with him.

Last night he'd been the hawk, predatory beak, sharp acquisitive talons. Last night she'd opened herself to those talons, given herself to the rush of desire, the fascination of the man who wore the mask.

In this bright cold afternoon he was as warm, as companionable, as easy to be with as Robin.

Again she touched the spot behind her ear with her gloved hand.

No, not Robin. Not remotely like Robin.

Thirteen

●

The moon had risen in a cloudy sky when they entered the substantial village of Gerrards Cross. Pen had attempted to draw from Owen some idea of how he intended to ask his questions in High Wycombe, but he had answered evasively. When she told him her ideas, he had merely raised an eyebrow. He was, it had seemed, prepared to talk about anything except the real reason they were on this journey.

Finally Pen had fallen silent, and Owen had made no further attempt at conversation. Pen sensed that he was secretly amused but she was damned if she was going to offer anything more. They rode in silence for the last hour as the evening drew in and Pen found herself fantasizing about supper, a blazing fire, hot milk laced with wine and spiced with nutmeg and cinnamon, and then a deep feather bed.

The latter image jerked her out of her reverie. Involuntarily she glanced at her companion, grateful for the waning light as she became aware that her cheeks had suddenly warmed.

Owen instantly turned to her. "Tired?"

"An understatement," Pen returned as coolly as she could. *Surely he hadn't read her thoughts?*

"Well, the end is in sight." He gestured with his whip to a large half-timbered building set back from the main street. The lights from its unshuttered front windows glowed through the gathering dusk. Pen's cob increased his speed as if scenting the stable, and Owen's horse followed suit.

"If Cedric has done his job well, all will be in readiness to receive us." Owen looked over at her. "By the way, I thought it would be politic to say that you're my sister and I'm escorting you to relatives in Oxford."

Pen forgot her momentary discomfiture at this absurdity. "We don't look in the least like siblings," she protested. "I'd have thought a spy would come up with something more ingenious."

He gave her a mock bow from atop his horse. "You'll have to forgive me, but I, too, am tired. I had had barely two hours' sleep before you woke me with such lack of ceremony."

"I doubt I had that much myself," she responded, and instantly wished she had bitten her tongue.

"You slept poorly?" He raised an eyebrow but she couldn't see his expression in the gloom. "I wonder why."

Pen was spared an answer as they came into the light thrown from the inn's windows and two grooms raced from the shadows to take their horses.

Pen tried to summon the energy to dismount.

Her limbs refused to obey. She made no objection when, wordlessly, Owen lifted her down.

He set her on her feet, keeping his hands at her waist, and for a moment neither of them moved. Then he said quietly, "Just why did you sleep poorly, Pen? An unquiet mind perhaps?"

Pen hesitated. His eyes were upon her, a penetrating gaze that felt almost as if it would pierce her skull to the thoughts behind. "Perhaps," she said deliberately. "I have much to keep me awake, Chevalier. I am close to finding the truth about my child." She stepped away from him. "Let us go in."

He followed her into the light and warmth of the inn, where they were greeted by a giant of a man, red-faced from years of sampling his own wares. His voice was as deep as if it had been steeped in port.

"I bid you welcome to the Bull, good sir. My lady." He bowed. "You'll take a glass of something to warm you?"

"I would go straight to my chamber," Pen said swiftly. "Would you send a hot bath and supper to me above stairs, please?"

"Aye, madam. I'll send Mary to help you. I'll have your baggage carried above stairs straightaway."

Pen paused. She hadn't considered the awkwardness of arriving at a respectable inn without a spare garment to her name. She didn't even have her hairbrush.

"Unfortunately my sister's baggage was stolen

from her horse while we were dining earlier to-day," Owen said swiftly. "Take my bag up to her chamber." He turned to Pen. "My dear, feel free to use whatever you think you might need."

"My thanks, sir," she said with a small curtsy.

He reached out a hand and caught her chin in a fashion that didn't strike her as at all brotherly. He tipped her face up to meet his warm and steady gaze. A faint smile lingered on his lips. His expression was all promise. His hand on her chin seemed to render every inch of her skin acutely sensitive.

"We shall sup together. Send the maid to me when you're ready to receive me."

"I am very weary, *brother*," she returned, twisting her chin from his fingers.

"Nevertheless, you must sup," he responded easily. "And we should discuss our plans for the morrow."

"I didn't think you wanted to," she retorted. "All afternoon you refused to talk about it."

"My plans were not fully formed," he said gently. "Now I'm ready to talk about them . . . over supper."

Pen felt like a worm on the hook. She couldn't argue in front of the landlord, who was already regarding them with some interest.

"As you will, *brother*," she said, her eyes shooting fire. "But our discussion must be short, lest I fall asleep with my head in my soup." She turned from him towards the stairs.

"Show her ladyship upstairs. I'll take a pot of

ale in the taproom in the meantime," Owen said to the landlord.

"Right y'are, sir. This way then, madam." The landlord moved ahead of Pen on the stairs.

He opened a door onto a well-proportioned chamber. "I trust this'll do ye, madam."

"Yes, it will do very well," Pen said, entering the chamber.

"I'll send Mary up with his lordship's bag." The man bowed himself out.

Pen unclasped her cloak and hung it on the peg beside the door. She sighed involuntarily.

She didn't want to resist him. The effort exhausted her. But she couldn't yield to desire again . . . it was too much of a betrayal of her mission and of Philip, and it would be putting her own needs ahead of her child's.

She was so close to the truth now. She could feel how close she was. She had felt it that morning when she'd first started out from Greenwich . . . felt it as an almost preternatural conviction.

There came a knock at the door and a cheerful young woman entered with Owen's leather bag. She was followed by three sturdy fellows burdened with a wooden tub and several steaming copper kettles.

"Master said as 'ow y'are wantin' a bath, madam," the girl said with a curtsy.

"Yes, I thank you." Pen shook her braids free of the netted snood as the men set down the tub before the fire and filled it with the hot water.

She smiled at the young woman. " 'Tis Mary, isn't it?"

"Aye, madam. At your service." The maid watched critically as the bath was prepared, then waved the men away with a commanding gesture. One of them winked at her and she blushed.

"I'll 'elp ye undress, madam."

"Thank you." Pen gave herself into Mary's deft hands and was swiftly divested of her gown and undergarments.

"Such a pretty gown," Mary said, smoothing the orange velvet and shaking out the damask folds of the underskirt.

"It needs sponging and pressing," Pen said, pinning her braids to the top of her head to keep them free of the water.

"I'll see to it right away, madam."

"And would you bring me a cup of wine? I've a mind to linger in the water."

Mary bobbed a curtsy and hurried to the kitchens for the wine. Pen lay back in the tub, closing her eyes, refusing to think of anything. When the maid returned she sipped her wine, still keeping her eyes closed, summoning strength for the battle she knew lay ahead. A battle she would fight only with herself.

The clock striking eight startled her out of her reverie. Mary said tentatively, "I thought you were asleep, madam. I didn't like to waken you."

"I probably was." Pen set her empty cup on

the floor. She rose to her feet and took the towel Mary handed her.

Pen saw that while she'd been dozing in her bath, Mary had set a low table before the fire with two stools, one on either side, in preparation for supper *à deux*.

She dried herself slowly, then, wrapped in the towel, began to examine the contents of Owen's bag. He had packed a clean silk shirt but it would barely reach her knees. In the present circumstances she could hardly sup with him half naked, she thought acidly. It would definitely send the wrong message. His night robe, on the other hand, would drown her. A much more satisfactory impression.

She put it on and then unpinned her braids, letting them fall in two heavy ropes down her back. She untied the ribbons and used her fingers to unknot the plaits. She had no hairbrush and neither, it seemed, did the chevalier, so her hair would have to remain in its unruly state. She was suddenly vividly reminded of the morning in Mistress Rider's inn. She'd had to tidy her hair with her fingers then also.

"You may fetch a supper tray now, Mary."

Mary went off and Pen wandered to the window. She opened the shutters and leaned out, breathing deeply of the cold air. Clouds had rolled over the moon and there were no stars to be seen. It was very dark and very quiet after the noise and bustle of London. She turned back to the chamber as the door opened to admit Mary with a laden tray.

"Here's supper, madam. Scalloped oysters, a nice breast of capon with a sorrel sauce, and a platter of custard tarts." The girl named each dish with obvious satisfaction as she laid them on the small table. "Cook says that'll tempt the most delicate appetite."

"And mine is far from delicate. . . . What a feast," Pen said appreciatively, surveying the table with a hungry eye. "I'm ravenous."

"My lord D'Arcy chose the dishes," Mary told her, hurrying out and returning almost immediately with a flagon of burgundy and two pewter goblets. She held up the flagon. "Best in the cellar. Your brother picked it out himself."

She arranged the goblets with the flagon on the table with a little flourish.

"Very pretty, Mary," Pen said, smiling at the girl. "Were you named for the princess?"

"Aye, madam," Mary replied with a curtsy.

"Your parents are very loyal," Pen said. "And it is a lovely name." The girl blushed and curtsied again.

"Would you inform my brother that I'm ready to receive him?" Pen said, closing her mind to the reflection that she'd never been less ready to take on Owen d'Arcy.

Mary took one last look at the table and nodded at her handiwork before going in search of the chevalier.

Pen poured wine into the two goblets. The deep red stream glowed in the candlelight like a ruby in the sun. Her mouth watered. How had Owen known that scalloped oysters were her favorite dish? Or had it just been a lucky guess?

"Enter," she called at a knock on the door, turning, goblet in hand, to offer Owen what she hoped was a coolly polite smile.

He stood by the door, regarding her with an air of appreciative appraisal that sent a jolt through her belly. Resolutely, she concentrated on rearranging the place settings that Mary had put out with such care.

"You're lost in that robe," Owen observed with a smile. "Wouldn't the shirt have been better?"

"I am not inclined to sit at table with you with bare legs," Pen said tartly, and then immediately regretted conjuring such an image. She could see a glint of arousal in his eyes and his smile changed to a clearly inviting grin.

She cleared her throat, saying as neutrally as she could, "I must congratulate you, Chevalier, on such a clever choice of supper."

"Somehow I knew exactly what would please you," he observed, crossing the floor with his soft, swift step. He cupped her chin in the palm of his hand and kissed her mouth. He pushed his hands up through her loosened hair, fluffing it out around her face.

"You're looking more than usually beautiful this evening, sweetheart. Fatigue appears to suit you." His eyes glowed with invitation and promise.

Dear God, how was she going to manage this?

"I cannot imagine how you could possibly know what would please me." Pen turned away from him to pick up the other goblet. "Wine, sir?"

"My thanks, madam," he replied with her own formality, taking the goblet. He sipped, regarding her over its lip with a comprehending smile in his black, black eyes.

"I've watched you at many a meal," he said. "I notice what you choose to eat. You prefer the breast of a fowl, you have little liking for beef, and you never pass up an oyster." He laughed as if his observations gave him pleasure.

"A spy's trick," Pen accused.

"Or a lover's."

"No," she said definitely. "One moment of weakness, Chevalier, does not make a lover." She sat down at the table, gesturing to the stool opposite. "Shall we eat?" She took up a serving spoon and dug into the dish of oysters.

"By all means."

Owen took his seat and, cradling his goblet, watched her as she served them both. "The moment of weakness was not mine, Pen. I gave in to nothing that I did not embrace with delight."

"Then you have nothing with which to reproach yourself," Pen observed. She broke into the loaf of barley bread and spread butter thickly onto a crust. She felt as if she were fighting for her life, with only her wits to keep him at bay.

Owen raised an eyebrow and carved a slice of

capon, laying it on her plate. "In general I try not to do things for which I might reproach myself."

Pen deliberately speared an oyster with her fork. "The cook in this inn is quite accomplished," she observed. "Rarely have I tasted such good oysters. The local river trout are very good too. You should try them while we're in these parts."

Owen refilled his goblet. He regarded her in silence for a minute. He was not going to get anywhere with wordplay. "So, you gave in to a moment of weakness. Why, Pen? You don't strike me as one who easily yields control."

Pen spooned sorrel sauce over her capon. "I daresay I was overdrunk," she said deliberately. "Besides, on Twelfth Night traditionally all scruples are laid aside. People do the most unlikely things. I imagine the atmosphere went to my head."

"Oh, Pen . . . Pen . . ." He shook his head in reproof. "I can tolerate much but not such blatant untruths."

"That is all the answer you are going to get, Chevalier." She faced him across the table. "And now, should we not discuss how we're to proceed on the morrow with my list of names?"

"In an orderly fashion, as is my invariable custom," he responded. He leaned forward and placed his hand over hers, exerting just enough pressure to hold her hand still on the table.

Once again Pen was aware of that strange sense of losing the definition of that part of her body that touched his. It was enclosed and melding with his, his warmth becoming hers.

"Pen?" he said, making of her name a soft question.

"No," she stated. "No, I do not want to, Owen."

He moved his hand from hers. His expression was intent, his eyes as piercing as ever, and she felt stripped bare, as if there was nowhere to hide, as if her true thoughts and emotions were laid out before him.

"Do not lie to me, Pen. You may tell me that you choose not to make love, but you may not tell me that you don't want to."

She had lost her husband and her child. She could not endure any more hurt, she had borne enough for one lifetime. She could not love a spy, a will-o'-the-wisp who would lead her into the marsh of hurt and betrayal. *She could not.*

"Very well," she said quietly. "I choose not to."

He was very still, his hands now resting lightly on the table. "Will you tell me why?"

So many reasons, such a confused morass of reasons. Pen seized upon the one she could easily explain, the one he would have to believe.

"Don't you know?" she demanded with a spurt of welcome anger. "You forced a repellent choice upon me, Chevalier, but it's almost over now. Once you've fulfilled your side of the bargain I will not willingly see you again."

"Now wait a minute —" he began, but she

swept his protest aside with a violent gesture.

"I don't trust you, Owen. I don't know that you're telling me the truth when you say the French are supporting Mary. I don't trust you not to lie to me just to get my cooperation. And even if you weren't lying, your government could change its position at any moment."

Impatiently she brushed away a lock of hair that had fallen over her face as she spoke. "And would you tell me?" she challenged. "Would you tell me if suddenly I was betraying the princess? No, of course you would not." She answered her own question, scorn lacing her voice.

"I cannot possibly make love with a man I don't trust an inch . . . a man who has used me and my despair for his own ends. You are despicable, Chevalier."

She heard the bitter, hurtful torrent as if it were detached from her, coming from some distance. She had told herself that if they once again joined in love, it was inevitable that they would part in bitterness, in anger and disappointment. And now she had made that happen anyway. But better now.

Owen rose to his feet. Without a word he left her, closing the door very softly behind him.

Pen buried her head in her hands as hot tears stung her eyes.

Owen strode from the inn. The door banged shut on his departure. He walked down the main street with an almost desperate haste, as if he

260

could leave behind the rage and the hurt and the confusion. *How dare she?*

How dare she say such things? He had always been honest with her. True, he had struck a bargain, a devil's bargain certainly, but he had never tried to deceive her. And she knew it.

She had been lying. That torrent of accusation had come from somewhere but not from her heart. Did she really think she could fool him? Or did she think that if she made him angry enough he would give up?

What was she afraid of?

He stopped at the far end of the village street and looked up into the cloudy sky. A gust of icy wind tore at his bare head but he didn't feel it.

Perhaps he should take his dismissal and be glad of it. Perhaps he was getting in too deep with this woman.

Perhaps he too should be afraid.

There was no place in his life for an enduring union, for the love and commitment that Pen deserved. Such a relationship would endanger both him and her. It had happened once, it would happen again. It was the price he paid for the life he had chosen.

He took risks all the time, calculated risks, never careless ones. Everything he did had some purpose behind it, a purpose that would advance his own work. What he was about to do now was reckless, and far from aiding his work it could well hinder it.

And he didn't give a damn.

He spun on his heel and strode back to the inn. The door banged again behind him and the landlord popped his head out of the crowded taproom. "Everything all right, m'lord?"

Owen didn't answer. He mounted the stairs two at a time.

The maid Mary was coming out of Pen's chamber carrying a tray of dirty dishes and the remnants of their supper. She looked startled as the chevalier caught the door before she could close it behind her.

She stared up at him. "Lord love us," she mumbled. The lady's brother had a full head of steam on him and no mistake.

He marched past her into Pen's bedchamber and the door closed in Mary's face.

"No," Owen declared, standing with his back to the door. "No, Pen, I will not accept this. I will hear the truth, if indeed you know it yourself, but I will not stand for one more word of a nonsense that insults us both."

Fourteen

●

Pen sat on the bed and gazed at him in stunned silence.

"I don't understand," she managed finally.

"Oh, yes, you do."

He sounded angry and yet she felt no anger surrounding him. His gaze was steady and quiet although she could see the tension around his mouth, in the set of his jaw.

He saw the slight redness of her eyes, the sheen of tears in their hazel depths, and he was filled with an emotion he couldn't name but he knew it was not as simple as lust. It was sympathy, pity even; it was love, and it was a deep hunger to hold her, to kiss away the grief and confusion . . . to heal her.

He came over to the bed and knelt before her, taking her hands in his. He lifted them to his lips, kissing her palms. "My poor Pen. How much you've had to endure," he whispered.

"I don't mean to add to your troubles, sweetheart." He smiled at her, releasing one hand to stroke her cheek, to brush away a strand of hair, sticky with tears. "Nothing will happen that you don't wish."

He came up to sit beside her on the bed, and

drew her into his arms. He heard her sigh, a deep exhalation that seemed to carry from her a world of pain and confusion. He felt her relax against him, her head resting against his shoulder.

Pen was aware of the steady beat of his heart, the scent of his skin, the warmth of his body. This was not the wild impulsive passion of Twelfth Night, this was simply a delight in his closeness, a need for his closeness. She let the wretched doubt and uncertainty slide from her. This would not hurt her. This that she needed so much, this that would bring her so much pleasure and joy.

Her fingers moved over the buttons of his doublet, unfastening it so that she could slip her hand inside to feel the strong, rhythmic beat of his heart that seemed now to become one with her own.

Owen shrugged the garment off as he took her face in his hands and kissed her. Deftly she loosened the laces of his shirt, exposing his throat. She laid the beating pulse of her thumb on the pulse in his throat. For the moment there were no words, only the silent communication of their hearts beating as one.

Moving his lips from hers for a moment, Owen kicked off his shoes. Then he uncurled his long, lean frame and stood up in his stockinged feet.

Pen's eyes were riveted on the taut lines of his body in the tight-fitting hose, the swell of his sex, the strong column of his throat, the broad expanse of his chest exposed by the opened shirt.

Her breath caught in her throat, and now a current of pure lust struck deep in her belly, banishing the lyrical quality of the last moments. She tightened her thighs as her loins seemed to open and fill.

She unclasped the robe at her throat and let it fall open. She stood there, her hands at her side, waiting for his touch on her skin.

Owen took her hands, holding them in his for a minute before turning them up and pressing his lips once more to her palms. He ran his hands up her arms beneath the loose wide sleeves of the robe, cupping her elbows, before sliding up to trace the flow of her shoulders into the rounded point of her upper arms.

He kissed her, his tongue moving delicately in her mouth; her own joined with his in the slow, measured exploration of cheeks and lips and teeth. The tip of his tongue touched hers, licked it, and she chuckled with pleasure at the strange sensation, her own tongue curling around his. It seemed as if nothing else existed now but the two of them in this firelit chamber, lost in the entrancement of love and desire. It seemed as if nothing could break the spell, nothing could intrude.

She freed the last of the laces of his shirt, pushed it off his shoulders and brought her mouth to his chest, her tongue flicking at his nipples until they were hard, tight buds. She kissed them, ran her tongue along his breastbone, up into the hollow of his throat. Her hands clasped his hips, her thumbs pressing into the hard points of his hipbones. Slowly she slid down his body until she knelt in front of him. Her fingers worked at the lace of his hose and her tongue darted into the deep indentation of his navel. She slid the hose over his hips, down to his ankles, and over his feet, sure, so sure of what she was doing.

He stood very still as her tongue trailed down over his belly, following the dark path of hair. She took his penis in her mouth, lightly flicking the tip with her tongue, her teeth grazing the shaft as her hands cupped his balls, kneading gently but firmly.

Owen's fingers curled in her hair, ran down over her bent neck, slid beneath the loosened robe to press into her shoulders. He gazed down at her, watching her mouth move over his sex, the dark circles of her lashes resting on her pale cheeks. And he thought he had never seen or experienced anything more erotic.

Pen looked up at him, holding his sex in the palm of her hand. Her lips were moist, her cheeks now faintly flushed, her eyes deep and bright. "That pleasured you?" The sound of her voice was shocking after the long silken silence of their bodies.

"Immeasurably." He drew her to her feet. He slid his robe from her shoulders and tossed it aside. He looked at her body and she made no move to conceal herself from the intense gaze.

She felt herself beautiful to his eyes, the imperfections of her body unimportant. And when he touched her, her skin glowed beneath the long smooth strokes of his caressing hands. Her thighs parted as he pressed them open, and when his mouth found the full, opened lips of her sex and he pleasured her as she had pleasured him she yielded to wave after wave of exquisite delight.

They fell together onto the bed, and Pen felt they were moving as if in the slow, graceful steps of a pavane to the soft lilt of a lute. He lay facing her, touching her cheeks, her eyes, her nose, her lips with tiny strokes of his fingertips. She put her arms around him, pressing her loins against his but without urgency, allowing that familiar sensation of their bodies merging to flow slowly through her. He curled a leg over her hip and with a leisurely twist of his own hips entered her as they lay facing each other. He cradled her cheek in the palm of his hand, tracing the curve of her mouth with a finger as he moved within her.

It was a slow, honeyed slide into delight.

After, they lay unmoving, gazing at each other open-eyed, both smiling slightly, savoring the deep satisfaction of their joining.

Owen touched the corner of her mouth with a fingertip. "You're tired, sweetheart. You should sleep now."

"Thank you," she said softly. "Thank you for not believing me."

He said nothing, merely kissed her eyes, and

then reluctantly but with determination he left her bed. He lifted her against him for a moment as he pulled back the coverlet and then tucked her beneath. "Sleep, Pen."

"Must you go?" Her eyes were already closing as a glorious languor crept over her.

"I have work to do," he said with a rueful smile.

"Oh, yes," she said dreamily. "I remember. And I told you you would have plenty of time for it as I would not be in your company this evening."

"So you did," he agreed solemnly as he pulled on his clothes. "Well, we all make mistakes."

Pen's chuckle was barely audible.

Owen put on his shoes and snuffed the candles before he left. He strode to his own chamber, realizing that his own fatigue had disappeared. He felt fresh and rested, filled with energy.

In his chamber he found Cedric huddled by the fire, the pigeon silent in its covered cage.

Owen greeted him cheerfully. "Did you find a decent supper, lad?"

"Aye, sir. I supped in the kitchen with the servants. Pickled tongue and a dish of sheep's brains," Cedric told him with an enthusiasm only slightly modified by a deep yawn.

"It sounds delicious," Owen murmured. "Did you enjoy the company?"

Cedric blushed. "That Mary's a right sauce box, sir. She gets quite above herself sometimes." He sounded disapproving but Owen was not deceived. Cedric was at an age when he noticed girls but found it easier to manage the puzzlement they caused him by criticizing them. Give him a year, Owen thought, and the lad would see the opposite sex with new eyes.

"She was probably trying to impress you," Owen suggested.

Cedric's blush deepened and he turned aside to busy himself turning down the coverlet on the canopied bed.

"Shall I help you to bed, sir?"

"No, no, I have work to do. Get you to your own rest." Owen gestured to the truckle bed beneath the poster bed.

The page kicked off his shoes, pulled out the cot, tumbled onto it, hauled the blankets over him, and was instantly asleep.

Owen smiled as the boy's even breathing filled the chamber. He had rescued Cedric five years ago from the streets of Le Havre. The lad had been six at the time.

Six. Andrew would be six this year.

Owen stood still and waited for the pain to die down. It would eventually, it always did. One day he would be able to go to his children. One day it would be safe enough. But he would be a stranger to them. He would have missed their growing.

He sat at the table beneath the window. He took from the inside pocket of his doublet a small round silver case, snapping open the clasp to reveal a double-sided miniature. He drew the candle closer and looked upon the sweet faces of his children, curly-headed babies with grave dark eyes and snub noses. A year separated them. Estelle had been annoyed when she conceived Lucy so soon after giving birth to Andrew. She had complained that it would spoil her figure.

Owen gazed for a long time at the portraits before folding them back into the little silver case. He replaced it in his pocket, then reached for a quill. He sharpened it with his dagger, then drew a very small tablet in front of him and began a coded report to the ambassador on what Pen had told him of Mary's concerns and her faked illness.

He had intended to visit de Noailles that morning and carry his information in person, but Pen's importunate arrival at his bedside had forced a change of plan.

He laid down the quill for a minute and tried to retrieve the glorious afterglow of their loving. But the images in the little silver case in his pocket intruded now. And with them the knowledge that he had let down his guard, allowed emotion to rule his head, and as a result possibly endangered Pen as he had endangered Estelle.

Resolutely he took up his quill. Work was always an anodyne and the code sufficiently complex to take up all his concentration.

Once or twice as the night wore on he rose to throw another log on the fire or to trim the lamp, but his thoughts remained engaged on his task.

As the false dawn showed through the cracks in the loosely shuttered window, he sanded the small sheet of paper with its series of letters and numbers on both sides, rolled it tightly, and inserted it into a bronze cylinder.

He took the pigeon from her cage, attached the cylinder to the ring around her leg, and carried her to the window. He opened the shutters onto a blast of frigid air, but the clouds had lifted and there was no sign of snow. He released the bird and watched as she flew arrow-straight, following her mysterious homing instinct. She would be in London by evening.

He lay down on the bed in his shirt and hose, arms linked behind his head, and let sleep claim him.

Pen slept as deeply as she had ever slept in her life. In sleep she curled her body into a tight ball, as she did every night when Nutmeg shared her bed. The cat, every night since age had put an end to his nighttime hunting and carousing, inserted himself beneath the covers to press himself against her belly.

In her sleep she felt soothed by the animal's regular breathing, his warmth, his need for her, and the comfort he brought her. And when she awoke in the dark chamber where the fire had burned down to gray embers she found herself smiling at the thought of how the cat had deeply resented Philip, who would not permit him to get under the covers, although after one failed attempt to banish him altogether from the bed he had wisely yielded and Nutmeg had taken his place at the end of the bed on Pen's feet.

The dream tangles faded. Pen remembered Philip now with a piercing intensity. It was as if he was with her once more.

She sat up, wondering if guilt had awakened her. Had she, by loving Owen, truly betrayed Philip? She probed the question, nagging at it as if she were exploring an aching tooth with her tongue. And yet she could set no nerve jangling.

Philip would not have wanted her to spend the rest of her life in mourning. It was time now to lay aside her grief. Once she had discovered the truth about their child, then she could lay her memories to rest.

She hugged her knees, resting her chin atop them. Philip's death had been so cruel, so sudden, she mused. One minute in the peak of health, stronger than she had ever known him, the next . . .

There was a knock at the door and it opened immediately. Owen came in carrying a large bundle of what looked like material.

Pen smiled dreamily at him. "I missed you. Did you finish your work?"

"I did. I even managed an hour's sleep," he responded. "I didn't expect you to be awake so early, though." He set his burden on the chest at the foot of the bed and went to throw back the shutters on the windows.

Sunlight flooded the chamber. "I hadn't realized it was so late," Pen contradicted.

Owen came over to the bed. He leaned over her, gently caressed the curve of her cheek, a flicker of anxiety in his questioning gaze. She reached up to cover his hand with her own.

"No regrets, Pen?" he asked softly.

"No," she said definitely. "No regrets and no guilt."

She was so honest, so upright. And she had been right that he had compromised that upright honesty by forcing his bargain upon her.

Pen slid off the bed and put her arms around him. She could feel his heart beating beneath his bare chest as she inhaled the deliciously rich male scent of his skin. It was just a hug, she was asking for nothing more, and Owen responded, wrapping his arms around her, kissing the top of her head.

Finally she drew back and looked up at him. "You look troubled."

"I am," he replied with a rueful smile. "Very rarely do I question my decisions, once made, but you, sweetheart, are turning my life inside out."

"Is that a compliment?"

He shook his head with the same smile. "I don't know, Pen. I really don't know."

"But is it a good thing for you?" she pressed.

He stepped slowly away from her. "That I don't know, either. It may be good for the soul, but it's not good for my peace of mind."

He went to make up the fire. Pen reached for

the discarded night robe, wrapping it around her against the cold morning air as she watched his deft, competent movements, the surging power contained in his lean, hard body. She wondered exactly what he had meant by his peace of mind, but something kept her from asking. She had a niggle of presentiment that perhaps she didn't want to know.

She looked for something neutral to say in the sudden awkward silence, and her eye fell upon the bundle on the chest.

"What is this you've brought?"

He straightened as the fire caught. "Ah, well, I have been thinking. It occurred to me, knowing the . . ." He paused, considering his words, a smile playing over his mouth. "The strength of your resolution, shall we say? — that you would probably not be willing to remain here today while I ask questions in High Wycombe."

"No, of course I wouldn't," Pen said with a touch of asperity.

He came over to her. "Consider for a minute," he said, holding her shoulders. "If there is an evil tale to tell, no one's going to tell it in your presence. You must see that, Pen."

"But I can't sit here twiddling my thumbs while you're having all the excitement."

"Excitement?" He raised an eyebrow.

"Well, all the *doing*," she explained. "I want to be *doing* something. It is my business, after all."

"Well, as it happens I anticipated just such a reaction." He stretched sideways to the chest.

"It occurred to me that Cedric is about your size. So I have here his spare suit of clothes, which he has been induced to lend you. Do you think you can play the part of servant?"

Pen's eyes gleamed as she took the britches, shirt, and doublet from him. "Why, yes, of course. What a splendid idea, Owen! This way I can accompany you and make my own judgments about what you hear, and I can tell you what to ask if I have some other ideas.

"But what about my hair?" she said, frowning.

Owen lifted a heavy swatch of her thick brown hair and twisted it around his wrist, bringing her very close to him. "When it's braided and coiled it'll be invisible under Cedric's cap. And if you pull the cap down low over your eyes and preserve the modest demeanor of a servant no one will give you a second look."

She gazed up at him bright-eyed with mischievous excitement. "Just the solution I would have expected from a spy."

His expression was suddenly grave. "Perhaps so, Pen. But understand this. If you compromise the investigation you must accept that I will have fulfilled my side of the bargain. I must be back in London the day after tomorrow, so this is the only chance. Is that understood?"

"Of course," she responded impatiently. "And of course I won't compromise anything. What do you think I am?"

"A very stubborn woman," he replied, taking another turn of her hair around his wrist so that her head was against his chest.

"My mother's daughter," Pen said, tilting her face up for the kiss she knew was coming.

It was a long kiss, one that possessed her utterly, and when finally he released her, unwinding her hair from his wrist, she touched her lips with her fingertips, feeling them swollen as if from a bee sting.

"Don't let anyone see you kissing your page in such fashion, Chevalier. It would certainly cause remark."

He laughed and strode energetically to the door. "Your own riding boots and hose will pass muster. When you've broken your fast I'll meet you at the stables."

As soon as he'd left Pen rang for Mary and asked her to bring up bread and meat. "Oh, and a jug of small beer, if you please," she added, laying her borrowed raiment out upon the bed.

Mary stared at the clothes. "Lord love us, madam, but you're not goin' to be a-wearin' of them clothes."

"Yes, I am," Pen responded placidly. "When you return you can tell me how well they suit me."

"It ain't right!" Mary declared, scandalized. "It ain't right for a Christian lady, an 'ighborn lady at that, to go around lookin' like that."

Pen merely laughed. "Fetch up my breakfast, Mary, there's a good girl."

That very same morning in London was cold and crisp, but Robin was oblivious of the glories of the bright blue sky, the freshness of the air that seemed for once to carry none of the fetid odors of the city. He was feeling somewhat the worse for wear, and reflected grimly that he had only himself to blame. He had spent the previous evening quietening his conscience with tankards of mulled ale, and had slept heavily but not restfully.

He didn't know whether Pen would hate him for what he was about to do or if in the end she would be grateful. But he had sworn to himself that he would find out everything there was to discover about the Chevalier d'Arcy. If Pen had drawn the chevalier into her obsession about her baby, then she had confided something to him that she would never, ever have told anyone with whom she was not deeply and intimately involved. Whether passion was the spur or the consequence of that involvement, she was in danger. Owen d'Arcy could not be trusted.

If d'Arcy had any unsavory secrets, then Simon Renard, the Spanish ambassador, would know them. He would know that d'Arcy worked for de Noailles, as spy networks were an open secret, and he would have made it his business to know all there was to know about his rival ambassador's master agent. Of course that didn't mean he would be willing to share what he had with someone as seemingly unimportant as Robin of Beaucaire.

Robin left his horse with a groom in the stable at the rear of the Spanish ambassador's tall narrow house in Cheapside and was admitted by a sober-suited individual whose saturnine mien strongly resembled his employer's.

He showed the visitor into a parlor where the rich hangings and heavy paneling merely added to the somber atmosphere, which was in no way enlivened by the sunlight slanting through the diamond-paned windows. The chamber was cheered by a fire, though, and Robin gratefully moved to stand in front of it, warming his backside at its bright glow.

He was nervous, although Renard had sent a pleasant enough response to his written request for an interview. However, this reflection didn't do much for Robin's confidence. His hands felt clammy and he was wiping them on his handkerchief when the door swung open.

He shoved the handkerchief into the pocket of his doublet in such haste that half of it hung out, a limp and scrunched scrap of less than pristine linen. The ambassador's gaze flicked over his guest and noticed everything, from the heavy eyes to the careless handkerchief. But what he knew about Robin of Beaucaire, and it was a great deal more than Robin suspected, was interesting. The young man was highly regarded both for his agile brain and for his probity, and it was always possible he could prove useful.

Simon Renard nodded at Robin. "You are well come, my friend. Pray be seated. You'll take some wine?"

Robin murmured his thanks and took the chair indicated. Renard poured wine into goblets of Venetian crystal, handed one to his guest, and then took his own seat, crossing one elegantly shod ankle over the other.

"So, what can Simon Renard do for Robin of Beaucaire?" His voice was soft and faintly accented. Although a smile touched his lips his eyes were sharply calculating as they rested upon the man sitting opposite him.

Robin took a sip of wine and found it heartening. He cleared his throat. "I have some interest in Owen d'Arcy, sir."

"Ah." Renard nodded slowly. "You come straight to the point. I appreciate it. But I ask myself why you would come to me."

Robin thought for a minute. He couldn't pull the wool over Renard's eyes and it would make him look foolish to try, not to mention that it would irritate the ambassador, which wouldn't serve his purpose at all.

"Spain's ambassador would know about France's spies," he responded.

Renard chuckled, although Robin found it a somewhat sinister sound. "Well, well, you are right not to play games, my friend. What interest do you have in this man?"

It seemed best to continue as bluntly as he'd begun. "He is paying considerable attention to my stepsister, Penelope, Lady Bryanston. Her well-being is very much my concern, and I would be certain that he means her no harm."

Renard nodded again, and sipped thoughtfully from his goblet. "So this is a purely personal matter."

"Yes, sir."

"I think you can safely assume that affairs of state lie behind everything d'Arcy does," the ambassador said. "He does nothing without purpose, and his purposes are all intricately bound up with French diplomacy. His pursuit of the lady will be at the behest of de Noailles."

Robin swirled the wine in his goblet. "I had expected as much. But I was wondering if there is anything else, anything personal that you might know about d'Arcy, sir."

"Anything that might cause the lady to look elsewhere for a love interest?" the ambassador asked with a lift of a thin eyebrow.

"Yes, sir."

There was a moment's silence. Renard turned his goblet between his hands so that the shaft of sunlight caught the crystal, revealing a rainbow of color in the glass. He could see a way to give Robin of Beaucaire what he wanted, and in doing so he would be banking a future favor. Always useful. And he could see no way that reviving the old scandal would upset the delicate balance between the French and Spanish embassies at the Court of St. James's. It would not, after all, be an affair of state, just a personal matter. And it was an old story, redolent of gossip and malicious rumor. But no one could say that in recounting it he had invented it.

He began to speak slowly, continuing to turn his goblet in his hands.

"I will tell you a story. You may make of it what you will. Once upon a time there was a man at the French court, a very clever, highly regarded young man of excellent lineage. His mother was Welsh, highborn if such a concept is possible among that barbarian muddle of clans and tribes." Renard's nose twitched in fastidious distaste.

"His father, however, was related to the Duc de Guise and therefore with royal connections. The man had spent most of his life in France, with occasional visits to his mother's homeland. He was bred to the life of a courtier, but it was clear his talents lay elsewhere. He was bored with court life and made no secret of it. This was a man who needed work, food for his brain."

He rose and fetched the flagon. He refilled their goblets while Robin sat in barely concealed impatience.

"In due course the young man took a wife. It was clear from the outset that it was an ill match, but it had been promoted by his father with the outspoken support of the king."

Renard shrugged. "Under such pressure, what's a man to do? The lady came with a handsome dowry." He took his seat again, straightening a crease in his silk hose before continuing.

"He made no secret of his impatience with life at court, or indeed of his impatience with his wife's frivolities. He began to spend time in Burgundy, ostensibly managing his estates. But those to whom it mattered knew that that was a front for his involvement in undercover diplomacy for the king. He was . . . is . . . very good at his work. Probably the best. He has few scruples as to his methods of gaining information."

Renard flicked the rim of the goblet he held and the sound rang true and pure.

Robin watched, fascinated by the play of the long fingers on the goblet, by the insidious innuendo in the tale Renard was spinning.

"His wife remained at court while the man was away on his frequent so-called visits to his estates. Their estrangement became the talk of the court. The man's wife was very beautiful, and could have had her pick of lovers. She was much sought after. Adoration is so seductive, particularly at a court where discreet liaisons were indulged." Renard gestured with an open palm as if to say: *What could one expect of a court as licentious as the French?*

The Spanish ambassador seemed to have little time for the customs of others, Robin reflected. He nodded politely, however, well aware that the Spanish court was excessively strict. It was not the first time he'd heard one of its members deride the laxer, friendlier rules and rituals of the French.

"In due course the woman bore two children. A boy and then a girl. At first, the man was a surprisingly doting father, making up, one might say, for the mother's apparent indifference. She appeared to find the children an embarrassment. It was thought she believed that motherhood made a matron of a woman, and the lady was not willing to be considered in the least matronly."

Renard paused again, took the scent of his wine before continuing. "There were whispers about the woman's fidelity, as one might expect. She was without her husband for long periods and certainly enjoyed flirtations. The man seemed as indifferent to the gossip about his wife as he was to the woman herself. He remained a doting father whenever he was at home. And then quite suddenly everything changed. The man announced that he had discovered his wife *in flagrante delicto*."

A thin smile touched the ambassador's mouth. "Now, you must understand that while there had been whispers about the woman's flirtations they were merely for amusement. No one at court actually believed that she had taken a lover. There had been no evidence of adultery, and it was generally held that she was too stupid to have succeeded in managing an affair discreetly. Her lack of wit, after all, was considered to be one of the contributing factors to her husband's indifference. So the husband's denunciation came as a great surprise to everyone."

Robin sat forward intently, his knuckles showing white against the glass he held.

The ambassador sipped his wine. "The denunciation surprised everyone, but not nearly as much as did the violence of his vengeance."

He stretched sideways and placed his glass on a small table beside him. "The lover was not named, apparently he had fled the scene in some . . . some disarray, and was never seen again. The man denounced him as a coward who had fled to avoid the inevitable duel. This certainly made sense. Our man was . . . is . . . a superb swordsman, not a man to run up against, I should warn you." He nodded significantly at Robin, who flushed but said nothing.

"The man then divorced his wife very publicly, repudiated her and his children in front of the entire court, then took her away. She has not been seen or heard of since."

"He killed her?" The question emerged as a shocked whisper.

Renard concealed a half-smile and shrugged. "Perhaps. Rumor has it that he had her locked away in a convent in the Pyrenees, a particularly strict order, a silent order committed to a life of abject poverty, as I understand it. It would be a savage existence for a woman whose lifeblood was the rich and exciting life of the court, a woman who needed adulation with every breath she took. She would probably have preferred death. Indeed, rumor yet again has it that she sought death at her own hands."

Robin said nothing. He could think of no adequate response to such a horror.

"A savage punishment, I think you would agree," Renard continued in his smooth manner. "Even for an unfaithful wife. If indeed she *had* been unfaithful."

The ambassador raised an eyebrow. "Very few people believed in her guilt, which she denied with her last breath. It was generally believed that the man had trumped up the charges in order to be rid of her. It was assumed that there was another woman involved."

Renard shrugged again. "If there was, she hasn't made an appearance. Anyway, he took the children, whom he'd publicly declared to be bastards. No one knows where he took them, but it's generally believed that he's not laid eyes upon them since. He then eschewed all society, which had anyway all but ostracized him, and he was seen in Paris only when he had business there.

"As far as the French court is concerned he has dropped out of sight . . . and, therefore, since a Frenchman has the attention span of a gnat, out of mind. He appears in London and elsewhere, of course, when he is about his business. But few people know his unsavory story."

Renard picked up his glass again. "There you have my little tale, my friend, and, as I said, you may make of it what you choose."

Robin was silent for longer than courtesy permitted before he recollected himself. "My thanks, sir." His reflective gaze returned to the now-empty goblet he held.

Renard watched him with his earlier hint of amusement. "Was that what you wished to hear, Lord Robin?"

Robin looked up again and his eyes were

bleak. "Perhaps so, sir. But I don't care to cause pain to those I love."

"Ah. In our world, my friend, that makes a man vulnerable. And that is very dangerous." Renard stood up and Robin took his cue.

"Thank you for your time, sir. I am most grateful." He set down his glass rather awkwardly and it tottered on the edge of the table. He caught it in time, replacing it with exaggerated caution in the center of the table.

"Not at all. I'm glad to have been of some service. My man will see you out." Renard offered a short bow and left the chamber while Robin was still executing a deeper bow to his host.

The saturnine servant appeared immediately and in silence escorted his master's guest to the street. Robin stood looking up at the house, which seemed fancifully to him to be as dark and devious and secretive as its occupant. Renard had been as forthcoming as Robin could have wished, but Robin knew his own business well enough to be certain that that was because the ambassador would call in the debt in his own time.

He'd warned Robin against an open challenge to a superlative swordsman. The warning piqued Robin's pride, but he took it to heart nevertheless. He was no mean blade himself, but not in the first rank of swordsmen.

But he'd cross that bridge if and when he came to it. His first duty was to Pen. And it was a duty that turned his blood cold. How did you tell your dearest friend that her lover was a monster?

Fifteen

●

Owen went into a peal of laughter when Pen appeared in the stable yard.

"What's so funny?" Pen demanded, pulling Cedric's cap down low on her brow. "Mary thought it was scandalous but she didn't think there was anything amusing about my appearance."

"It's just so unlikely," Owen said through his laughter. "You're far too pretty for a page."

Pen considered whether to accept this as a compliment or as an adverse comment on her disguise. She decided it was both. "Well, I can't do much about it," she stated, tugging at the hem of Cedric's short doublet as if she could thus lengthen it to cover more of her thighs.

"It has its alluring aspects," Owen observed. "I hadn't realized you had quite such a deliciously round backside."

At any other time she might have been flattered, but not in the middle of an inn's stable yard. Pen flushed to the roots of her hair. "Someone will overhear you!"

"There's no one around," he returned with perfect truth. "The groom has gone to fetch Cedric's horse for you. I believe we'll make better progress if you ride Nugget."

"Does Cedric mind?" Pen asked doubtfully.

"No more than he minds lending his spare suit of clothes and being excluded from my business for the day. If he wants to go abroad he knows to use the cob, although I doubt he'll subject himself to such an indignity." Owen's smile was affectionate.

Pen had observed both Cedric's adoration of his master and Owen's easily affectionate manner with the lad. It had struck her that there was a strong bond between master and page. It was another of the mysteries that thickened around Owen d'Arcy.

The groom appeared from the stable leading Cedric's dun-colored mare. He barely glanced at the page. "I'll fetch the black now, m'lord."

Owen nodded and turned to Pen. "Let me put you up."

Pen didn't trust his somewhat wicked smile, but the dun stood too high for her to mount unaided. In her present costume she would be able to ride astride, though. She disliked the new sidesaddles that were now considered de rigueur for ladies of the court. They restricted movement too much.

She bent her knee for Owen to toss her up into the saddle. As she'd expected, he took the opportunity to run his hands over her bottom, and for one instant that left her breathless he slipped one hand between her thighs in a darting intimate caress before he boosted her into the saddle.

"Nice," he observed with the same wicked smile. "Very nice indeed."

Pen had not the slightest desire for sex play. The business at hand was far too serious, and yet Owen was behaving as if they were going on a jaunt. She refused to smile, and stared straight ahead.

Owen mounted his horse, the smile still playing on his lips, but he made no attempt to elicit a response. He turned his horse out of the stable yard and onto the road to High Wycombe.

It was barely seven o'clock but the world was already stirring. They passed a milkmaid with her full pails and a young goatherd yawning as he drove his flock through the village to the fields beyond. A knot of ragged children were clustered around the village well, throwing stones at one another, laughing and playing tag, until an irate woman emerged from one of the cottages lining the street and came towards them flourishing a broom. She smartly boxed the ears of the first two children she reached, and the others hastily fell into an orderly line with their buckets.

Cottage doors stood open as women swept debris into the street; the smoke from cooking fires curled in the crisp air. A tiny girl chewing a lump of black bread ran barefoot into the roadway chasing a chicken. She was oblivious of the horses coming towards her and suddenly veered sideways, trying to cut off the chicken's path.

Owen dragged his horse aside, avoiding the child by an inch. He was swearing, a stream of

French that Pen, whose command of the language was more than competent, barely understood.

The child picked herself up, and seemed only then to realize the danger she'd been in. Owen switched to English as he scolded her for not looking where she was going.

Frightened out of her wits, the child stared up at this angry man on his great black charger, then she turned and raced back into the cottage from whence she'd come, abandoning her pursuit of the squawking chicken.

Owen sat very still as his horse settled down. He looked shaken and he seemed to Pen to have lost color, his lips almost white, his eyes blank with shock. She didn't know whether it was anger or distress at the child's near miss or both, but she knew she had never seen him affected in this way.

She herself could still not believe that the child had escaped unscathed. The stunning speed of Owen's reaction, the strength in his hands as he'd pulled up the horse, had amazed her. It was as if the horse was an extension of himself, a weapon almost, to be controlled just as he controlled his rapier. Deft, certain, deadly. But when he'd wielded his rapier to lethal effect he'd behaved afterwards as calmly as if nothing had happened. But there was something about his reaction now that was quite different, and she didn't know what to say.

Owen stared into the past. He saw little Andrew, all of two years old, toddling into the sun-lit courtyard of the château in Burgundy flourishing a little wooden sword. The boy had seen his father returning from the hunt and with excited shrieks tottered towards him, tripped, and fell straight into the path of Owen's great horse, an animal built to carry a man in full armor in the jousting lists or across a battlefield. The horse had reared as Owen, in terror, hauled him back, and an iron-shod hoof had caught the child a glancing blow to his shoulder. A glancing blow, but enough to dislocate the fragile joint. His son's screams of agony still lived in Owen's memory, almost as vividly as if he was hearing them now.

Pen could bear the silence no longer. Alarmed by his expression, she leaned over and touched his arm. "Owen?"

He jumped as if stung and looked at her as if he didn't know who she was.

She said, her fingers pressing into his arm, "It's all right, Owen. The child's not hurt. You reacted so quickly . . . like lightning. *She's not hurt.*"

Her words and her touch reached him through the shock of memory. His eyes focused again and the color returned to his cheeks, his mouth once more relaxed. "No, you're right. Come, let's get on."

Pen didn't immediately set her horse to follow him. It had been a bad moment, but she'd never before seen Owen look lost. Indeed, she could never have imagined that he could be. He'd handled the situation with his customary efficiency, but he *had* looked lost. The more time she spent in his company the less she seemed to know about him.

"Pen!"

At the imperative summons she nudged her horse into a canter to catch up. Owen glanced at her. "We don't have time to daydream."

Pen offered no defense.

He rode fast but Pen, comfortably astride a young and steady horse, kept up easily. It was twelve miles to High Wycombe and they reached their destination in just under two hours.

"Where do we go first?" Pen asked, looking around the familiar village from beneath the pulled-down brim of her cap.

"The tavern," Owen said. "The fount of all gossip." He had barely spoken since they'd left Gerrards Cross, and Pen had not interrupted his reverie. She had put the mystery aside for the moment and given herself over to her own thoughts as they drew closer to the place that contained so many memories for her, the happy ones almost obliterated by the terrible ones.

"Is that the Bryanston house?" Owen gestured with his whip to a pair of closed iron gates set into a high stone wall on the outskirts of the village.

"Yes, the manor," Pen said with an inner chill. She had not been back here since her mother and Hugh had taken her away after the baby's birth. She and Philip had enjoyed country life and had done much to enhance the beauty and convenience of Bryanston Manor. She wondered whether Miles had continued the improvements . . . Miles and his mother.

"The Bryanston Arms is on the green," she said.

Owen rode towards the large expanse of grass in the center of the village. It was ornamented with a whipping post and stocks occupied by a miserable-looking vagrant liberally splattered with refuse.

"Nothing changes," Pen murmured, recognizing the vagrant as Old Tom, whose fecklessness and propensity for helping himself to anything he fancied frequently landed him in the stocks.

The tavern was small, its thatched roof in need of repair. In fact, Pen noticed, there was a general air of neglect in the village that had not been apparent during Philip's tenure at Bryanston Manor. It was the earl's responsibility, or rather that of his steward and bailiff, to keep the tenants' housing in good order, but there were crumbling roofs, broken gates, dismantled walls, and thickets of weeds in the hedgerows. Everything she saw spoke to an absentee lord of the manor.

She mentioned this to Owen, who said, "Good. That should work in our favor. If the family are rarely here and their tenants have reason to bear a grudge they're more likely to talk."

He drew rein at the tavern's ale bench and swung down. "Take the horses to the stables and see them baited and watered. I'm going inside to lubricate some tongues."

"Wait!" Pen exclaimed, swinging herself from the dun. "I'm coming in too. That's the whole point of my disguise."

He turned back, his eyes once more alight with amusement, and Pen, to her heartfelt relief, saw that whatever mood had enveloped him had vanished.

He said, "Unfortunately it's less convincing than I'd hoped. But if you play the part of servant, it might add verisimilitude to an otherwise implausible tale."

"I'm a page, not a groom," Pen protested.

Owen laughed. "Don't take offense, sweetheart, but besides being too pretty, you are a little too old to make a convincing page. Go and talk to the grooms and ostlers and see what you can glean from them, but I should avoid talking to anyone who might have known you in your customary guise."

With that he sauntered into the tavern, leaving Pen torn between indignation and acknowledgment that he was probably right.

She took the horses' reins and led them round to the stables. At first it seemed that they were deserted, and they were certainly not as well ordered as she remembered them. The cobbles were slippery with ordure, the straw filthy and stinking. She led the horses to the water trough and broke the film of ice with her riding whip. The water beneath was green and foul.

"Ye want summat?"

She spun round at the rough voice and found herself face-to-face with a man she vaguely recognized. Young, with a surly air, he would have been little more than a boy four years ago.

"Fresh water for the horses," she said, trying to deepen her voice, but it still sounded lighter than she would have liked.

"Well's on the green," he said carelessly. "Bucket's over yonder." He gestured to a bucket in the corner of the yard.

Pen hesitated. It occurred to her that she didn't recognize the youth but that she had known his father, or maybe his uncle. He too had had a surly twist to his mouth and a greasy lock of hair falling across his eyes. But he had been cooperative; it was more than his livelihood was worth to be otherwise in those days.

"Things have changed since I was here last," she observed, fetching the bucket.

The youth spat on the cobbles. "Aye. Them up at the manor. Don't do nothin' fer us no more."

"You don't need them to clean the stables for you," she said acidly.

"Eh, you watch yer tongue, you!" He took a step towards her, and prudently Pen grabbed up the bucket and hurried from the yard. An altercation would do no good at all.

She drew water from the well, and staggered

back with the heavy bucket to the stables wondering what Mary's ladies would say if they could see her now. The princess's confidante up to her elbows in muck and manure.

She watered the horses, led them into the stables, forked unappetizingly damp hay into their troughs, and headed for the inn. Apart from her eagerness to see how Owen was faring, she was thirsty.

Owen was holding court at the taproom counter. He was surrounded by men from the village, all sporting foaming pitch tankards, and even the landlord held his own as he leaned over the stained counter.

"So why'd ye be a-lookin' fer Granny Wardel, sir?" the landlord was asking as Pen slid into the dim room. "A fine city gent like yerself?"

"I'm a lawyer," Owen informed him. His voice had changed, the soft melodic tones accentuated so that he spoke with a pronounced lilting cadence. "I've some news for her . . . something to her advantage," he added with a conspiratorial wink.

"God's bones!" exclaimed a farmer. "Nellie Wardel, come into a fortune!"

"Not quite," Owen temporized. "But if you'd give me her direction . . . ?"

He caught sight of Pen in the shadow of the doorway. She took a step towards him, but with a barely perceptible movement of his hand he waved her back into the shadows.

"Mine host, draw a pint of ale for my servant,

296

if you please." He tossed a coin on the counter. The innkeeper drew ale from a keg and sent the pot skimming down the counter to where Pen stood in isolation.

She took it up without a word and drank thirstily. The name Nellie Wardel had been the first one on the ledger page. Pen had never heard of her, but it seemed she was well known. Granny Wardel. She tried to remember, to picture the faces that had crowded around her in her agony. Was there one that would fit the sobriquet *Granny?*

She couldn't think. All her memories of that dreadful time lurked in the shadows of pain and terror.

Owen turned from the counter and came over to her. He gave her a nod that clearly indicated she was to finish her ale and accompany him. Pen drained the pot and followed him outside.

"I hate to leave the horses in those stables. They're a disgrace," she said in a low voice.

"We'll need them anyway to pay our visit to Granny Wardel. She lives some two miles away across the fields." His voice was his own once more.

Pen needed no instruction. "I'll fetch them then." She gave a mock tug on her forelock and went off on her errand.

She waited until they had remounted and were once more in the relative seclusion of the lane before asking, "What about the other names? Did anyone know anything?"

Owen shook his head. "They seemed to think they were outsiders. A quality that I gathered found little favor with the men of High Wycombe."

"It's the same with all the villages around here. They keep to themselves except for market days and even then they bargain with great mistrust."

"Mmm." Owen seemed to consider this fact. "Useful," he murmured.

"How so?"

"Divide and conquer," he said. He seemed absorbed and Pen wisely left the master to his plotting undisturbed by the flood of questions, reflections, and possibilities that sprang to her lips. She rode quietly beside him as they crossed three fields and approached a small cottage set in a tiny garden beside a pond, where ducks picked their way across the ice.

"You may come in with me, but if you recognize the woman you must leave immediately. That will confirm for me that she was involved in the birth and ensure that she doesn't guess at your identity." He spoke crisply. Pen only murmured an affirmative.

They tethered the horses close to a hedge where they could crop something more appetizing than the stale hay of the stables at the Bryanston Arms. Owen walked briskly up the path and rapped on the door. Pen stood behind him, trying to make herself small and inconspicuous.

The door creaked open. A wizened face

peered out at them. "Well?"

"Mistress Wardel?" Owen inquired politely.

"An' who wants 'er?"

"Esquire Rhoscolyn," Owen said in the same soft lilting cadences he'd used in the tavern.

Welsh! Pen realized. A perfect Welsh accent. She couldn't see the woman clearly as she still stood inside the cottage, the door only opened a crack.

"If I might talk with you for a moment, mistress?" His smile was warm and open. "You had a brother in Highgate, as I understand it."

"Aye?" She still looked suspicious but she opened the door a little wider. "Our Ned. What of 'im?"

"He asked me to bring you something. I'm a lawyer," Owen said. "If we could just go inside . . . out of the wind . . . ?"

With a bemused expression Granny Wardel opened the door wider. Owen stepped into the clean-swept interior of the one-room cottage. He glanced over his shoulder and saw that Pen, who now had a clear view of the woman, was still standing on the pathway.

Granny Wardel had been there that afternoon. She had bathed Pen's forehead with lavender water during one of her more lucid moments.

Pen felt the surge of excitement even as the remembered terror and despair threatened to overcome her. That woman had been there. She would know something. She *must*.

Owen emerged from the cottage after half an

hour. His expression was abstracted, his purse rather lighter than it had been when he'd begun his chat with Granny Wardel.

"What did she say?" Pen asked, unable to keep silent. "Does she know what happened to the baby?"

Owen shook his head. "She wasn't there at the moment of delivery, but she believes that the child was stillborn."

Pen felt disappointment like a suffocating black blanket. "She told you nothing then."

"I didn't say that." He looked at her. She looked so desperate, as if all the life and energy were being pressed out of her.

He said gently, "We have another stop to make, one that I trust will bear fruit."

Pen mounted the dun in silence. "Where are we going now?" she asked finally as they left the cottage behind.

"To Wycombe Marsh. A woman by the name of Betsy Cosham lives there."

The third name on the ledger page. "Betsy Cosham was paid more for her services than any of the other women," Pen said, seeing the page clear in her head.

"So I believe. It didn't help to improve Granny Wardel's opinion of Betsy Cosham, which was very enlightening." He turned his horse through a gap in the hedge beside the lane. "This is a shortcut, I believe. Tell me . . . does the name Mistress Goodlow mean anything to you?"

Pen frowned. "Why, yes, she's Lady Bryanston's herbalist. She has a cottage in the grounds of the estate, and her own herb garden. She physics the entire household."

"Did she attend your labor?"

"I don't remember her being there in particular. She always attended a sickbed so I probably wouldn't have noticed her. She gave me physic during my pregnancy, when I was being sick all the time. Did Granny Wardel mention her?"

"Only in passing. I gather she's no more popular in the neighborhood than Betsy Cosham. Bred from the same bone . . . or birthed from the same cauldron, to use Granny's more vivid terms," he added.

He shook his head. "Witchcraft is an easy accusation, but there's no denying that the power to do good is easily turned to evil's hand. Either way, there's no love at all lost between the midwives of High Wycombe and anyone who might trespass on their territory."

"That's why Granny Wardel told you so much?"

"That and money, my dear. Golden sovereigns will unlock most tongues," he responded sardonically. "She believed I was bringing her a few sovereigns from her brother Ned who had belatedly remembered his duty to his impoverished sister."

"Oh, but I must reimburse you," Pen said hastily. "I have money . . . only I left it in the inn at Gerrards Cross with my own clothes."

301

"We will have an accounting anon," he said.

Pen heard the mock solemnity in his tone. "We *will*," she stated firmly.

"Certainly we will," he agreed. "In fact, I will probably bill you for my services."

"I have already paid for them," Pen said with a taut smile.

Owen had meant it as a light sensual tease, one that he had hoped would lift her mood. "I thought we put that to rest last night," he said.

"Yes," Pen agreed in a low voice. "We had. Old habits die hard, I suppose."

"I suppose," he agreed coldly.

They rode in silence to the hamlet of Wycombe Marsh, and Owen without hesitation drew up at a sizable cottage set well on the outskirts of the hamlet.

"The woman has resources and doesn't care for neighbors," he observed, almost to himself. They dismounted and tethered their horses to the gatepost. "Come in, and if you recognize her, leave immediately."

Betsy Cosham opened the door at the first knock. She was a blowsy woman in her middle years. Her small pale eyes regarded Owen closely. "What's it that you want, sir? I've got most things. And I can lay me 'ands on others."

"May I come in?" Owen asked, reverting to his Welsh accent.

She nodded and held the door for him. She cast Pen a shrewd glance and nodded again. "Best come in," she said, leaving the door open for Pen to follow.

In the dim interior of the cottage Betsy Cosham sat down at the table and surveyed her visitors. "Girl's in trouble then, is she?" She indicated Pen. "Good family is she? That why she 'as to come to Betsy dressed as a boy?" Betsy threw back her head and roared with delighted laughter. "God's blood, girl, you couldn't fool me! No one can put one over on Betsy Cosham."

Except that you've got the wrong end of the stick this time, Pen thought, creeping shyly into the shadows, hunching her shoulders in a fair imitation of a guilty party. She didn't recognize the woman, but that didn't mean she hadn't been in the birthing room. And it seemed a reasonable assumption that the woman wouldn't recognize in this shadowed figure the barely conscious Lady Bryanston, her face a rictus of agony in the throes of labor.

Owen ignored this by-play. "What can you do?"

"Depends 'ow far gone she is." Betsy got up from the table, her stool scraping on the flagstones, and went to a shelf of dusty vials and small boxes. "What are ye, girl? Less 'an three months? 'Tis a lot easier then."

Pen shook her head in mute distress and Owen said brusquely, "Six."

"She never is!" Betsy exclaimed. "I never seen a six-month that skinny."

"It's not for her, it's for her sister," Owen said.

Betsy's eyes narrowed. "Well, I got summat

that'll bring it on early. A six-month won't live."

Pen was so cold she thought she would die. Right there in this vile cottage with its shelves of evil potions. Had Philip's mother come to Betsy for the means to bring on premature labor? Or had she sent Mistress Goodlow?

"And what if it does?" Owen inquired. "What if it's more than six months and it does live?"

"Not my business," Betsy mumbled, but the sudden flash of suspicion in her eyes was like lightning in the dimness of the cottage.

"Take your seat again, Betsy," Owen said, gesturing to the stool. There was something in his voice that electrified the cottage. Pen stepped even farther into the shadows. Betsy almost involuntarily took the stool.

"This is something that *is* your business," Owen continued, his voice now silky smooth. "Let us assume that some two and a half years ago an eight-month child was forced early into the world, but was safely delivered and, against all expectations, managed to survive. What do you think would have happened to this child?"

Betsy had gone as white as chalk. She stared at Owen, her tongue flicking over her lips. A fleck of saliva nestled in the corner of her mouth. "Don't know what y'are talkin' about."

"No?" He took a purse from his doublet and laid it on the table. It chinked. Then he withdrew his dagger from its sheath at his hip and laid it beside the purse. "Let me help you to understand, Betsy."

Betsy's eyes were riveted on the purse and the dagger, on the elegant white hands that rested beside them. Elegant yet embodying strength.

"I offer you your choice of gifts, Betsy. Answer my questions correctly and the purse is yours. Or you could choose the other." He clasped his hands lightly on the table and looked at her.

The dagger was plain, a business tool. No jeweled hilt, nothing but that razor-keen blade. Pen told herself he would never use the knife. Of course he would not follow through on such a threat. An unspoken threat.

But then she realized that she didn't know . . . didn't know whether he would use it any more than she knew anything truly *real* about Owen d'Arcy. He was a spy, and he used a rapier like an assassin. How could she possibly expect to know what he would do?

She felt Betsy's fear, felt the other woman's conviction that this stranger in his dark clothes with his intense black eyes and soft voice would indeed use that dagger.

"I ask again, Betsy. What do you think would have happened to this child?"

She licked her lips, catching the fleck of saliva. Her eyes were scared, her skin gone pasty. "There's places," she muttered finally. "Places to board such a babe. When they're not wanted like."

Not wanted! The words screamed in Pen's head but she stood immobile, barely breathing.

"Who took the child?" Owen's fingers flickered suddenly, lightly touched the blade of the knife, seemed to caress the hilt. Betsy quivered.

"My lord," she said. "My lord took it. Wrapped it in flannel and took it. That's all I know, honest. An' they'll kill me if they ever finds out I told."

"They won't," Owen said calmly. "Where did they take it?"

"I dunno. Truly I dunno," the woman said, wild-eyed with fear.

"Guess!" The knife point drove into the table. His movement was so quick that it eluded even Pen's fixed gaze.

Betsy shuddered. "I 'eard 'em talk of Lunnon."

Owen sheathed the dagger very slowly. As slowly, he pushed the purse across the table. Then he rose and without a word of farewell strode to the door. He put an arm around Pen's shoulders, easing her ahead of him out of the cottage.

"You wouldn't have, would you?" Pen asked, too stunned to take in Betsy's information, her head full of what she had seen Owen do.

"Do what?"

"The knife . . . you wouldn't have hurt her?"

"I knew it wouldn't be necessary," he said quietly.

Pen realized that he had not answered her question, just as she realized that she wouldn't ask it again. There were things better not known.

Slowly what she had heard became real. "My

child," she murmured. "She said the child lived."

"Yes," he agreed. He hesitated, then said, "That does not mean, Pen, that the child *still* lives."

"My child is alive," she stated. "I just have to find him." Her voice was calm and full of a conviction that Owen knew no doubts of his would shake.

"How were you so certain she was lying when she said she knew nothing?" she asked as they reached the end of the path.

"A trick of the trade," Owen replied. He looked down at her and his eyes were cool. "The spy's trade, Pen. I have an infallible sense of when people are concealing information. Isn't that why you wanted my help . . . my professional expertise was how you put it, I believe? You should not balk at the methods I use to achieve the results you want."

"I ask your pardon," Pen said without hesitation. "There was no reason for me to refer to our bargain just then . . . or in that tone. I understand it offended you."

Owen looked at her closely. He was surprised at how hurt and disappointed he had felt when she had started to pick the old bone. But he could see in her candid gaze only genuine regret.

Finally he smiled, and the warmth returned to his eyes. "We will put it behind us, then."

Relieved, she returned his smile. They untied

the horses and set off back to the road to Gerrards Cross.

"So, we look for the child in London," Owen stated.

"But *where?* The city's huge."

"Let me think about it." It was an evasion; he was convinced he knew where Pen's child, if he still lived, was held. Owen was remembering when he'd met Miles among the South Bank stews coming out from one of the more insalubrious alleys. There were very few reasons that would take a man of Miles Bryanston's lineage and wealth into the dangerous, disease-ridden hovels of Southwark.

Owen could think of one, and it filled him with a cold and savage fury.

Sixteen

●

The Duke of Northumberland paced the antechamber to the king's sickroom. It was close to noon. The king's apartments looked out over a courtyard from whence rose the unruly sounds of the crowd gathered to pay homage to their sovereign. Every day a crowd gathered hoping to catch a glimpse of Edward. And every day for weeks now they had been disappointed.

"We must show him today," Northumberland stated. The king's physicians had been summoned to Edward's bedside and the Privy Council now waited impatiently without for their verdict on the king's condition. Would he be fit enough to appear before the people?

The Duke of Suffolk pulled at his short beard as he joined Northumberland. "The people are clamoring to see him," he muttered.

"I have ears. I can hear them myself," Northumberland said irritably. He frequently had difficulty controlling his impatience with his somewhat slower-witted companion. It wasn't that Suffolk was unintelligent, but Northumberland's wit far outstripped his.

Suffolk didn't take offense. He endured too much of his wife's acidity to find the duke's occasional tartness offensive.

"Perhaps we could keep him under wraps for a few more months," Suffolk suggested. "The danger of the cold, of winter chills . . . People will understand that."

"Aye," agreed his companion. "But in a few months he could be dead. And then we have Mary marrying herself to Philip of Spain and clawing back the country for the damned Catholics."

Both men were silent, considering how much of their own personal wealth they would lose if Mary reinstated the Catholic church, as they knew she would. Both men, like their fellows in the king's antechamber, had benefited greatly from the dissolution of the Catholic church, seizing lands, estates, and treasure. Power and titles had followed. They had too much to lose if Mary succeeded Edward.

"Perhaps we could persuade the king to name Elizabeth in Mary's stead," Suffolk suggested hesitantly. "On religious grounds. He always finds religious arguments persuasive. He's such a fanatical Protestant he cannot wish to see his Catholic sister on the throne. Elizabeth professes to be a committed Protestant —"

"Elizabeth is a tricky little bastard," Northumberland interrupted savagely. "She'll say whatever she thinks is politic. No one knows her well and she makes damn sure it stays that way. She's all sweetness and duty to her brother, and has only understanding smiles for her sister. But what goes on in that red head is anyone's guess. She's a damn sight cleverer than she lets on, I'll tell you that, Suffolk."

"So you think she couldn't be managed? She's barely twenty, after all."

"She might be easier than her sister," Northumberland allowed. "But if I can contrive, we'll have neither of 'em."

Suffolk looked as startled as he felt. "You cannot set aside the succession."

"*I* cannot, certainly. But that poor invalid in there might be so persuaded," Northumberland said, his voice very soft, but his eyes burning with a sudden passion.

Suffolk's expression was as suddenly cunning. He stroked his beard again, his fingers twisting and twining in the short graying hairs. "If he puts aside his sisters, my wife, as Henry's niece, is next in line." He looked slyly at Northumberland.

"Aye," Northumberland agreed with a placid smile. "But there'd be little satisfaction in such a resolution for me, Suffolk. The marriage that we have talked about will satisfy all our needs."

"Jane and your son?" Suffolk looked puzzled.

"Precisely." Northumberland waved him down as the door to the king's bedchamber opened and the procession of black-clad physicians emerged, one shaking his head over the lidded chamber pot he held out in front of him.

"Bad, my lord duke. His Highness is very bad," announced the leading physician. "The stimulant we gave him earlier in the hopes it would enable him to rise from his bed has had an ill effect, I fear."

"How so?" snapped the duke. "Apart from the fact that it didn't work."

"Unaccountably it seems to have caused an inflammation of the gut." The physician gestured to the chamber pot. "His Highness has passed much blood."

Northumberland grimaced. "Can he be taken to the window?"

"I would not advise it, your grace."

"Your advice be damned!" Northumberland's raised voice caused a silence to fall over the antechamber.

"Pembroke, tell the king's attendants to wrap him up well and carry him out."

"I most strongly protest, your grace! His Highness will suffer a relapse," the physician protested as the Earl of Pembroke hastened to do the duke's bidding.

"He is already suffering a relapse," Northumberland declared with ice in his voice. "May God preserve us from physicians."

The physician drew himself up to his full height. "I am considered the most skilled of my profession, my lord."

"Aye, and such skill gives me a very poor opinion of your profession," the duke declared rudely. He turned his back on the man, who left the antechamber with an air of self-righteous chagrin.

Someone coughed discreetly at Northumberland's shoulder. "My lord."

The duke glanced at the man who had appeared beside him. He frowned as if searching for his name.

"Bryanston, my lord duke," Miles supplied with an ingratiating smile.

"Oh," Northumberland said testily. "What brings you to the king's antechamber?"

Miles knew that only the members of the Privy Council had unrestricted rights to this holy of holies. But he had his mother's orders and they were ringing in his head.

"I was thinking, my lord duke, that perhaps His Highness's physicians are no longer effective," he said. "It seemed to me that perhaps you share that feeling." He rubbed his hands together nervously, aware that sweat was beginning to trickle down his face.

"What if I do?"

"There are other avenues, my lord." He wiped his face on his turquoise brocade sleeve and turned to pull forward an elderly woman who had been hidden by his bulk. "My family has an old retainer who is a most skilled healer. She has many secrets and wishes to offer her services to the king."

Northumberland stared at the old woman, who surprisingly met his stare with a steady gaze of her own from washed-out gray eyes. There was something assured about her, something that inspired confidence. "Your name, goodwife?" the duke demanded.

"Mistress Goodlow, your grace," Miles answered for her. "A very skilled healer and herbalist. My mother thought —"

"I have no interest in what your mother thinks, let the woman speak for herself," the duke interrupted.

"I have the touch, your grace," the woman said in a soft voice. "I have healed many cases where life hung in the balance."

"Your grace, it would do no harm to let her examine the king, since the physicians don't appear to be doing any good," Miles put in eagerly.

"That is certainly the case," Suffolk declared. He regarded Northumberland speculatively. "We have little to lose."

Northumberland glanced at the Earl of Bryanston, who looked, the duke thought, like a large and overanxious puppy wanting to be let out. "You and Mistress Goodlow may wait in the far antechamber. After the king has been shown to the people, we will talk again."

Miles beamed. His mother would finally be pleased. Now he had access to the real seat of power. He would make himself indispensable to Northumberland and the Privy Council. Mistress Goodlow would attend the king, the healer *he* had placed at the king's bedside. From now on his position would be assured.

The door to the king's bedchamber opened and a stalwart attendant came out, in his arms a slight blanket-swathed bundle.

Northumberland strode across the antechamber. He spoke softly to the bundle. "Highness, the people call for you."

"They are my subjects," Edward said, his voice a bare thread. "I would greet them. Take me to the window, Samuel."

Northumberland gestured that the long windows should be flung open, and as he approached there was a great roar from below. "The king! The king!"

Northumberland stepped to one side so that the attendant carrying the young king could step into view. Bonnets flew in the air and a rousing cheer sent startled pigeons aloft in a flap of beating wings.

Edward could not stand but he insisted the blanket be loosened so that the crowd could see his face. It was a miscalculation. At the sight of the ravaged countenance the crowd fell silent. Edward tried to wave but the effort was too much and he was racked by a violent coughing fit.

Northumberland gestured to the attendant to bring the boy back into the antechamber and himself closed the windows on the crowd, already dispersing in an atmosphere of dejection.

"Take him to his bed," he instructed and followed the attendant to the king's room, Suffolk on his heels. They waited by the door as Edward was once more installed in the huge four-poster.

His body made a barely discernible lump under the covers. The air in the chamber was fetid, reeking of sickness. The windows were tightly shuttered, the fire blazed in the hearth.

The dukes approached the bedside. Edward coughed weakly now and the stench of decay on his breath made his visitors step back.

"Forgive me, Northumberland, but I could not stay longer," he whispered.

The duke waved away the men attending at the bedside and came closer, ignoring the foul odor.

"Northumberland, I am dying," the king whispered. "But there is so much to do first."

"Yes, Highness," Northumberland agreed calmly. There was neither time nor point in denying the truth since the king himself had accepted it. "You must consider well whether you wish to name Princess Mary as your successor."

"She is already named," Edward responded. "My father named her."

"But *you* are king now, sir," Northumberland said gently, holding his pomander to his nose. "You have ruled over a Protestant realm. Would you see it returned to the Catholic church? Your sister will marry Philip of Spain, and Protestant England will fall into the fires of the Inquisition."

Edward groaned. "I would rather burn in hell's fires myself. But how can it be done?"

"I will explain, Highness. When you feel a little stronger." The duke stepped back from the bed. He nodded at Suffolk and the two slipped quietly from the king's bedchamber.

Northumberland pushed through the press of people in the antechamber, ignoring their questions. He passed Miles Bryanston and the old woman but didn't acknowledge them. Instead he made his way to a chamber at the end of the passage, closed the door after Suffolk had entered, and then swiftly and in silence went to work. He looked behind every arras, moved pictures aside to check the walls behind, peered into the fireplace, knocked on the paneling with his knuckles.

"You can never be sure," he said. "Whenever I leave this chamber I'm afraid someone will make it insecure." He ran his hand over a knot in the paneling, frowning, trying to remember if it had been there before. It could well conceal a peephole.

Satisfied at last, he sat down in a carved chair behind a massive table and drummed his fingers on the oak. "The king cannot die until we have arranged the succession to suit us."

He reached into his purple silk doublet for a key and unlocked a drawer in the table. He reached in, felt for the spring that would release the false bottom, and then drew out a sealed package. This he laid on the table in front of Suffolk.

"As we agreed, I have drawn up marriage contracts betrothing your daughter, Lady Jane, to my own son, Guildford Dudley. You and your wife should look them over carefully, but I think you will find that they are exactly as we agreed."

Suffolk picked up the sealed package and tapped it against his palm. "I take it the marriage should take place without delay."

"Within a few weeks."

Suffolk nodded. "Lady Frances will inform Jane. The girl may have some silly objections since there is a precontract with Lord Hertford, but my dear wife will have no difficulty overriding any objections."

"I am sure not," Northumberland agreed. He had little doubt that the formidable duchess would prevail over her timid dab of a daughter. "In the meantime, we should perhaps try the skills of Bryanston's herbalist. The king has to live long enough to alter the succession in favor of his cousin Jane. He must exclude both sisters and settle the throne on Jane."

"And by extension her husband, your son," Suffolk said rhetorically.

"And my son," Northumberland agreed. "In the meantime we must calm the jittery nerves of the French, who are terrified that with Edward on his deathbed, Mary will marry Philip of Spain. No one must have an inkling of what we intend. I suggest we inform the French that we are making plans for Mary's marriage to the Duc d'Orleans. An alliance they have long sought. It should keep de Noailles busy for a while."

Suffolk regarded him closely. It was clear to him that Northumberland knew where he was going with this. "And?" he prompted.

"Beaucaire's sister," Northumberland said,

steepling his fingers. "She appears to have taken up with a French agent. It occurred to me that it might be a useful connection so I told Robin to leave it alone, let it develop."

"You would use her to pass information to the French?"

"Precisely. Robin is very close to her, she would never question anything he told her. He will tell her what we want the French to know." Northumberland smiled his thin smile. "Neat, don't you think, Suffolk?"

"Very."

"Meanwhile, we must ensure that Mary remains in the palace under our eye. She still insists that she's too ill to leave her chamber, and she continues to importune the king for a visit, but of course the king doesn't receive her messages."

Northumberland rose abruptly, as if he'd said all he was going to on the subject. "Let us see this woman Goodlow again. If she does the king any good I suppose that fool Bryanston will want some favor in exchange. We'll find him another earldom or something." He left the chamber in his usual energetic fashion, Suffolk on his heels.

Pen stretched and gave a languid yawn. It was still dark. The embers of the fire glowed and her bedchamber in the Bull inn was warm and quiet and secluded as the womb. She turned on her side, pressing her lips into the hollow of Owen's shoulder, licking the salt tang of his skin as he slept.

He murmured something and put out an arm, sliding it beneath her so that he held her close.

"Are you still sleeping?" she inquired against his skin. "Can I not wake you?"

"I sleep the sleep of the just," he returned and she could hear the smile in his voice. "And in justice should be permitted to return to my dreams."

Pen moved a hand beneath the covers. She smiled in her turn as she felt his flesh grow hard in her grasp. "Justice demands that I reap my just deserts." She rolled over him, settling astride his thighs. She ran her hands up over his belly, over his ribs, pressing the hot wet furrow of her body against his hard jutting sex. "I don't believe that you're still sleeping."

"No, it appears not," Owen agreed. He cupped her knees, slid his hands along the smooth planes of her thighs, held her hips.

Pen lifted her hips a fraction and guided him within. Her body closed around him and she held herself still, savoring the feel of him as he grew to fill her, as his penis pulsed against the tight sheath that enclosed him.

Owen threw his hands up over his head and raised his hips. He moved within her in a leisurely rhythm. Pen laughed softly, matching his rhythm, as the pleasure built slowly, inexorably. It was only the fourth time they had made love and yet it seemed she knew his body as intimately as her own. She fought to hold off the orgasmic joy, to hold on to the edge for one more glorious second. But at last she let go, yielded to the wash of pleasure, let it take her where it would.

She buried her face in his shoulder, tasting the sweat of his fulfillment. The air was rich with the smell of sex, of their conjoined flesh. His penis was small and soft within her now. Slowly, reluctantly, she rolled away from him to lie at his side.

Owen stroked the curve of her cheek, twisted his hands in the tangle of her hair as it lay tumbled over his shoulder.

"This time we were not careful," Pen whispered. "I preferred it thus."

"I too," he replied. "But I'd not wish for any undue consequences." He hitched himself onto an elbow, leaning over her. "You would not, either, Pen."

"Not now," she agreed. She raised her eyes to his, a question now in her steady gaze. "But what of you, Owen? Would you one day like to have a child?"

Owen's face closed, and while his position didn't change she felt his sudden withdrawal. "There's no room in my life for children," he said, sitting up and flinging the coverlet aside.

Lucy and Andrew. They both had their mother's eyes. Green as moss.

Pen lay still as he sat in silence, staring into the middle distance. Her skin was cold and her spirit suddenly weighted with dismay. She should not have asked such an intimate question. They were lovers but there was so much about him that she did not know. So much about himself that he would not reveal. Was it simply the excessive caution that a spy's life made necessary? Or was it something else, something essential to the man himself?

She stretched out a hand to touch his back. His skin was as hot as hers was cold. There was something badly wrong. She could sense his hurt through his skin. It was as if he was lost again, as he had been the day before when his horse had nearly trampled the child. Unable to keep silent, she asked softly, "Owen, what's troubling you?"

There was a moment's silence in which she wished she had not probed further. Then he seemed almost visibly to shake off that moment of depression. "Nothing . . . an old story." He leaned over and lightly slapped her turned flank. "Come, get up now. We have to be on the road to London at first light."

What old story? She wanted to know, but even if he hadn't closed the subject, there was no time to pursue it. The sooner they got back to London, the sooner she would find her child. Owen had too many mysteries to be solved in a moment. This one too would wait.

She jumped from the bed, hurried to the coffer for her shift and hose that Mary had washed for her and laid in lavender the previous day while she was roaming the countryside in Cedric's clothes.

She bent to open the coffer. Owen looked at her, aroused once again by the pearly glow of her bare skin, the delicious curves of her out-thrust backside, the line of her spine, the sweet hollows behind her knees.

She stood up with the garments, holding them against her as she turned towards him.

"You couldn't do it again, could you?" she said with a degree of astonishment as she saw his arousal.

"Very easily," he replied.

"Well, we haven't time," Pen declared, hastily dropping the shift over her head to cover her inviting nakedness. She sat on the chest at the foot of the bed to put on her hose. "Should I call for Mary or will you lace me?"

"Call for Mary. Much as I would enjoy it, I have to dress myself." He thrust his arms into his own night robe and strode to the door.

"I know you're not going very far but will you not kiss me goodbye after such a night?" Pen smiled at him, holding out her arms. It seemed too unceremonious to part with such sudden haste after the long glorious hours of their love-making.

He turned back. "I was trying to resist temptation," he offered. He put his hands at her waist and kissed her mouth. She closed her eyes automatically, then suddenly opened them. Something didn't feel right. It felt as if he wasn't truly there. Owen's eyes were wide open and he seemed to be looking over her head even though his mouth was warm and firm on hers.

Chilled, Pen pulled back. She laughed a little awkwardly. "Your mind's on other things."

"Forgive me, I was distracted," Owen agreed. He smiled apologetically. "My only excuse is that my mind is on your business, Pen. I'm anxious to be on the road."

"As am I," Pen said, stepping away from him. She believed him but it still made her uncomfortable to think that he could appear to be so physically close and yet actually be a world away. "I will join you below stairs as soon as I'm dressed."

Owen hesitated, as if he would say something more, then he kissed her again quickly and left her.

In his own chamber he awoke Cedric and dressed rapidly. There were times when his ability to separate his mind from his actions was something of a liability. He had kissed Pen because she'd asked him to, but his mind had been elsewhere. Most women didn't notice, but Pen was a woman of a different order, and until that moment their lovemaking had always engaged him completely. It was not surprising that she had noticed his distraction.

But he had been thinking of how to approach the next step in Pen's quest. He didn't want to go sniffing around the South Bank stews too obviously in search of stray children in case it alerted the Bryanstons, so he needed a device. He needed a reason to go from brothel to brothel, and the only foolproof plan he could think of would have to involve Pen. He had not yet told her what he suspected of the child's whereabouts. Indeed, he didn't know how he was going to, but she had to know.

And then they would face another problem. Would Pen be able to identify a two-year-old child on whom she had never laid eyes?

Seventeen

●

It was early evening when they returned to Greenwich Palace. Owen left Pen at the road entrance to the palace. It was the back way in and people still thronged the road, pressed through the gates either coming or going, merchants and barrow boys, laundresses and cooks, heralds and grooms, all serving the palace's needs.

"I will await you at the water steps at eight o'clock," Owen said quietly. "You will be free for the evening then?"

"I would think so. Mary, even when she's behaving like herself and not an invalid, generally retires early to her prayers and a few hours of quiet study. . . . Oh, do be still, William!" she exclaimed as the gelding pulled against the reins, anxious to return to the familiar stable.

"I would be very happy if I were never to lay eyes on that animal again," Owen observed, surveying the restive horse with acute disfavor. William had made the latter part of their day's ride after they'd retrieved him from the inn at Northolt somewhat eventful.

"He behaves beautifully in the country," Pen said defensively.

"That I do not believe," Owen stated. "The

sooner you're off his back the happier I will be. He's a thoroughly dangerous mount."

"I own I had expected him to behave better," Pen said with a sigh.

"Well, we will go by water tonight. Wear a thick cloak, it will be cold."

"If I cannot get away by eight . . . ?" She regarded him anxiously.

"I will wait until nine. After that it'll be too late and we must try another night."

"I cannot wait another night!" Pen said in a low voice that throbbed with urgency. "But where are we going to start to look? I know you have some plan . . . some idea."

Owen hesitated. He'd managed to evade her questions all day because he couldn't bear the torment the truth would cause her. She would have too long to dwell on it, to imagine it. Too long to suffer the agonies of inaction.

Pen's clear-eyed gaze rested on his face. She saw the sudden spurt of rage in the black eyes that met hers. She recoiled from it and William snorted and stamped.

"I do have a plan," he said, the flatness of his voice doing nothing to diminish that flash of fury. "But it needs some refining and I would keep it to myself for the moment."

He smiled at her, and his expression was once more calm and seemingly untroubled. "I am never comfortable sharing my plans until they're perfectly in place, Pen. It's a trick of my trade, I'm afraid."

"Very well," she said. "I'll meet you at eight at the water steps."

"Until then." He leaned over and lightly brushed her lips with his before he turned his horse back onto the London road.

Pen joined the throng passing through the gate into the rear courtyard of the palace. No one remarked her. A groom took William from her in the busy stable and led him away, the horse throwing up his head against the hand on his bridle as he surged eagerly towards the stables.

Pen entered the palace and hurried to her own chamber, keeping her hood up, her head lowered. She had no wish to be accosted by anyone who knew her until she'd remedied her appearance, which she was sure was far from courtly.

Nutmeg was as usual curled on the end of the bed. He raised one eye and turned his back, showing his disapproval of Pen's absence.

She pulled his ears and tickled his chin until he relented and greeted her with a rough tongue on her hand and a deep-throated purr. "Stupid cat," she said. "You knew I was coming back. I always come back."

She rang the handbell for her maid and cast aside her cloak, examining her reflection in the glass. Her suspicions had been correct. The ruff of her gown was bedraggled, the hem of the figured silk underskirt splashed and muddied from the road. Ordinarily she would have worn a safeguard to protect her gown while riding but she'd been in such a hurry she'd forgotten such niceties.

Ellen muttered when she saw the condition of her mistress's gown. She announced that she had been very surprised Lady Pen had gone to the Earl and Countess at Holborn without taking her. And to go without a word and without taking so much as a night bag.

"It was very sudden, Ellen, and I have clothes enough there," Pen said soothingly. "And you know Tilly would not let anyone but herself take care of me."

This was so true that Ellen was somewhat placated, although she kept a ruffled silence while she fetched hot water and towels, then helped Pen into a fresh gown and readjusted her coiffure.

"Just a simple linen hood and coif, Ellen," Pen instructed. "I'll not be supping in company tonight."

When she was dressed in a plain gown of gray damask with a white pleated partlet to the throat, a dark gray hood and crisp white coif, Pen felt as modestly attired as a nun. Mary would approve it as suitable for a sickroom, she reflected as she smoothed the folds of her skirts.

"Ellen, I will sup alone in my chamber after I've seen the princess. Then I shall retire early. I will not be needing you after seven o'clock."

"Very good, m'lady. Oh, and Lord Robin's been here, asking for you. He wanted to know if you'd returned. Quite surprised I was. I'd have thought he'd know when you'd be back, seeing as how you were with the family at Holborn."

Pen thought quickly. Pippa must have told Robin the truth, otherwise he would have assumed like the rest of her family that she was closeted with the princess. He would not betray her, though.

"Oh, Lord Robin's been kept busy with the duke," she said vaguely. "I'm sure I'll see him later."

It had all seemed so simple in the single-minded urgency of her planning. Now, amid all the familiarities of her ordinary life, the difficulties she had so blithely dismissed took on a new dimension. She couldn't begin to imagine how she could continue to deceive both her parents and the princess about her whereabouts over the last four days. Ellen, for a start, could well say something about her mistress's unorthodox departure which would get back to Guinevere.

But if she found her child none of that would matter. Everything would be explained. Even Mary would have to understand.

But if she failed to find her son . . .

No, she would not even consider that possibility.

"I'm going to the princess now." She hurried away to the princess's apartments before Ellen could make any more awkward observations.

A chorus of voices greeted her when she entered the antechamber.

"Oh, Pen, the princess is so sick," Lady

330

Matilda said, jumping to her feet in a shower of embroidery silks. "Since you left she won't admit any of us to her chamber. She sees only the physician and Lucy."

Lucy was Mary's handmaid, a woman as passionately devoted to her mistress as she was to the Catholic church, a woman whose hands were as deft as her tongue was still.

"And the king," another lady began. "While you were gone they carried the king to the window to show him to the people calling for him in the courtyard. He was too weak to walk but the duke insisted he be carried to them. But when the people saw his face no one cheered or threw up their hats." She gave an exaggerated shudder. "So ill as he looked!"

Pen listened in a kind of despair to the flood of information. She wasn't interested in any of it. Indeed, it seemed to her that the person who would have been interested four days ago no longer existed. This babble merely interfered with the only thing that concerned her. All her energies were devoted to getting to the water steps by eight o'clock without hindrance. And yet she had to pay the expected attention to the chatter around her. The king's health was a matter of huge moment to Mary, but Pen at this moment wouldn't have cared if Edward had died in her absence.

"Forgive me, but I must go at once to the princess." She interrupted the chatter with a brisk gesture and turned to the door to Mary's bedchamber.

"Madam, are you truly ill?" she exclaimed, hurrying to the bed, for a moment forgetting her own turmoil in her anxiety at the princess's appearance. Mary lay propped on pillows, her face whiter than the fine linen on which she lay. Her eyes were sunken, dark bruises beneath them.

"Oh, Pen, I have had such need of you," she said weakly. Her hand seemed like a skeleton when Pen took it.

Mary looked at death's door and Pen's first thought was poison. "Have you eaten anything unusual, madam?"

"Nothing that Lucy hasn't tasted," Mary said. "No, I think the good doctor has been overly zealous in the purging and the cupping. I can barely move."

"Why did you not stop him?" Pen demanded. "It was for you to say, madam, surely?"

A flicker of annoyance appeared in the princess's cloudy eyes. "Northumberland paid me a visit this afternoon. I had no choice but to convince him of the seriousness of my condition. Had you been here, Pen, you could have managed him for me."

Pen made no response. Shocked though she was at the princess's appearance, she wasn't about to encourage Mary's petulance with voluble apologies.

"Has your request to visit the king been granted?" she asked neutrally.

"I do not believe Northumberland relays my requests," Mary declared, sounding stronger by the minute. "But I think he came here to assess my condition himself."

"Then maybe, since he cannot help but be persuaded of the gravity of your illness, he will now pass your message to the king."

"No," Mary said definitely. "He will not. I would take some gruel, Pen. It's time to regain my strength."

Pen gave her the silver porringer and sat beside the bed while Mary ate several spoonfuls.

"I understand that the duke insisted your brother be shown to the people," she said, handing Mary a goblet of wine. She was relieved to see some slight color reappear in the princess's countenance.

She added, "I understand that it was not a successful appearance."

"No, Lucy told me as much," Mary replied, her voice much stronger.

She took another sip of wine. "My brother is near death and I must find a way to leave here without delay, Pen. In the morning you must help me. We must think of how I may leave this place secretly and make my escape back to Essex. My cousin's ships are waiting off the coast. If my danger grows too great, one will take me to Flanders. On Edward's death I will return as rightful queen with the emperor's army at my back."

The film of weakness had lifted from her eyes and her intense gray gaze fixed upon Pen's countenance as she made this declaration with quiet determination. "Northumberland shall *not* get the better of me."

Pen would not dampen this resolution with doubts about the Holy Roman Emperor's willingness to launch a bloody war to secure his cousin's throne. The emperor was a cold and calculating monarch. He could well decide that Mary's throne was not worth risking his own men. Once she was in his hands, he would be able to marry her off wherever he needed an alliance.

Mary's throne depended on her remaining on English soil. But Pen said nothing of these reflections.

"No, madam," she agreed. "He will not. Let me think tonight how best to proceed." She rose to her feet. "I'm certain we can find a way. But if you have no further need of me now, I would go to my chamber. I find myself very fatigued."

It was Mary's turn to look concerned. "I trust you've not caught a chill, Pen. I would expect Lady Kendal to have taken a care for your health."

Pen gave a little laugh. "No, madam, I have no chill, but my sister has little need of sleep and she and I sat up late most nights and rose early. Pippa has always fatigued me, dearly though I love her." The lie tripped off her tongue with surprising ease. She had not thought herself particularly adept at falsehood.

"Well, if that is all . . ." Mary looked relieved. "Go to your rest, Pen, and in the morning we will discuss what I should do next."

And in the morning I might be holding my child in my arms.

The reflection made Pen dizzy. She put out a hand against the intricately carved and gilded bedpost. If tonight she found her child, there would be no need for further lies. Mary, even in her present danger, would *have* to understand Pen's deception. Selfish, arrogant, petulant, Mary was all of those things. She was after all her father's daughter. But she had a deep core of decency and justice. And loyalty to those who stood by her.

Mary as queen would have total power over her subjects . . . power to sign a death warrant or a pardon.

Power to help a friend establish the legitimacy of a stolen child, and power to punish the thieves.

The moment of dizziness passed and Pen was relieved to see that Mary hadn't noticed it. She bade the princess good night and left her, pausing only for a few minutes in the antechamber, where the ladies pressed her to join them for supper.

"No . . . no, I'm very tired," she demurred. "I shall sup in my chamber." She left on a chorus of good-nights, forcing herself to resist the urge to run to her chamber, forcing herself to nod at acquaintances she passed in the corridors, to exchange polite greetings with others. To all she said she was on the princess's business, and no one attempted to delay her.

Ellen brought her supper, with a saucer of minced rabbit for Nutmeg, who rose high on his legs, arching his back in a leisurely stretch before jumping off the bed and approaching the saucer with a supercilious air.

"I won't need you again tonight, Ellen," Pen said, buttering a piece of wheaten bread. "You may leave and attend me in the morning."

"You don't need me to help you to bed, madam?"

"No . . . no, I can manage myself, thank you." Pen took up a chicken drumstick and smiled dismissal at the maid.

As soon as Ellen had left, Pen put down the chicken with a grimace of distaste. She had no appetite, her stomach was churning with excitement and terror.

She sat and watched the clock.

The knock on the door was so unexpected, so startling and unwelcome, that at first Pen didn't react. It came again and this time Robin's voice accompanied the knock.

"Pen? Pen, I know you're in there. I need to talk to you." He opened the door as he spoke and stood in the doorway, his hand still on the latch, as if waiting for permission to enter. It was not something he ordinarily waited for since Pen would never refuse him such permission, but this evening he was hesitant. The woman he knew had changed and he wasn't sure the old rules, or the absence of them, still applied. And what he had come to say, had steeled himself to say, was so abhorrent to him that he felt strangely as if he was forcing himself upon her.

Pen glanced at the clock. It was close to seven. In half an hour she would go. It would take her fifteen minutes to reach the water steps and she wanted to leave plenty of time.

"I'm very tired, Robin," she said, leaning her head against the chair back with a wan smile. "Can we talk in the morning?"

"This won't take very long." With a resolute air he came fully into the chamber and closed the door at his back.

Pen felt a surge of desperation. She had to get rid of him. "Robin, please, can't this wait?"

"No," he said. "You have to believe me, Pen, I don't want to tell you this." He pulled off his gloves and blew on his hands, cupping them over his mouth as he frowned into the fire. "But I can't stand aside. I love you too much to keep silent."

"This is about Owen d'Arcy, I assume." Her voice was cold. She could think of no other way to drive him away. "I have told you before, Robin, that that is my business."

"Where did you go with him?"

"That is also my business. If this is all you've come to talk about, I tell you straight I will not hear you." Her eyes flickered again to the clock. "I don't wish to quarrel with you but I will *not* talk of Owen with you."

"You don't need to talk. I'm going to talk and

you must listen to me." Robin gave her no time for a response. "The chevalier is a French agent, Pen. He's working for the French ambassador."

"I know that," Pen said scornfully. "He told me so himself . . . presumably to forestall any tale-telling," she added sardonically. She had to keep up the offensive.

Robin flushed and his discomfort was translated into aggression. "And did he tell you about his wife, also? And his children?"

Pen found it hard to breathe for a minute. "He told me he wasn't married," she said softly.

"He's not . . . not now." Robin saw that at last he had her attention. He began to pace the chamber, slapping one fist into the palm of the other hand. "I'm sorry, but you have to hear me out, Pen."

"I'm listening," she said, her voice flat. She stood up abruptly as if better to withstand a blow, her arms unconsciously crossed over her breast. Robin paced as he told her the tale Simon Renard had told him. He didn't embellish, and he left out nothing.

"He declared his children to be bastards?" Pen said when he had fallen silent. It was said more to herself than in expectation of a response.

"So I understand."

"And he hasn't seen them since?" She shivered, and tightened her arms across her chest.

"So I understand. My informant is . . . is reliable," he said.

"Another spy?"

338

"In a manner of speaking."

"And that world is yours too," Pen stated. She required no confirmation but this was the first time it had been openly acknowledged between them.

"I ask that you keep that knowledge to yourself," he said.

Pen merely shook her head with a touch of impatience. Robin knew she would never betray him.

By the same token, she knew he would not lie to her. She had to believe what he'd told her. Not only would Robin never make up such a tale, but it answered so many questions, solved so much of the mystery that surrounded Owen. But was he capable of such cruelty? She had accused him of using her unhappiness for his own ends. It was true that he had. But he hadn't pretended any other motive.

He had not wanted to talk of children, said he had no place for them in his life. He had been so distressed over the little girl in the lane. . . .

Guilt . . . remorse . . . regret. Was that what dogged him at those moments when he looked so hurt and lost? Was he helping her find *her* child because of guilt over his own?

Her eyes flicked again involuntarily to the clock. It chimed the half hour as she looked at it. *His reasons didn't matter.*

"Pen?" Robin moved towards her and she shook her head.

"No . . . Go. Go now. *Please.*"

"Pen . . . Pen . . . I'm so sorry. I hate to hurt you."

"I know. But leave me *now!*" She held up a hand as if to push him away. "I need to be alone."

Robin hesitated, uncertain, unwilling to leave her alone when she looked so white and desperate. He wanted to comfort her, stay with her until she was herself again.

Pen stared at the long hand of the clock creeping to the seven. *"Get out!"*

Robin knew he could not stay, whatever his own needs. He turned and left without another word.

Feverishly now Pen swathed herself in her cloak, pulled on her gloves. Whatever Owen d'Arcy had done, she needed him. Until she had her child in her arms she would not see him as a man capable of disowning his own tiny children. She would not think of him as capable of such savagery towards a woman whom the world considered blameless. She would not think of him at all except as a means to an end.

Why, in God's good grace, did Robin have to choose tonight of all nights to spill his tale?

No! There was no room in her head for anything but what this night would bring. She drew the hood of her cloak well over her head and opened the chamber door, peering down the corridor half afraid that Robin would be mounting guard in the passage. But there was no sign of him.

She left the palace as she had done before by back corridors used mostly by servants. A light cold rain had begun to fall when she stepped outside. She glanced up at the moonless sky and wondered distantly if this weather would suit Owen's plan. Whatever plan the spy had concocted.

She hurried along the redbricked path beneath the dripping archway of yews, her way lit by the pitch torches planted along the path that led to the river. Lights flickered from the cressets of barges drawn up at the dock, and the wherries and sculls waiting in midstream in the hopes of a passenger. The river was as busy by night as by day.

She emerged from the shadows and saw Owen immediately. He was standing at the edge of the dock, looking towards the path from the palace. He raised a hand when he saw her, an almost infinitesimal gesture of both greeting and warning — as if she needed the latter, Pen reflected.

She scanned the various groups of people on the dock awaiting transport into London, but to her relief she saw no one she knew. She retreated farther into her hood and walked casually to the edge of the dock where Owen stood.

Without waiting for her to reach him he stepped aboard a substantial barge that she saw had the luxury of cabin housing. It must be a private barge. But whose?

She stepped aboard as nonchalantly as he had. The oarsmen glanced at her, and the man at the

341

tiller yelled an order as soon as her foot touched the deck. Men rushed to untie the barge. Pen ducked into the cabin, feeling the boat move beneath her as it swung away from the dock.

"Good, you're early," Owen said as Pen stepped into the cabin that was lit only by a swaying oil lamp hanging from the low ceiling. His voice was rather clipped, his expression detached, and Pen welcomed the distance. She could not have endured kisses and soft words.

She was struck immediately by something different about him. She peered up at him in the shadowy light of the flickering lamp. He was shrouded in a long, thick, black cloak edged with some unidentifiable dark fur. She realized that the jewel on the turned-back brim of his black cap was paste. And then she saw the faint scar running down the side of his face and the odd twist of his mouth; even the shape of his chin had changed.

He looked disreputable, she realized with a shock. The elegant Frenchman had been replaced by a disreputable, slightly seedy man in cheap and unremarkable clothing. And it wasn't just the clothing, it was the way he was holding himself, everything about his posture. His shifty gaze added to the impression of a man who dabbled in unsavory business.

It was easy to imagine that this was a man who could betray women and children.

She closed off the thought as if she were plugging a leak, and looked around the small cabin that was furnished with rich hangings at the small windows and heavily cushioned benches set into the hull. It was as luxurious as one of the royal craft.

"Whose barge is this?"

"The ambassador's," he answered. "There are some advantages in the connections I have."

Pen merely nodded. She was as tense as a coiled spring, her thoughts and emotions a turmoil of wretched bewilderment, agitation, determination, conviction. She wouldn't have cared if the ambassador himself with an entire army of French spies was on board so long as they didn't hinder her.

It was stuffily warm in the brazier-warmed cabin and she loosened her cloak. Owen suddenly smiled and for the first time looked like his familiar self. "You're dressed for a convent, sweetheart. Not at all suitable for the role I would have you play tonight."

"What role is that?" Her hands were now clenched, the nails biting into her palms. He mustn't touch her. She couldn't bear it.

He made no move to do so, however, answering simply, "A whore. Fortunately I've brought the costume for you."

"And what role are you playing?" she asked, her body as taut as a bowstring.

"A pimp," he replied as if it was the most natural thing in the world.

Pen inhaled slowly. It certainly explained his altered appearance. She'd never knowingly encountered a pimp, but this seedy, slightly menacing figure that the elegant Owen had become would surely fit the bill. It still seemed extraordinary, however.

"Are you serious?"

"Deadly so. If one is to frequent whorehouses 'tis wise to look the part."

Pen stared at him as the implication sunk in. "My son is in a *whorehouse?*"

"If I'm right," he responded. Quietly he told her how he'd seen Miles Bryanston emerging from the back alleys of the South Bank stews. Owen had dreaded making this revelation but saw to his surprise that Pen didn't seem particularly shocked.

She listened in silence. Owen's suspicions didn't have the power to horrify her. For two years she had lived with such terrible depths of uncertainty that knowledge itself, however grim, was a relief.

"These places board unwanted children," she said almost to herself when he'd finished. Her eyes darted to his face, watching for some reaction to such a description. There was no change on his countenance or in his eyes.

"I think, in general, they tend to be the unfortunate consequences of their mothers' profession," he replied aridly. "One child more or less isn't going to cause much trouble, and I'm sure the Bryanstons are paying heavily for both the privilege and the silence."

Pen stood clasping her elbows. "So what is your plan?"

"I am going to sell you to the highest bidder."

She stared, uncomprehending. "What do you mean?"

"We'll visit each establishment, and at each one I'll be offering you for sale. I won't like the price so we'll move on to the next until we find what we're looking for."

"Children?"

"Or evidence of such. Once we've narrowed the field, we'll decide how best to proceed."

"If I find my child tonight, I'm taking him," she declared with a fierce light in her hazel eyes.

"Will you recognize him?" Owen asked, watching her closely.

Pen shook her head. "I don't know," she said, and the fierce light died under a wash of despair. "How could I possibly know? I've never laid eyes on him."

"Well, we'll cross that bridge when we come to it," Owen said briskly. "Now, to make our preparations." He heaved a leather bag onto the table, which was bolted to the floor in the center of the cabin.

Pen watched as he took out a ragged gown of blue linen and a grimy petticoat. "Those are for me?" She couldn't help wrinkling her nose at the stale smell coming from the garments.

"You need to look the part. Let me unlace you."

Pen submitted, although her muscles tensed as she waited for his touch on her skin. His fingers were deft, accomplishing the task swiftly and without straying. Pen understood that the spy on business had no time for loverlike caresses.

She relaxed slightly but couldn't help a shudder as she donned the petticoat and the gown. "Where have they been? They could be diseased."

"No, I assure you they look worse than they are," Owen responded. He laced the blue dress, which was so low cut it barely covered her nipples.

Pen stared down at the white mounds rising from the décolletage. "I didn't know I was so well endowed," she muttered.

" 'Tis the gown as much as anything," he replied.

In other circumstances Pen would have offered a humorously ironic response to this unflattering albeit true statement. But she had no laughter in her tonight.

He turned back to the bag and took out a small tin. "Come under the light."

Pen did so. He opened the tin and took out a brush, some blackish powder, and a chalky gray paste. He turned her face up and went to work.

"What are you doing exactly?" Pen asked as his fingertips smoothed the powder under one of her eyes.

"Making you look like an abused whore," he told her.

Pen grimaced but asked no more questions.

Finally he stepped back and examined his handiwork. "I think that'll pass muster."

"I wish I had a mirror."

"You won't like what you see, but if you must, this'll give you some idea." He took a small circle of beaten copper from his bag of tricks and held the swaying oil lamp steady for her.

Pen saw a complexion gray with grime and ill health. One eye had a dreadful purplish bruise that spread down her cheekbone. Her lips had the appearance of being slightly swollen. "This is horrible," she whispered.

"It's meant to be." He sounded suddenly detached. "The women in these places are not there through choice. They're in the gutter with nowhere else to go. If you went there looking fresh and untouched it would instantly arouse suspicion. You'll have no need to say anything, just keep behind me, look afraid, cower . . . whatever strikes you as appropriate. And just follow my lead."

Pen nodded and turned away from the dreadful image in the copper. The reality of where they were going had now become hard-edged and she was filled with dread. If her child *was* alive, how would she find him? Neglected, hurt . . .

Dear God, she couldn't bear to think of it.

Eighteen

●

"Robin? I'm glad I ran into you. I want a word."
The Duke of Northumberland loomed out of
the shadows in the great hall, stepping out from
behind a pillar, almost, Robin thought, as if he'd
been lying in wait.

Robin stopped, not sorry to have some distraction from the turmoil of his own thoughts.

"My lord?"

Northumberland glanced around. The hall
was crowded even at this hour. "Come to my
privy chamber in half an hour." He walked off on
the instruction.

Robin shrugged. It struck him as rather late
for such a summons even from Northumberland, who had no schedule for his scheming, but
it was not a summons to be ignored.

Exactly half an hour later he presented himself
to the sentry who stood at the door to the duke's
privy chamber. The sentry, obviously warned to
expect him, opened the door for him immediately.

He was not at once acknowledged by the three
men in the chamber, who continued their conversation.

"The marriage date is fixed for Whitsunday,"

Northumberland said. "The young people should improve their acquaintance in the meantime. Guildford will wait upon Jane in the next day or two. . . . Ah, Robin, there you are, good." Northumberland from the carved seat behind his massive oak desk waved him to an armless chair.

Robin bowed to the Duke of Suffolk and the Earl of Pembroke, who were standing together beside the arched window that looked down onto the torchlit courtyard.

They nodded at Robin and went to take chairs on either side of the desk. He thought they both looked tense, and he sensed an air of expectation in the chamber.

Robin took his seat, none of his speculation apparent on his countenance. He'd had his suspicions that Northumberland was planning to marry off his youngest son to Lady Jane Grey, Suffolk's daughter, and now he had his confirmation. But what was the marriage designed to achieve, apart from the simple uniting of two ducal houses? Northumberland would have something more devious in mind, Robin was convinced.

"We are to celebrate a marriage, my lord duke?" he inquired placidly.

"Aye, my son and Jane Grey," Northumberland said, rubbing his chin. "The king has given his blessing."

"My felicitations to both parties," Robin said, even as he wondered how poor little Jane was taking the news of her impending nuptials. Not well, he was certain. She had little liking for any of the Dudley sons. They were rough and had often bullied her as a child.

Had this summons anything to do with the wedding? For the moment he forgot his preoccupation with Pen and Owen d'Arcy. These three men were the most prominent members of the Privy Council. He knew them well but had never before been invited to participate in their deliberations.

"Well, enough of that," Northumberland said, steepling his fingers. "Robin, we would talk of your sister."

The preoccupation flooded back. Robin said nothing, but he was now very still, every nerve stretched.

"Lady Pen still keeps close company with Chevalier d'Arcy," Northumberland continued. He raised an inquiring eyebrow. "That is still the case, I believe. They were much together over the Christmas season."

"Aye, very close," Suffolk put in. "Lady Pen shows a distinct partiality for the chevalier's company."

"What of it, my lord?" Robin demanded, his tone curt to the point of discourtesy.

Northumberland waved Suffolk into silence and stated as if answering Robin's question, "The chevalier is a French agent."

So that was it? Northumberland had finally come up with a way in which Pen's connection with the spy could be turned to good use. In grim silence Robin waited for enlightenment.

Northumberland leaned forward over the desk. "Is your sister aware of that fact?"

"Of course not, my lord duke," Robin replied, his gaze clear, his expression calm as a millpond, no hint of his inner turmoil as he sought the best way to protect Pen.

"My sister knows nothing of spies. She has had a great deal of tragedy in her life in the last few years and it seems that the chevalier has offered her some distraction. Her family have seen no harm in it." His voice was bland and only someone listening for it would have heard the challenge running deep beneath.

Northumberland was not listening for it. He drummed his fingers on the desk, the great ruby on his finger glowing ruddy in the light of the lamp. "I see a way to turn the situation to our advantage. We need to get some information to the French . . . information that's not exactly true." A thin smile flickered over his mouth.

Robin's nostrils flared as he sensed what was coming but he waited with every appearance of polite attention.

The duke continued, gesturing to Suffolk and Pembroke, "My lords and I have decided that we will use Lady Pen in this business. Whatever she tells the chevalier that is pertinent to French interests, he will inevitably pass on to his masters. We need right now to give them something that will keep them too busy to meddle in our real business." He chuckled. It was a sinister sound, quite without humor.

"Robin, you will use your sister to pass on certain information to her lover."

He rubbed his hands together and the ruby flashed red fire. "Through your sister we shall tell the French that we are promoting a marriage between Mary and the Duc d'Orleans. It's a project dear to their hearts and it'll keep them off the true scent. They shall hear through Lady Pen regular bulletins about the king's health . . . that he grows stronger by the moment . . . and that his sister is now definitely looking to wed with France and not with Spain."

"A splendid falsehood," Suffolk said, nodding vigorously. "There is nothing that France would like better than to dance on the grave of an English–Spanish alliance."

Robin straightened his ruff, which seemed to have found its way to the side of his neck. Did this have anything to do with Jane's marriage to Dudley? It had to. Northumberland never dabbled in random schemes.

"And what is the true scent, my lord?" he inquired.

The duke seemed to consider before he said with an assumption of geniality, "All in good time, Robin. You shall know all in good time. For the moment let us concentrate on your sister's part."

Robin wondered fleetingly if Pen would agree to such a thing now that she knew the truth about her lover. Not that he intended to find out. It had been many months since he had begun to distrust Northumberland's commitment to his country's well-being, and several years since he had understood the depths of the duke's personal ambition. He had offered his services to the duke as a result of his close connection with Suffolk, in whose household Robin had passed most of his youth. But now it was time to declare those old loyalties dead.

Whatever he thought of Pen's relationship with d'Arcy, Robin would not involve her in Northumberland's dirty business. Whatever the duke was planning, it was to the greater glory of the house of Northumberland. Let him find some other way to manipulate the French spy.

He stood up and said quietly, "My sister is no spy, my lord. I will not make one of her."

Northumberland stared at him in utter disbelief. He couldn't remember when anyone had had the temerity to deny him. "What did you say?" he demanded, cupping an ear as if questioning his hearing.

"I said, my lord duke, that I will not involve my sister, wittingly or unwittingly, in any such scheme."

There was an indrawn breath followed by a taut silence in the chamber. The fire crackled, candlewax dripped onto the table. Robin held his ground against the duke's livid glare.

Then Northumberland spoke, his voice soft and deadly. "Make no mistake, Beaucaire. If your sister fails to pass on this information she will find herself in the Tower. There are many pretexts on which she, as the princess's closest confidante, could be arrested. If you cannot persuade her to cooperate, she will pay the full penalty for treason. Not even her family will protect her."

Robin was in no doubt that the duke would carry out this threat. It was, of course, much more effective than threatening Robin himself. There was little else that he could say, so he bowed and left the chamber.

Northumberland frowned at the closed door for a minute. Then he shook his head, dismissing the odd notion that his threat had not achieved Robin's cooperation.

"The king is working on what he calls his *Device for the Succession*," he said after a minute. "He is preparing to leave the throne to Suffolk's daughter. But the new deed of succession must be signed and ratified by the entire council before the king's death."

The Earl of Pembroke sighed. "I doubt it will be easy to get the council's agreement."

"Oh, they'll agree," the duke said impatiently. "After all, they will have the fine example of the most loyal Earl of Pembroke to follow."

Pembroke flushed slightly but said nothing. He rose to his feet. "I give you good night, my lords."

"The woman, Goodlow, is she doing the king much good, do you think?" Suffolk asked when the door had closed behind the earl.

"He seems worse if the truth be told. But something's keeping him alive," Northumberland replied. "He's working frantically on this *Device*, and perhaps he's rallied a little. I think he's probably living on his determination not to see his country returned to the Catholics."

Suffolk shook his head. "His sufferings are so great, Northumberland. I can barely endure to see them."

"Well, as long as he does what's necessary before God has mercy on him," the other said coldly.

"At least on his death we'll be done with the drunken posturing of that fool Bryanston. For as long as his creature tends the king, he can claim access to the highest realms of the court. He seems to have decided he's my dearest friend and confidant. Everywhere I go he's on my heels, whispering into my ear, looking around to see who's remarked him in such close company with *Northumberland*." His lip curled.

"I'm sure you'll think of some way to have him lodged in the Tower," Suffolk observed somewhat aridly.

"Oh, never fear it." Northumberland got up. "I take it you've had no trouble with Jane over the betrothal."

"Some small resistance, but nothing her mother and I could not deal with." Suffolk followed him out of the chamber. "The wedding plans are well under way."

Robin knocked on Pen's chamber door. There was no answer. Softly he opened the door and slipped into the darkened room. He knew immediately that Pen was not there; there was no sense of her presence. The cat on the bed opened one eye, then closed it again.

Could she be with the princess?

Robin looked around and with a shaft of despairing frustration saw that her cloak had gone from its hook by the door. He had had but one thought: that he had to get Pen out of the palace and safely under his father's roof by morning. The Earl of Kendal would protect her even from Northumberland, whatever the duke might say. They would have to take her far from London to evade the consequences of the duke's wrath but Lord Hugh would know how to do it.

"Where in hell are you?" he demanded of the room in general and the inattentive cat. But he knew the answer. She would be with that damned spy. Was she so infatuated with him that she couldn't bear to spend a night apart? Or had she gone to confront him with the information Robin had given her?

Either way, she wasn't here. But she would have to come back by morning.

He sat down to wait for her beside the dying fire.

What lay behind the marriage of Suffolk's daughter to Northumberland's son?

It was an interesting enough puzzle to occupy

his restless mind as the night wore on.

"Which one?" Pen stared down the dark, fetid alley set back from the South Bank of the Thames. The ground beneath her feet was thick and rank with mud and the contents of the over-flowing kennel. The lane was so narrow that the gabled roofs of the opposing houses almost met above their heads, offering some slight protection from the steady drizzle.

"We'll start with the first one." Owen gestured to the closest of the two lamplit doorways.

Pen shivered. She didn't think she had ever been anywhere so wretched, so utterly desolate and filled with menace. She glanced up at Owen and saw that he had his knife in his hand. She could feel his body as he stood close to her. The taut alertness of every muscle and sinew was quite at odds with the hunched and somewhat furtive posture he had assumed with his disguise.

They approached the first doorway and a man pushed past them on his way out into the wet night. He was straightening his doublet, lacing his hose even as he went. He cast Pen a swift appraising glance.

"Keep your eyes off her, she's mine," Owen said in a voice so harsh and rasping that Pen could barely believe it belonged to him. He reached for her wrist and encircled it tightly. "Come here."

She obeyed the sharp jerk on her wrist with a

frightened little whimper. The stranger gave a sly half-smile. "Mebbe I'll find 'er 'ere one of these fine days."

"Aye, maybe," Owen said and stepped into the dimly lit hallway, dragging Pen behind him.

"Well, well, what can I do fer ye, dear sir?" A woman spoke from the door of a parlor. "Come you in an' see what I've got." She gestured behind her even as her sharp, calculating, bloodshot eyes assessed her visitors.

"I've come to sell, not buy," Owen stated, "but I'll take a look at what you've got." He entered the parlor, still dragging Pen behind him as if she were a dog on a leash.

She kept her head down and tucked sideways into her shoulder, finding it shockingly easy in these surroundings to act like a beaten woman. She listened for the sound of children.

A cry came from an upper floor and she stopped, pulling back against Owen's hand. He jerked her forward again and raised a hand. She shrank. The cry came again but it wasn't a child's. Pen felt cold and sick as she pictured what was going on upstairs.

The parlor, if such it could be called, was a sparsely furnished chamber. A sullen fire smoldered in the grate, tallow candles flickered in sconces. There was a smell of cheap perfume and rank flesh.

Three women sat on stools beside the fire. Each wore only a chemise, unbuttoned to reveal her breasts. They regarded the new arrivals with blank stares from dull eyes gazing out from tangled masses of lank, greasy hair.

"Here." Owen swung Pen under the light from one of the candles. He caught her chin and pushed it up. "What d'ye think?"

The woman came closer. "Mistress Boulder's the name," she said, peering at Pen. "Looks as if she's been in the wars. A mite troublesome is she?"

"Needs to know her place," Owen said shortly. "But she pretty well knows it now."

"Well, well, dearie." Mistress Boulder walked all around Pen. She stopped and pinched the flesh of her upper arms. Pen couldn't help recoiling.

The woman gave a coarse laugh. "Doesn't look strong enough to 'andle the customers we gets 'ere. 'Ow much d'ye want fer 'er?"

Owen seemed to consider, then he said, "I'll take a look around first, mistress. See if it might suit her." He winked and the woman laughed. "Oh, I know what you wants, sir. You wants a look at what's upstairs? Well, I've a choice morsel or two up there, but they're with customers at present."

"I'll take a look," he said. "Then we can discuss terms." He released Pen's wrist abruptly and spun her into the corner of the parlor. "Don't move!" He followed the whoremistress outside to the rickety staircase that gave access to the upper floor.

Pen turned slowly back to the parlor. The

three women at the fire regarded her with un-friendly eyes and she guessed that they didn't like competition. She swiped the back of her hand across her eyes as if wiping away tears. It was a bid for sympathy that fell on stony ground.

"I've a baby," she whispered. "Will she let me keep him?"

One of the women spat into the fire. "You don't want to bring no baby 'ere, girl."

"But would she let me?"

"Nah! No time fer 'em lest someone's payin' fer their keep."

Her heart jumped. She said in the same whisper, "Does she board any like that now? Mine'd be good as gold. I'd pay for his keep out of my wages and maybe help to look after the others."

The women shook their heads at her. "Y'are new to this, ain't yer?" one of them observed. "Right namby-pamby way o' speakin' you got."

"Aye, one o' them lady's maids, I reckon," one of her companions commented. "Got 'erself a swollen belly an' out on the streets, I'll wager."

They were talking about her as if she weren't there, Pen thought. But it seemed they had spun a convincing tale, one she could use at the next place if this one bore no fruit. "Are there any here?" she pressed. "If there are I'd tell my man I'd stay."

At this they laughed delightedly. "No, there ain't any 'ere at the moment. Was one a few weeks ago. But, bugger me, dearie, you thinks to tell yer man where you want t' stay?" They all laughed again.

Owen reappeared. He jerked his head at Pen and she scuttled from the parlor, ducking as she passed him as if expecting a blow. Once outside, even the reek of the alley seemed fresh and clean.

"No children," he said tersely.

"No, they told me. But there had been one."

"Let's try the next one." He stopped for a second and looked closely at her. "How are you holding up?"

"Well enough," she said, and it was true that energy coursed through her now that she was grappling with reality. She *would* find her child tonight. If he was alive behind some vile door in these vile streets she would find him and she would take him.

"Come then."

The next whorehouse was much like the first. Pen told her tale to the women while Owen explored the place with the whoremistress. There were no children here either.

Owen came down the outside stairs, his voice angry as he accused the mistress of the establishment of trying to cheat him. He shouted for Pen and she hurried to join him in the street. The woman stood on the stairs, a stream of profanities pouring from her lips.

"Sounds like you were asking too much for me," Pen observed with strange gallows humor.

Owen didn't respond. His face was grim as he stood in the street, rain dripping from the upturned brim of his hat. He'd had his share of whores in his time and he knew the harsh realities of their lives, but these two houses had filled him with a violent disgust.

"Where now?"

"I'm thinking," he said curtly. "Let's go back to the river." He walked briskly back to the South Bank. Lights glowed through the rain from the more substantial establishments. He looked around, trying to picture the moment when he'd seen Miles Bryanston emerge from one of the alleys running back from the river. He'd thought he'd been right the first time, but clearly not. He stared fixedly at the openings to the remaining lanes, hoping that something would jog his memory.

Pen huddled into her sodden cloak and waited. Now more than ever she realized how much she depended upon Owen. She could not possibly have ventured into this place without him. Whoever or whatever he was, whatever his reasons for helping her, he was all she had.

All the damned lanes looked alike, Owen thought. Particularly in the rain. But he thought there was something about a particular house at the end of the row on the corner of the alley directly in front of them. It was crooked, and the unsupported side leaned so far over it looked as if it might tumble at any minute.

The more he looked, the more convinced he became. Bryanston had emerged from that lane.

"This way." He took Pen's elbow and propelled her ahead of him. There was but one lantern here, and if it were possible the lane was fouler than the one they'd just left.

The door beneath the lantern was very firmly closed. Owen lifted the latch but it was fastened from within. "Not too eager for custom," he muttered. He banged imperatively with the hilt of his sword.

After a minute they heard shuffling feet and mumbled grumbles and the door was opened a crack. A wizened crone peered at them in the lamplight.

"You open for business, woman?" Owen demanded in the harsh rasp he had been using all evening. "Light's on."

"Depends," the woman said. "What's that you got?"

"A girl. You want her and the price is right, you can have her." He pulled Pen into the lamplight. "Fresh meat, she is. She'll clean up nicely . . . suit your choosier customers." He gave a short laugh and pushed into the house, thrusting the woman aside whether she would object or not.

He looked around what seemed to be the only room on the ground floor. It was deserted. "Quiet tonight."

"I 'ave me regular customers," the crone declared. "Out back." She examined Pen. "I don't want no troublemakers," she said, gesturing to Pen's marked countenance.

Pen shrank back behind Owen. Her eyes

darted around the chamber and her heart jumped into her throat. There was a cup of milk on the table with a rag dipped into it. A memory came back, fresh and vivid from her childhood in Derbyshire. A woman sitting in the sun, holding a baby on her lap, dripping milk into its mouth from a soaked rag. Tilly had told her that the woman couldn't suckle her infant because her own milk had dried up.

"You've got a baby in this house, mistress?" she asked in a whining, cajoling tone. She plucked at Owen's sleeve. "Please, sir, ask her if she'll take my baby too? Please, sir."

Owen snarled at her and she cowered, covering her face with her hands.

"I heard tell on the street, mistress, that you run another little business on the side," he said, pulling at his chin. "Baby boarding."

"An' what of it?" The crone's eyes shifted slightly. "You got summat in that line you want taken care of?"

Owen jerked his head towards Pen, who still stood covering her face with her hands. "Anywhere we can talk alone, mistress?"

The woman glanced at Pen, then shuffled to the rear of the room, where Owen now saw a narrow door. He followed her into a squalid scullery.

He lowered his voice. "I'd make an arrangement with you, mistress. A lucrative one. I want to get rid of her child. It gets in the way of her work and she thinks of nothing else. Take her and the brat and see the whelp off. Until the brat's gone you can have her for free, and I'll pay you well once the job's done."

"Seems like a deal of trouble for a whore," the crone muttered. "Summat special about her?"

Owen smiled, and it was a most unpleasant smile. "She has some special talents for those who like what she has to offer. They pay dearly for them, I can assure you. But she's been no good to me with the child."

"Why don't you see him off yourself?"

Owen shook his head. "Not my line of work, mistress. I'd prefer to pay to have it done." He dug into his pocket and tossed a handful of sovereigns on the table.

The crone stared at them. "And I get the girl for free?"

"Aye," he said shortly. "When the brat's gone, we'll discuss a fair price if you still want her."

"Well, let's just see now." The crone moved a hand to sweep the coins off the table.

Owen clapped his own hand over the money. "Talk first, mistress. I want to know what I'm paying for."

Nineteen

●

Pen waited until the door was shut on them, then she raced outside. She paused to look up at the top floor, where she saw two very small shuttered windows. She scrambled up the wooden staircase at the side of the house, grabbing at the broken rail when a rotting step crumbled beneath her. There was a door at the top.

"Please let it be unlocked," she whispered into the rain. She raised the latch. The door creaked open into a dark, noisome space, cold as the grave.

For a second she stood there, her hand still on the latch. She was paralyzed by an icy fear of what she would find . . . of what she wouldn't find . . . that having come this far she might find nothing. Then strength returned in full flood, and with it the hard conviction that she *had* found what she sought.

She had no lantern but stepped inside, leaving the door ajar behind her. Her eyes were already accustomed to the dark of the street and now in the dimness she could make out three bundles on the floor.

"Whassat?" The startled question came from one of them and Pen stepped cautiously across the uneven floorboards, desperate not to make a sound that could be heard below.

She knelt beside the first bundle. An emaciated girl blinked up at her, her eyes huge in her filthy face. Beside her slept a tiny baby. "It's all right," Pen whispered, adding absurdly, "It's only me," before shuffling on her knees to the next bundle.

A small boy lay curled in a ball, sleeping on the pile of straw that made his bed. She looked down at him. He was stick thin beneath the ragged scrap of blanket and she tried to guess at his age, but in the dimness it was hard to be certain.

She crept to the third and last pallet. Another small boy. This one was awake though. He stared up at her, sucking on a grubby thumb.

Despair hit her with the force of a tidal wave, threatening to drown out all her conviction, her dreams, her determination. Surely she should know which of these was hers? A child she had carried for eight months, a child she had labored through hours of agony to deliver alive into this world.

Surely there was some maternal instinct that would enable her to recognize her own son.

Pen squatted on her heels and fought her tears. They would do no good. How much time did she have? How long could Owen keep the woman talking? Not for one minute did the possibility occur to her that neither of these children belonged to her.

She bent and lifted the boy. The straw beneath

367

him was soaked and he wore only a ragged shirt. He stared up at her with shocked eyes. "Hush . . . hush, little one," she whispered, cradling him against her bosom. His thumb dropped from his mouth but he didn't cry out as she'd feared.

She carried him to the door, where there was a little more light. She examined his dirty face; she was looking for Philip's eyes, his nose, his mouth. She could not see them. There was nothing remotely recognizable in this child's face. She held her breath as she clutched him close, wondering if she would sense something, some kinship, but she felt only a dreadful pity for the neglected scrap she held.

She set him down just inside the doorway and he stood swaying, sucking his thumb, watching her in mute curiosity. Pen picked up the second boy and carried him to the door. He awoke and blinked, startled and then afraid, his mouth opening on a wail.

"Shh." Pen put her hand gently over his mouth. "It's all right." She explored his face, looking for some sign, and again there was nothing.

What kind of mother couldn't recognize her own child? she thought wretchedly.

She set the boy down next to the other one. They were much of a height, both thin as twigs, both filthy. She guessed them to be around two years old. She squatted down before them. "What's your name?" she whispered to the thumb sucker.

He shook his head.

" 'E don't 'ave no name." The girl spoke suddenly out of the darkness, and as she came up to the door Pen saw that she was older than she'd thought. Probably six or seven. She clutched the infant to her bony chest.

"Don't suppose 'e's stayin' long enough to get one," she informed Pen. "Them's me charges. What d'you want wi' 'em?"

"Where do you all come from?"

"Me mam works in the cribs out back," the girl told her, gesturing into the darkness behind the house. "This 'ere's me sister." She held out the baby, who gave a thin wail. "Don't know about them two. Not been 'ere long." She looked at Pen hungrily. "Got any food on ye?"

Pen wished she had had the forethought to bring something, but how could she have imagined anything like this? Owen hadn't warned her until they were on the barge, and even then, even in darkest nightmare, she could not have pictured this hideous world.

Her desperation had receded in this exchange with the girl and she knew now what she had to do. She hitched a boy on each hip and turned with her burdens to negotiate the rickety staircase.

"Eh, you can't take 'em away, them's me charges!" the child exclaimed. "Mistress'll flay me!"

"I'm not taking them away at the moment," Pen said over her shoulder. "Come with me if you wish."

"Don't got no choice," the girl informed her, following on her heels. "I dursn't let 'em outta me sight."

They reached the street without mishap. Pen's two burdens were so light she barely noticed them. They felt like paper in her arms, flimsy and easily torn. She'd left the door ajar and now she kicked it wide open and marched in.

"Owen?" Her voice was peremptory as she strode to the door at the rear of the parlor and kicked it open.

Both Owen and his companion turned to the door. "Ah," he said.

"Eh, what d'ye think y'are doin'?" the woman demanded, her voice rising. "Them's my children. Nellie!" She grabbed up a wooden ladle and advanced on the girl, who was cowering behind Pen. " 'Ow many times 've I told ye to let no one near 'em? 'Ow many?" She brandished the ladle.

The girl grabbed Pen's cloak. "Oooh, it weren't me fault. 'Onest it weren't."

"All right, that'll do!" Owen's voice cut through the scullery with the cold edge of steel. He caught the woman's raised arm and expertly liberated the ladle, not once taking his eyes off Pen. He had never seen her look the way she did now, afire with a brittle desperation as she tightened her grip on the two children.

He understood immediately the reason for that desperation and it did not surprise him. It would have been too much to expect her to know her son at first glance, unless the child had some unmistakable distinguishing feature. But Pen had expected the impossible of herself, he could see it at once, and his heart filled with compassion. But compassion alone was not going to see them safely and successfully out of this situation.

Pen intended to force the truth out of the baby-minder, and Owen could see no better way to achieve their purpose swiftly. He could only hope that one of those pathetic scraps was indeed the rightful Earl of Bryanston. If not, they'd have the devil's own job continuing their search. The entire Southwark brothel network would be alerted.

"One of these boys is *my* child," Pen stated, stepping closer to the woman. "One of these was brought to you by the man who calls himself Lord Bryanston. *Which one?*" She fixed the woman with a stare of such piercing intensity that the brothel keeper drew back.

"I don't know what y'are talkin' about," she said. "Them's my children. None o' your business."

She glared at Pen, but there was a flicker of uncertainty in her narrowed eyes. Her visitor's outward appearance was still that of a beaten whore. But everything else about her was radically changed. She stood erect, her body poised and taut as an archer's ready to loose her arrow. Fire raged in her hazel eyes. There was a contemptuous curl to her mouth, and a set purpose in the line of her jaw. She looked capable of murder.

Pen sat the children on the stained trestle table and turned again to the woman, keeping the boys at her back. "Which one?" she demanded again, her voice frigid yet somehow distant. "My friend is very skilled with a knife. I'm sure you wouldn't want me to ask for his help."

She seemed to be doing very well without it, Owen thought with a flicker of appreciation, but he stepped forward, his knife now in his hand. He would prefer to use bribes rather than threats, but Pen had set the course and for the moment he would follow.

The woman glanced over her shoulder at Owen, her gaze going to the serviceable knife in his hand. "I dunno what y'are talkin' about," she muttered.

Owen adjusted his grip on the hilt of the knife. "Oh, I think you do, mistress. Tell us which child was brought to you by the Earl of Bryanston."

"I dunno nuthin' about no earl," she said, stepping backwards while keeping her eyes on the knife. She seemed to abandon the fiction of her own maternal stake in the children. "Didn't give no name. None of 'em does."

"Fat, red-faced, nasty little brown eyes," Pen supplied promptly.

Behind her the children began to whimper. The girl, Nellie, still holding the infant, stood in the doorway poised for flight, although she gazed with fascination on the scene unfolding in the scullery.

The woman backed another step towards a broken dresser, her hand sliding behind her. Owen moved with the lightning speed that Pen was now so used to. The woman shrieked and the heavy carving knife she'd reached for fell to the earthen floor. Owen had her arm twisted behind her back, his own knife held with apparent negligence at her throat.

The children's whimpering became outright wailing and the heart-rending sound filled the filthy scullery.

Pen stepped up to the captive crone. She put her face very close to the woman's, ignoring the stale reek of her, and repeated slowly, "Fat. Red face. Little brown eyes. Short-cropped mouse-colored hair. He would have been richly dressed, carrying a sword. He probably stank of drink. Now which of these boys did he bring you?"

The woman's eyes darted to the screaming children, and Owen with his usual supreme sense of timing released her arm and returned his knife to its sheath. It was time for the carrot.

Pen looked at him in surprise and indignation but he gave her a short, reassuring nod and turned to the woman again.

"Mistress, let's have no more talk of knives," he said affably. "Let's talk of coin instead. I'll take the child off your hands and pay you three times what Bryanston is paying you. You may tell him that the child died of the fever if you wish. I doubt he'll question it in this place." He cast a derisory look around the scullery.

There was sudden quiet, even the children's crying now diminished to hiccups and the occasional sob.

Pen turned to them, gathering them against her, heedless of runny noses and wet filthy faces pressed to her whore's habit.

Owen looked at her for a second, then said in the same pleasant tone, "Now, mistress, let us come to terms."

Pen lifted the children onto her hips again and turned around, leaning for support against the trestle table. Her eyes never left the old woman's face, and the woman seemed to retreat from the intensity of her gaze, her own eyes shifting sideways, darting around the scullery, resting nowhere.

"Which one?" Pen demanded again.

Owen took a leather pouch from his pocket. It was very like the one he had given Betsy Cosham. It flitted across the hard clear surface of Pen's concentration that she hadn't yet repaid him for those sums disbursed in her cause.

The woman's eyes fixed upon the pouch that Owen held in his palm. " 'Ow much?" she asked thickly.

"Five guineas."

Her eyes narrowed and a greedy, speculative glitter appeared in their shallow depths. "The lord pays two guineas a month for 'is board."

"Nonsense!" Pen exclaimed involuntarily.

"His mother would never let him out with such a sum." Lady Bryanston, as Pen knew to her cost, was as miserly as a woman could get.

Owen's demeanor changed abruptly. All signs of affability disappeared and his eyes were black stones in a suddenly impassive countenance. He said coldly, "Two guineas a month would feed an entire nursery of two-year-olds. You don't appear to be feeding *one* adequately. I will pay you five guineas. Or shall we try the alternative method of persuasion?"

The old woman looked at the two children in Pen's arms. Pen held her breath.

"The lord brought that one." She pointed at the child whose thumb was once again in his mouth. "Said 'e'd give me two guineas a month." She turned and spat into the sawdust at her feet. " 'Aven't seen 'alf that."

"Well, you shall now see five guineas," Owen said, opening the drawstring of the pouch. He shook out five coins and laid them on the trestle.

Pen gazed into the filthy face of her child. He sucked steadily on his thumb and sleepily returned her stare. His eyes were brown like Philip's, she thought. She waited for a rush of maternal adoration and felt nothing. Only a curious cold detachment. Her quest was finished. She had her baby. He was alive, he would get well. But instead of relief there was just this sense of absence, of something missing.

She looked at Owen. He was so calm, so . . . so indifferent, she thought. Indifferent to this miraculous moment when she held her child for the first time. He had done what he'd promised. Was that all it meant to him? But of course he had no place in his life for children, not even his own.

Now, as the end drew near, the information that Robin had given her, the knowledge that she had pushed to the farthest reaches of her mind during the night's urgency, surged forward. She looked at Owen, at her lover, with the eyes of a stranger now. She did not know this man, had never really known him. He was a stranger with whom she had had a bargain now completed, merely now a stranger to whom she owed money.

Pen looked at the second child she carried. He snuffled against her chest. She said flatly, "Pay her for this other child too."

Owen inhaled sharply. "Do *what*, Pen?"

She met his gaze steadily as she held both children. "I cannot abandon a child, even though you can, Owen."

She hadn't meant to say that but the words spoke themselves. Instantly she wished them unsaid. At the very beginning of this night she had told herself that Owen's past, the spy's past, was no concern of hers and of no interest. Once she had her child, their bargain was complete. She need never face him with what she knew, need never express the revulsion that now hit her with full force. They would part as they had to, a natural end to what could only ever have been a

376

brief idyll before the spy went about his business elsewhere.

There was love mingled with undeniable lust, but she had always accepted that it was a love without a future, that she would take away with her only memories of lust and its satisfaction. Just that. No more. And now she realized how deeply she had been fooling herself. It *did* matter. Her memories would be sullied irreparably by the knowledge of this part of his past. And she wanted to understand *why* he had done what he'd done.

Owen stared at her for a long minute, a puzzled question in his eyes. Then his gaze hardened suddenly and his mouth thinned.

Who had told her?

"Pay that vile creature what she wants for this child," Pen demanded, desperate now to get the business over with. Whatever lay now between herself and Owen d'Arcy could not take place here.

"And what of the other two?" he demanded, and his voice was hard-edged, his gaze unpleasant as it rested on her face.

"They have a mother, such as she is," Pen said, her voice flat and dull. "But I'll not leave this other one."

The crone looked between them, her eyes sharp and hungry. "Twelve guineas for the two of 'em." Her voice became wheedling. "I'll 'ave trouble on me 'ands when they comes to get 'em, my lord."

"Pay her! I'll not negotiate the price of a child's life," Pen snapped. She turned and pushed through the door of the scullery and out into the street, clutching her children.

Outside, she took off her cloak and wrapped them both in its thick folds. It was hard to carry them wrapped together but she hoisted them up against her shoulder and, without waiting for Owen, set off down the alley towards the river-bank.

Owen threw money on the table, and as he passed the little girl with the baby he slipped a sixpence into her clawlike hand. More than that he could not do. One could not rescue every half-starved child from the desperate existence in the London alleys. Even Pen seemed to have acknowledged that.

Outside he saw that the lane was empty. With a muttered oath he set off towards the faint light of the riverbank.

Who had told her? Who had given her that twisted version of the truth?

Owen knew she could not have heard the truth. No one knew the truth except himself and his mother. If anyone remembered the scandal now, it was with a shrug. Estelle was long dead, her husband no longer visible at the French court. It was an old and irrelevant story. So who had decided to resurrect it? And *why?*

He caught up with her easily, hampered as she was with her awkward burden. She was drenched, the blue gown pressed to her body.

378

Her hair, no longer protected by the hood of the cloak, had escaped from its pins and tumbled soaked down her back.

He unclasped his cloak and swung it around her shoulders. "Shutting the stable after the horse has bolted," he muttered. "Give the boys to me." He took them from her before she could protest, and began to walk fast with them through the rain towards the quay where the ambassador's barge was still docked.

Pen ran to keep up with him. She jumped after him onto the deck of the barge, and the lantern from the cabin threw a path of light across the decking.

Owen ducked into the cabin with his charges, and Pen, stumbling in her haste, almost fell in after him. The brazier burned brightly; its warmth and the light from the lantern made a magical cave of the small space.

Owen set the children on the floor. He turned to Pen, who, shivering, knelt in front of the boys, unwrapping them from her cloak.

Owen rummaged in a bulkhead cupboard and took out a pile of towels and two blankets. "Here." He tossed them across to her. His voice was curt, his movements brusque and matter-of-fact. "Dry them first and then get into your own dry clothes."

He toweled off his own hair before stripping off the wet homespun jerkin he had worn beneath his cloak. His shirt joined it on the floor and he rubbed his torso dry, bending over the warmth of the brazier.

Pen was barely aware of him as she stripped the babies of their shirts, murmuring distressfully at the thinness of their frail bodies. But they didn't seem bruised or marked in any way and she took some comfort from that. She wrapped each one in a thick blanket and sat them on the velvet-covered bench set into the bulwark.

"I wish we had some food, some milk, *something* to give them."

"There's bread and cheese, milk and ale in the cupboard on the other side," he said, gesturing with his head. "But before you do that get yourself dry. You'll be no good to either of them with lung fever."

There was sense in this, and Pen swiftly stripped off her own soaked garments and swathed herself in a towel, reflecting that where she had failed to anticipate a child's need, Owen had not. Her confusion grew beyond the point where she could begin to untangle the knot.

The children sat solemnly side by side, not making a murmur. They looked shocked, apprehensive, and yet somehow resigned, as if sudden removals in darkest night by strange faces to new places were quite ordinary occurrences in their short lives.

"Here." Owen handed Pen a flask of aqua vitae and she took a deep gulp, spluttering as the fiery liquid burned her throat, but slowly the warmth spread through her belly and her shivering subsided.

She began to scramble into the clothes she'd been wearing when she'd first stepped onto the barge. They were blissfully dry and warm. Now she noticed that Owen was dressed in dry garments, dark woolen britches, linen shirt, plain woolen doublet.

He helped her with the laces of her stomacher without asking if she needed assistance, again brisk and matter-of-fact, then while she buttoned her sleeves he took out bread and cheese. With his knife he sliced chunks of both and gave them to the children on the bench.

They stared at the offering in wide-eyed wonder, then looked up at Owen, then across to Pen, as if expecting this largesse to be snatched from them as suddenly as it had appeared.

"Eat," Pen said quietly. She came over to them and knelt smiling before them. "Eat. Aren't you hungry?"

They nodded in unison and again in unison crammed bread and cheese into their mouths.

"They haven't said a word," Pen said. "Do you think they can talk?"

"I've no idea. I don't suppose people have talked much to them," Owen responded.

Pen flinched at the cold indifference of his tone. They would have to have a reckoning. But not now. Not when she had two cold, starving, confused two-year-olds on her hands.

Owen continued in the same tone. "What do you want to do with them now? We can't keep the ambassador's barge tied up at Southwark steps for very much longer."

She had not thought carefully beyond this moment when she would have her child safe. It seemed obvious that she must take her son to her mother . . . to his grandparents. Guinevere and Hugh would keep him safe. But how was she to take him . . . them . . . alone in the middle of the night? And she needed to be back in Greenwich by the morning, when she had promised to help Mary escape from the palace that was now her prison.

That escape had now become a matter of personal urgency for Pen. Mary's support could make all the difference when it came to establishing her son's identity. As heir to a throne occupied by a dying king, Mary should have the power to declare Philip's son the legitimate earl. But while Northumberland kept her a virtual prisoner she had neither power nor influence. Once she had regained her freedom she would gather the people's support. They were absolutely loyal to Mary, and would rally to her with a power that would withstand all Northumberland's scheming.

But first she had to be her own mistress, and for that she needed Owen's help.

Pen turned away from Owen and back to the children, offering them milk, averting her face from Owen's intent scrutiny.

Regardless of what she knew of him, regardless of this breach that yawned between them, could she enlist the spy's help just once more? If his government was genuinely interested in supporting Mary's claim to the throne then he would surely help, whatever differences existed between them.

Owen leaned against the table in the center of the cabin, crossing his legs at the ankles. "I have to give the boatmen instructions. Do we return to Greenwich?" he prompted with a touch of impatience.

"Yes . . . yes, we must," Pen said. "I don't know what else to do. I must take the children to my mother at Holborn, but I can't do it until I have helped the princess get away from Greenwich."

She set down the milk and turned back to him, rising slowly to her feet. "You know as well as I do that Northumberland is keeping her an unofficial prisoner. He is turning her brother against her and she lives in fear of the Tower every minute of the day. Any day Northumberland could succeed in persuading the king to impeach her. If she's out of his hands he'll find it much harder to do that. I need you to help me secure her freedom. Once she's free, as heir to the throne, as queen on Edward's death, and he cannot live much longer, she will be able to have Philip's son legally acknowledged."

She waited, her hands at her sides, her eyes never leaving his face. When he said nothing she went on into his silence, her voice flat and determined, "If your government truly supports Mary's cause, then you will help me."

She threw the challenge at him. Would he now deny that the French interest was no longer served by supporting the princess? Would he tell her now that he had been deceiving her all along?

Her body felt heavy as lead, her spirit as disheartened as it had ever been. Even when she glanced over at the bed and looked upon her child, there was no lightening of her load. She knew nothing of this man. His body, yes. But the man himself, of what drove the man, Owen d'Arcy, she knew absolutely nothing.

Owen did not respond to the challenge. "You can do nothing encumbered with children," he declared. "I will leave you at Greenwich and I will take the children to your mother. Then we will talk of Mary's position."

"No!" Pen exclaimed involuntarily. "No, you cannot take the children." How could she allow someone who had abandoned his own children to be responsible for hers?

"And why not?" His voice now was pure ice; his expression set off a thrill of alarm in the pit of her stomach.

Hastily she said, "Now that I've found my son, how can I let him out of my sight?" But she read his disbelief in his eyes. He had known what lay behind her impulsive rejection.

Owen's mouth was twisted, his eyes dark and fathomless as pitch. He turned from her and called to the boatmen, "Greenwich!"

"Aye, m'lord." There was a flurry of activity and the barge swung into midstream.

384

Owen resumed his position leaning against the table. "Well?" The one word fell like a stone into the heavy silence.

He was demanding an explanation, and Pen couldn't find the words to lay before him an accusation of such enormity.

She turned back to the children. "I think you know." Her voice was low as she laid the babies down on the velvet and covered them in blankets. "Your wife . . . your children?"

"They are no business of yours," he declared, and there was a contemptuous edge to his voice that astonished her. It was as if he were placing *her* in the wrong. He was offering neither denial nor defense. She hadn't asked for this tale of his past, but it had to be common knowledge in certain circles, else how could Robin have discovered it?

"No," she agreed with a welcome flash of anger, her voice ringing with sarcasm. "Of course they have nothing to do with you and me. How could your past have anything to do with your present? But there is much that I understand now."

"You?" he questioned with insulting incredulity. *"You?* You understand nothing. . . . *Nothing!"* He snatched up his wet cloak and left the cabin.

Pen sat on the bench opposite the children. They seemed to be asleep. *What didn't she understand?*

She knew that Robin could not have made up

such a story. She knew his sources would be reliable. And it all fitted so neatly. All the little puzzles and the bigger mysteries, all were somehow explained by such a tragedy. And all the guilt and regret in the world couldn't undo such a tragedy.

She got up and went to look at her son. He was easily identifiable from his companion, whose hair as far as she could tell through the dirt was probably carrot-colored. She bent over her child and drank him in, waiting for the moment of revelation, the instant of absolute certainty, the flood of the love that knows no limits.

Finally she turned away, still unsatisfied by her response. She took up her cloak and went up on deck. Owen was standing in the stern, looking back at the flickering lights of the receding city.

What didn't she understand?

She had to know. She loved him . . . *did* love him. Even if they had no future, she had to understand.

It took courage to approach him, every line of his body was forbidding.

"Why, then?" she asked, standing just behind him. "Why did you do it?"

He didn't turn around but his voice was hard as iron, sharp as his rapier. "You know *nothing* of my world. How dare you presume to judge! Go below!"

She heard the dreadful anguish in his voice and knew that she had done something terribly wrong. And now she didn't know how to put it right. If he wouldn't talk to her, how could she put it right? If he wouldn't explain, how could she understand?

She returned to the cabin and the sleeping children, and sat still on the bench, hands folded into her lap, waiting until the barge nudged the dock at Greenwich, and the sky was touched with the gray promise of morning.

Robin awoke with a sudden start. He realized that the gentle chiming of the brass clock on the mantel had shaken him from his light and disturbed doze. He glanced at the clock. It had just struck five.

There was still no Pen. But at some time during the long reaches of the night, his mind had lit upon a motive for Northumberland's eagerness to marry his son to the king's cousin. It was a wild, treasonous idea. But it suited Northumberland's overarching ambition, the deviousness of his sharp intellect.

It would require the king's cooperation, but Northumberland's power over the king in his frailty was absolute. And it meant that Princess Mary and her half sister, Elizabeth, were in grave danger. And anyone close to them.

Robin got stiffly to his feet and stretched, cramped and cold. He went to the window and looked out at the gray dawn. Northumberland would have reasoned that if the French were distracted with the promise of a marriage between

Mary and their own candidate, the Duc d'Orleans, they wouldn't look too closely at what else the Privy Council was up to.

Once the duke had what he wanted, the French could complain and threaten retribution as much as they liked. Once Jane was crowned queen, the two princesses safely locked away, not all the French and Spanish armies combined could dethrone her. But until then, he had to work in secret.

Pen by her very proximity to Mary was in danger, whether she refused to do the duke's bidding or not.

She would have to return to Greenwich this morning. If he could catch her in time, he could get her back into a barge and away to Holborn before she set foot in the palace. But first he must discover where she had disappeared to.

A short while later, Robin ran from the chamber, swinging his cloak around him as he went. A few servants gave him indifferent glances as he ran past them. He skipped over the mop of a burly man washing the marble floor of the great hall and took a side door out onto the redbrick path leading to the river; the same path one of the servants had seen Pen traverse last night. Men were extinguishing the pitch torches that lit the path but seemed incurious about this early-morning courtier's hasty progress.

It had stopped raining but the yews still dripped in melancholy fashion and the path was slippery beneath Robin's feet. The river was an oily ribbon.

At this dead hour, when the night traffic was done and the day's work had not begun, the quay was for once deserted. There were a few craft bobbing far out in the water, dim shapes in the waning dark as they waited for the first morning customers.

At the dock was the French ambassador's barge. Robin stopped at the end of the path, for the moment hidden from the barge while keeping it in clear view.

Pen stepped out onto the dock. She held something in her arms. Owen d'Arcy came behind her. He too held a bundle in his arms.

Robin moved out from concealment. "Pen?"

Twenty

●

Pen looked in dismayed astonishment as her stepbrother hurried across the quay towards her. What on earth was he doing here in the gray dawn? She glanced uncertainly over her shoulder at Owen, who was carrying the little red-headed boy. Owen's eyes had narrowed; his mouth was taut.

The child in her arms, as if sensing her distress, woke up and began to cry, bewildered little sobs as if he was catching his breath.

Owen stared at Robin of Beaucaire, a cold anger building with the realization that here was the source of the poison. He had expected some kind of trouble from Pen's brother, but he had expected it earlier. And he hadn't expected the venomous form it had taken.

And Pen had swallowed the whole dreadful story without question. She had had not an ounce of faith in him.

Pen felt Owen's cold gaze piercing her like a shaft of ice. She hesitated, comforting the child in her arms, unsure what to say or do as Robin approached across the quay.

Then quite suddenly the first wave of jubilation hit her.

She was holding her child.

And it was so right that Robin should be the first of her family to acknowledge her son. She and Robin were closer than any siblings could be, and Pen wanted him now to touch the child, to smile upon him, to anoint him with the full blessing and acknowledgment of all their family. Then it would be real. Then she would know that the long nightmare was over.

She began to run to meet him. "Robin . . . Robin . . . I have my son. I've found my child." She arrived breathless in front of him, hugging the little boy to her.

"See . . . See . . . Philip's son. See his eyes. They're Philip's eyes." She didn't know when she'd decided absolutely that the child's brown eyes were his father's, but now it seemed self-evident.

Robin stared at her in bewilderment, then he looked blankly at the filthy scrap of humanity in her arms.

"Pen . . . Pen . . . dearest Pen." He reached for her, wanting to hold her. "What is this, Pen? What are you talking about? What is this child?"

Pen stepped away from his arms, the light dying from her eyes. "I told you. This is my son. I have found my son. Don't you believe me, Robin?"

For a moment Robin could find no words. He could think only that Pen had slipped off the edge of reason, and there was only one person who could have led her to make such a desperate error.

He spun around on Owen d'Arcy. Almost without his being aware of it his sword was in his hand.

"Don't you understand what you've done to my sister?" Robin declared, his sword arm unmoving, his brilliant blue eyes ablaze with a wild fire. "How could you let this happen? Why would you encourage her in this insanity?"

"Robin!" Pen cried out as she saw the streak of silver.

"Don't be a fool," Owen said coldly. He put down the child he was carrying. The boy instantly curled against Pen's skirts, hugging her knees.

"Robin, I know it's hard for you to believe," Pen said urgently. "But this is *my* child. Owen helped me find him."

Robin turned to her, although his sword still remained pointed at Owen. "Pen, how could you trust this man after what I told you . . . after what you know of him? *Why* would he help you? A man who disowned, abandoned his own children, a man —"

He broke off abruptly at a jarring pain in his arm. A savage blow to the blade of his sword had bent his wrist and sent the weapon spinning to the ground. Owen d'Arcy stood still, his black eyes mere pin pricks, his rapier steady in his hand, its point now resting lightly on the ground.

Robin clasped his wrist, numbed from the force of the blow that had disarmed him.

"Dear God in heaven!" Pen whispered. She could feel both children shaking against her as the ugly violence thickened the air around them. "Stop this! Stop it!"

Owen sheathed his rapier and took a deliberate step away from them. Then with a mock bow at Pen, and another towards Robin, he turned back to the barge.

"No . . . no, Owen!" Pen cried, stumbling after him, her step impeded by the child still clinging to her skirts. Had he forgotten that she still needed his help? Her quest was but half over.

Owen stopped, one foot already on the deck of the barge. He turned slowly back to her, and a flicker of hope showed in his eyes.

Pen didn't see it. "Owen . . . Owen, we have to help Mary escape. You have to help me . . . for my son's sake." She came to a stop just in front of him, one arm encircling the child at her knee, the other holding her son to her hip.

Hope faded. He said nothing.

Robin, still holding his numbed wrist, came out of his trance. He looked again at the child in Pen's arms.

Could they all have been wrong?

Horror filled him.

A stranger had believed Pen when her family had deserted her. But why were there two children? Such pathetic, ill-used babes. How could the child of Pen and Philip be in such a condition?

Dear God, what had they all done?

He took a step towards Pen, desperate to find the right words amid the questions flooding his brain, but she ignored him. She had eyes now only for Owen.

"Owen . . . please?" Pen said. Nothing else mattered. At this moment she had no interest in anything but gaining Owen's cooperation. No one else could do what needed to be done. She had her child. Now she needed that child to be safe.

She continued with a flat single-minded determination, "This has nothing to do with whatever lies between *us*. I cannot understand that if you won't explain . . . and now there's no time."

She paused for a heartbeat, waiting for something, some softening of his expression, but there was none. No offer to explain later, no hint of emotion in his hard gaze. Nothing at all.

Once again she closed her mind to anything but her present goal. "I'm not asking you to do this just for me, Owen. Mary's freedom will suit both sides of our bargain, I believe."

Robin found his tongue at last. "What bargain?" he demanded, his eyes still on the child in Pen's arms.

Pen turned to him. "The chevalier and I struck a bargain. I would spy on Mary for him, and in exchange he would help me find my son."

Her jaw set as she saw Robin's appalled expression. "I doubt you have the right to throw the first stone," she said.

"You are wasting my time," Owen stated, turning impatiently back to the barge. "I am not interested in your family squabbles."

"No, wait!" Pen demanded, desperation edging her voice as she realized how frail now was the tie between herself and Owen. "This is not a squabble. Defeating Northumberland is in all our interests."

Robin's head was spinning. He seemed to be caught in a vortex that threw him from one drama to the next. He said urgently, "God's blood, Pen! That's why I was waiting for you. I need to talk to you alone. About Northumberland." He laid a hand upon her arm, shaking it slightly. The child she held whimpered, and Robin dropped his hand instantly.

"Pen . . . please. We need to talk."

"If this concerns Northumberland, it would probably save time if I were a party to the secret," Owen observed. He glanced at the sky. It had stopped raining and the clouds seemed to be lifting.

Robin exhaled sharply. He shook his head as if in denial, then said, "Pen?"

She faced Owen. "Owen, will you help me, regardless of how things are between us? Will you do this one last thing for me?"

"And just how are things between us, Pen?" he asked with an ironic, mocking light in his eye.

It tore at her heart. She said quietly, "Broken, I believe."

Owen merely nodded. He looked again at the

gloomy sky, the lines of his face harsh and sharply etched in the gray light, but when he turned his eyes once more upon his companions, Pen recognized the return of the spy's detached concentration as he considered the issue.

"Let us get onto the barge. The quay grows public now and we'll be remarked."

Robin bent to pick up his sword, and thrust it back into its sheath with a rough gesture. He and Pen followed the chevalier onto the barge, Pen still hampered by the child she held against her skirts and the other in her arms. But she found she could not let go of either of them. And it seemed, by their limpet-like clutches, that they were not prepared to let go of her either.

"So, what is so urgent that you had to catch Pen in the dawn?" Owen asked without preamble, perching as before on the edge of the table, legs stretched in front of him, ankles casually crossed. His posture suggested a certain insouciance but there was nothing careless in the penetrating black gaze.

"Northumberland is demanding that she pass false information to . . ." Robin hesitated, seemed to swallow before he could continue. "To you . . . to her lover. If she refuses, he threatens to charge her with treason. She has to leave here, go at once to safety."

Robin glanced at Pen, at the children. What were they to do with them? *How could he think clearly at the moment?*

"The slimy, crawly bastard!" Pen exclaimed.

"I am not frightened of Northumberland."

"Then you should be," Owen said, his mouth grim. "What is this information?" He gave a short laugh. "You may as well tell me since I'm supposed to hear it."

Robin accepted that somehow he was now hip deep in French diplomacy. He could have no loyalty to a man who had threatened Pen, a man whose ambition showed every sign of threatening the security of the kingdom. He had no choice now but to offer his services to a man who had involved Pen in the serpentine undercurrents of conflicting diplomacies.

It was a hideous tangle, and yet Robin could see but one logical course of action. And, if the truth be known, he was so much at sea, so confused and distressed, he could almost welcome the detached professionalism of the seasoned French agent.

He told Owen d'Arcy what Northumberland wished the French to believe.

Owen's mirthless laugh came again. "The man must think we're fools. It's a stalling tactic, but why?"

"I think I know," Robin said, and quietly explained his suspicions.

"If Jane is crowned queen, Northumberland's son will become king and his father will be the real sovereign power in England," Robin finished. "But he'll need the consent of the Privy Council even if the king has changed the document of succession, and he needs to keep his plans totally secret until the moment he reveals them as a *fait accompli*. So if the French are busy planning Mary's wedding to one of their own, and the Spanish are fretting about the possibility of a French alliance, Northumberland can get on with things in peace."

Owen nodded and observed aridly, "A shrewd piece of deduction. My congratulations, Beaucaire."

Robin looked as if he would rather have such a compliment from anyone but Owen d'Arcy.

"Mary is in even greater danger then," Pen declared. She was sitting on the bench, the children lying beside her, their heads on her lap. She was impatient with all this talk, all these plans, that postponed the moment when she could be alone with the boys, the moment when she could begin to know her son and he to know his mother.

"The duke will need her well out of the way," she said, her gaze bent upon the two heads in her lap.

"And he'll need Elizabeth out of the way too," Robin said. "But, Pen, you're also threatened, as is anyone close to Mary, and particularly since you're not going to spy for Northumberland. You cannot go back to the palace now."

Owen had put all emotion from him, in the way he had perfected over the years. His mind was detached, focused only on the task at hand. He said crisply, "She has no choice. If we're to secure the princess's freedom, Pen must behave exactly as normal. Indeed, for the moment, Beaucaire, you must tell the duke that your sister has agreed to do his bidding. That should buy enough time."

He turned to Pen. "If asked, you will tell Northumberland that you will do anything to serve your country, and, of course, anything to serve the duke. Is that understood?"

Pen nodded. "And what of Mary?"

"We have to do this in two stages." He tapped the back of one hand into the palm of the other as he explained. "There are only two ways out of Greenwich, by road or by river. She'll be apprehended on either route before she gets more than a mile. We have to get her out of Greenwich and back to Baynard's Castle. From there, there are any number of routes out of the city. It will be a simple matter to confuse the pursuit and get her to safety."

"A simple matter?" Pen queried. "The Earl of Pembroke owns Baynard's Castle. He's part of whatever scheme Northumberland is hatching."

"There is a way," he said, his tone curtly dismissive of this cavil. "And I believe that if she seeks Pembroke's protection he will not immediately know how to refuse it."

"I think that's true," Robin said. "I have observed how he often stands in opposition to Northumberland . . . not for long, I grant you, but he does mutter sometimes."

"Yes, so I have been told," Owen said carelessly.

Pen assumed that he had his own spies with their own ears and eyes. Others like herself . . . doing what she had done.

"Northumberland will suspect nothing if the princess wishes to take an airing on the river," Owen continued. "After her illness it would not be surprising, and he'll know that she cannot possibly escape his vigilance on the water. This afternoon you and a few of her ladies will accompany her. Obviously she can take nothing with her, nothing that will imply she's expecting to be gone more than an hour or so. She will land at Baynard's Castle and take up residence again there."

"But what then?" Robin asked.

"I'll arrange for her departure at first light tomorrow. Pen, you may look for me at Baynard's Castle this evening, when I will tell you what to do. In the meantime, Beaucaire, you will distract Northumberland so that he doesn't think too much about the princess's decision to take an airing. Tell him about your sister's willingness to do his bidding. Suggest other ways she can be useful . . . I'm sure you'll come up with something inventive." Owen made a dismissive gesture that set Robin's teeth on edge, but he made no comment.

Pen stood up, gathering the children to her. She hesitated, looking at Owen, wanting to say something, hoping that he would say something, but he only returned her look with cold detachment.

"We will go then," Pen said.

"Yes." He didn't move from his perch on the table as Pen, the children, and Robin made their way in silence around him and out into the daylight.

They stepped onto the quay, which was now abustle. The French ambassador's barge pulled away almost immediately, and Pen stood watching as it swung into midstream.

For all Owen's apparent detachment, she had read the hurt and anger and disappointment in his eyes, and it pierced her soul. But why wouldn't he defend himself?

If he had told her it wasn't true, she would have believed him. Wouldn't she?

Pen looked down at the child in her arms. For now this was all that mattered.

"This is my son," she said her eyes radiant.

Robin looked at her helplessly. "How can you know?"

Pen's explanation was succinct. "We went into High Wycombe. The woman who delivered him told us that Miles took him away as soon as he was born. She told us where to look for him. And we found him tonight."

Robin gazed down at the child. He could not bear to think of what she had suffered in the last two years . . . she and this scrap of jetsam in her arms. "And what of the other?" he asked.

Pen exhaled softly. "I don't know what plans to make for him yet, but I could not leave him in such a place. Such a dreadful place, Robin. I think I will kill both Miles and his mother."

It was said with such low-voiced ferocity that Robin at that moment believed her capable of it.

"There are other routes to retribution," he said. "Leave that to your mother and my father."

"Yes, but establishing his identity, his rightful title, that will be more difficult." The words now tumbled over themselves in her urgency. "But Mary can do it. Mary is the heir to the throne; once she's free she'll have the power to declare my son's legitimate right to his father's lands and title."

Pen stopped talking. There were many people on the quay now, boatmen with wherries laden with produce for the palace kitchens, servants hurrying to unload them. Soon there would be courtiers, people who might recognize her. Maybe even Miles. The future was a grim tangle, but now the immediate needs of the two small lives she held took precedence.

"I have to take care of them," she said. "Find them clothes . . . food . . . milk . . . warmth . . . baths. Robin, I don't know where to start. Look at them, poor mites. They don't speak. They barely cry."

And she remembered how Owen had thought of the needs of small children. He had brought food where she had not thought to do so. Food, milk, and blankets. He knew more than she did about such matters. He was a father.

It made no sense.

But she was a mother. A mother of two. Their

lives were now her responsibility. *That made sense.*

"Should I take them to Holborn now?" Robin suggested. He had no idea how he would do such a thing, but he assumed he would find a way.

"No," Pen said. "They are my children. I won't let them go again."

She bent and with some difficulty scooped the other child into her arms. She considered for a second, then stated, "I believe his name is Charles."

Robin gave in to the inevitable. Soon his step-mother would unknot this skein. "What if some-one comes looking for him?"

"They dumped him . . . abandoned him in a hellhole. They'll not come looking for him."

Robin scratched his head. Pen was making this sound so simple, so obvious. "Pen, you have to help the princess leave Greenwich. How can you do that with two babies in your arms? How can you even imagine keeping them in your own apartment without the whole palace knowing? Without Bryanston knowing?"

"Oh, he's going to know soon enough," Pen said grimly. "But for the moment, fetch Pippa. Ellen will help me care for them now, she has a whole host of younger brothers and sisters, so she's bound to know what to do. When you get back you can arrange transport so that she and Pippa can take them back to Holborn. I will stay with Mary until Owen has arranged her escape.

When Mary is free, then so will I be."

Robin hesitated before asking, "Do you trust d'Arcy in this?"

"Absolutely." Pen hoisted both children higher in her arms so that Robin could no longer see her face. "It will serve his own interests."

Again he hesitated. "Do you love him?"

Pen did not answer the question. Instead, keeping her face averted, she repeated, "Fetch Pippa, Robin. I'm going to take the boys to my apartments. Ellen will look after them while I wait upon Mary and tell her of Owen's plan."

Bitterly Robin wished that they could do without the assistance of Owen d'Arcy. But he knew that the full resources of the French ambassador and the agile mind of his top agent could do what he himself could not.

"Let me carry Charles." He took the red-haired child from Pen. The boy allowed himself to be moved from one set of arms to the other with a mute passivity that made Robin want to weep.

Pen's chamber was still empty, as Robin had left it. Ellen always waited for her mistress's summons in the morning, although she expected it soon after dawn, when Princess Mary would be ready to receive her ladies.

"Tell Pippa the truth," Pen said, taking Charles from Robin's arms. "She'll understand."

"She won't be surprised." Robin took out his

own less than pristine handkerchief and kneeling, wiped both runny noses. "She and I were talking about how maybe there was something in this obsession of yours . . . I can't get this off. It seems to be encrusted."

Pen laughed, and for a moment she was light-hearted. "You won't recognize them when Ellen and I have finished." She smiled then and said, "Well, I always thought Pippa would see the light in the end."

Robin, still on bended knee, looked up at her. "We were so wrong. Can you forgive that, Pen?"

"Yes," she said simply. She paused with her hand on the bell that would summon Ellen. "It was a strange story, Robin. I'm sure I seemed crazed with grief. I can understand how difficult it was."

They had all done what they had believed was in Pen's best interests. And Robin thought now of how in the same mistaken belief he had interfered between his sister and Owen d'Arcy. He had done what he thought right, but he could see now that he had meddled where he should not. Pen's family had caused her enough grief as it was. He went to the door.

"I'll be back with Pippa in three hours."

He glanced back at Pen, who was on her knees in front of the children, unwrapping the blankets. "Yes . . . yes, hurry back," she said absently.

Robin left her, passing Ellen on his way. She bobbed a surprised curtsy at the sight of him coming from Pen's chamber so early in the morning. He offered her a distracted nod and hurried on his way.

Ellen entered her mistress's chamber, then stood in the doorway, jaw hanging. "Lord love us, madam. What's all this?"

"My son, Ellen," Pen told her. "And his brother. We need to bathe them, feed them, and find some clothes for them."

"Lord love us!" Ellen muttered again, sinking down on a stool, fanning herself with one hand. She knew, as did every member of the Kendal household, of Lady Pen's tragedy; now she could only stare, mouth agape.

Pen had expected such a reaction. She said sharply, "You don't need to understand at the moment, Ellen, you just need to help me. You must fetch everything yourself because *no one*, and I mean *no one*, must know that they're here. As soon as Lord Robin and Lady Pippa get here, you and my sister will take them to Holborn, to my mother and Lord Hugh. Now, fetch me hot water."

Ellen rose slowly. She was by no means a stupid woman and Lady Pen didn't strike her as someone who had lost her wits. "I thought there was only one, my lady."

"Well, that's another story," Pen said, relieved to see that Ellen was at least willing to cooperate.

Ellen came over to the children. They gazed blankly up at her, naked and shivering in the early-morning chill. "Oh, it's a crying shame," she said. "Look how thin they are."

"Hurry!" Pen said with sharp urgency. "I'll make up the fire while you're gone." She wrapped them again in the blankets and then threw fresh kindling on the fire, poking it into a blaze before piling on logs.

She sat down on the floor before the fire, taking the boys onto her lap. "Do you talk at all?" she whispered. "Can you say something to me?"

But they remained silent, both gazing at the fire as if mesmerized by the flames and the warmth, her son with his thumb firmly in his mouth.

Ellen came back with two silver porringers. "I thought we'd best feed 'em first, Lady Pen. I doubt they've seen hot water in their lives, poor little mites, don't want to shock 'em to death."

"Oh, yes, Ellen. A good thought," Pen said with approval. "Food will soothe them. Will you feed Charles?" She lifted him from her lap.

Ellen set him on a stool and lifted the lid of the porringer. The child grabbed for it as the fragrant steam curled in the air. "Slowly does it," Ellen said, taking his hands in one of hers and holding a spoonful of honeyed gruel to his mouth.

Pen held her son on her lap and fed him in the same way. His eyes never left the spoon, following its progress from bowl to his mouth and back again.

"Do you think he looks like his father, Ellen?"

Ellen glanced over. "Hard to say, madam, under all that dirt," she replied diplomatically.

"Yes," Pen agreed, scraping the last of the gruel from the porringer. The boy licked his lips and it seemed to her now that some of the blankness had left his eyes, some of the shocked rigidity gone from his body. He reached for the empty bowl. She let him have it and he ran his finger around, licking it before upending the porringer.

"They need more, Ellen."

"Yes, but not too much at once," Ellen said with authority. "After a bath, we'll try a coddled egg and some more milk."

Pen reached under the bed for the copper bathtub and pulled it in front of the fire. "We shall need clothes for them."

"Aye, madam, that's easily done," Ellen declared. "I'll fetch water."

Pen took both children on her lap again and rocked them gently, singing a soft nursery song from her own childhood. It seemed the natural thing to do. They had to learn to trust; they had to learn to expect good things to happen.

Tears pricked behind her eyes as she thought of all the time wasted, of all the desolate months that these scraps had been on earth without hope or expectation.

But from now on they would know only love, and warmth, and full bellies.

The bath was much less of a success than honeyed gruel. They kicked and struggled but still astonishingly made very little sound, just a whimper that occasionally approached a wail.

They put both of them in the water at once. Charles instantly scrambled out and ran dripping into a corner.

"Leave him for the moment," Pen said. "It's going to take both of us to handle just one of them."

She held her son firmly as Ellen soaped him and rubbed him. It was like cleaning tarnished silver, Pen thought, watching the pale clean skin emerge beneath the application of the wash cloth. His face was small and angular, pale with lack of fresh air and adequate food, but she thought she could see Philip now in the line of his nose, the shape of his mouth. And definitely his eyes. He had the same long lashes that Philip had had. Heartbreaker's lashes, she used to say, teasing him.

"He is like his father," she murmured, more to herself than to Ellen.

"Aye, there's something there," Ellen agreed, rinsing off the child's head. The still downy baby hair was a soft brown, curling against his neck.

He had stopped wriggling now and went passively into Pen's arms as she wrapped him in a towel. His thumb was back in his mouth and his eyes closed abruptly.

"Exhausted, poor mite. Let him sleep while we do the other one."

Pen wrapped him securely in a dry towel and laid him on her bed. Nutmeg regarded him warily, and moved to the farthest edge of the bed. Little Philip didn't stir, but slowly his thumb slipped from his mouth.

Charles beneath the dirt was revealed as freckle-faced, green-eyed, with a very pale complexion. His hair once washed was a bright carrot red; much more abundant than the little earl's, it stood up in a spiky halo.

"I have to go to the princess now," Pen said, once Charles had joined his brother in sleep on the bed. "Stay here with them, Ellen. Don't leave the chamber." She reached behind her to unfasten her laces. Her gown was in no fit condition for visiting the royal apartments.

Ellen hurried to help.

"Just unlace me and then fetch more food and clothes and whatever they'll need while I'm gone," Pen instructed. "You must stay with them with the door locked when I'm not here."

Ellen went off to fetch what was needed. Pen changed her dress, keeping an eye on the sleeping children as she did so. She tidied her hair, tucked it away under a plain linen coif. There was no time for an elaborate coiffure this morning.

As soon as Ellen returned Pen hurried to the door. "If I'm not back when Lord Robin and Lady Pippa arrive, let them in. But no one else!"

"Forgive me, madam, but I'm no fool," returned Ellen.

Pen smiled. "No, I know." She closed the door, then stood for a minute, bracing herself for the visit to Mary. It was so hard to switch her mind from the domestic concerns of her children to the harsh reality that lay ahead. The scheme she had to manage.

And there was no time, no time at all, to consider what she had lost.

Twenty-one

●

"Why would the French help me in this?" Mary mused as she placed a silk ribbon in her book to mark her place.

"For your favor, madam," Pen returned, even though she assumed the princess's question had been rhetorical. "I understand that they hope to promote your marriage with the Duc d'Orleans."

Mary's laugh was ironic. "I'm sure that they do. And it does no harm to let them think that I might agree . . . one day." She rose from her chair and went to the lectern placed to catch the daylight from the embrasured window. "Do you trust your chevalier, Pen?"

Pen saw no point in disputing her personal connection with the chevalier. "Most assuredly, madam." She stood by the fire, her hands clasped against her skirts.

"He is one of de Noailles's spies, I imagine?" Mary's tone conveyed little interest in the question or its answer.

"I believe him to be the ambassador's master spy."

Mary flicked the pages of the great tome that rested on the lectern, as if she was looking for a particular passage. "How long have you believed that, Pen? Or should I not ask the question?"

"Perhaps you should not, madam." Pen became aware that her nails were digging into her palms, that there was an ache between her shoulders. She tried to relax her tense posture and slowly uncurled her fists.

Mary looked up briefly. "I trust you, Pen. Therefore I will trust your agent. We will put ourselves in the hands of the French." A thin smile touched her mouth. " 'Tis not as if we have much choice in the matter, and it will annoy Northumberland most powerfully."

"Aye, madam." Pen turned her head from side to side in an effort to release the crick in her neck. She realized that she was exhausted. Sleepless nights seemed to be her lot these days.

"I will accompany you, of course. But who else would you have? No more than one or two others. It must not look as if you're going out for more than the briefest time."

"Who do you think is best suited to such an enterprise?"

Pen considered the members of Mary's retinue. "Matilda and Susan."

"Very well. I leave the organization to you. But I will not go without my books. They must be crated somehow and taken aboard."

Pen didn't bother to argue. It was just one more logistical issue she would have to deal with.

"How does the chevalier propose I leave Baynard's Castle?"

"He hasn't said, madam."

"I see. How reassuring." Mary was suddenly tart. "I go into the lion's den without a sure means of emerging." She moved towards the prie-dieu, saying in dismissal, "I would needs pray, since all reassurance lies with God."

Pen curtsied and left the bedchamber. Mary had a considerable cross to bear, but there were times when she made life very irksome for those around her.

She took Susan and Matilda aside and explained the situation. They had been attendant upon Mary for almost as long as Pen had. Matilda was soon to be married for the second time, to one of the king's equerries, and Susan, like Pen, was a widow.

"Taking a crate of books without being remarked won't be easy," Matilda said.

"No," Pen agreed. "We'll have to pretend it's a picnic hamper."

"A very heavy one," said Susan. For some reason this made them all smile, for a moment forgetting the danger in which they all stood.

"Well, let's get on," Pen said. "There's much to do. Matilda, would you order the barge for noon? Try if you can to ensure that Master Braddock is at the helm. His loyalty to the princess is unquestioned." Matilda nodded and they parted to make their own preparations.

The clock in the tower in the central courtyard

struck nine. Pen looked down from one of the tall arched windows in Mary's antechamber. Robin had left at seven. She could not expect him back before ten at the earliest.

Her heart seemed to be beating far too fast, and her skin felt dry and tight. Fatigue, she knew, but there was more. She was tense, filled with an apprehension that was somehow mingled with excitement at the prospect of the day ahead. The danger of the day ahead.

One false move, and Northumberland would have all the excuse he needed to impeach Mary, not to mention her companions in flight. The plan, at least up until they reached Baynard's Castle, rested entirely on her shoulders. Then Owen would step in, but she'd still have a part to play.

Owen. Excitement, apprehension, dimmed. When this was over she could not imagine that she would ever see him again.

When this was over she would have her child in peace and love and safety. She must concentrate all her emotional energies on that. Her relationship with Owen d'Arcy had begun with that and ended with it.

Instantly Pen left Mary's apartments, her step quick, her jeweled slippers silent on the waxed oak floor. Her children awaited her.

"Lady Pen?"

The unpleasant voice of the Duke of Northumberland arrested her. She turned slowly. "I give you good morning, my lord duke."

"How does the princess?" His cold gaze flitted across her face and she was glad of the somber light in the corridor.

"A little better, I believe, my lord duke. She talks of perhaps taking the air later today. It seems that the sun has shown itself for once."

"Taking the air?" He stroked his neat beard. "She must be feeling quite improved."

"Her physician believes a little river air might do her good, sir. She intends to be carried by litter to the barge for an hour on the water."

"I see. At what hour?"

"After her prayers, my lord duke. When the morning mists have lifted and yet the sun is not too bright." That, Pen thought, was evasive without being obviously so. There was never a set period for Mary's prayers and they would often continue for hours.

Northumberland regarded her from beneath heavy brows, a slight frown in his eyes. It struck him that Pen Bryanston was a little too like her mother for comfort. Something in the set of the head, the gleam in the eye. And yet she appeared perfectly correct in manner.

"Have you seen your brother since last even, madam?"

"I had brief speech with him an hour ago, sir." Pen smiled.

The duke again touched his beard. Perhaps it aided his thinking, Pen reflected.

"And did your speech touch anything of moment, Lady Pen?"

"I believe so, my lord." She curtsied but kept her eyes on his face. "You will find, sir, that I know my duty, as does my brother."

Northumberland took this in, his hand still at his beard. Then he bowed, as if satisfied. "Pray, madam, give the princess my felicitations on her return to health."

"And the king . . . how is the king's health this morning?" Pen asked, her tone pleasant and concerned.

Northumberland's frown deepened. "His Highness's health improves daily," he said stiffly, and went on his way.

In a pig's ear! Pen thought, waiting until he had rounded the corner of the corridor. On impulse, she turned down a passage that would take her past the king's antechamber on her way back to her chamber. It would be useful to know which members of the Privy Council were at Greenwich when Mary made her escape.

She heard the voice of Miles Bryanston braying down the passage long before she reached the entrance to the antechamber.

"Mistress Goodlow, my lord duke, has always had the most beneficial results."

Goodlow.

Pen stopped. She held herself still in the shadow of the walls, glad that her dark gown blended with the gray light.

Goodlow! Lady Bryanston's pet herbalist. The woman Granny Wardel had said was Betsy Cosham's colleague. A woman who had been at

417

Philip's bedside during his illness . . . had watched him die.

A woman who had given Pen tonics to strengthen her during her pregnancy. Herbs, potions that she had perhaps acquired from Betsy Cosham, who knew any number of ways to end an unwanted pregnancy.

What had Owen said? Something about how the gift to do good could as easily be turned to evil.

Philip had been well, much stronger than usual during that winter. His cough had barely troubled him. Then so suddenly he had started to sicken . . . and had started so quickly to fail. Mistress Goodlow had attended him.

Before he became sick or after?

Pen stood in the shadows, one hand on her throat, as her memory of that dreadful time cleared. His mother had hovered, all solicitation. She had summoned the herbalist when Philip began to sicken. Only the herbalist, no other physician had been allowed to approach Philip's bedside. Pen couldn't remember whether Mistress Goodlow had given Philip any medicines or not. If she had, nothing had worked. His cough had grown worse and worse. Pen from her own sickbed had heard him day after day, night after night.

Pen saw again Philip's gray countenance, the greenish pallor as he'd started to vomit, to sweat, the dreadful desperation in his eyes as he'd accepted the inevitability of his death. They had all

418

watched him die. His mother had stood quietly, dry-eyed in the shadows. Mistress Goodlow, so calm as to be almost indifferent, had closed Philip's eyes, drawn up the sheet.

Pen stared into the corridor, her breath paused in her throat as a dreadful thought took shape.

Philip's mother. A woman capable of inducing a premature birth, of condemning an infant to the living death little Philip had endured . . . a woman who consulted Betsy Cosham about the disposal of unwanted children . . .

Such a woman would be capable of watching her son die. Her unsatisfactory and uncooperative son.

Philip's mother had never liked him . . . no, much stronger than that. He had threatened her, threatened her control. Miles, on the other hand, had slavered at her hand like a trained boarhound ready for the signal to kill. Had Lady Bryanston taken advantage of Philip's weak constitution? Had she allowed him to die?

Pen listened intently to the continuing discussion in the antechamber.

"Mistress Goodlow's results don't seem to be particularly beneficial at present, Bryanston," the duke declared with a sardonic sniff. "She appears to be doing no better than the physicians. Indeed, worse, I would have said."

"A few more days, my lord duke. Just a few more days and I am certain you will see some improvement," Miles wheedled.

"Indeed, my lord, Mistress Goodlow's physic is renowned."

Pen froze at the odiously familiar voice of her mother-in-law. Panic shot through her, but she couldn't seem to move a muscle. Her son . . . the children . . . they were only a few yards away. She had a sudden desperate fancy that her mother-in-law would smell her grandson's presence, like some beast of prey, scenting the wind.

"You will find, my lord duke, that Mistress Goodlow's physic works over time," Lady Bryanston was saying, the customary sharpness of her voice effortfully mellowed.

Oh, yes, Pen thought. Her mind was as cold and clear as crystal. She could taste on her tongue the bitter liquid Goodlow had given her in the days before her labor began. Her stomach muscles clenched in involuntary response to the vivid memory.

Was this the way Miles and his mother had chosen to curry favor with the duke? To introduce their own herbalist into the king's bedchamber? The woman had shown herself utterly loyal to Lady Bryanston, and presumably she could do good as well as evil.

But what if she failed? What if the king's condition worsened? Who would Northumberland hold responsible?

Lady Bryanston, for all her viciousness and ambition, had a crude mind. Her strategems were without subtlety and she had played straight into her daughter-in-law's hand.

420

Pen moved away from the concealing shadows. She walked into the king's antechamber, her soft skirts swaying gently around her. She was smiling.

"I give you good morning, Lady Bryanston . . . Lord Bryanston." Her curtsy was impeccable. Her brother-in-law recovered from his surprise quickly enough to offer a passable bow in return.

"Do I understand that Mistress Goodlow attends upon the king?" she inquired of Northumberland. The chamber was as always crowded, some with reason for being there, most without, but her quick glance showed her the Earl of Pembroke standing in a knot of courtiers. He was here, not at Baynard's Castle. All to the good.

"Aye, madam. You know of this woman?" The duke looked at her intently.

"Indeed, sir. She presided over my husband's death, and over my own premature labor." Pen continued to smile. "I am of a superstitious nature, my lord duke. I prefer an angel of mercy to an angel of death."

Lady Bryanston drew breath in an audible hiss. Her son turned dark crimson.

"I can see that you would, madam," the duke said. "How unfortunate that two such misfortunes should have followed so closely upon one another."

"I have always thought so," Pen agreed. "But ill luck attends many bedsides. Is that not so, madam?" She turned her brilliant smile upon her mother-in-law.

"Mistress Goodlow's reputation reaches far and wide, my lord," the dowager countess said through rigid lips.

"Yes," Pen agreed. "She's a woman who inspires confidence. For some reason," she added with a tiny shrug, still smiling. "You'll have to forgive me if my experience has given me little faith in her *healing* powers." The emphasis was minute, but sufficient for Northumberland, whose intent gaze had not left Pen's countenance.

The seed was sown. Pen said blandly, "If you will excuse me, I have duties to attend to." She curtsied again and made her way back to the corridor through the thronged chamber.

Miles, ignoring a warning look from his mother, pushed through the crowd in her wake.

"Wait!" He seized Pen's arm, his fingers hurtful on her forearm.

"So rough, Miles," she chided gently. "If you would have speech with me, pray do so. I am at your service."

"You can prove nothing!" A shower of spittle flew with the words although his voice was barely above a whisper. "Nothing!"

Pen wiped her face with a fastidious grimace. "What would I be interested in proving, Miles?"

"That's enough, you dolt!" Her mother-in-law was there, her mouth thinned with malice and fury. "Get back to the duke."

Miles glared at Pen. *"Nothing!"* he declared, ignoring his mother's jabbing elbow. Then he pushed past his mother and obeyed her instruction.

Lady Bryanston regarded Pen as she stood with her back to the wall, rubbing her arm where his fingers had bruised the flesh. The hard brown eyes held just the suspicion of alarm lurking beneath the naked loathing that made Pen's flesh crawl.

"I don't know what game you play, Pen, but I warn you. Do not set yourself up against me. Miles is right. You can prove nothing."

"Indeed, madam?" Pen raised one eyebrow, slipped sideways away from the countess, and walked swiftly down the corridor.

Indeed! she thought. My child is living proof. *And by God, madam, it shall come back to bite you.*

She knocked lightly on the locked door of her chamber. "Ellen?"

The door opened immediately and Pen swept inside, turning to lock the door at her back.

The children gazed solemnly at her. They were dressed now in Holland smocks and petticoats, as befitted boys not yet breeched. Each held a piece of marchpane in his fist and wore an expression somewhat resembling bliss.

"Have they said anything?" she murmured, kneeling on the floor to put her face at their level.

"Not as such, my lady," Ellen replied. "But they've been all round the chamber, exploring.

423

Mostly they need feeding up."

"Yes." Pen bent to kiss her son and said distressfully, "No . . . no . . . I won't take it away," as he recoiled, snatching his fist behind his back.

She straightened, made a move to stroke his head. He shrank away from her, and when she tried the same with little Charles he too retreated, scuttling backwards across the bed.

"I will kill her!" Pen said with soft savagery. "So help me, God, I will see her rot!"

She stood looking at the children, clasping her elbows. "Toys . . . they need something to play with."

She felt a wave of helplessness wash over her. She didn't know how to be a mother. She'd had no experience, no opportunity to learn. And now she had two damaged babies who'd never been mothered, who didn't know a loving caress from a threatened blow.

But she was not alone, she reminded herself. She had her own mother, who knew everything about loving parenting, to guide her. It would be all right.

And Owen? What kind of father had he been before he'd disowned his children? Now that she looked at it, she knew that something was wrong with Robin's story. She had been forcing a piece of the puzzle that looked right into the wrong part of the picture. Just because there was a patch of blue, didn't mean the piece had to fit in the sky. It could be the sea, a snatch of color from a piece of clothing.

A knock at the door jerked her out of her reverie.

"Who is it?"

"Me!" came Pippa's impatient exclamation.

Ellen opened the door. Pippa bounded into the chamber, Robin on her heels. She flung her arms around Pen.

"Oh, Pen, dearest, I am so sorry . . . so very very sorry. Mama and Lord Hugh were out riding so I haven't had a chance to tell her, otherwise she would have come with me."

She turned with tear-wet cheeks to the bed, saying softly, "Oh . . . there he is . . . but . . . but which one, Pen?"

"Don't you see any likeness?" her sister asked with painful anxiety.

Pippa dashed the tears from her eyes and squatted in front of the boys, managing to produce a cheerful grin. "So, who have we here? Is that marchpane? It's quite my favorite sweetmeat."

They regarded her solemnly and continued to suck on the confection.

"I don't think any child of Philip's could have red hair," Pippa said with a tiny laugh. "And this one has his father's eyelashes. I'd know them anywhere."

"Oh, Pippa!" Laughter and tears mingled in Pen's voice as she embraced her sister. "They are Philip's eyelashes, aren't they?"

Robin approached the pair on the bed. " 'Tis extraordinary," he murmured. "But there *is* a likeness."

"What are you going to do?" Pippa asked, rising to her feet. "How will you have him declared Philip's son?"

Pen glanced at Robin. He gave her a slight warning shake of his head and she understood that not even Pippa could be let into the secret of Mary's impending flight.

"I have an idea," Pen said. She turned to the interested maid. "Ellen, would you fetch meat and ale? I haven't yet broken my fast."

Ellen looked none too pleased at this dismissal but curtsied and went on her way.

"Now," said Pen. "If we can discredit Miles and his mother in some way, have them arrested even, then it will be a great deal easier to establish Philip."

"How are you going to do that?" Pippa inquired, her gaze lively with interest.

"I've already begun." Pen sat on the bed and put an arm casually around her son. This time he didn't pull away, but rested his sticky face against her breast.

"If Northumberland can be persuaded to believe that Goodlow might once have used poison in the Bryanstons' interests in the past, he will see treason, will he not?"

Pippa and Robin stared at her in silence for a minute. Then Pippa said, "Do you believe Lady Bryanston used her to induce your labor, Pen?"

"Oh, yes," Pen replied, her mouth twisting. "She tried to force me to miscarry. And I believe she allowed Philip to die. But I cannot prove it, as she and Miles both said."

"They would hardly say you could prove nothing if there was nothing to prove." Pippa ran her fingers through a bowl of potpourri on the table, her expression distracted.

"It will serve," Robin said with a grim smile. "Northumberland sees treason in every corner and he's already out of patience with Bryanston, who follows him around like an eager puppy, always boasting about his close connections with the *Grand Master of the Realm*."

Pen nodded. "Then you can nurture the seed I sowed, Robin. The duke trusts you, and because of the family connection you'd be in a position to voice suspicions about Philip's death . . . speculate a little out loud. From what I heard, the Goodlow woman is not doing the king any good with her ministrations, quite the opposite, so the duke would have no reason to contradict what you implied."

Robin rose to his feet. "Then I will be about this business." He went to the door just as Ellen entered with a tray.

He laid an arresting hand on her arm and took the ale jug off the tray. He tipped it to his throat and drank deeply before setting it back. "My thanks, I had a thirst to rival a camel's after a month in the desert."

He wiped his mouth with the back of his hand as he glanced over at Pen. "Until later then."

"Yes, until later."

"A carriage is waiting below to take Pippa and

Ellen, with the children, to Holborn."

"They'll leave directly," Pen replied.

Robin nodded, repeated as if it reassured him, "Until later then," and left.

"You should eat," Pippa said, indicating the tray that Ellen had set on a low table.

Pen nodded and broke bread, laying upon it a slice of sirloin liberally spread with mustard.

"So Ellen and I are to take the children to Holborn," Pippa stated, instinctively taking Pen's place on the bed between the boys. Idly she reached a hand behind her to stroke Nutmeg, who was still regarding the proceedings warily. "You cannot leave Mary? Not even for something this momentous?"

Pen shook her head and swallowed her mouthful. "I haven't told her. I can't risk the Bryanstons getting wind of this while the children are still in the palace."

"No, I suppose not." Pippa raised an eyebrow. "There's something you're not telling *me*, though."

When Pen made no reply, Pippa didn't press further. It was to be her task to break the news to her mother and Lord Hugh. There was no room for distraction.

Ellen bustled around the chamber assembling the necessaries for their journey. "We'll be taking Nutmeg with us then," she observed, tucking the cat into his carrying basket without waiting for an answer.

Pen picked up her son, holding him against

her shoulder. His head lolled sleepily. She kissed the top of his head, inhaling the soft, clean, baby smell of him. So different from when she'd first seen him.

"We'd best go," Pippa said. She moved to take Philip from Pen as Ellen picked up Charles.

"Yes," Pen said, but she kept hold of her son. Her arms would not make the necessary movement to hand him over.

Then she said, "No . . . no, I cannot let him go. Take Charles to Mama. I will bring Philip when I can." She kissed his cheek.

"But, Pen . . . Pen . . . how can you look after —" And then Pippa stopped. "We'll see you both as soon as you've done whatever it is that you're about to do," she murmured instead into her sister's ear as she bent to kiss her. "I don't think any member of the family will ever argue with you again, Pen."

At that Pen smiled; it was typical of Pippa to make such a joke.

The two women left with the bundled child and the cat in his basket. Pen carried Philip to the window. How she was to explain him to Mary, she didn't know. But neither did she care. He was her son. And she would not let him go again.

Twenty-two

●

"Get rid of it!" Lady Bryanston commanded, her voice for once agitated, her skirts swinging around her as she paced the library.

"But how, madam?" Miles asked. He knew what his mother was referring to but this abrupt command took him by surprise.

"I have no idea!" she snapped. "Just *do* it!"

"But no one could have any idea where he is," Miles protested. "He's buried as safely in the stews as if he were six feet in the ground."

"I should have dealt with him at birth," his mother said, pausing by the table, her hand unconsciously caressing a massive piece of granite carved into a lion's head that served as a paperweight.

"If you'd kept your mouth shut this morning, everything would have been fine. Instead of which, you have to lay hands on her and prate about how nothing can be proved! You are an idiot, Miles!"

Miles sighed and tucked in his chin. This refrain had continued ever since they had left Greenwich Palace after his confrontation with Pen. He'd rarely seen his mother so unnerved, but then he'd never seen Pen so curiously triumphant. And she had been triumphant, complacent, so extraordinarily sure of herself. It was that, Miles knew, that had shaken his mother.

"What does she know? What *could* she know?" Lady Bryanston muttered. She picked up a paper knife and Miles took an involuntary step backwards. His mother, while not being averse to employing others in such matters, was not herself prone to physical violence — her tongue wreaked all the damage necessary — but her mood at present was most unpredictable.

"We have to get rid of it!" she repeated, driving the point of the paper knife into the desk. The gesture merely bent the tip of the blade, but its symbolism was obvious even to her thickheaded son.

"The child is the only possible link. While he's alive, there is always the danger that he might be found, and the whole story will come out."

"You didn't think so before, madam," Miles said tentatively. "It's been two years and more."

"I assumed that in those conditions he would have died long since," she declared with what sounded to Miles remarkably like a hiss. "But you heard what Pen said about Mistress Goodlow. If she starts making those connections, there's no knowing where it will lead."

"No, madam," he agreed, ducking his head. "But how is it to be done?"

"Find a way!" Her hard brown eyes glared their contempt, her voice dripped icy scorn.

"Yes, madam."

Miles bowed and hastened from the library, replacing his bonnet as he did so.

Lady Bryanston looked up at the portrait of her son Philip that hung above the mantel. At least he'd had brains, she reflected. But he would not bend to her will . . . not even as a child. He'd always followed his own path, his own conscience, and he'd married a woman who was exactly the same. Both of them pig-headed, unmovable, both of them without a smidgeon of ambition, except to see Philip's poetry in print.

If only she could have harnessed Philip's brain to her own ambition . . .

She sighed and shook her head at the waste of such talent and opportunity.

"My lord duke." Robin approached Northumberland in the king's council chamber. The duke stood alone by the window embrasure, his face darker than usual, his mouth seeming thinner, his eyes more piercing.

"Robin?" His voice was curt.

"I talked with my sister, my lord," Robin said in confidential tones. "She is, of course, very happy to do your bidding."

"Yes, I talked with her myself," the duke said, his frown deepening. "She made her obedience known to me. I will assume your moment of insolence was an aberration."

Robin bowed his head. "I ask pardon, my lord. I was taken aback and forgot my duty for a moment."

The duke nodded, his expression still dour.

"How does the king?" Robin asked, looking over his shoulder towards the door to the king's antechamber.

"Ill . . . very ill," Northumberland said.

"The herbalist's remedies do no good?"

"No. If anything the king is worse."

"We are a superstitious family and do not ourselves have too much faith in Mistress Goodlow's abilities," Robin said casually. "She had but ill luck when attending my sister's husband, and then my sister, who miscarried late in her pregnancy despite Mistress Goodlow's best attentions."

"Yes, so I understand." The duke looked shrewdly at the younger man. "Lady Bryanston, however, recommends her most highly."

"Yes," Robin agreed. "A triumph of hope over experience, one might say."

"One might." Northumberland rubbed his fingertips over his mouth. "Lady Pen implied as much."

"My sister is understandably prejudiced," Robin said smoothly. "But Lady Bryanston has much at stake." He smiled.

"Oh?" The duke quirked an eyebrow.

"To have one of her own servants in such close proximity to His Highness . . ." Robin paused. "It cannot help but add to her consequence, and, of course, to that of her son."

"I had noticed," Northumberland said dryly. He looked away from Robin, gazing out of the window at the river glittering under the feeble rays of the winter sun.

Robin glanced up at the clock on the mantel. It was close to one o'clock. Mary's barge would be long gone from the palace dock, but it would be several hours before she reached Baynard's Castle. His primary task was to ensure that the duke failed to notice her prolonged absence, and Robin was deriving a savage satisfaction from the business at hand.

He murmured, "My sister's husband died very suddenly. It was such a puzzle to us all, one day he was hale, the next he had taken to his bed, never to leave it, despite all the attentions of both Mistress Goodlow and his mother."

Northumberland turned back to Robin. "And of his wife, I assume?"

"Lady Pen was not well herself at the time. It was assumed the usual frailty of pregnancy, although she had been well up until then," Robin said with a half shrug. "She was not strong enough to attend at her husband's bedside much of the time."

"I see." Northumberland again touched his mouth. "Do you make a point here, Robin?"

"If you would take one, my lord." Robin's vivid blue eyes never wavered as he met the duke's stare, his mouth was unusually grim, his body very still and straight. "The king does not improve."

"No," Northumberland said, and without a word of excuse pushed past Robin and stalked from the council chamber.

He entered the king's bedchamber but remained in the doorway, wafting his pomander in a vain attempt to freshen the air. Only the woman Goodlow attended the king, holding a small copper pan over a candle flame. She glanced up at the duke, but offered no obeisance, her lips moving all the while in some incantation.

"How fares the king?" Northumberland demanded.

"He will be well within the week, my lord," the woman said, her expression calm, her eyes quietly confident. "The physic takes some time to work."

Northumberland frowned, hesitated. What had Beaucaire been implying? That the Bryanstons had introduced a poisoner into the king's bedchamber? It was impossible to believe, not least because Northumberland couldn't imagine what they would hope to gain by the king's death. And yet the king grew worse, not better. Maybe the woman was simply a charlatan.

His mouth thinned. Charlatan or worse, she was the Bryanstons' instrument.

He strode to the door of the bedchamber and bellowed, *"Guards!"*

They came running, six of them, weapons drawn.

Northumberland pointed to the Goodlow woman. "Question her about the death of Philip Bryanston," he instructed coldly.

Mistress Goodlow, for the first time since Northumberland had met her, paled; terror stood out stark on her countenance.

"Put her to the question," he said with icy dispassion. "And send for the king's physicians. They must repair the damage this woman has done."

If God gave them the power for such an impossible task.

"I do not understand any of this," Mary said for the tenth time as she looked across the cabin to where Pen sat holding her child. "How can we possibly flee across country with a baby on our hands?"

"I do not believe he will cause any difficulty, madam," Pen said calmly. "He hasn't so far." She kissed the top of the child's head.

Philip had barely uttered a sound since they'd left Greenwich but she was relieved to see that he seemed to be taking notice of his surroundings now. His dark eyes were wide and roamed constantly around the cabin, resting every now and again on the faces of the women, all three of whom returned his solemn gaze with a kind of horrified bemusement at the tale they had just heard.

If the situation hadn't been so grave, Pen would have been amused at the speechless astonishment that had greeted her arrival on the barge with a baby in her arms. She had waited until Mary, with Susan and Matilda and a very heavy picnic basket, had boarded the barge before joining them, giving the helmsman the order to depart as soon as her foot touched the deck.

That had been over an hour ago, an hour in which she explained what had happened, and in the face of Mary's objections declared with quiet resolution that she had no intention of being separated from her son again in the foreseeable future.

"The chevalier helped you find him," Susan said, still bemused.

"How could anyone be as evil as your mother-in-law?" Matilda's tone was awed. "To do such a thing? 'Tis well nigh impossible to believe."

Mary was for the moment silent. She was thinking of how her own father had had her declared a bastard, his marriage to her mother incestuous; how he had stripped her of her title and forced her to serve her half sister as lady-in-waiting. On his orders she had been kept short of food and decent clothes, imprisoned in cold, drafty houses, deprived of her mother's company. Even when Mary had been at death's door, when she and her attendants were convinced she had been poisoned and had only days to live, Henry had not permitted her mother to tend her.

Parents could do dreadful things in the name of dynasty and ambition.

"Your chevalier is clearly resourceful," she said after a minute. "Which is fortunate since all our hopes rest on that resourcefulness. Has he made provision for the child's presence?"

"No," Pen confessed. "But I have little doubt it will not be beyond his resources to manage."

"Let us hope not." Mary shook her head as if in resignation.

"How will you establish his identity, Pen?" Susan leaned over and hesitantly touched the child's fragile hand. He jumped as if startled but made no sound.

Pen tightened her hold on him and glanced at Mary. "I am hoping that my mother and Lord Hugh will have some knowledge of the legal issues, but my cause would be greatly helped by your approval, madam. If you were to declare yourself satisfied that he is indeed the true Earl of Bryanston it will carry much weight."

Mary shook her head bitterly. "Not in my present position, Pen. I have no more power than a street vendor."

"That will not last, madam," Pen stated. "You will be queen on your brother's death."

"One would hope so," the princess returned with an arid smile. "How close are we?"

Pen rose with Philip and went up on deck. They were close now to Whitehall Palace on the north bank. She lifted the child onto the rail and crooned softly to him, nuzzling his cheek. He seemed now to accept her caresses, but he still spoke not a word.

She picked up his hand and felt the tears prick behind her eyes at how thin and fragile, almost clawlike, it was. She remembered how Anna's hands at this age had had dimpled bracelets at the wrists, and pudgy little fingers. How her arms and legs had been so round.

But soon, she promised herself. Soon little Philip would look as he should. And soon she would see the day of vengeance.

She turned and went below. "Wind and tide are with us. We should reach Blackfriars in an hour or so, and I see no sign of pursuit, madam."

Antoine de Noailles drew his cloak tighter around him as a bitter wind gusted off the river. "Why must we walk outside?" he grumbled to his companion. "My parlor is perfectly secure and a damn sight warmer."

"I prefer the outdoors for this discussion," Owen said. "There are times when walls have ears. Besides, it's a beautiful afternoon; a little bracing, I grant you, but quite exquisite." He gestured to the bare trees along the riverbank. Their branches were starkly white against the brilliant blue sky, their twigs glittering with a filigree of ice.

De Noailles sighed, unimpressed by the day's winter beauty. He glanced up and sideways at the taller man. He could feel the brittle edge to the chevalier's mood, see it in the hard jut of his set jaw, the disturbing light in his eye. Something was badly wrong with Owen d'Arcy.

He clapped his gloved hands together and returned to the main topic of conversation. If

439

Owen wanted to confide his troubles, he would do so in his own time. "So, we are to help Mary get safely away to Essex," he said. "Do you really think Northumberland is planning on rerouting the succession?"

"I think it's highly likely," Owen said, breaking off a twig from the box hedge beside the path. "It seems the most plausible explanation for these sudden plans to marry his son to the king's cousin."

He rubbed the greenery between his hands, inhaling the scent. "Her house at Woodham Walter is but two miles from the coast, so, if she needs to flee the land, she's within easy reach of the emperor's ships there."

"Aye," muttered the French ambassador, pulling his hat down farther over his ears with an emphatic tug. "Northumberland could have her arrested on a charge of treason at any moment since she insists upon practicing her own religion against the king's express edicts."

"He'll find it harder to do that if she's no longer under the king's roof." Owen turned away from the river and began to walk back up the path to the house, his companion hurrying to keep up with his long stride.

"I wonder if Simon Renard has come to the same conclusion about Northumberland's intentions," de Noailles said. "I must ask our ears in the Spanish embassy."

Renard! Of course. Owen stopped dead on the path and the ambassador nearly ran into his back. Renard would know the old scandal, and if he thought it would do him any good he would have no scruples about relaying it to someone like Robin of Beaucaire. And what more natural than that Beaucaire would know where to go for unsavory tidbits of information? The French wouldn't tell him anything, but their rival, the Spanish ambassador . . . ? Of course.

"What is it?" demanded de Noailles, withdrawing his nose from between Owen's shoulder blades.

"Just a revelation," Owen said, his mouth taut. "The answer to a puzzle."

"What puzzle?"

"A personal one."

De Noailles grimaced at the curt tone but knew better than to pursue the subject. "So you'll winkle the princess out of Baynard's Castle in the morning. I'll arrange for a goodly crowd to be at the gates just before dawn. Our men will spread largesse around the taverns tonight."

"Aye, and spice the coin and the drink with a few hints that Northumberland means the princess some harm. That should get them going."

De Noailles nodded. "Will you escort her yourself into Essex?"

"That depends," Owen said, his mouth still taut.

"On what?"

Owen gave a short laugh that was quite without humor. "On whether I decide I have something better to do, my friend."

The ambassador found this answer less than satisfying but he gave a very Gallic shrug and said merely, "God and good fortune go with you, then."

"And with you, Ambassador." Owen left the garden and directed his steps along the ice-crusted lane towards a tavern that he knew. There he ordered a pitcher of mulled wine while he waited for evening, when he would make his approach to Baynard's Castle under cover of darkness.

Pen.

He stared down into his tankard, inhaling the fragrance of cloves and nutmeg. She had failed him, he thought savagely. She'd believed her brother's tale, Simon Renard's tale. She had believed the worst without hesitation.

He drained his tankard and set it down hard on the table. He swung his heavy gaze to the fire, watching the patterns in the flames. He had begun to think there could be a future to their loving, although he hadn't thought how it was to be achieved.

He would have had to tell her the whole wretched tale then, for her own safety. But she would have understood. She would not have endangered either of them as foolish Estelle had done. Poor, foolish, vain Estelle.

Owen stared into the flames and allowed his anger and hurt to flare high with the spurt of scarlet and then diminish as the sudden flame fell back. He wasn't prepared to let Pen go. It was as simple as that. He was still bitter, still raw. He wanted to hear her beg his forgiveness, he wanted to withhold it, watch her dismay. He wanted her to be as distressed as he was. And yet he wasn't prepared to let her go.

It was what he had meant, of course, when he'd told the ambassador that he didn't know what his plans for the morrow would be. They would depend on Pen. On where she went, what she had decided to do. Or rather, what she decided to do when faced with a choice.

He rose abruptly, swinging his sword to his side, catching up his cloak from the bench beside him. For the moment he had a spy's business to transact.

The tide had turned and the current was running strongly when he returned to the river. He hailed a skiff to take him to Baynard's Castle.

It was a bitterly cold evening, the sky a mass of stars, throwing silver light onto the dark, fast-flowing waters of the Thames. A small boat full of eel fishermen bobbed against the mud flats along the riverbank and their voices drifted clearly through the brittle air.

Owen pulled his chin into the collar of his cloak like a snail withdrawing its head and reviewed his plans.

"Baynard's Castle, guv. Looks like ye've got company."

The oarsman's voice brought him back to the

443

freezing night. He sat upright and gazed across to the mouth of the Fleet River where it flowed into the Thames. The bulk of the castle rose above, dominating the view up and down the river. Three barges were jostling for position against the current as they tried to maneuver alongside the quay. The lead barge, which was also the smallest, flew the Duke of Northumberland's pennant.

"Stay your oars," Owen said in a bare whisper, remembering how clearly the voices of the fishermen had carried over the water. "Hold up in midstream."

The boatman shipped his oars and hunkered down on the bench, pulling his frieze cap down and his collar up over his ears.

Owen turned on the thwart and swiftly doused the light from the cresset. The starlight offered little shadow but the boat was small and sat very still on the water.

He sat immobile, concentrating on the scene. The boatmen were having trouble docking the first barge with the swift-flowing current, and the two others swinging in the water sometimes perilously close to each other. Muffled curses flew on the wind. Three men emerged from the cabin as if in response.

Northumberland, Pembroke, and Suffolk.

Owen nodded to himself. He had expected word of the princess's arrival at Pembroke's residence to reach Greenwich by midafternoon. The three council members had wasted no time,

444

it seemed. Which meant that Owen had no time to spare.

The three men huddled against the deck rail, deep in conversation as they watched the docking. Owen could hear nothing. But he didn't need to. His gaze swept the shoreline.

"Pull into the bank just beyond the mouth of the Fleet," he whispered. His voice was a mere breath on the air but the oarsman had no difficulty hearing.

He took up his oars again and pulled strongly into the bank. Owen paid him and stepped into the shallows. The mud had a thick coating of ice that protected his boots and hose from the ooze beneath. He trod carefully, and the watching oarsman thought that it was as if he glided over the slick surface, so little sound did he make. He seemed to find footholds in the bank as if he knew they were there, and within a minute he was standing securely on the riverbank, his feet and garments not a whit disturbed by his unorthodox approach.

Owen listened. The castle's water steps were concealed from him by the bend that formed the mouth of the Fleet river, but he could hear voices clearly now. He was no more than a hundred feet from the steps.

He moved closer, seeking the concealment of a screen of rushes. The three men were now standing on the quay as a small troop of soldiers disembarked behind them.

"I don't like it," Pembroke was saying. "Not

without the king's direct orders."

"The king still will not issue an order for his sister's arrest without a deal of persuasion," Northumberland declared impatiently.

"I had hoped to work on him over the next day or two while she remained at Greenwich, safe in our custody, but the princess has taken matters into her own hands. I wish to God I knew who's advising her, who's helping her. She couldn't have planned this alone. Was she even sick?"

He spat over the rail with an oath. "But I'll find out soon enough. Now, we need to take her, before she leaves London."

Owen moved away, up towards the castle walls, his step swift and assured as he climbed through the undergrowth, ice crunching beneath his boots. The three men continued their discussion on the quay beneath him.

At the top of the hill, he turned aside along the wall to a small, little-used postern gate that he had discovered on previous visits, before the princess and her retinue had gone to Greenwich.

One minute the watchman was gazing morosely into the freezing darkness trying to find the source of the whisper that had hailed him, the next he was resting in blissful unconsciousness beneath a bush.

Once inside, Owen strode rapidly with the air of a man who knew both his way and his business, grateful in his haste for the straw that had been laid on the cobbles and flagstones to prevent slipping on the ice. Pitch torches flared in sconces high up on the walls of the cloistered courtyards that led to the west wing of the castle, where Mary had her apartments.

A soldier stood at the foot of the wide, curved flight of stone steps that led to the great oak door to the princess's lodging. He yawned and leaned back against the wall. This was routine duty and he was thinking longingly of the sentries' fire-warmed antechamber, the mug of ale and the dice cup waiting for him when he was relieved in half an hour.

Owen stopped in the shadow of the cloister leading to the stairs. He took from his doublet pocket a handful of pebbles that he'd picked up from the riverbank. The sentry yawned again and shifted his pike on the flagstones.

Owen tossed the pebbles into the cloister ahead of him. They fell in a clattering shower. It was an old trick, and, like most old tricks, it worked.

The sentry spun around towards the noise and took a step into the cloister. Owen slipped behind him, soundless as a woodland deer. He was halfway up the stairs, his dark clothes blending into the shadows, before the sentry had dismissed the clatter as unimportant and returned yawning to his post.

Owen lifted the latch on the door at the head of the stairs.

Twenty-three

●

The domestic running of the castle had been thrown into near chaos by the princess's unexpected return. Her apartments had not been readied for her and servants ran hither and thither through the series of rooms with fresh linens and hangings for the beds, buckets of hot coals for the fires, jugs of steaming water for the comfort of the guests.

The princess stood before the newly kindled fire in her parlor, her eyes on the Psalter she held between her hands. Her lips moved in soundless prayer.

Pen came into the parlor, carrying Philip on her hip, followed by two maidservants with laden supper trays.

"Since our picnic hamper only contained books I thought we should have supper," Pen said cheerfully.

"I have little interest in supper. 'Tis pesky cold in here." A shiver went through Mary's slight frame and she bent to the still sullen coals. "I don't know why it is that sea coal doesn't burn as well as wood. The fire's been lit this hour past and yet it throws off no heat at all."

"They have so little wood in the city, madam.

But you'll have log fires aplenty at Woodham Walter." Pen tried to disguise a note of exasperation. They were all three cold, hungry, and anxious, and Mary's complaints didn't improve the shining hour. In truth Pen was interested only in Philip's welfare. The baby was beginning to grizzle; a good sign, she thought. At least he was expressing himself, and maybe with some expectation that now his needs would be gratified.

The servants set the trays on the table and left. Mary put down her Psalter. "Well, let us eat then. When will your chevalier come, I wonder?"

"When he considers it right, madam," Pen said. Still holding the baby, she took a silver porringer and spoon from the table. Philip, from his perch on her hip, lunged for the bowl, and she laughed. "Yes . . . yes . . . it's coming."

She carried him, wriggling and wailing in frustration, to the window seat. She sat him down on the cushioned seat and sat beside him, spooning the honey-sweetened, milky gruel into his ever-open mouth. The tears dried on his cheeks and he waved his skinny arms in his eagerness.

Mary regarded them with a frown. She didn't mind children, and, indeed, had been moved to horror and pity by Pen's story, but the child was distracting Pen when all her attention should be on the princess's plight.

The door opened and Pen looked up, spoon poised. Philip wailed at the pause in his feeding just as Owen d'Arcy stepped into the chamber.

He closed the door, turned the key, and dropped the heavy bar into place.

He stood for a second with his back to the door. His black gaze swept the chamber and the energy coursed from him. He was dressed in a dark gray doublet slashed with black silk, the high collar opened to reveal a fashionably narrow ruff. His shirt was of dark gray edged in silver lace; his hose of black silk. He reminded Pen of nothing so much as the deadly silver-gray rapier in its black sheath that he carried at his hip.

"You've brought the child," he said, his dark gaze unreadable as it rested on her countenance. "Was that wise?"

"I had no choice," Pen returned simply, aware that her cheeks were suddenly flushed, aware of the surge of longing . . . longing to see his conspiratorial smile, his dancing eyes lit from behind with a warmth that she had sometimes thought could only be love. Instead, he was distanced, detached, his expression impassive.

"I could not bear to be parted from him. I don't believe he will hamper us," she said in a quiet, uninflected voice.

"I am glad to see you, Chevalier." Mary rose to her feet, and despite her calm tone fear danced in her eyes. He had brought peril with him, it crackled around him like an aura. "We had been awaiting you. Is there any news from Greenwich?"

"In a minute, madam." Owen spoke

brusquely. He strode into the connecting chamber, his step swift and silent. The princess's apartments consisted of a series of chambers, some little more than closets, others large and commodious bedchambers, all connecting to each other to form a corridor.

Pen gathered up Philip and followed on Owen's heels. He hastened through the deserted corridor of rooms. In the seventh and last chamber, an antechamber for the princess's pages, at present deserted, Owen locked the door and dropped the bar.

He turned to Pen, who stood breathless at his side. "Is there any other door that gives access to the castle beyond these chambers?"

She shook her head. "Not that I know of."

"Then come, we have little time. They will be here any minute." He moved past her, hurrying back to the princess's parlor.

Pen followed, running now to keep up. He entered the parlor and the three women rose to their feet. The sense of urgency and its attendant fear spread through them like an infection.

"What is happening, Chevalier?" Mary spoke steadily, but her hands shook as she pressed them against her skirts.

"You are in danger of immediate arrest, madam," he said, going to the four narrow glassed windows in the outside wall. He looked through them, down into the courtyard. A party of archers emerged from the gatehouse. "I had hoped that Northumberland would be more

451

cautious, but it seems his need is desperate."

Mary touched her throat. The pulse beat fast beneath the white lace partlet she wore at the neck of her gown. She said nothing.

Owen turned back from the window. "However, we can circumvent them so matters are not in such dire straits." He smiled suddenly, and Pen noticed how everyone except herself seemed unaccountably to relax.

The smile was designed simply to hearten the three women, to give them confidence. Why didn't they realize it? Pen wondered. It was as clear as day to her that Owen was in no mood to smile, however confident he might be in his ability to pull the chestnuts out of this fire.

Philip whimpered and she jiggled him against her shoulder. Maybe they were simply impressed by a show of raw male power. The thought in any other circumstances would have made her laugh and long to share it with Pippa. Lady Guinevere's daughters had not been bred to be impressed by such displays.

"No one knows I'm here so they won't know that you're aware of the immediate threat," Owen continued in his calm way. "They'll come to you expecting to gain peaceful entrance. They will not attempt to force their way in here. Such a tale would be quickly spread and it would enrage the people. The council's intention I'm certain is to lure you out and then speed you away while the city sleeps."

Mary nodded at the chevalier, her color returning. "The people do love me," she said with perfect truth.

Owen didn't reply but turned back to the window. The dukes and the Earl of Pembroke were entering the courtyard from the main gate on the heels of the archers and flanked by the party of soldiers. Quite a force to take one slight woman, he thought aridly. But, of course, it was the people of London they were concerned about. Londoners were a law unto themselves, intimidated by nothing, and they were fiercely loyal to Princess Mary. Therein lay the key to Owen's plan.

"Pen, extinguish all but a single candle in this chamber."

Pen obeyed without a word.

Owen spoke now in a whisper that nevertheless carried to every pair of ears. "When they come, madam, they will see that there is no light beneath the door. On no account must the door be opened. Pen, you will inform the earl through the oak that the princess has retired for the night. The journey has tired her and there's fear that she's taken a fever again."

Pen nodded briefly. Somehow she seemed to be standing outside the situation, watching the drama as if it were taking place on a stage. She hitched Philip higher on her shoulder, rubbing his back. He had fallen asleep but he was so thin she barely felt his dead weight.

"At first light, madam, you will be on your way to Woodham Walter," Owen declared with the same quiet confidence.

No one said anything as they heard the tread of heavy boots on the stone stairs outside. It sounded as if a sizable crowd had come to a halt outside Mary's door.

Mary was very still; she felt for her rosary, concealed beneath her overgown. Her lips moved silently. Now there was light only from a single candle and the sulky glow from the fire, and the five figures in the chamber seemed frozen in the shadows.

There was a knock at the door and the Earl of Pembroke spoke in warm and friendly tones. "Madam, I am honored you have returned to my house. May I have speech with you?" The latch rattled.

Owen nodded at Pen but she had already moved to the door. "My lord, the princess is awearied and has retired to her bed. I would not disturb her."

"But 'tis barely eight of the clock," the earl protested jovially. "I would sup with Princess Mary."

"My lady's fever has returned, my lord. She will not be disturbed this even." Pen stood calmly before the door, her voice steady as a rock.

"Then we should send for the physician." The earl was now almost pleading.

"The princess has taken a sleeping draft and will not be disturbed this even," Pen repeated firmly.

There was a rustle of movement beyond the

door and then the imperative sound of what had to be a sword hilt against the oak. "Lady Bryanston?"

"Yes, my lord Northumberland," Pen responded sweetly.

"You will give us entrance. We have need to speak with the princess." There was a barely perceptible pause before he said, "I bear a message from His Highness."

That was a swiftly concocted lie, Pen thought, but she could tell by Mary's sudden movement behind her that it could have worked. She glanced over her shoulder and saw that Owen had laid a restraining hand on the princess's arm.

"My lord duke, the princess is asleep. But I'm certain she will be pleased to receive you in the morning."

"I would hear that from the princess herself!" Northumberland sounded flustered.

Philip stirred against her shoulder and she rubbed his back again, anxious that he should make no sound. Again she repeated calmly, "My lady has taken a sleeping draft, my lord. She can speak to no one."

Owen stood outside the shadowy light thrown by the candle and the fire. His hand rested on the hilt of his rapier. He watched Pen soothe the restive child, and thought that in the few short hours since she had found her son she had grown more assured in handling him. They seemed to have grown together. Fanciful, of course, and yet he could almost see the bond strengthening between them.

There was a pause, much whispering, scuffing of boots on the cold stone outside the door. Then Northumberland said, "Lady Bryanston, pray give the princess our earnest wishes for her speedy recovery. We will wait upon her in the morning."

"I am certain she will be pleased to receive you, my lord duke," Pen said again.

Northumberland glowered at the massive oak door closed against him. Suffolk and Pembroke stood in silence, and the small troop of soldiers gathered behind them stared into the middle distance.

Northumberland muttered almost to himself, "There's nothing to be done at the moment. She's safe enough in there for the night. I'll return to Durham House until morning and be back here soon after dawn. She has only the three women with her, they'll have to open the door at some point. We'll simply wait her out."

"Aye, that seems best." Pembroke sounded relieved. The idea of forcibly removing the princess from his residence had alarmed him greatly. If Northumberland's plans did not succeed, and by some hideous miscalculation Mary did become queen, anyone present tonight would be facing the executioner's ax.

Everyone in the dim chamber remained immobile, listening as the sound of many boots receded down the steps to the courtyard. Then there was a collective exhalation.

"So, it seems you have bought us some time, Chevalier," Mary said in a low voice.

"Time for you to take some rest, madam," Owen said. "We cannot leave until first light."

"I could not sleep." The voice was haughty; the rosary beads clicked.

"Then, madam, you may pray," he returned brusquely. He turned back again to the windows behind him, watching the activity in the courtyard as Northumberland and Suffolk emerged from the castle. Horses were brought for them and they rode out through the opened gates. Presumably they were staying in their London residences for the night, so that they would be well positioned to make a speedy return in the morning. That would leave the princess with a very small window for her escape.

Mary felt that the chevalier had somehow dismissed her. There was insolence in his impatience, as if he gave not a fig for royal blood. But she found that she could not gainsay his assured assumption of command. "How are we to leave here undetected?"

"We cannot leave undetected," he stated. "But surprise and the dawn light will be on our side. You may leave the details to me. Go to your rest, madam."

Mary had lived for too much of her life in mortal danger to argue, however much she disliked the peremptory tone. She left the parlor, gesturing to Susan and Matilda that they should accompany her.

Pen closed the connecting door. She stood with her back to it, one hand behind her still resting on the latch, her other arm encircling the sleeping child.

Owen turned back to the room. The sight of her with the child stirred him and at the same time filled him with bitter envy.

"If he's sleeping perhaps you should put him down," he said, bending to poke some life into the fire.

Pen laid Philip on the window seat and covered him with a blanket. His thumb was in his mouth and she thought his cheeks had filled out a little; they certainly had more color.

"He's wet," she said. "But I'll wake him if I change him."

Owen straightened from the fire. "Where's the other one?"

"Charles . . . I call him Charles," Pen said. "He'll be tucked up in the nursery at Holborn by now. I didn't think I could manage both of them at the moment."

The exchange was curiously stilted, she thought, as if between two quite other people, two strangers. She felt empty when she looked at him. Empty and hopeless. His eyes were so hard, so pitiless, and she couldn't read anything behind them. No softening, no understanding.

But she had failed him, she reminded herself,

and Owen it seemed had no forgiveness for failure.

He merely shrugged. "You won't be able to carry him out of here yourself. You'll have to relinquish him for a few minutes, I'm afraid."

"Why?" She could hear a ripple of panic in her voice as if Philip had been threatened. Her eyes darted to the sleeping child and she had to force herself to leave him undisturbed.

Owen made no immediate reply and in the quiet Pen heard the absolute silence in the chambers beyond the parlor. It was a frightened, waiting silence. Outside, the faint sounds of marching feet drifted upwards. A voice called an order. A horse stamped on the cobbles.

Owen looked at her and she looked back at him, her hazel eyes deep pools of confusion and trouble in her pale, tired face.

"Owen?" she said softly. "Owen, I cannot bear to be broken like this. Can we not try to mend it?"

He moved then, came over to her, his step sure and determined. He stood directly in front of her without touching her, but so close she could feel the heat of his body. He spoke with slow deliberation, his eyes still without warmth, and he spoke to her as if she were a stranger.

"I am a man of five and thirty. I have had a wife and two children. I have done many things in my life. I have fought on battlefields, and on the decks of a ship slippery with blood; I've been tortured in a Moorish prison and escaped from a

Spanish one. I'm a fighter, not a courtier, by nature. And my business is espionage. I have never pretended otherwise with you."

"No," she agreed, feeling for words. "And you're telling me now that I may not know many things about you . . . about your past . . . about the things that you have done . . . have had to do. That these things are not for me to know. I must accept you, trust you, without necessarily having a reason to do so."

"But you can't do that," he stated harshly.

She lifted a hand towards him but didn't touch him. "Maybe," she said. "Perhaps . . . I don't know."

Smoke billowed from the fireplace as wind gusted down the chimney. The glass windowpanes rattled. The bright clear weather had turned around.

Owen stepped back. His eyes, black as polished obsidian, gazed into her own as if he would see into her very soul.

She waited for him to say something, offer her something, some inkling of his thoughts, but he said nothing and the silence seemed to smother them.

She said dully, "So how are we to get out of here unhindered? What of Philip? Why may I not carry him?"

"I will explain," he answered, his voice once more calm and detached. "You have a considerable part to play, and I see a way to put the child's presence to good use."

★ ★ ★

Half an hour later, they made their way soundlessly through the corridor of darkened, deserted chambers. Susan and Matilda were both asleep, fully dressed, sharing a bed. The curtains were drawn tight around the princess's bed and there was no sound from within.

Pen went to the night table and took a small round box. She handed it to Owen, who slipped it into his doublet pocket. In the pages' empty antechamber, Owen eased open the door and peered into the narrow corridor beyond. It was deserted, as he had hoped. Pembroke had no reason to suspect that his guest might attempt a midnight backstairs departure from a closely guarded castle.

He slid from the room and disappeared into the shadows.

Pen locked the door after him and dropped the bar. She ran back to the parlor where Philip still slept soundly. Apprehension close to terror, exhaustion, the dreadful empty shell of her love for Owen, all threatened to overwhelm her. She forced herself to eat some bread and meat, then sank down on a low chair by the fire.

Twenty-four

●

"Pen?"

Pen came to with a start and realized that she must have dozed. She jumped to her feet. "Madam? You are awake."

Mary stood in the doorway, fully dressed except that she had discarded her hood. Her hair lay in soft coiled braids on her shoulders. It made her look younger than her thirty-six years.

"I have not slept," she replied. "Where is the chevalier?"

"He has gone to arrange for our departure."

Mary came over to the fire. "And how does he intend to manage that?"

"With great fanfare, madam." Pen bent to add more coals to the dying fire. "But it was necessary to borrow your seal." She glanced up at the princess, whose expression betrayed no emotion.

Pen continued calmly, "He has given order for transport to be ready for us as soon as it's daylight. No one will have the authority to prevent your leaving so unexpectedly. Northumberland and Suffolk left the castle after you refused them entrance, but the chevalier expects them to return soon after dawn, so we must move quickly."

"I see." Mary took the stool that Pen had vacated.

"The chevalier believes that your safety cannot be threatened in London in the daylight. We will set out as if to attend early service at St. Paul's. The French ambassador has arranged for a large crowd to gather outside the gate waiting to cheer your departure and accompany you on your way to church. You will not be arrested in the presence of a popular mob."

Mary cupped her chin in her hand as she looked into the fire that still failed to produce more than the impression of warmth.

"Simple and probably true," she observed. "But am I to claim sanctuary in St. Paul's then? Surely when we are on the country roads beyond London the duke could send a warrant after me."

"No, madam. When we enter the church you will slip out by a side door and leave the city by a secret route, whilst I remain in church in your stead. The chevalier will provide you with an escort. I'll remain at my prayers for a while after you've left, and that should give you sufficient start. You should reach Woodham Walter by early evening. Then you will be under the protection of the emperor's ships."

"And what of you, Pen?"

Pen turned her face to the fire. "I will take my child to Holborn and seek the protection of my family."

She paused, choosing her words; Mary was

very conscious of the dignity due a princess. "As an added precaution, I will take your place when we leave the castle. You should be disguised as a maid, carrying Philip to make the deception more complete. Susan and Matilda will accompany us so that it will look as if I have remained behind."

She looked back at Mary and saw the expression she expected. She went on swiftly, "Everyone knows that you often invite members of the household to worship with you. The presence of a maidservant with a child in your small party will not cause undue remark."

Mary stared at Pen. "*I* . . . I dress as a maid?"

Pen said quietly, "A maid's kirtle for a throne, madam. No one will pursue a maid through the countryside."

Mary was silent, her gaze once more returned to the fire. If this deception would enable her to stay alive and outwit Northumberland, the throne would be hers. She said heavily, remembering her youth anew, "It will not be the worst of indignities.

"I suppose I should count myself fortunate that the French interests also serve mine at present." She shrugged, leaned towards the fire, extending her hands to the flames. The rings on her fingers glittered. "I have learned always to use what comes to hand."

Pen inclined her head in acknowledgment, and then went to the window. She gazed down into the courtyard where the torchmen paced their allotted beat. The wind had dropped again and it was quiet and still, a few flakes of snow drifting to the cobbles.

When he left Pen, Owen took a series of twists and turns through the narrow servants' corridors. He wondered if they had increased the guard at the main door to the princess's lodgings and thought it unlikely. They would see no threat. How could she and her three ladies possibly, without help, leave the secured environment of Baynard's Castle?

He had not spent enough time in the castle to learn its secret passages, but he had certainly learned its back ways, and within a short time he found himself in the kitchen courtyard. Beyond lay the stables.

He found a sleepy groom on duty ready to sound the alarm if the earl decided to leave his castle on a late-night errand. It was not an unusual occurrence.

Owen gave his instructions. He showed the princess's seal and gave his orders with succinct authority. The befuddled groom tugged a forelock and swallowed a yawn.

The princess had decided to attend early-morning worship at St. Paul's with her ladies. The carriage should be ready and waiting in the central court at first light. The groom thought nothing of it. Such an excursion would be within character for the deeply religious princess.

Owen left Baynard's Castle through the same little-used postern gate through which he'd entered. The watchman was still beneath his bush, a livid bruise blooming on his temple. He moaned as Owen bent over him, feeling for a pulse. Owen hesitated, glancing up at the sky where the evening star was fading fast. He had little time to do what had to be done, but the man had been lying out in the frigid night for too long. He hitched him up by his armpits and dragged him into the shelter of the small watchman's hut. It wasn't much warmer, but at least the roof kept the snow out. He set the man down, propping his back against a wall. Then he left to go about his own business before ensuring that the ambassador's men were doing their job of raising a mob of Princess Mary's noisy and loyal supporters.

"We should leave now, madam." Pen turned from the window where she had been watching for the fading of the evening star.

Mary stood dressed in a maidservant's plain serge gown and cloak. They were old garments that belonged to her maid Lucy and had been left behind at Baynard's Castle when they went to Greenwich. Mary was smaller than Lucy and the ill-fitting costume made her look even shabbier. No one would see the regal Princess Mary in this gown with the dragging hem and overlong sleeves. Matilda and Susan stood beside her, pale and frightened.

466

"Are you certain they will not stop us?"

"No," Pen said frankly, lifting a sleepy Philip from the window seat. "But I think this is the best chance we have."

"Very well. You will need to precede me." With the slightest touch of irony Mary gestured to the door.

Pen handed her the child and it was like tearing off her own skin. She watched critically anxious as the princess held the child awkwardly against her.

"Let me cover him more securely, madam." She wrapped the blanket tightly around the child, covering his head. "Just hold him steadily so that he doesn't become frightened."

"I think I can carry a child," Mary said sardonically. "At least as far as the carriage. Then you may have him back."

Pen curtsied. Susan lifted the heavy bar on the door and turned the key. Pen, heavily veiled, swept through. Behind her the other women fell into place.

Pen's heart raced but she found that she had absolute confidence. The carriage would be there, the gates would open as they must for a daughter of Henry VIII, and they would gain the freedom of the streets. Owen would ensure that it happened.

The guard at the foot of the stairs scratched his head as the party swept down. He had had no orders to prevent anyone leaving the princess's apartments, his job was simply to check the credentials of anyone entering them. As far as he knew, the princess was simply an honored guest of the Earl of Pembroke.

"The princess is attending morning worship at St. Paul's," he was informed by one of the two haughty ladies accompanying the slender, veiled and cloaked figure of Princess Mary.

"Yes, madam," the guard returned with a low bow. He cast an incurious glance at the humbly attired maidservant carrying the baby, and guessed that the princess had decided the woman was in need of a little spiritual counsel.

He stood still scratching his head until the party had passed into the cloister, then he abandoned his post and made his way to the guardroom, where he found the sergeant dozing beside the fire.

"What're you doin' 'ere?" the sergeant demanded. "Yer detail ain't up until eight."

"Well, seein' as 'ow the princess an' 'er ladies 'is gone to church, I thought I'd get meself a bit of a warm like." He held his hands to the brazier gratefully.

"Gone to church?" The sergeant sat up. His opened tunic gaped over an overhanging paunch. "We wasn't told."

The guard shrugged. "Someone forgot, I reckon. Or mebbe she jest decided on the spur o' the moment."

The sergeant stood up, rebuttoning his tunic. "I'd best tell my lord." He hurried away to the earl's chambers.

★ ★ ★

Pen tried to walk slowly, casually, setting the pace for the others. It was hard not to hurry but they mustn't give the impression of any unusual urgency. All her senses were concentrated on Mary and Philip behind her, her ears alert for the child's faintest whimper. He would need feeding again soon. How could she feed him while she was on her knees in the Lady Chapel of St. Paul's? The question seemed to take precedence over all else.

The castle was coming alive for the new day. The torchmen were leaving their posts in the central courtyard, and servants scurried around, extinguishing the pitch torches along the cloister walls. Everyone stopped what they were doing to bow as the group of women went by. The veiled princess inclined her head in acknowledgment.

Pen heaved a sigh of relief. In the cold gray light of the freezing morning the carriage was there in the central court, flanked by two outriders, the horses' breath steaming.

Pen took her place in the vehicle. The others climbed in after her, the maid last.

Pen held the leather curtain aside so that she could see out. Mary shrank into the darkest corner of the carriage, staring at the arms engraved into the panel behind Pen's head, and thought of the crown.

The carriage driver cracked his whip above the horses' ears at the moment when the Earl of

469

Pembroke emerged from the castle, his clothing in disarray, a cloak hastily thrown over his furred night robe. He ran across the court to the carriage, almost tripping over the hem of his gown.

Pen's heart jumped into her throat. In an urgent whisper she instructed the outrider on her side of the carriage to signal that the castle gates that gave onto Ludgate be opened immediately. She dropped the curtain, concealing herself in the vehicle's dark interior.

"Madam . . . madam, I beg you . . . pray stay for a moment. I will accompany you."

Pen coughed into her handkerchief and without moving aside the curtain said in a muffled voice, "I cannot stay, my lord. I intend to worship at St. Paul's this morning." She coughed again.

"Madam, you sound quite hoarse. You shouldn't be out in the dawn air, really you shouldn't," the earl said desperately.

The carriage began to move. "My lord, I go to my prayers," she stated in a fair imitation of Mary at her most haughtily dismissive. "Move forward."

The earl raised a hand to order the gates closed again but then saw what awaited beyond them. A substantial crowd was gathered along the route to Ludgate. The princess's name rose in a great roar.

Pembroke's hand fell to his side. He watched helplessly as the carriage moved through the gates and was engulfed in the fervent crowd beyond.

Hats were thrown into the air, cheering folk ran alongside the carriage.

Pen leaned over, moved the curtain aside, and raised a hand. Her veil was thick and black. She saw faces raised in adoration and a shiver ran through her. This was the adulation of royalty. This was what Mary would not give up.

And why should she?

She dropped the curtain and leaned forward to take her son from the very willing princess. He looked up at her with his great solemn brown eyes, then suddenly smiled. Her heart filled with an unutterable joy and she gave a little cry of delight, smothering his face with kisses.

The carriage climbed Ludgate Hill, the steep incline slowing their progress so that the crowd was well able to keep up with the horses.

"Pembroke will have sent immediately to Northumberland," Mary said. "He will know within the hour."

Pen, still enthralled by her son's smile, said vaguely, "You'll be long gone by then, madam."

Mary chewed her lip; beside her Susan and Matilda sat in rigid, terrified silence. Even the escorting crowd's riotous support had a frightening edge, as if it could suddenly tumble from wild good humor into violence.

They drew up outside the main doors of the church. One of the outriders opened the carriage door, and Pen, having handed the child back to the princess, descended, raising one hand as the mob cheered. The others followed, and in minutes they were safely within the church's dark interior. A priest in plain robes stood before the altar preparing to conduct the Protestant mass.

Mary stiffened, her nose twitching. Only under compulsion would she attend a Protestant service. The absence of incense in the air offended her. When she was queen, all the old rituals would be restored, she promised God as she followed Pen into the Lady Chapel. There would be scarlet robes and incense, the full panoply of the mass, the eucharist, everything that her brother had forbidden.

Now out of sight of the main body of the church, she gave the baby back to Pen. She knelt before the chapel altar, her hand going to the hidden rosary beneath her gown.

"Madam, this is no time for prayer," Pen whispered.

"There is always time for prayer," Mary replied.

"I trust then that you can pray on horseback, madam." Owen d'Arcy stepped out of the shadows behind the altar. "Come this way. There's no time to lose."

Mary rose reluctantly, despite what was at stake. "Do my ladies come with me?"

"All but Pen," he said. He moved aside a tapestry beside the altar depicting the crucifixion, and opened a small door behind it. Mary hastened past him into the darkness of a narrow passage, Susan and Matilda following.

Owen glanced over his shoulder at Pen. "Stay here until I come back for you."

"How long?" she whispered, her mouth dry at the prospect of kneeling alone with her helpless baby, unprotected in the shadowed darkness of this dank-smelling chapel, waiting for she knew not what. She held the child tightly to her breast, pressing his mouth against her bosom in case he began to cry.

"Not long." And he was gone, closing the narrow grilled door behind him.

The three women had stopped in the dark passage. With a murmur of excuse he slipped past them, leading the way over the uneven flagstones, down a staircase into the crypt that smelled of damp and old bones. A single candle illuminated the space.

Owen wasted no time on words. He crossed the crypt and led the way up another narrow staircase. A door at the top opened onto an alley running between the walls of the cathedral and a great mansion next door.

Three men sat horses with pillion saddles. Owen helped the princess onto the pillion pad behind a burly man well wrapped in a homespun cloak, a wide-brimmed hat pulled down over his brow. He offered no greeting and received none.

"You will stop to change horses twice on the road, madam," Owen said softly. "Be prepared to ride fast. These men know the route to take and how to evade pursuit, so you may trust them absolutely. I doubt you will run into any difficulties, you have enough of a head start. God go with you."

"And with you, Chevalier," Mary murmured. "You may thank your masters for their help. I will not forget it."

Owen bowed and turned to help Susan and Matilda onto their own pillion pads.

As they rode off, Cedric slid out of the shadow of the house wall. "Shall I fetch our horses now, sir?"

"When the clock strikes the half hour. Have you packed the panniers as I instructed?"

Cedric looked hurt. "Aye, sir. Of course, sir. I haven't forgotten one thing. Even all the breechclouts?" There was a question in his voice, although he didn't directly ask why such things were necessary on this upcoming journey. He received no answer to the unspoken question however.

"Good. Then be here when the clock strikes the half hour." Owen turned back to the secluded door into St. Paul's, and Cedric hurried off, reflecting that he had not seen his master smile once since they'd returned from the journey to High Wycombe.

Pen started as the tapestry over the door rustled. Philip lifted his head from her breast. Owen entered the Lady Chapel and went immediately to the grilled gateway that opened onto the nave. There was a scattering of worshipers in the body of the church, but none of the crowd that had accompanied the princess had ventured into the holy place. The priest's voice intoned still from the altar.

He came to kneel beside Pen at the rail before the chapel altar. "We will leave in five minutes."

"I must go directly to Holborn," she whispered back. "Northumberland will know of my involvement in Mary's escape. He's bound to —"

"No, you will come with me," Owen interrupted, in the same murmur. Despite his outward calm, his blood was racing, every nerve stretched at the gamble he was about to take. He was committing himself absolutely to one course of action. If it failed he had lost everything.

"But where?" She turned to look at him, lifting the heavy veil with her free hand. Her gaze searched his in the dim light of the single candle that burned on the altar.

"I wish you to come with me without seeking any answers," he replied.

Pen pushed her hand up beneath her veil, rubbing the back of her neck.

"I wish you to come with me without seeking any answers, and without hesitation," he repeated.

This was a test. She knew it immediately. A test, and possibly the second chance she had longed for.

But her spirit rebelled even as she understood that he was asking her now for her complete trust, her complete faith. But she was an independent, free-thinking woman. Not some cipher willing to yield all free will.

She stared back at him, and then saw behind the dark eyes the plea, the desperate anxiety, the hope he would not express. He had staked everything on this one demand. She had to go with him on these terms or not at all. But go *where?* To *what?*

"My child . . . what of Philip?" was all she said.

"He will come with us."

"My parents?"

"You will send them an explanation through Cedric."

"I have no explanation," she pointed out.

"You are with me. That will be sufficient."

There was silence in the Lady Chapel. As if from far away she could hear the congregation making the ritual responses. He had asked for no hesitation, and yet he was not pressing her. She understood that he was frightened that she would refuse him.

And she too was frightened that she would refuse him.

She rose fluidly to her feet, hitching Philip more comfortably onto her hip. "Do we go this way?" She gestured to the tapestry.

Owen nodded and lifted the tapestry aside for her. He didn't know whether she had agreed or not. His heart still raced; he was aware that his palms were damp inside his gloves.

Pen entered the narrow corridor. They moved

swiftly and in silence across the crypt, out into the cold morning. The clock struck the half hour as Owen closed the door behind him. Cedric was riding down the alley, leading two horses.

He dismounted hastily, took off his bonnet, and bowed to Pen, his eyes darting to the baby in her arms. It seemed he had an explanation for the peculiar contents of the panniers.

Owen didn't know whether she had agreed or not, but now he took the initiative, hoping that he could carry her indecision on the tide of his own affirmation.

He instructed crisply, "Cedric, you will go at once to the Earl of Kendal's residence in Holborn. You will ask to speak only to the earl or to Lady Kendal. You will explain that Lady Pen and her son are under my protection. They need have no concerns for her safety, and I will return her, with her son, in due course."

"No," Pen said. Such a message would infuriate her parents, but it would also perplex and distress them. The thought of the pain and confusion they must be feeling now, now that Pippa had arrived with Charles and told of their grandson's rescue, filled her with sorrow. She should go to them now, at once.

And yet she could not. Not if she was to follow her heart.

They would understand. In the end they would understand.

She glanced at Owen and saw his mouth twisted with pain and disappointment. He had taken her sharp negative as a final rejection.

She said urgently, "Cedric, you must say that the chevalier and I have some further business to transact concerning my son. Tell them that I would give anything to be with them now, but I will come as soon as I can. Tell them that I am content with what I am doing now."

She touched Cedric's arm. "That is most important, Cedric, you understand. Tell them that I am content, say that they are not to worry."

Cedric looked surprised at the urgency of her tone, the pressure of her hand on his arm, but he said only, "Yes, madam. I understand."

Pen wondered what Robin would tell them of the chevalier. Would he tell them what he saw as the truth? Or would he have the sense to keep his tongue still and let Pen tell her own story in her own way?

"Where shall I meet up with you, sir?" Cedric asked.

Owen didn't immediately hear him. Her words brought him joy, but also a greater understanding of the difficulty of her decision. It was not just about him at all. A humbling reflection, but Pen had prompted many of those in their time together.

He thought how he could barely remember his own family life, the strong ties that bound parents and child. His father had been a distant figure, his mother loving, but at an early age he had been sent away from her to live in another aristocratic household as courtly tradition dictated. As for his own wife and children . . .

He became aware that Cedric was repeating his question and collected his thoughts with some effort. "I make this journey alone, Cedric. You will report to the ambassador. You will tell him that I follow the beacon. He will understand. Then you will offer your services in whatever way he can use them. . . . Pen, give me Philip while Cedric helps you mount."

Pen handed Philip over, watching covertly as Owen, with seemingly natural ease, shifted the child to his hip, waiting until a disgruntled Cedric had helped her into the saddle of a broad-chested chestnut mare.

He handed the child up to her without a word, then mounted himself on the big black that Pen remembered from their previous journey.

Cedric trotted off down the alley, heading towards Ludgate and Holborn. Owen set off in the opposite direction, towards Watling Street.

Pen had to ride behind him until they reached the wider thoroughfare, then when she came up beside him he said in neutral tones, "We have close to a hundred and fifty miles to ride. I would do it if we can in five days. We will ride late into the evening and start at dawn each day. Can you manage the child without the help of a nursemaid?"

"Yes, of course. But I have nothing for him."

"In the panniers."

She looked down at the panniers that hung on either side of the saddle. She hadn't noticed them before. Her sense of being detached from reality intensified. There was something dream-like about going she knew not where for a reason she had not been given. What had he meant by following the beacon? Some code, presumably, that the ambassador would understand.

She had given herself up to Owen d'Arcy, to whatever purpose he had. And yet, despite that, she could feel no closeness between them. It was as if they didn't know each other at all, and had to start all over again. And perhaps they did.

It was a daunting prospect, and yet it held the promise of a satisfaction and contentment she had not known in so long. And if she wondered how it could be possible, practical, to love a spy, to live in domestic harmony with a man like Owen d'Arcy, she pushed it to the farthest recess of her mind.

They left London through Bishopsgate, and only when she was beyond the walls did she begin to feel safe. The immediate danger was past. Northumberland would not know where or how to follow them.

"Gone?" Northumberland stared in heavy-eyed disbelief at the Earl of Pembroke, who, although dressed, looked almost as rumpled in the duke's bedchamber in Durham House as he had in the courtyard at Baynard's Castle, rather as if he'd dressed in the dark.

"Aye," Pembroke responded. "She went to early mass at St. Paul's. She was seen to enter with Lady Susan and Lady Matilda. The carriage remained outside, but when I arrived, the service was over and there was no sign of the princess or her ladies."

"And what of Lady Pen?" Northumberland demanded. "She accompanied the princess to London yesterday. We spoke with her last even. What does she know of this?"

"She was not seen with the princess, but she too has disappeared," Pembroke said, chewing his lip unhappily.

Northumberland let loose a string of vile oaths at his valet, who was helping him dress. The man endured in stoic silence lest blows accompany the oaths.

"Who's behind this? Who got them away?" Northumberland demanded of the air. "Lady Pen certainly has a hand in it."

"And perhaps the Chevalier d'Arcy?" Pembroke suggested. "We know there's a connection there."

Northumberland picked up a cup of wine and drained it. "Aye, the French," he said bitterly. "But is Beaucaire involved in this too? The entire Kendal clan?"

He slammed the empty cup back on the table. "Kendal is no true friend of ours. He has never made any secret of his loyalty to Mary. I see his hand here also."

He snatched his cloak from his valet's hands with something resembling a growl. "We return to Greenwich, Pembroke."

He strode from the chamber, saying over his shoulder, "The king must sign his *Device* today, and the council ratify it immediately. Mary is out of our hands for the moment, but all is not lost."

"And what of Lady Pen?"

"When I have the king's signed *Device* in my hand, I can arrest Mary. Then I'll deal with the rest," the duke stated with a grim smile. "For the moment, we cannot afford to show any discomfiture in the princess's removal to Essex. We must allay suspicion, not give it credence."

They took horse and crossed the river on the Horseferry, the duke in fulminating silence, staring out over the oily water as his mind selected and rejected the options that lay open to him.

They reached Greenwich before noon, and Northumberland, with a brusquely dismissive wave at his anxious companion, strode into the king's bedchamber. The stench knocked him back like a physical blow. Since his last visit he had gone no farther into the chamber than the doorway.

He approached the bed. The king lay on piled pillows, his body a mass of ulcerated sores, his breath barely stirring the air.

" 'Tis done, Northumberland. My *Device for the Succession* is complete." Somehow a wasted arm managed to gesture to the side table, where lay a sheet of parchment, closely written in the king's exquisite handwriting.

Northumberland marveled as he took up the paper at how this boy, at death's door, had managed to produce a work of such perfection. It was all there, not a legal point to be disputed, and the king's signature and seal were duly affixed.

"This is good, Highness," Northumberland murmured. "But now you must rest." He looked down at the poor heap of wasted flesh with a surge of desperation. The boy could not die until the council had approved the new deed of succession.

But, dear God, how long could he last?

Twenty-five

●

Guinevere looked at the page as he finished his re-hearsed speech and said, "I don't understand. Where is she going?"

Cedric clutched his cap to his chest. "I don't know, madam. My lord wouldn't tell me. I was just to say that Lady Pen says she is content."

Hugh laid a hand on his wife's shoulder. "The boy knows no more than what Pen told him to say, Guinevere."

She placed her hand over his. "I know. But it's so hard to understand, Hugh! I need her to be here, Pen and her child . . . our grandson. I *need* her . . . to talk to her, hold her . . . tell her how sorry I am." Her words caught and she clasped her throat with her free hand as if she could smooth out the obstruction.

"We all do," Hugh said quietly. He nodded dismissal at Cedric. "My thanks, lad."

Cedric bowed and hurried away with relief. The atmosphere in the house had felt uncom-fortably like mourning.

Guinevere still stood immobile at her hus-band's side. "Perhaps Robin will know some-thing," she said.

"Robin knows no more than I do," Pippa declared. "And perhaps less. He's not a woman."

"What do you mean?" Her mother looked across at her where she stood by the table, her fingers twisting, her pose unusually taut and tense for the mercurial, sunny-tempered Pippa.

"Pen is in love with Owen d'Arcy," Pippa said. "*Passionately* in love." Her hazel eyes glittered as she emphasized the word. "She was in love with him before he helped her find Philip, but now she owes him everything. 'Tis quite simple, really." She shrugged her bony shoulders.

"She's in love with a French agent," Hugh said. "Does she know that?"

"Oh, yes," Pippa said. "I believe she's always known it. I don't know what she's going to do about it, but I expect that's what she's trying to find out now."

Her parents absorbed this. It was an explanation that fitted Pen's steadily determined character. She was not one to give up, as her extraordinary battle to retrieve her son had proved. She would do whatever was necessary to come to a decision, to do what she considered right.

"I think she's probably in the safest possible hands," Hugh observed, pressing Guinevere's shoulder. "From what I can gather, the chevalier has a formidable reputation." His voice took on a somewhat dry note. "Multitalented it would seem, as a swordsman, strategist, spy, diplomat. Utterly competent at pretty well anything you could mention."

"Including seduction," Guinevere observed tartly.

"Pen didn't go into anything with her eyes closed."

Slowly Guinevere nodded. "There's nothing we can do for now, anyway, except help that poor little mite she's called Charles." She shuddered slightly. "What a terrible, terrible story, Hugh. How could we . . . ?"

"We did, and we had only Pen's best interests at heart," Hugh responded. "We made a mistake. We will do everything we can to make up for it."

"Yes." Guinevere seemed to stand straighter, to draw strength from her husband's firm declaration. Hugh never repined over the past; with a soldier's blunt purpose and clear sight, he would always move ahead, rectifying where he could, accepting where he couldn't.

She continued decisively, "And in Pen's absence, the first order of business is the Bryanstons. I will have that woman's head, and her son's."

"Well, Pen and Robin have already started on that," Pippa said, and told them of Pen's plan. "We think the duke will take the bait."

Hugh gave a grim smile. "What a splendidly devious plot. I wouldn't have thought Pen had such a mind."

"She's been keeping company with a spy," Guinevere reminded him.

Hugh gave a short laugh. "I think you had

better grow accustomed to it, love. Our task now is to rid the world of Miles Bryanston and thus clear the way to establish Philip in his stead. I care not what tools come to hand."

"No," Guinevere agreed. "I will go to the nursery now and see how Ellen is managing with the little one. By the time Pen returns, I intend that he should be plump and talkative." She moved away from her husband, and left the parlor, her step as graceful as ever.

Hugh nodded to himself. Such work would help Guinevere to assuage her guilt. And he thought it was all to the good that Pen should have Philip to herself for a while. They had a bond to forge that should have been forged more than two years earlier.

The setting sun that night told Pen that they were journeying westward. They entered ever-deeper countryside, riding down narrow lanes, along bridle paths, through woodland.

The weather had turned beautiful, brilliant blue winter skies, a chilly sunshine. It wasn't warm enough to soften the hard-packed mud of the paths and lanes and the horses made easy work of the travel. Although they rode a long day, Owen didn't press the pace, and stopped several times to bait and water the horses.

Country inns were few and far between. They stopped that first night at a roadside tavern that could offer them only a stable loft for accommodation. Pen regarded the flea-ridden straw mattresses and said bluntly that she would prefer to sleep on the earthen floor.

Owen didn't argue. He left her in the sorry chamber, reappearing some minutes later with his arms piled high with dried bracken.

"Prickly but no fleas," he said succinctly.

Pen was amazed at his competence as he created a nest of bracken before the fire that he himself had lit in the stone hearth. He had brought in the panniers from the horses and now he laid out blankets over the bracken and set a flagon of wine on the floor.

"I'll see about supper and water."

Pen laid Philip on the makeshift bed to change his breechclout. He was sucking his thumb, gazing up at the ceiling, his eyes following the flickering shadows of the fire on the beams. She tickled his belly and he gave a little chortle, drawing up his knees.

She bent to kiss him and he thrust his fists into her face with another chortle. "Do you know I'm your mama?" she whispered. "I think you do."

She turned at the sound of Owen's booted feet on the ladder that served as stairs. She offered him a rather self-conscious smile as if he had caught her doing something foolish.

"I was talking to him," she said. "I keep wishing he would say just one word, but at least he's started to chuckle."

"He has a great deal to catch up," Owen said, setting down a wooden bucket and a kettle. "There's hot water in the kettle. Not much, but you might be able to refresh yourself and the child."

"I'll save some for you."

He shook his head. "Don't bother. I'm perfectly content with cold. I'll fetch supper now."

"And milk," Pen called after him.

She opened another of the panniers that Owen had assembled for Philip. There were flannel cloths as well as the linen breechclouts, two small blankets, two new petticoats and Holland smocks. She wondered how he had managed to acquire these things. When had he decided that they should make this journey?

She dampened one of the flannel cloths and washed Philip quickly lest he get too cold. His thinness as always distressed her. He wailed at the washing, but once he was clean and dried he smiled at her again, looking expectantly towards the pannier from which throughout the day had emerged bread, cheese, winter apples.

"You shall have some milk," Pen said, setting him on his feet, watching as he toddled around, examining his surroundings. Maybe he was not articulate yet, but he was certainly lively and interested, she thought, as she dampened the cloth and washed her face, the back of her neck, and her hands.

Owen returned with a jug of milk, a loaf of bread, and a cauldron of what looked like stew. "The sleeping quarters aren't up to much, but the food seems passable," he observed, setting down his burdens. He rummaged in the pannier and produced two spoons and knives.

Pen marveled anew. He had forgotten nothing, it seemed.

When they had finished she left him with Philip while she went in search of the outhouse. The night was filled with stars, the ground bathed in silver light. It was very quiet after the noise and bustle of Greenwich and the city. She was so tired, she felt she could fall asleep on her feet, and the thought of the bracken bed filled her with longing.

She had the sense that Owen would not approach her tonight. In fact, she thought that he would make no attempt to make love until what lay between them was resolved in the way he wanted, or had decided. It was strange, like living in limbo, being in such close, intimate contact, yet conscious of a vast distance between them that was also somehow contrived.

They lay that night beneath their cloaks, the blanket-wrapped baby nestled in the crook of Pen's arm, the bracken sweet-smelling beneath them. While Owen said nothing, indeed lay motionless, his breathing deep and even, Pen was aware of every muscle and line of his body. She ached with fatigue, but also with a pure physical longing for his touch. But sleep claimed her, and when she awoke in the gray dawn she was alone on the bracken.

Her heart banged against her ribs. Philip was gone. She was alone. She scrambled to her feet, her loosened hair tumbling around her face, her eyes wild with fear. She ran for the ladder, then heard Owen's voice from the stables below.

He was talking in a soft monologue, and when she stumbled down the ladder, almost landing on her knees in her haste, she saw him holding Philip, encouraging the child to pat the neck of one of the horses in a stall.

Tentatively Philip put out a hand, touched the horse, then withdrew it with another of his chortles.

Owen became aware of Pen and turned to her. The wildness had not yet died from her eyes and he understood what she had feared. It would be a long time before she would be truly secure, truly certain that she would not lose the child again.

"We were just looking at the horses," he said calmly, handing Philip back to her. "If you will pack up the panniers, I will see about breakfast and provisions for the day. Then we must be on the road."

Pen cradled Philip's head to her breast, drawing deep breaths as she calmed herself.

Owen went past her, back to the cottage. It was so hard to hold himself away from her. When he'd seen her terror-stricken face he had had to restrain himself from going to her, taking her in his arms, soothing her, kissing that soft mouth, kissing the fear from the forest pools of her eyes.

If she turned from him when she knew the

truth, then there was nothing more he could do, but he had sworn that if there was to be another time when they touched each other in the ways of love, it would be a beginning, not an end.

The strange sense of living in limbo persisted for the remainder of the journey. Each night they lay all three of them in one bed, sleeping chastely, considerately moving as little as possible on the various rustling mattresses they were offered.

While they rode, Pen pointed things out to Philip as he sat on the saddle before her, cradled in the crook of her arm. Trees, birds, rivers, a scarecrow. She repeated the names of these objects. His solemn stare would follow her pointing finger while he chewed on a slice of apple or a crust of bread. She wondered if he had ever seen a tree, or a bird, immured as he had been in the vile darkness of a Southwark stew.

When her arm grew tired Owen would lean over and take the child from her. He never asked her if she was tired, but he seemed always to know the exact moment when she was ready to relinquish her son.

Pen relaxed into the strange, quiet, waiting rhythm of those days as they continued to travel westward. On the fifth day they took the Horseferry across the Severn River into Wales. Now she knew definitely what she had suspected for the last two days. But she said nothing, and neither did Owen.

Philip had been fascinated by the ferry and the river, and for the first time threw a fit of pure temper when Pen would not let him race around the flat deck between the horses, or stick his head through the rough wooden railing.

"He's cross," Pen said in astonishment. "Isn't that wonderful?"

Owen laughed, and for an instant she glimpsed once again the warm, teasing companion and lover who held her heart.

But the laughter died as swiftly as it had arisen, and his expression grew once more closed, his eyes unreadable. When they rode off the ferry Pen could feel his tension, felt how it grew as they rode through what seemed a much softer air, across a verdant countryside that stretched along the banks of the wide Severn. Ahead of them in the clear air they could just make out the dark crags of the Brecon Beacons. Now Pen understood the meaning of his strange message to the ambassador.

"That is the beacon?" she said, pointing to the mountains.

" 'Tis a code we set up many years ago. I have never had cause to use it before," he replied. "If I'm needed, if there's danger, the ambassador — and only the ambassador — will know where to find me."

Pen accepted this in silence. It reminded her anew of the unpredictable, perilous life he led for the sake of his country. She thought of Robin and wondered with a touch of fear what had happened to him as a result of Mary's escape. Had he been implicated? Proved a traitor to Northumberland's cause?

They turned through fieldstone gateposts set into a soft gray fieldstone wall and rode up a grassy track, fields on either side. The track curved, and ahead lay a small manor house of the same soft gray stone, with a slate roof and mullioned windows. Smoke curled from four chimneys, chickens scratched in the small court in front of the house, there were ducks on a pond to one side, and doves cooing from a dovecote.

Pen glanced at Owen. He had stopped his horse and just sat there gazing at this bucolic scene. He inhaled deeply.

When he spoke, his voice was shocking in the taut silence. "I thought never to see this again."

Pen didn't ask why not. She knew she would find the answer here.

The front door opened and a woman stepped out. She was tall, thin, gray-haired beneath a simple white coif, elegant, despite a worn countenance and the apron she wore over a kersey gown. Two green-eyed children peered around her skirts.

The woman raised a hand to her eyes as if to shield them from the light. She took another step forward.

"Owen?" Her voice was soft, lilting, incredulous.

Owen dismounted. He walked towards her. "Mother." He bent to embrace her. They clung together for a long time, watched by the two children from the doorway, and by Pen, who remained mounted.

Slowly they moved apart. Owen came back to Pen, his mother beside him. He reached up and lifted Pen and her child to the ground.

"Mother, this is Pen Bryanston and her son, Philip. Pen, this is my mother, Esther, the Lady d'Arcy." He turned slightly towards the house. There was a catch in his voice. "And those are my children, Lucy and Andrew. They do not know their father."

Pen looked at the woman, looked at the children, who were gazing at the strangers with frank curiosity. Then she turned her gaze helplessly on Owen.

Owen said quietly, "Mother, I need you to tell Pen."

Owen's mother looked between them. Her expression was grave but there was a light behind the clear gray eyes. "You are sure, Owen?"

"Yes. I cannot do it myself."

"Very well." Her tone was decisive despite its melodious lilt. "You and your child are welcome indeed to my hearth, Pen Bryanston, as you must be welcome in my son's heart. Only thus would he have brought you to me. Let us go inside."

She turned back to the house.

Pen looked at Owen. His expression was open now, in his eyes a look of relief, as if finally he had laid down a great burden.

"Will you go?" he asked softly.

"Yes . . . yes, of course."

"I will be waiting for you."

Pen nodded and hurried after Lady d'Arcy into the warmth of the house, where the air smelled of new-baked bread, woodsmoke, dried lavender and rose petals.

Lady d'Arcy led Pen into a small parlor at the back of the house. A child-sized spindle stood in one corner, a half-spun ball of wool on the distaff; a rag doll drooped lopsided on the window seat. Pen stepped over a spinning top, noticed the sheet of parchment on the table with the letters of the alphabet painstakingly copied in a childish hand.

Lady d'Arcy noticed Pen's swift observations. She smiled a little. "Owen's children have sharp minds. They learn quickly, much as their father did."

She subjected her visitor to a close and candid scrutiny. "My son must love you very much to bring you here," she observed. "I thank God for it. These last years have been hard for us all."

Pen said simply, "I love Owen, madam. But there are questions . . . problems . . ." She shrugged slightly, and turned a little so that Philip could look over her shoulder out of the window.

"Yes, I imagine there are. Pray sit down." Lady d'Arcy gestured to the settle beside the fire. "Take a cup of elderflower wine." She poured from a jug that stood on the table, then selected an apple from a basket on a low table and gave it to Philip.

"Not Owen's son?" she said in soft question.

"No," Pen said. "My late husband's and mine. But Owen has played a part in his life that I can never repay."

Esther d'Arcy smiled at that, and the smile grew behind her eyes, showing Pen the beautiful woman she must once have been, before care and sorrow had settled upon her.

"I think you have already repaid it," she said as she sat with her own cup on the settle opposite Pen. "By bringing him home." She gazed meditatively at the broad oak boards at her feet, before finally raising her head.

"Owen was married some ten years ago, at his father's behest. His father belonged to the royal family of de Guise. It was a good marriage, a good alliance for a member of that family and for Estelle's. Set the child down, there's no harm he can do in this room," she said, seeing Philip wriggling on his mother's lap.

Pen set him on his feet and he set off around the room on one of his voyages of exploration.

"Estelle was very beautiful, rather vain, not very clever," Esther continued. "She knew nothing of Owen's activities for France." She looked sharply at Pen, who nodded her understanding.

"Owen is very dedicated, he was often away. Home sufficiently to father two children, however," she added dryly.

"To be brief, Estelle enjoyed flirtation, maybe

even more than that, I don't know and I won't speculate. She was ignorant of Owen's life; Owen failed to warn her or to take sufficient care of her. He failed to anticipate the danger into which her vanity led her, and thus failed to protect her."

Pen said nothing. Owen's mother spoke this criticism of her son without emotion, but she was watching Pen closely for her reaction. Pen gave her none, merely sat upright on the settle, her hands circling the cup she held in her lap, her eyes checking Philip every few minutes.

"Owen had . . . has still, I assume . . . his enemies. The enmity is not personal but professional, you understand?"

Pen nodded.

"He had some information about a member of the Spanish court that would lead to that man's arrest and execution. In order to prevent him from divulging that information, the man and his faction set a trap for Estelle. They presented her with a courtier, one so attentive she gave him her complete trust. She was a trusting soul," Esther added, taking a sip of her wine.

"She was inveigled into a clandestine meeting and was abducted, together with her children. She had hired a new nursemaid a few weeks previously, ardently recommended by her suitor. . . . More wine?"

"No, I thank you."

"Very well. Owen's wife and children were held hostage. Unless he agreed not only to bury his information deep as the grave but also to play turncoat, enter the service of the Spanish as a double agent, they would die.

"This was no idle threat," she said with soft emphasis.

"No," Pen agreed, reaching out a hand to steady Philip, who had stumbled against the table as he reached for another apple.

"Owen rescued his wife and children. He has friends of his own, many of whom would give their lives for him."

Pen had little difficulty believing this. She was mesmerized by this story, discarding now the mismatched pieces of Robin's version.

Esther sighed suddenly. "When he had his family safe he decided that the only way he could guarantee their safety while continuing his work was to take them out of his life. If they were seen to have no meaning for him, they would be of no value as blackmail. He repudiated his wife, disowned his children, gave himself completely to the causes of France."

Unconsciously Pen massaged her temples. It was still a chilling tale of one man's ability to cut himself off from emotional attachments, to cut himself off from his children.

"His choice was very simple," Esther said, watching Pen closely. "Either he gave up his life's work, or his family. He paid the penalty for his foolishness in not warning Estelle, in not guarding her more carefully. He loved — loves — his children deeply. He has never forgiven himself, I believe. But neither do I believe that he considers the choice he made between country and family to be wrong."

"For Owen," Pen said. "Not wrong for Owen."

"But for others maybe," Esther said. "Yes, I can see that."

"Did you consider it wrong?"

Esther hesitated. "For Lucy and Andrew's sake, yes. They have never heard their father's name spoken since they came to me three years ago. Andrew then was three, Lucy two . . . about the same age as your little one." She smiled a little, her gaze soft as she followed Philip's concentrated progress around the parlor.

Then she sighed again. "Owen believed it was the only way he could keep them safe."

Pen continued to press her temples, as if it would help her mind pick its way through this thicket. Owen's mother was telling her the bare, unvarnished truth. She had not shirked from criticizing her son, had not shirked from expressing her own doubts as to the wisdom of the course he had taken.

But Pen knew in her blood and her bones how his separation from his children had devastated him. She remembered the little girl who had run in front of his horse, the deep shadows in his eyes when he'd talked of children, the competence with which he'd anticipated the needs of a two-year-old on their journey, the ease with which he handled Philip, and her own

500

child's comfort in his arms.

"What of Estelle?"

"She died two years ago. Plague visited the town where she lived."

"She was not in a convent . . . a silent order?"

Esther shook her head. "No. That was the fiction. In fact, she was living on one of her family's estates in Provence. She lacked the excitement of the court, but little else. She enjoyed the social life of a provincial court, and I believe she had a lover. She was not unhappy . . . and she was safe."

"I see." Pen frowned. "Why would Owen not tell me this himself?"

"I imagine because he was afraid he would try to justify his actions, and he knew I would not," his mother said quietly. "He has never been a coward."

Pen picked up Philip, who was leaning against her knees, sucking on the core of the apple, his eyelids drooping.

Owen needed her to understand, to accept, to forgive. Pen held the child's head until his eyes closed and his body went limp against her. "May I leave him here?"

"Of course."

She rose and laid the child carefully on the settle, then she left the parlor.

The soft notes of a harp drew her down a passageway and across a hall to the half-open door of a paneled chamber at the front of the house.

Owen sat at the instrument, his eyes closed,

501

his fingers moving over the strings. It was the sweetest melody. Pen stood in the doorway listening. She could hear yearning, sorrow, and hope in the sounds he drew from the instrument. His two children sat on the floor, listening in rapt silence.

Owen opened his eyes and looked at Pen. All the yearning, sorrow, and hope that he had put into his music was stark in his gaze.

She smiled at him, holding his gaze, then quietly she went to sit down on an armless chair behind the children. Owen's fingers moved over the strings, and now he plucked a magic filled with hope and promise.

"The woman has confessed to the use of witchcraft and sorcery in her work in the Bryanston household, my lord duke." The black-clad guardsman held his cap to his chest and bowed as he delivered his information.

Northumberland looked up from the papers on his desk. "And what of the king? Does she confess to treason?"

"No, my lord duke. Even on the rack, she held to the story that she had been sent at Lady Bryanston's behest to do all she could to aid the king's recovery."

"Did she administer poison to Philip Bryanston at his mother's behest?"

"She denies that, my lord duke. But she admits to doing nothing to help the earl during his illness, on Lady Bryanston's orders. She also confessed to giving Lady Pen Bryanston a potion to induce premature labor, again at Lady Bryanston's order."

"Well, well," Northumberland declared, stretching his legs beneath the table. "So Lady Bryanston and her crawling son introduced into the king's bedchamber a known poisoner, a confessed witch, a woman they had used for their own purposes." He ran the flat of his hand over the papers in front of him, smoothing them with a rustle.

"Arrest the lady, her son, and her son's wife on a charge of treason. Have them taken to the Tower and let us hear what they have to say."

"Aye, my lord duke." The guardsman bowed again, turned with a salute, and left the duke's privy chamber.

Northumberland rose from the table. There were no heirs to the Bryanston earldom. It would now be available for bestowal for services rendered. As he remembered, it was a considerable estate, with lands in Oxfordshire and somewhere in the north of England. Rich lands that had once belonged to several monasteries, dissolved under the old king's regime. They would make a useful bribe to some member of the Privy Council in exchange for a signature on the young king's *Device* to alter the succession.

Miles Bryanston left the brothel, drawing on his jeweled gloves. The child had gone. The woman said it had died of a fever, but there was something about her shifty eyes, her wheedling tone, that made Miles uneasy. Better just to tell his mother that it had died, though. Not give her any ideas.

His eyes gleamed. Maybe he'd just tell her that he'd done what she'd ordered. Maybe he'd say he had dropped it in the river. That way he'd get credit, and no one would be any the wiser.

He hailed a skiff at the steps. "Westminster!" He sat down on the thwart, pulling his cloak more securely around him. It was a neat plan. Take the credit, quieten his mother, and all's right with the world.

He was whistling to himself as he entered the Bryanston mansion. Joan was crossing the hall, looking distressed, which was not unusual.

She greeted him with upflung hands and a great sigh. "Oh, Miles," she said.

His good mood evaporated. "What is it, woman? Why do you always look so miserable? 'Tis enough to curdle the milk."

Joan sighed again. "Lady Bryanston . . . your mother . . ." Tears filled her eyes. "She has been so unkind to me all morning. Dolly had another little accident, just the littlest one, and Lady Bryanston threw her out into the kitchen yard and has forbidden her ever to come in the house again. And now she's so sick . . ." She gave another shuddering sigh, and the tears trickled down her cheeks.

"Oh, Miles, I could almost believe she's been poisoned."

Miles grimaced. Dolly was Joan's pet spaniel, a thoroughly useless animal in his opinion, with an unfortunate habit of having what Joan euphemistically referred to as "accidents."

"Probably she ate rat poison in the yard," he said with scant sympathy. "Where is my mother?"

"In the library, above stairs." Joan wafted off, weeping bitterly.

Miles ascended the stairs and entered the library. Lady Bryanston glanced up from the ledger on the desk. She was looking frustrated. Accounts always flustered her. The sums never came out right, and this time was no exception.

"Well?" she demanded.

"I dealt with it," Miles declared, leaning against the door in a posture redolent of self-satisfaction. "He's gone."

"Ah." Lady Bryanston leaned back in her chair and regarded her son with something remarkably like approval. "Good. Then we have nothing further to concern us."

She turned back to the ledger, saying irritably now, "I wish you'd do something about your wife. Her sniveling is driving me to distraction."

Miles opened his mouth to reply just as a violent banging echoed through the house.

"What the devil is that?" He opened the door to stick his head into the corridor. The banging resounded.

"Someone's at the door," his mother said, rising to her feet. "It doesn't take the mind of a genius to understand that." She swept past him into the corridor.

Raised voices reached them from the hall. Loud, rough tones. Joan's voice, shrill and frightened, came in response.

"God's blood, what's this?" demanded Miles as he saw the great hall filled with men . . . men armed with pikes and swords.

He stepped off the last stair and was instantly engulfed.

"Lord Bryanston, I have a warrant for your arrest and that of your mother on the charge of witchcraft and treason," intoned a man wearing a silver chain of office and carrying a heavy mace.

Miles was ashen. "What . . . what do you mean . . . what witchcraft . . . what treason?"

Lady Bryanston, herself surrounded now, said in rising tones, "What nonsense is this? There must be some mistake."

"You are hereby arrested, madam, for introducing a confessed witch into the king's bedchamber, and for plotting the king's death by poison."

Lady Bryanston swayed suddenly, her hand at her throat. "What proof? What evidence for such charges?"

"The confession of the woman Goodlow, introduced by you into the king's chamber. She admitted inducing your daughter-in-law's premature labor at your command, and to the frequent preparation of venomous potions and the casting of spells, also at your command."

"Confession!" The full implication seemed to take a long time to sink in. She stared at the official, looked around at the stony faces of the guards surrounding her.

"You are to be conveyed to the Tower for questioning," the official said. "You, your son, and your daughter-in-law."

Joan gave a shriek and fell to the floor in a dead faint. Miles's pallor took on a greenish tinge. Lady Bryanston continued to stare as dreadful comprehension dawned.

The Tower . . . the Question.

They were allowed no further words, and indeed were capable of none as they were escorted by boat to the Tower, where they entered beneath the portcullis of Traitor's Gate and were soon entombed in the dungeons beneath the Tower.

Twenty-six

●

Pen stepped outside into the soft air of the June evening. She held Philip's hand, listening to his babbling recitation of the objects he saw, his constant repetition of "Look, Mama, look."

Lucy and Andrew had been as responsible for his rapid grasp of language as had Pen. Philip seemed to respond to their cues more easily than he did to an adult's.

Owen, arm in arm with his mother, came around the house from the vegetable garden. He carried a basket of new carrots. He was dressed in country clothes, the rich embroidered silks and velvets of London discarded in favor of woolen hose, linen doublets, homespun jerkins.

But he was never without his rapier or his dagger, even when engaging in a task as simple as pulling carrots from the ground for supper. And not a day passed when he didn't practice his swordplay, tilted at the old quintain in the tilting yard behind the house, loosed arrows at the target on the butt. These activities fascinated his children, and Andrew ran around flourishing his own wooden sword in imitation. But Pen and Esther knew there was no play behind this concentrated practice.

Pen waited for them to reach her. She had sensed in the last weeks a certain growing impatience about him. She guessed that this quiet interval of healing, renewal, learning to know each other was coming to an end. And, in truth, she was impatient herself to return to her family.

She reached into her pocket for the letter she had just received from her mother. She had written to her family in care of the French ambassador, and Guinevere had replied using the same courier. They had exchanged little communication in the five months since Pen had left London. Owen still considered it dangerous to risk revealing his mother's home to outsiders. But the letters they had exchanged had carried in a very few words all the emotion they felt, all the unspoken understandings that were now held among them.

Owen and Esther reached her. Owen kissed Pen's mouth as she lifted her face to the evening sun. Esther smiled and bent to talk to Philip, who eagerly placed his hand in hers when she suggested they go into the kitchen garden to pick some strawberries for supper.

"Your mother always seems to know when we need to talk alone," Pen said, shading her eyes against the setting sun as she watched them go. The slender band of gold on her ring finger glowed against the sun's rays.

"I saw the courier's horse," Owen said. "You have news?" He indicated the letter she held.

"Miles and his mother were exiled two weeks ago," she said.

"A good riddance," he replied.

"Yes. Apparently no evidence was brought against Joan, but she was banished to her own family's estates in Lincolnshire. The earldom lies open."

"Then it is perhaps time we returned to claim it for your son."

"I thought so, although I don't know how. It lies in Northumberland's gift at present."

She gave a rather puzzled smile and said, "It doesn't seem to matter very much anymore. Philip's plump and talkative and happy. I don't know how much he remembers of the bad time, but it doesn't disturb his sleep. Maybe his inheritance is of no importance."

"I think it is," Owen said. "If it can be fought for, then we must do it."

"Perhaps," Pen said. "I'm so content, so sleepily smug like Nutmeg. I seem to have no stomach for mousing."

She gave a tiny laugh, but then her eyes grew serious. Tentatively she broached the subject that could not be avoided any longer. "But I thought also that it was perhaps time for you too to pick up the threads of your life."

He took her hand, twisting the ring on her finger. "Our life, Pen."

"We have not talked about how we are to conduct it," she said.

"No," he agreed, stroking her hair. "There's

been too much else to talk about."

She laughed, leaning into him, inhaling the sun-dried scent of his shirt, the tang of fresh sweat from his garden work, feeling the ripple of his chest muscles beneath her cheek. "I believe we've done more loving than talking."

" 'Tis a form of talking." He continued to stroke her hair, which in this quiet countryside she wore unbound most of the day. The evening breeze took up the finest of the gold-brown strands and sent them wisping across her forehead.

"Will we take Lucy and Andrew?" She looked up at him and saw the old shadows cross his eyes.

"No," he stated. "They are best with my mother for the present. London is too dangerous for them, and they won't be happy. Later, when we can see things clearly, then I'll fetch them."

Pen didn't argue. They were Owen's children, although a bond was growing between them and herself. But Owen had to decide for himself when it would be safe to acknowledge them publicly again.

For herself, she wore his wedding ring and would stand up as his wife, but she knew the dangers, and her family would know them. If it came down to drawn swords to protect her, if Owen was not there, then she would have Hugh and Robin and all who stood beside them. This was a risk they had discussed and settled between them. But Owen was not yet prepared to expose his children . . . or prepared to ask someone else to protect them.

Pen knew that he was wrestling alone with the decision whether to continue in the service of France or to settle into unadventurous domesticity. She would not push him to make such a decision. She thought she had reached her own peace, and would make her own life according to what course he took. He would always love her.

Esther, like Pen, had sensed Owen's impatience. She accepted their plans for departure without surprise, although it was hard for her to hide her sorrow.

Lucy and Andrew clung to Owen even as he explained carefully that he would not this time be gone too long. He and Pen would come back for them.

"But you're taking Philip," Andrew pointed out.

"Yes," Lucy agreed, her chin trembling, tears standing out in her eyes. "We want to come, and we want to bring Grandmama too."

"Not this time," Owen said gently. He drew them against him, kissing them, holding them tightly. It was a physical effort to release them into his mother's waiting arms. "Soon, I promise you."

Pen felt her own tears pricking. She understood how hard it must be for him to leave them again, how it must remind him of the dreadful time when he'd sent them from him before. But she also knew that when the time came for him to take them again, Esther would suffer the loss most grievously.

Why was it that love, the most generous of all emotions, should cause such pain?

They left Wales at the end of June, and this time there was no urgency to their journey. The sun shone, the hedgerows and orchards were thick with blossom, their fragrance heavy in the air.

On the second evening, as the sun set, they came upon a stream. Owen dismounted and lay full length upon the bank. He rolled up his sleeve and plunged his hand into the gently moving water. He came up with a brown trout thrashing in his grasp. He dropped it to the bank and stunned it with a stone, all in one movement it seemed to Pen, who had dismounted with Philip.

"Une nuit sous la lune," Owen said, looking up at the shadow of the moon in the still bright sky. "Food, fire, blankets."

"Oh, yes," Pen said. "And we can bathe in the stream." She turned to Philip. "Would you like to swim, love? Paddle in the stream?"

Philip regarded the stream with some gravity. He stretched out as he'd seen Owen do and reached down a hand, trying to touch the water. When he couldn't reach it, he frowned and inched forward on his belly.

Pen moved to grab him before he toppled headfirst, but Owen was there before her, lifting the boy high into the air so that the child laughed uproariously.

Pen undressed him, then stripped off her own clothes. She twisted her hair into a knot on top of her head, picked up Philip, and carried him into the stream.

Owen watched from the bank, his eyes narrowed appreciatively. He loved the back of her neck, the sweep of her narrow back. He loved the smooth indentation of her waist, the slight roundness of her belly, the rich flare of her hips. He thought that she had put on a little weight just recently, that the happiness of the last months had somehow rounded her out. She had never been thin, not like her sparrow of a sister, but unhappiness had given her a drawn, taut look. Now she was luscious as a bowl of thick rich cream, or the ripest peach, and he loved every inch of her body.

Aware of his scrutiny, Pen turned around, her nipples hardening with the coldness of the water. Philip kicked his legs with squeals of glee, sending a shower of water across the surface, the drops winking in the sinking sun.

"Aren't you coming in? Or do you prefer to play voyeur?" she called.

"For the moment the latter," he responded. "If you weren't holding the child it might be a different matter."

Pen laughed. Philip's presence was somewhat inhibiting. She played with him in the water awhile, washing off the dust of travel from her own skin, enjoying the freshness. When she came in, setting Philip on the bank first before scrambling inelegantly up herself, Owen had lit a fire, and two more trout lay beside the first one.

He wrapped the child in a towel and had him giggling as he dried him. Pen dried and dressed herself, then sat beside the fire while Owen cooked the trout.

Later, under the stars, while Philip slept curled in his own blanket, Pen moved over Owen's body, relishing every familiar inch of skin, her tongue painting in broad strokes, her teeth nibbling at his nipples, grazing the length of his penis as she drew him deep into her mouth, inhaling the rich fragrances of his arousal, her cheeks brushed by the crisp curling hair of his inner thighs.

He lay back, arms stretched above his head, legs spread wide, giving himself up to her possession. The night air was soft, the silvery light of moon and stars rippled on the still waters of the stream.

She raised her head from his loins and gazed up the muscle-planed length of his body. She ran a hand lazily in the deep concavity of his belly, a finger found the even deeper pit of his navel. She pulled herself up on her elbows and kissed the pulse at the base of his throat.

He brought his hands down then to grasp her head, his fingers twisting in her thick brown hair. She obeyed the leisurely pull that brought her face up to hang over his. She smiled down into his eyes, her body lying full upon his, the outward curve of her belly nestled into the inward curve of his, the softness of her thighs supported by the hard muscle of his own lean length.

"Kiss me," he demanded, and she lowered her head, fraction by fraction, teasing him, watching the glow in his eyes, until her lips met his. A mere brush at first, the tip of her tongue darting into the corners of his mouth, pushing between his lips to stroke his teeth, the inside of his mouth, tasting the wine they had drunk with their supper. Then he began to return the kiss, his tongue fencing with hers, stroking the inside of her cheeks, his teeth nipping the tip of her tongue, before he clasped her face in both hands and his tongue delved deep within her mouth.

She raised her lower body and he entered her with a long slow thrust. Their mouths were joined, their bodies were joined, and the wondrously familiar rhythm took hold of them, familiar and yet as always different. Some different nerve touched, some different emotion that each drew from the other.

Pen slowly left his mouth and sat back, leaning against his drawn-up knees. He reached down between her wide-spread thighs and touched the engorged lips of her sex, caressing the hot wet furrow. When it was right, he touched the erect and swollen nub of pleasure. She bit hard on her lip to keep from crying out on this quiet stream bank as her loins convulsed with the ecstatic rush and her thighs seemed to dissolve in liquid joy. She fell forward over his body again, and again as his own orgasm pulsed deep within her, a second wave ripped through her. She moved her loins against his and held her breath for the third, diminishing surge of pleasure.

"Women are so lucky," Owen murmured, stroking her hair as she stretched limp and sweaty along his length. "It seems unjust."

" 'Tis payment for the pains of childbed," she murmured when she could get her breath.

He chuckled weakly, stroking down her back, his hand coming to rest on her bottom, idly caressing the soft curve.

After a while, Pen struggled up so that she was once more sitting astride him. She heard her voice as if coming from a great distance, saying what she had promised herself she would not say.

"I do not know how I will endure living without you." She brushed the hair from her eyes. "I know you will be gone often, and I know I won't know where, and I don't know if I can endure it, the uncertainty, the danger. I thought I could. I swore to myself that I would never say this, but, oh, Owen, I don't know how I will do it."

She added fiercely, "I will, of course I will. I just don't know how."

She looked down at him, her eyes now grave, haunted with the anticipation of sorrow, the fear she knew awaited her, and regret that she had spoken at all.

He put his hands at her waist and lifted her

away from him. He sat up beside her. He took her hand, where she wore his wedding ring.

He spoke quietly, looking down at her hand. "Family, friends, they have always given way to my work. Until now, I have lived for my work. It was what defined me to myself as well as to others."

"I know," she said swiftly, placing a finger over his lips. "There's no need to say more. It was just a moment of weakness." She tried to smile. "Ecstasy weakens me, I find."

He took her wrist and moved her hand down, holding both her wrists in one hand tightly against his knee. "I said, *until now*, Pen."

She let this sink in, feeling the air cool on her sweat-slick skin, a light breeze lifting her hair. "But you could not give it up," she stated. "And I could not live with myself if I thought that I had made you do so."

He shook his head in reproof. "In this, sweetheart, you could not compel me. I have always done what I considered to be right, even if . . ." A shadow crossed his face. "Even if others suffered for it."

He smiled suddenly, ruefully. "But I'm thirty-five, maybe it's time to acknowledge the advancing years and find a profession a little less unpredictable."

"Advancing years!" Pen scoffed. "What nonsense."

"I have a wife and three children," he said. "And for all I know, there could be others." He placed his free hand on her belly. "It isn't as if we aren't providing nature with opportunity."

"No," she agreed, unsmiling, aware that this was perhaps the most important conversation they would ever have. If he felt she had pressed him, maybe he would feel resentment later; if she felt that he had denied her fears, maybe the resentment would be on her side.

"But what would you do, love? I don't see you farming, or playing the courtier, or idling your time away, even with such delights as music."

"Antoine detests England," he said. "If a suitable replacement could be found, I think he would gladly return to Paris."

Pen stared at him. "You would be ambassador to Mary's court?"

"I have every reason to believe King Henri would approve it, with Antoine's support."

Pen absorbed this. Diplomacy, overt diplomacy. Much safer than the covert world of an agent. And yet, from one point of view, perhaps as exciting.

"You would still spy?"

"No. I would run spies," he said. "Something I do already. Again an area of expertise that would stand any ambassador in good stead." His smile was a touch sardonic in the moonlight.

"We would live in London, then. All of us?" She seemed to be feeling her way to understanding exactly what he was saying, desperately anxious not to misinterpret and rejoice too soon.

"If this works out, yes." He released her hand

519

and stood up, his long lean body glistening in the moonlight. He stood with his hands on his hips looking out over the silvered stream and the countryside beyond.

"I couldn't promise it would be forever. We might have to live for some time in France. Would you object?"

She rose and came to stand behind him, putting her arms around his waist, resting her chin on his shoulder as she looked out over the same landscape. "If I am with you, I would live in Suriname, or among the Cossacks in the Wild Lands."

He turned and drew her against his chest.

It was early evening on the sixth of July when they rode through the gates of Lord Kendal's house in Holborn.

Pen could barely contain her excitement, an excitement mingled with a curious apprehension. She knew she would be welcomed, that there would be no reproaches, not even for her marriage, which had taken place in the small church in Owen's mother's village. She had written and told them, and they had written to welcome Owen into the family with warmth and gratitude for all he'd done. Nevertheless, she couldn't help her anxiety.

Would they like each other? How would Owen, an only child, a man who had always lived his life alone, at least emotionally, feel clasped to the exuberant, loving, intensely close bosom of her family?

The gatekeeper had sent his son racing up the drive through the trees to warn the family of the new arrivals, and as they rode onto the gravel sweep in front of the house, the door opened and a wave of people flowed out, the air filled with glad cries.

Pen was engulfed. Philip, startled into silence, was passed from hand to hand. Owen dismounted and waited, watching the scene, wondering how he would ever find a place in it.

"Don't let it overwhelm you," Hugh said at his elbow. "Guinevere and her daughters can overwhelm any outsider. For the rest, they are family retainers who've known Pen since she was born. It'll settle down in a minute."

He smiled at Owen and held out his hand. "You are most welcome, Owen d'Arcy. You've looked after my daughter with such care. I haven't seen her so well, so happy, so *radiant* since before Philip died."

"I am glad of it," Owen said, taking the other's hand and returning the strong grip. "And I thank you for your welcome." He looked again at the noisy group, observing, "Robin's not here?"

"No. Northumberland's kept him close to his side these last months. Princess Mary's departure and Pen's disappearance didn't please him. He's keeping close watch on Robin."

A worried look entered Hugh's brilliant blue gaze. "If Northumberland decides Robin betrayed him, then —" He broke off abruptly. "But that's a concern for another day. Come, you must be welcomed by the distaff side."

Pen was exclaiming over little Charles, whose hair seemed spikier and redder than ever atop a round, freckled face, and a well-fed body. "Does he talk?" she asked Pippa.

"Nonstop," Pippa said with a laugh. "Especially if there's food around."

The sound of hooves pounding the gravel interrupted the melee. Robin on a lathered horse galloped onto the sweep, gravel spraying from beneath the animal's hooves.

He sprang from the saddle, for the moment barely noticing Owen and Pen. Hugh hurried over to him. "What is it?"

"Edward's dead." Robin was breathing heavily, sweat running down his face. "Sometime this morning, but the duke will not have it proclaimed. He has sent to Mary at Hundson, and to Elizabeth to attend their brother's bedside. If they come to London they will be seized immediately and taken to the Tower."

He wiped his face on his forearm, staining the silk of his doublet.

"He intends to have Jane proclaimed queen as soon as he's locked the city gates, and had troops in the outlying cities prepared to deal with any uprising."

His gaze fell on Pen, on the child in her arms. She came swiftly to him, kissing him. He hugged her tightly. "I'm so glad you're back, but you would have done better to have stayed in hiding." He glanced over at Owen, and the two men exchanged a look that was neither hostile nor particularly warm, but there was acceptance beneath it.

Then Robin continued flatly, "Northumberland will be avenged upon us all once he has Mary and Elizabeth in his hands, and Jane wears the crown."

"That cannot happen," Owen said. "Mary must be warned not to come to London."

"Aye," Hugh agreed, moving towards the house. "She must fly north, where the Catholic support is greatest. I'll go at once to Hunsdon. Robin, you'll accompany me. Send to the stables for my horse and a fresh one for you."

Guinevere said nothing. Her husband had chosen his side. If Mary's cause was lost in this fight for the crown, then Hugh and his son would lose their heads.

Pen glanced at her husband. "Owen?" She made of his name a soft question.

"I have no part to play in this fight," he said. "France supports Mary's cause, as do I, but it is not my place to take up arms in England's civil battles. You understand that, Pen?"

He frowned at her, wondering if she would understand why he had to maintain a political, diplomatic detachment in a cause that her own family had embraced, their loyalty putting their lives at risk.

"Yes," she said. "I understand. Your loyalties are with France."

Owen nodded, his relief greater than his satisfaction. "My place is at the ambassador's side." He turned to Guinevere. "Madam, my wife and adopted son are under the protection of France."

Guinevere nodded. "That is good. Take them to the safety of the ambassador's roof."

"And Pippa and Anna and Charles," Pen said. "I know you will not come, Mama, but they should."

Guinevere looked a question at Owen, who said, "Of course. They are related to France by marriage. Are you certain you won't seek the same protection, Lady Guinevere?"

"No, I thank you. My place is under my husband's roof," she said quietly.

Hugh emerged from the house as Robin appeared astride a fresh horse and leading Hugh's charger. Their farewells were brief but no less intense for that. Then they rode off down the driveway.

"Gather some things together," Guinevere said to Pippa. "And take Tilly and Ellen. They'll help with the children."

Four days later, Jane Dudley was proclaimed queen and taken in state to the royal apartments in the White Tower in the Tower of London to await her coronation.

As the great culverins sounded along the river to herald the queen's progress, Pen, Pippa, and

Anna left the ambassador's residence at Whitehall and went to the river to watch the procession leave Durham House. The crowd along the bank was silent, sullen, no cheers, no thrown caps, as the magnificent procession of barges made their stately progress.

"The country will not stand for it," Pen whispered, her lips barely moving because there was no knowing who might be planted in the crowd.

Pippa merely nodded her agreement and held tighter to Anna's arm.

They returned to the residence, filled with a depression that verged on fear. The whole city, hot and muggy in the summer swelter, felt as if it would erupt at any minute into a riot of the mob violence of which Londoners were so capable.

Owen greeted them with relief. " 'Tis dangerous to be out there," he chided, making no attempt to hide his annoyance.

"It was safe enough," Pen said, unfastening her hood. "But we didn't linger. What news of Mary?"

"A messenger arrived just now." The ambassador answered her as he came out of the parlor into the cool hallway. "Mary is safely away to Framlingham. Your father and brother are with her. The duke has had proclamations issued in every market square but the people are turning out in droves in support of the princess."

"We can only wait now," Owen said. He put a hand on Pen's shoulder. "And if you do not mind, madam wife, you will wait within doors.

You and your sisters." He tried to sound as if he was teasing her, but neither Pen nor Pippa was deceived.

Anna regarded him with a hint of alarm. She didn't dislike her new brother-in-law but she found him intimidating at the best of times, although he was never less than unfailingly polite and considerate towards her. He made Pen laugh, though, and Pippa teased him with an ease and confidence that amazed her little sister.

Pen smiled. She thought she should have found this concern and stricture annoying, and yet she didn't. Owen had not protected his first wife, and his second would have to put up with the consequences of that failure.

They waited for nine days, during which they never left the house. Owen came and went, sometimes leaving Pen's bed in the early hours and not reappearing until late afternoon. Messengers arrived almost hourly from the north, where Mary was gaining overwhelming support. Northumberland was trying to raise troops against her across the country and meeting only resistance.

It was midafternoon on July 19 when Pen, sitting with her sisters, trying to teach Philip and Charles to play cat's cradle in the ambassador's parlor, heard the first roars from the streets.

She jumped up, the wool falling in a tangle to her feet. "What is it?"

They ran to the windows overlooking the

street. People poured down it, singing, dancing, weeping.

"What *is* it? Where the devil is Owen?" Pippa demanded. "He keeps us immured in here, and then isn't around us to tell us what's happening."

"I'm here." Owen's light, melodious voice came from the door. "It's over. Mary has been proclaimed queen. Northumberland is expected to surrender by nightfall."

Epilogue

●

Queen Mary rose from the chair beneath the cloth of state in the royal apartments in the White Tower and stepped forward to receive her visitors.

"Pen, my dear."

Pen curtsied, her damask skirts spreading across the rich Turkey carpet. "Highness," she murmured, bowing her head low.

Mary took her hand and drew her to her feet. She kissed her warmly. "I have missed you, Pen, but I understand you're to be congratulated."

She laughed gently. "Your chevalier has done us much service, and I understand we may see much more of him at court, in a rather more . . ." She laughed again. "Rather more conventional guise."

"It is my hope, madam," Pen said.

Mary was dressed with dazzling magnificence, her kirtle sewn with gold and jewels, her overgown blazing with gems. The royal apartments in the Tower were richly hung with many-hued tapestries, richly carpeted and furnished, and Mary, although it had been but a week since her triumphant entry into London, inhabited them with all the gracious ease of one who had never doubted they were her due.

Mary turned her attention to Owen, who stood at Pen's side. "Chevalier, when the formalities are done I will welcome you most warmly as a friend of England's queen to the Court of St. James's."

Owen bowed, his black velvet bonnet clasped to his chest.

"And who have we here?" Mary bent her gaze on the small figure between Pen and Owen. Philip, holding tightly to their hands, was dressed in a gown and petticoats of embroidered white silk. He surveyed his queen with wide-eyed curiosity.

"You and I have met before, I believe," the queen said, her smile benign. "Some considerable improvement has been wrought in the child's appearance since then," she observed, turning her intense, myopic gaze to Pen.

"Love and good food, madam," Pen said, smiling.

Mary nodded. She played with the heavy jeweled cross lying on her breast. Sapphires and rubies glowed so bright it was hard to look directly at them.

"Pen, I believe you have a favor to claim." The warmth in her voice, and the smile in her eyes, left no doubt but that the favor would be granted.

"Yes, Highness. The Bryanston earldom lies vacant since the exile of Lord Bryanston. I would claim it for my son, the son of Philip Bryanston."

"An evil tale," Mary said. She bent down to the child, whose gaze was riveted on the jeweled cross. He blinked and tugged a hand free from his mother's, reaching to touch the bright toy.

"So you touch the cross," Mary said softly. "You will grow in the ways of the true faith, my child, as England returns to the sacred ways of worship."

A shudder went down Pen's spine; she knew the depths of her queen's religious fervor, but she held herself very still.

"Philip, Earl of Bryanston, I restore you to your father's title and lands," Mary stated. "Grow strong in faith, and in loyalty to your queen."

Philip, overcome by the solemnity of the occasion, burst into tears.

Pen bent to comfort him, picking him up, awkwardly because her ceremonial gown gave her little room to maneuver. Owen took the child from her and soothed his tears against his own gray silk doublet.

"I shall miss you in my service, Pen, but I release you now to your husband's," Mary said formally.

Pen curtsied, hiding the flash in her eyes. She was no more in Owen's service than he was in hers. She backed away and saw Owen's amusement.

"Handmaid mine," he whispered into her ear.

"I welcome you to my service."

Pen gave him a look of mock indignation, and left him in order to greet her parents, who stood at the far side of the state chamber with Pippa, and a woman who had her own mother's red hair and her father's features. Elizabeth, the daughter of Henry VIII and Anne Boleyn.

Pen curtsied to the princess, to Hugh and Guinevere, and embraced her sister, who was looking more than usually exuberant.

Pippa waited impatiently for the greetings and formalities to be completed before drawing her sister aside. "I am to accompany Princess Elizabeth after the coronation," Pippa informed Pen in an undertone. "She won't remain at court but has requested my companionship. Do you think 'tis a sensible thing for me to do?"

"I don't know," Pen said doubtfully. "If she's not to be at court, it could be rather quiet for you."

"Oh, there's always excitement somewhere," Pippa said. "You managed to find an exotic and dangerous husband while in the service of a princess, I'm determined to try my own luck."

Pen laughed. "You are absurd."

"Oh, you'll see," Pippa said. "You'll see." She returned to Elizabeth, her step seeming more like a dance than a glide.

Pen and Owen, with Philip, left the royal apartments a short while later, the Tower ravens flocking on the grass of Tower Green, their discordant cawing rising in the evening air. They walked swinging Philip between them towards the Tower entrance.

Pen glanced over at the Gentleman-Gaoler's lodging, a handsome two-story building that faced the green. She thought she caught a glimpse of a figure at one of the windows. A slight figure in a somber gray gown, hair drawn back into a neat white coif.

Jane Dudley.

"Poor girl," Pen said softly. "She's not yet sixteen. A queen for nine days, and now a prisoner. All for an ambition that was not hers."

She bent to kiss Philip's cheek. "Such evil as there is, Owen. This child's father died for a parent's ambition. Poor little Jane faces I know not what for the ambition of the Suffolks and Northumberlands."

She stepped through the gates onto the water steps at the Lion's Gate.

"Our children will not suffer from *anything* we can avert," Owen said, swinging Philip onto the waiting barge.

"No," Pen agreed, taking a seat in the bow as the barge moved away from the dock. " 'Tis time to fetch Andrew and Lucy."

Owen smiled, standing feet braced on the deck, hands on his hips as he watched the city slide past.

"I love you," Pen whispered.

"And I you, sweetheart," he returned, still smiling.

"Love you," Philip announced, bouncing on

the seat beside his mother. "Love you . . . love you . . ." He shrieked with laughter as if he had said the funniest thing imaginable.

Pen came to stand beside Owen at the rail. He put an arm around her and she let her head drop to his shoulder. Behind them her son continued his joyful chant, and it was the most wonderful sound in the world.

"Kiss me," she demanded softly, turning her face up to Owen's.

"Always," he said, cupping her cheek in his palm. He brought his mouth to hers. "I am going to spend the rest of my life kissing you, sweetheart. Like this . . . and like this . . . now, and for always."

The employees of Thorndike Press hope you have enjoyed this Large Print book. All our Large Print titles are designed for easy reading, and all our books are made to last. Other Thorndike Press Large Print books are available at your library, through selected bookstores, or directly from the publishers.

For more information about titles, please call:

(800) 223-1244
(800) 223-6121

To share your comments, please write:

Publisher
Thorndike Press
295 Kennedy Memorial Drive
Waterville, ME 04901